DARK

in the City of
LIGHT

DARK
in the City of
LIGHT

a novel

PAUL ROBERTSON

BETHANY HOUSE PUBLISHERS

Minneapolis, Minnesota

Published by Bethany House Publishers
11400 Hampshire Avenue South
Bloomington, Minnesota 55438

Bethany House Publishers is a division of
Baker Publishing Group, Grand Rapids, Michigan.

Printed in the United States of America

Library of Congress Cataloging-in-Publication Data

Robertson, Paul, 1957–
    Dark in the city of light / Paul Robertson.
       p.   cm.
    ISBN 978-0-7642-0569-9 (pbk.)
    1. Upper class—Fiction.   2. Paris (France)—History—1870–1940—Fiction.
I. Title.
    PS3618.O3173D37   2010
    813'.6—dc22

                                                            2010011009

Dedication

ELLEN FAITH,
bright and shining, made for a world of light and wonder:
blessed are you, Pure in Heart, for you shall see God.

GREGORY SCOTT,
watchman on the city wall, sword in your hand:
blessed are you, who hunger and thirst after righteousness,
for you shall be filled.

JEFFREY ALAN,
seer of visions, dreamer of dreams:
blessed are you, Peacemaker, for you shall be
called the Child of God.

AND LISA:
rejoice and be exceedingly glad,
for great is your reward in heaven.

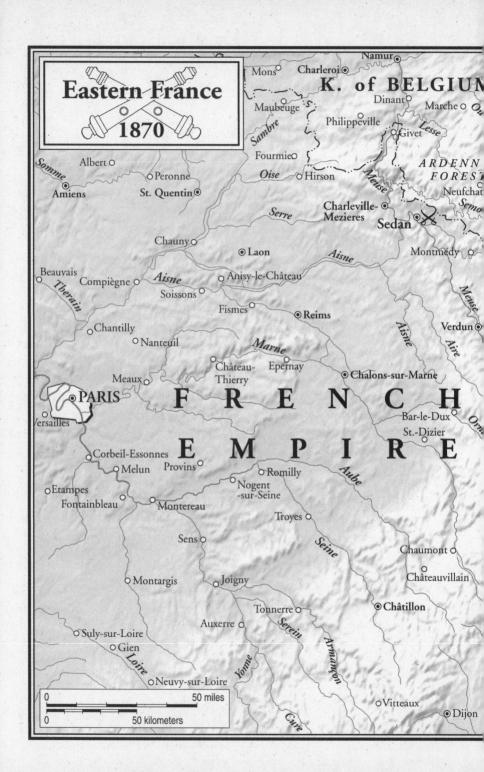

Eastern France
1870

K. of BELGIUM

Mons
Charleroi
Namur
Maubeuge
Dinant
Marche
Ou
Philippeville
Givet
Lesse
Sambre
Fourmie
Oise
Hirson
ARDENN
FOREST
Meuse
Neufchat
Semo
Somme
Albert
Peronne
St. Quentin
Serre
Charleville-
Mezieres
Sedan
Amiens
Montmédy
Chauny
Laon
Aisne
Beauvais
Compiègne
Aisne
Anisy-le-Château
Verdun
Therain
Soissons
Aisne
Aire
Chantilly
Fismes
Reims
Meuse
Nanteuil
Marne
Château-
Thierry
Epernay
Chalons-sur-Marne
Meaux
PARIS
F R E N C H
Versailles
Bar-le-Dux
St.-Dizier
Orn
Corbeil-Essonnes
E M P I R E
Melun
Provins
Aube
Etampes
Romilly
Fontainbleau
Montereau
Nogent
-sur-Seine
Sens
Troyes
Seine
Chaumont
Montargis
Joigny
Châteauvillain
Suly-sur-Loire
Tonnerre
Châtillon
Gien
Auxerre
Serein
Loire
Armançon
Neuvy-sur-Loire
Yonne
Vitteaux
Dijon
Cure

| 0 | | | 50 miles |
| 0 | | | 50 kilometers |

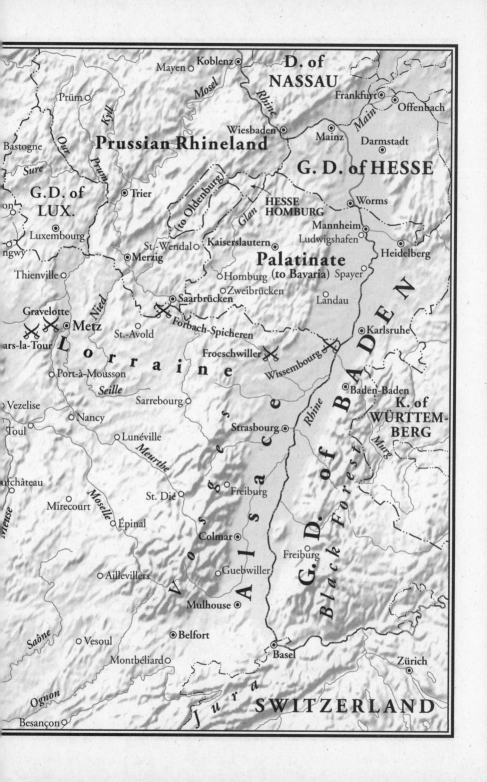

Central Europe 1870

Copenhagen

SWEDEN

Baltic Sea

Königsberg

Bornholm (Denmark)

Danzig

West Prussia

East Prussia

Narew

RUSSIAN

Hamburg

MECKLENBURG

Pomerania

P R U S S I A

Warta

Posen

Vistula

Warsaw

Bug

Poland

R U S S I A N

UNSWICK

Berlin

Brandenburg

Elbe

Silesia

Oder

E M P I R E

THURINGIAN

K. of SAXONY

Dresden

Koniggratz

Austrian Silesia

Galicia

STATES

Elbe

Prague

Bohemia

Moravia

Brünn

K. of

Danube

E M P I R E   of

Tisza

BAVARIA

Upper Austria

Lower Austria

Vienna

Munich

Salzburg

A U S T R I A

Budapest

Klausenburg

Salzburg

Styria

K. of HUNGARY

Tyrol

Carinthia

Drava

Banat

Idria

Slovenia

Sava

Slavonia

Venetia

Venice

Croatia

Bosnia

Belgrade

P. of Serbia
(semi autonomous)

Adriatic Sea

OTTOMAN

K. of ITALY

MONTENEGRO

E M P I R E

Rome

0			300 Miles
0			500 Kilometers

The thief comes only to steal and kill and destroy . . .

Chapter One

THE THIEF COMES

— 1 —

On a violent, black winter evening, Baron Ferdinand Harsanyi in Paris received a telegram from his wife in Vienna. It was delivered to his lodging on the Rue de Saint-Simon, and by candlelight at his desk he read its three words, *I AM ILL.*

"Will there be a reply, *monsieur?*"

The messenger, an old man, shuddered from the cold and stood close to the fire. The heavy coat of his uniform seemed to do little to warm him. Outside, hard gusts of the tempest outside assailed the window. It rattled and shook in its casing and the wind whistled through it. These were the only sounds inside as the man stood shivering and the Baron Ferdinand sat, uneasy as the storm.

Finally, the baron took the form and touched his pen to the ink bottle. "Today is Monday?"

"Yes, monsieur."

He scribbled, *WILL LEAVE TOMORROW ARRIVE THURSDAY.* "There, take that."

The messenger returned reluctantly to the night, and Ferdinand stood and began to pace the room. His steps were silent on the thick carpet, a slow tread that soon became quicker and more troubled. His path was wall to wall beneath two portraits, one behind his desk, of the Austrian emperor, and the other opposite, of a woman. At last, he stopped beneath it. The woman, in her youth, with long black hair and striking features, was wearing the fashions of an earlier time. The baron faced her, looking up; he was two hard decades at least past his own youth.

"Zoltan."

His valet appeared.

"Yes, master."

"We'll depart tomorrow for Vienna. I'll call on the ambassador at his residence this evening to ask his leave."

"Yes, master."

The cold gale had swept the Rue de Saint-Simon clear of men and light. Above the wind's howl, shutters creaked and half-loose things beat against hard walls.

Yet even against the hurricane blackness, curtained light crept from the buildings, side against side, lining the lane. No shaft of it touched the stones of the street. The glimmering windows were only pictures framed in night of the rooms and the lives hidden like jewels from the thieving storm.

It was upon this wailing sheet of shadow that Baron Harsanyi opened his door, its light spilling even onto the pavement, capturing an island from the blackness. He stepped onto the small square. Then he closed the door and the light surrendered back to the dark.

But the baron did not surrender himself to night. He wrapped his thick cape about him and advanced into it.

In a warmer season it would have been a short, pleasant stroll to the Rue de Grenelle. In the cold, he still chose to walk. A few carriages passed, and no one on two legs. For most of the way he was invisible in the shadows, the only witness of the war between the powers of the air and the strongholds of earth. He reached the Austrian Embassy and pulled the bell; it was a short but chilling wait for the front gate to be opened.

– 2 –

Prince Richard von Metternich, ambassador of Franz Joseph, the emperor of Austria, to Louis Napoleon, emperor of France, stood by the mantel in his private apartments, a goblet in his hand and a hot fire dancing at his side.

"Your Excellency." Ferdinand Harsanyi bowed.

The room was warm and close and fitfully bright. Flames roared in hearths at either end, and candle flames floated in their silver holders.

"Baron. What brings you out on a wretched night?" The prince's careless posture was in contrast to the baron's military straightness. His youth and finery were, as well; he was barely forty, and his emerald satin jacket shimmered like cat eyes.

"I must request your leave to return to Vienna."

"As you wish, of course." He set aside the formality with a gesture. "A personal matter?"

"My wife is ill." The baron's attention was pulled aside, toward the far hearth and the two chairs beside it. All the light made the shadows blacker, and the shadows leaped with the fire.

"How unfortunate," Prince von Metternich said. "My wife just visited her a few weeks ago when she was in Vienna. Did your wife tell you? Possibly not." The prince glanced toward the far fireplace, indecisive, but then shrugged. "They are such good friends. I'll not delay you. Please give my regards to the charming baroness, and my hopes for a speedy recovery." He gestured again in dismissal.

"Thank you, Your Excellency." Baron Harsanyi paused. His hair was gray iron and close-cropped. He would have been handsome as a young man; now he was hidden. "Do you have any instructions for me?"

The ambassador pretended surprise. "Instructions?" His head seemed to always be in motion, tilting, swaying, nodding.

"I'll be in the capital. Do you want me to convey any messages?"

"You would take precious hours from your poor, ill wife for a tedious visit to the Foreign Ministry?"

It would have been easier to see without such light. And over the growling flames, there had been another slight sound coming from the opposite fireplace.

"I would have the opportunity. If you wish." Ferdinand spoke slowly and carefully. "I would be expected to call on the foreign minister. It would be an affront to him on your behalf if I do not."

"And he would deserve it!" The ambassador's own fires flared. He took a deep breath and calmed himself. "But if I wish to insult the foreign minister, I should do it myself." His demeanor changed again, to give the baron his full attention. The mocking tone was gone. "Be innocuous, be bland, and say nothing. Tell him the usual, that relations between France and Prussia are as difficult as ever, and we have fears the current crisis may make them even worse."

"Which particular crisis do you mean, Your Excellency?"

"Pick one, any of them. Make one up if nothing new has happened by the time you get to Vienna. There's always a crisis between France and Prussia." He lifted his hands in annoyance. "The Spanish throne if you need a particular one. But . . ." The ambassador became more forceful. "Stress that this embassy is diligently working to calm the French government. Because the greatest harm would be that the ministry gives us instructions. You know as well as I, Baron Harsanyi, it is very delicate at the moment, and I think it is best for us to manage it ourselves. There will be war between Paris and Berlin within the next twelve months, I'm sure of it, but it's far better for the Austrian government in Vienna to not meddle. Be careful what you say."

The baron was satisfied. "I understand, Your Excellency."

He stared more closely at the chair facing the far fireplace, but the shadows were too deep. Prince von Metternich drew his attention away. "And will you also visit the office of the Army General Staff?"

"If possible. Again, it would be an affront not to. An affront on my behalf."

"I have no instructions to you about that. What will you say to them?"

"As the military attaché to the embassy in Paris, I will report to them on the state of the French army. That will be all that is necessary."

"Armies are useful, in wars and for other purposes, but they do not interest me." Prince von Metternich shrugged and his careless manner returned. "Perhaps this will be one war that Austria will avoid losing."

"I hope, Your Excellency, that if a war does come between France and Prussia, that Austria would not participate in it."

"Quite, Baron. That is the only way Austria ever avoids losing. We had our own defeat by Prussia four years ago and that is enough."

But now Baron Ferdinand was sure. Of the two heavy chairs that were set by the far fireplace, one was not empty. Prince Richard saw that Baron Harsanyi had seen. He smiled, as if he'd just remembered the two of them weren't alone. "Monsieur Sarroche?" he laughed. "You have been discovered."

The man stood and displayed himself in the tricking light. He was needle-like, short and very thin. Even his nose was long and pointed and unpleasant. His hair was the only feature about him that was abundant, brown and longer than was fashionable. "Monsieur." He bowed slightly and briefly. Baron Harsanyi stiffened, even more.

"Baron Harsanyi is the military attaché assigned to the embassy," the ambassador said. "And Monsieur Sarroche is an official of the French government in their Bureau of Armaments."

"I already know the pleasure of the baron's acquaintance," Monsieur Sarroche said. His voice was also unpleasant.

The baron remained silent.

"Of course you would know him," Prince von Metternich said. "I should have realized. The baron makes it his business to know everything admirable about the French army. Perhaps, Baron, you can guess the reason for the monsieur's visit."

Baron Harsanyi broke his stiff silence. "I wouldn't guess."

"Then perhaps you actually know. Monsieur Sarroche is here to discuss the French government's desire to make purchases from Austria."

"Military materials," Sarroche said. "As Your Excellency suggests, we may have great needs very soon."

"And we were just getting started," Prince von Metternich said, "when you were announced; I had even thought I should ask your assistance. But of course you are in a hurry to prepare for your travels."

"We particularly want mercury." The Frenchman spoke abruptly. He was watching Baron Harsanyi very closely.

"I really do feel as if I'm the one who's stumbled into the conversation," Prince von Metternich said, now pretending amusement. "Do you know something about, um, *mercury*, Baron?"

"The baron knows a great deal about mercury," Sarroche answered for him. "Austria's largest cinnabar mines are at Idria, in Slovenia, on the baron's estate."

"Cinnabar?" Prince von Metternich asked. "Not mercury?"

"Cinnabar is the ore; the mercury is produced from it," Baron Ferdinand said. "And mercury is used to manufacture mercury fulminate, which is an explosive. But the mines are on my wife's estate, not mine."

"Oh, that's what those mines are? We've known your wife for years, but I never could remember what exactly it was they dug out of the ground there."

"Yes, your wife's estates," Sarroche said to the baron. And then, slowly, "I am so greatly sorry to hear that she is ill." He let the silence hang, then added, "But not entirely surprised."

The baron inhaled sharply.

"Yes, it is unfortunate," the ambassador said, not taking notice of

Sarroche's last comment. His always mocking smile was sympathetic for a moment. "And how long will we be without you? A week? Two?"

"A week, I hope."

"A week then." The lights in the prince's eyes narrowed, and his head, moving like an adder, turned straight toward him. "That would be only two days at her side? Will it be enough?"

"Three days. I hope it will be enough."

"Take what time you need."

"And when you return," Sarroche said, "we will continue our discussion."

– 3 –

On the return to his apartment, the wind had decreased and a heavy snow fell. Where the lights of windows and streetlamps had before not penetrated the black, now their radiance had the slow white flakes to illuminate. Every light became a floating globe of falling grains.

With even greater speed, the baron retraced his steps. Inside the front hall of the building, he knocked on the concierge's door.

"A carriage," he said. "Fifteen minutes."

"Zoltan," the baron said at the door of his apartment. "We're leaving tonight. Quickly. We'll catch the last train." He looked out the window. "I hope the snow doesn't block the tracks."

"Ten minutes," Zoltan answered. He had black hair, straight down over his heavy brow, and a similar mustache over his mouth, and he wore a clerk's short coat over his loose white shirt and burly shoulders. He bowed and left the room.

Ferdinand's motions were fast and urgent. He opened a drawer of his desk and quickly removed papers and sorted them into a portfolio. In only eight minutes Zoltan had pulled a trunk from the bedroom and a smaller portmanteau from his own room. Baron Harsanyi searched the room with his eyes, looking for anything else to be taken.

A knock sounded on the door, its echo smothered in the drapery and carpet.

"The carriage, master," Zoltan said. A boy, the concierge's grandson, had brought the driver to the apartment.

The baron gave the boy a few *sous*, and Zoltan and the driver lifted the trunk and the portmanteau through the hall and down the stairs.

The baron blew out the last lamp, took his portfolio, and locked the door of his dark apartment behind him.

For the final time that evening, Baron Harsanyi ventured out. The snow was not yet deep and the carriage wheels cut through it without resistance. The first corner was the Quai d'Orsay, and they rode for a time along the left bank of the Seine. The road was well lit, and even the gaslights on the far bank were visible. The carriage turned onto the Pont de la Concorde and crossed the Seine; then they were on the other bank, beneath its lights, and the d'Orsay side was faint beyond the snow and fog. The whole river smoked and curled and cloaked itself and its banks in vapor.

On the right bank they still followed the water, on the Quai des Tuileries. The gardens were on their left, and then the bulk of the Louvre, and then on their right, the Ile, and barely, the blunt spires of Notre Dame ghostly in the snow. They turned on the Boulevard de Sebastopol and the river was lost behind them.

The new boulevard was as straight as a cannon shot, which was part of its purpose, to break up the nests and warrens of neighborhoods that had always bred uprisings and unrest.

But the boulevard's other purpose was to make Paris wondrous, and the long lines of lights and endless lines of gray stone mansions and bright windows and the sinuous lines of pedestrians on the sidewalks, and carriages on the paving stones, were beautiful and glittering, a street of light.

Then Boulevard de Strasbourg continued Sebastopol's line, and soon the grand front of the Gare de l'Est train station was in sight. But before they reached it, the baron spoke to the driver, "Turn here."

They turned onto the Boulevard de Magenta and then a second time onto a small side street; the sign said Rue de Valenciennes. They stopped at the third building, once but no longer a house. Now a small brass plaque was set beside the door that read, *Partington and Manchester, Ltd.*

One light glowed in the uppermost window. Despite the late, dark hour, the baron rang the bell and knocked, as well. There was no answer, but he was undeterred. He continued to knock, and finally the door creaked open. A wide, pasty face looked out.

"What is it?" the face asked in English-accented French.

The baron's English had only a slight accent. "Mr. Henry Whistler. Where is he?"

"Not here!" The clerk changed to English. "Not now."

"Is he in Paris?"

"No, sir. He's away."

"Where?"

"I'm not to say, sir."

"Is he in Vienna?"

The white face hadn't nearly the guile to deny that the baron's guess was the truth.

"I thought as much," the baron said, and turned away.

In an even greater hurry, the baron rushed into the station, leaving behind Zoltan and a porter with the trunk. Though the night had long been dark, it was still before nine thirty and the last trains were standing at the platforms.

"Two first class to Strasbourg," he said at the window.

"Yes, monsieur." The agent eyed him with suspicion. "You are Prussian, monsieur?"

"That isn't your business."

"It is the business of the police," the ticket agent answered. "I am required to ask. Travel by Prussians must be reported."

"I am Hungarian and I am a diplomat of the Austrian Empire."

"Very well, sir! Your tickets!"

The baron turned to go, but then he paused.

"Perhaps I should ask for an apology, for being mistaken for Prussian."

The agent scowled, but caught a gleam of humor in the dark eyes, and smiled. "I will apologize to an Austrian. To be called Prussian, it is a terrible insult, is it not?"

– 4 –

The suburbs of Paris fell behind and the moon rose over the train's eastward course. The farms and villages of the valley of the Seine crowded the track, and the train and the fields each sped past the other in the night, very close but different worlds.

The falling snow was left behind. The fields were silver white from the train's windows; the windows were gaslit yellow from the snowy fields.

At midnight the train stopped at Chalons, and at four in the morning in Nancy. Finally, the winter day dawned as the track rounded the heights of the Vosges Mountains and came to rest at the platform in Strasbourg.

Baron Harsanyi waited in the first-class lounge, wrapped in his heavy coat and unnoticed by his fellow passengers.

"What did you think?" he asked Zoltan, beside him.

"The rails are single track. Every kilometer from Paris."

"When the war begins, how long would it take Marshall Frossard to bring his first fifty divisions from Paris to the Rhine?"

"The first five, one week," Zoltan said. "After that the trains get too confused and the mobilization is a swamp. The trains can't run both ways on the same track."

"The Prussians have four double-track lines from Berlin. Trains both ways at the same time."

"They would move twenty divisions in ten days."

"But their army is conscripts. They'll have to be called up from their farms and villages. Their mobilization would take longer." He looked out at the night. "And the French would have the Vosges Mountains as a defense, and the fortresses in Froeschwiller and Forbach. It won't be easy for either side."

"It will be murder," Zoltan growled.

The train that departed Strasbourg en route to Munich wound slowly at first through the half French and half German spires and villages of Alsace. Then gathering speed it launched onto the Rhine Bridge, a kilometer of iron trusses and spans. The sharp lines were blurred by the mists and fogs rising from the river.

"One company of *dragoons* would take the French side," Zoltan said. "Then the Rhine is nothing to stop the Prussians."

"That's not Prussia," the baron said, nodding to the approaching bank. "It's the Grand Duchy of Baden. Baden isn't allied to Prussia yet."

"It's all German."

Halfway across, the train began to slow, and well onto the eastern bank in the village of Kehl it stopped. The passengers waited as officials of the Grand Duchy passed the length of the cars, verifying passports.

Outside the baron's window, two young guards stood on the platform of the station with rifles.

"Your papers, please?" The compartment door had opened, and a white-haired guard waited politely. "Austrian, yes, they are all in order. Thank you." He laid his hand on the compartment door.

"A moment," Baron Harsanyi said. "You're an old man to have to work hard, and in the cold."

"The young ones are drilling. It is the training."

"Like those?" He pointed out the window at the guards.

"Those two, yes. All those young ones are drilling and practicing."

When the door was closed, Zoltan shook his head.

"The rifles they have? *Zundnadelgewehr*." He spoke the German contemptuously. Then he returned to Hungarian. "Needle guns. They are trash."

"The Dreyse factories are supporters of Prime Minister Bismarck. He won't let the army change to a new rifle. Even here in the south, they haven't changed. The French rifles are far better. Quite accurate."

"The *Chassepots* rifles," Zoltan said. "I hit a target at a thousand meters. The needle guns only four hundred."

The train started and they began their journey through the south of Germany. After two hours they'd crossed the narrow waist of Baden and entered Württemberg. The black shadows of the German forest enclosed them.

"The forest of the Grimm tales," Baron Harsanyi said. "Did you know, in English, *grim* means austere and frightening? To see the place, that name is fitting."

"I don't know English."

Before noon they had passed Stuttgart and in the early afternoon they crossed the next frontier, into the Kingdom of Bavaria, and in the evening they came to the capital, Munich.

"Baden, Württemberg, and Bavaria," the baron said. "Von Bismarck and his Prussia have all Northern Germany in their hands, but these three Southern German states are still on the fence. The question is whether they will join a war with France. They have an alliance, but it only comes into effect if France declares war first."

"France would be foolish to attack," Zoltan said.

"Von Bismarck is a genius at making other countries do foolish things. That's why he's been so successful as Prussia's prime minister."

"If France attacks, all Germany will fight against her."

"There is no Germany," Ferdinand said. "They are all separate countries. Bavaria has its own kings, the Wittelsbachs, and they don't like the Prussian Hohenzollerns."

"So far, they have their king, and the Prussians have their king, and Hanover and Brunswick and Baden and all these little places," Zoltan said. "The people, they want one Germany. They always have. Where Germans are, that is Germany."

"The French will never allow Germany to unite."

"Unless they are forced."

"So, war is inevitable?"

"Only God could stop it."

They ate dinner in the station restaurant in Munich. At nearly midnight, they boarded the overnight train from Frankfurt. Zoltan slept, but the baron was lost in remorseless thought, staring out the windows at something beyond the Danube valley.

The day was well begun as they reached the outskirts of Vienna.

Beneath high, steam-shrouded arches of steel he stepped from the train onto the Vienna Westbahnhof platform. The station was crowded with passengers.

"A carriage?" Zoltan asked.

Ferdinand shook his head. "It's too early to arrive."

"The household will be awake."

But the baron was looking out the front doors of the station, toward an opulent marble building. He turned back to Zoltan. "I want to wait until the children have left the house. Check the bags here at the station. Then take a cab to the house. Don't go in, though. Wait at the corner where you can see who goes in and out, and don't let them see you. Wait for me. I'll be at least an hour."

"Yes, master."

– 5 –

Once Zoltan had left him, Ferdinand stood for a moment on the front steps of the station. Other people passed by, aiming for the imposing building directly across the street. Gold letters set above the second row of windows read *Imperial Hotel.*

He walked up the steps and the door was opened for him by a doorman. Inside, wealthy travelers ambled between the door, the front counter, the stairs, the dining room, and among the chairs and tables of the lobby.

At the desk he paused, and then asked, "Is Mr. Henry Whistler in this morning?"

"Just a moment, sir." The clerk studied the hundreds of squares in the wall behind him. Some of the pigeonholes had keys in them, some letters and notes, and some were empty. "Yes, he is in," the clerk said.

"Please have a message delivered to him."

"Yes, sir?" The man slid a sheet of paper forward, but the baron shook his head.

"Inform him that Baron Harsanyi would like to speak with him in the lobby."

The clerk nodded and rang a bell on the counter. A young man in hotel uniform sprang forward.

"Inform Mr. Whistler in room 225 that Baron Harsanyi wishes to speak with him in the lobby."

Ferdinand took a seat in a leather armchair in a far corner, and waited.

"My good baron!" The language and deep musical voice were English. The man was in a gray wool suit and bowler hat, with an ivory-handled ebony walking stick in his hand. His clothing was simply quiet and affluent, but his face was conspicuous. His cheeks were ruddy and his nose rounded above a bushy white mustache, and his eyes were very sharp. "Good morning! What an absolute surprise."

"Good morning to you," the baron answered.

Mr. Whistler sat beside him. "Quite a shrewd guess to find me here." Most of his smile was hidden behind the mustache. "But you're a shrewd man. And you're in Vienna to see the baroness?"

"I am here to see her."

"It was a guess that you'd find me here, wasn't it? Or did she tell you I was here? No, I doubt that." He smiled again, and for a moment the eyes were wickedly amused. "She's ill, you know."

"I do know."

"She was unable to see me yesterday," Whistler said. "I met with her three days ago, and she didn't seem well."

"She won't sell you any cinnabar," Baron Ferdinand said. "You've wasted your trip."

"I hope I haven't. But it seems to be a slim hope."

"Why did you even try?"

"We'll just say I'd heard a bit of a rumor that the wind might have changed."

"What rumor?"

But Whistler just smiled even more broadly. "And besides, you refuse to talk to me in Paris. It was worth a try to come here. And when she did talk to me, three days ago, she was as unfriendly to me as you have been." The sneering look reappeared in his eyes. "It must be the one thing in which the two of you are in agreement."

Ferdinand met his look with one just as sharp. But he responded calmly.

"Tell me what you proposed to her."

Whistler stared into Ferdinand's eyes for a moment, and his smile faded. "Why do you want to know?" He waited, and then said, "Perhaps I should have stayed in Paris after all. Was that where the new wind was blowing from?"

"I still don't know which wind you mean."

"I heard through one of my agents that Austrian cinnabar might soon be coming on the market. Are you the seller, Baron? I had assumed that it would be your wife."

"The cinnabar mines are part of my wife's estate," Ferdinand said. "She would have to agree to any sale."

"But you are her husband, and women have no legal rights to sign contracts. You have to sign it for her."

"I wouldn't accept anything against her wishes."

"You accepted your posting to Paris. But I suppose that wasn't against her wishes." Whistler tapped his fingers together, considering the baron's blank stare. "If your wife is ill and can't speak for herself, you might presume to speak for her." The sneer disappeared as he studied Ferdinand's face. "The French government has an urgent, desperate need for mercury fulminate and I would like to sell them some."

"The French have their own facilities. They can produce fulminate without buying it from you."

"But our good friend Monsieur Sarroche has no mercury to produce it with. There are only two sources in Europe large enough and developed enough to supply enough cinnabar ore: the Spanish mines at Almaden, and your Idria in Slovenia. Spain is even more unfriendly at the moment. Partington and Manchester will buy the cinnabar from you, produce the mercury fulminate in our own factories, and sell it to the French. You and I will both make a comfortable profit." He allowed another smile. "Herr Bismarck and Louis Napoleon are creating fortunes right now with this war they're trying to start against each other. Why not take our share?"

"The war may not happen."

"What could possibly stop it?" He paused. "Nothing. There is nothing more certain than war."

"You would sell the fulminate only to the French?" the baron asked.

"Not to the Prussians, if that's what you mean."

"That is what I mean."

"I would not sell it to Prussia. I can't," Whistler said. "Unfortunately, von Stieff has the whole German market all to himself. And the Austrian government would never allow the cinnabar ore to be exported to their greatest enemy anyway." He frowned in thought. "But I could find a way. War and greed are the two constants of human nature. For the right price, I'm sure I could find a way."

Baron Ferdinand ignored him. "So, again, tell me what you proposed to my wife."

"Here we get to it, don't we?" Whistler shook his head. "But I think I'll keep my cards to myself. First let me know if you can convince your wife to sell cinnabar to me. Or"—Whistler was back to smiling—"if you simply decide to sell it over her objections."

"I wouldn't do that."

"Don't tell me that your tender regard toward her prevents you from acting against her wishes. I wouldn't believe you."

"Austrian law doesn't give me complete freedom to act," Ferdinand said. "My wife does have some rights concerning her property."

"Then you'll have to start convincing her."

"That is my concern."

"It is, and you'd best get at it." Whistler frowned, and the mocking had returned. "The war won't wait, and the French are impatient." He stood to leave. "Sarroche has sent his own agent after her, you know, here in Vienna at the moment."

"Who?"

"That's another card I'll keep to myself."

"Tell me."

"You'll know where to find me, Baron," Whistler said, not answering. "I'll leave for Paris tomorrow. In the meantime, I wish your wife a speedy recovery." He leaned forward. "Or at least a speedy resolution. That would make things easier, wouldn't it?"

– 6 –

"What have you seen?"

Zoltan stepped back from the corner. "No one has entered."

"Have the children left?"

"Your son left as I arrived. On a horse."

"He's riding. And Therese?"

"She left ten minutes ago in a carriage. It came to get her."

"Who was in it?"

"I couldn't see."

"Most likely a friend. Then I am ready to arrive."

They both got into the cab that Ferdinand had brought from the train station. "On to the front door," Ferdinand said to the driver. Then he spoke to Zoltan. "I may go back out after the children have returned. Go to the stable and reintroduce yourself to the grays."

"Yes, master."

And then they had covered the last thirty meters to the front door. The house was stone and brick, as elegant and quiet as the street. With his cloak billowing unheeded about his shoulders, Baron Harsanyi stepped into the snow and mud and then onto the wide steps and up to the oak doors.

He opened them, and the sound echoed through the empty hall before him. He stood only a moment on the threshold and then walked slowly to the stairway and even more slowly upward. Doors above him opened.

"Master!" A servant woman met him at the top.

"Where is she, Maria?"

"In the bed. We expected you tomorrow. Today is only Wednesday!"

"Where is Rudolph?"

"He is out, and Therese, also. They would have been here if we had known you were coming."

"How is my wife?" he said, starting toward her bedroom.

"Sleeping. She is better than yesterday, less shaking."

The baron stopped. "Shaking?"

"Yes. Trembling."

"When was she awake?"

"Two days ago when we sent the telegram, and a little yesterday. She's breathing better than yesterday, too. The doctor says it is influenza. He says another week—"

But he passed her and came to the closed door.

"When will Rudolph return?"

"By noon, master. He's riding."

"And Therese?"

"She was with . . . with a friend. She's buying a hat."

His hand was on the door and he drew himself straight to open it. When he gently had, he stepped into the room, slowly and hushed but with no hesitation.

It was dim in the bedroom. Only a thin line of light entered through the drawn curtains. The shaft fell on the bed, on a heavy white coverlet that was like the snow outside, formed it seemed by the wind into a drift from foot to head, and at the end another mound of pillow blown against the headboard.

On the pillow her head lay still, and beside it a braid of dark hair. Her face was as white as the sheets. Her eyes were closed and only slow gasping breath showed that any life still coursed within.

He stood over her.

There was a sound behind him. "Master?"

He didn't turn. "Leave me, Maria. Close the door."

The echoes quickly died and he was alone with his wife. He knelt close and studied the pale complexion and listened to her fragile breathing. She was still very much the same as the portrait in his apartment in Paris; age hadn't changed her.

"Irene," he said, but there was no motion.

A ticking clock on the mantel was the only sound in the room. He glanced at it, then looked more carefully around the room. The walls were papered satin white with delicate gold-flowered columns. The furniture was heavy and old-fashioned, also painted white with gilded ornaments. Four red candles, two on each side of the bed, burned brightly. Their red was the only strong color in the room.

The fire in the fireplace was well kept; he crossed the room to the hearth and shoveled as much coal into the box as would fit.

He returned to the bed. He caressed his wife's cheek, feeling the dry parchment skin and measuring the heat of her blood and feeling it pulse. He even touched her eyelid and drew it open. He stared into her eye, and she stared back at nothing.

He drew back the cover from her shoulder and arm. He knelt, found her hand and grasped it in his.

Still holding it, with his other hand he took a handkerchief from his pocket and laid it out on the white cover. The cloth was dark red like a stain on snow, the same color as the candles. He folded it twice, into quarters, all with his one hand as his other held hers.

He took a deep, weary, sorrowful breath.

Then he cupped the handkerchief in his free hand and gently, firmly, held it down over his wife's still mouth and nostrils.

A tremor shook the bed as her frail body unconsciously struggled. He maintained his pressure; no air could pass into the lungs. Her hand in his quivered.

Her eyes fluttered open.

Then they closed. The struggle hadn't been long. There was a final shuddering and she was still.

Even so, he kept his palm in place for moments longer. Then he released her and now there was no breath at all, and no pulse in her veins.

He stood for several long minutes watching her, his own face hard and still as hers. Then he pulled the cover back over her arm and stepped away.

"I will be in my study," he said as he closed the door behind himself.

Maria was waiting in the hall. "Did she know you?"

"No. She didn't wake." He started slowly down the stairs. "And I tended the fire. There will be no need to disturb her. When the children return, send them to me."

– 7 –

The baron's study was small and sparsely furnished. One wall was shelves of books and one held only the door. In the corner of the other two walls, beneath a window, was an old, worn desk. Its antique character and archaic carving matched its owner.

The baron was seated at the desk. The portfolio he'd brought from Paris was unopened on it. The only other objects on the desk were an ink bottle and a blotter. Unmoving hours had gone by and it was noon.

A knock sounded on the door. He opened the portfolio, took out a paper, and held the pen over it.

"Enter."

The door opened. "Father?"

"Rudolph."

He stood from his desk and moved to embrace the young man standing uncertainly in the doorway, briefly and formally. They matched eye to eye in height and in width of shoulders, but the son was still in his first clean strength of manhood. His hair was jet-black and curling; he was square-jawed and dark-eyed and unweathered.

Rudolph stepped back. "I didn't know you were coming today. I would have been here."

"I changed plans."

"Have you seen Mother?"

"Of course, at the very first moment I arrived. She didn't wake."

"She'll recover. She's strong."

"Yes, I know. She will. You've grown, Rudolph."

The son's eyes glowed. "Yes, sir."

"And your schooling? She writes that you still plan to attend University in the fall."

"Yes, Father. At the Institute, here in Vienna. Mother has made all the arrangements."

The baron's eyes were unreadable. "And to what end?"

"There will be a position in the foreign office."

"A good Austrian, Rudolph. Like all your mother's family."

Rudolph's uncertainty, which had never entirely been absent, returned. "Yes, Father."

"And not the army?"

"Mother insists on the foreign office."

"And your wishes?"

"A career as a diplomat seems honorable. I would be following your footsteps."

"I'm not a diplomat. I'm a soldier."

"Well, yes, Father, of course, but—"

"I'm serving the ambassador as a military advisor."

Rudolph was silent, a silence that lasted very long, until another voice broke it.

"Father?"

"Therese! Come."

Rudolph stepped away to make room. Baron Harsanyi embraced his daughter in a true fatherly embrace.

"What are you doing?" she said. "You came early."

"I have business with the ministry."

"And have you seen her? She's in bed."

"Yes, I have. She didn't wake."

"I want to ask her about hats." She was like her mother, with a rounded face and gentle features betrayed by sharp eyes. Her hair was like her brother's, black and curling, even though it was very long.

"Maria said you were getting a new hat," Ferdinand said.

"Yes, it's being made. What are they wearing in Paris, Father?"

He paused. "Soon you'll come and see for yourself."

"Come to see? Paris? Oh, Father! I couldn't! Mother wouldn't let me."

"We'll ask her when she wakes."

"I can't leave until she's well."

"Of course."

"Father?"

Rudolph had stood still through their entire conversation.

"Yes?"

"If you don't need me, I'll be at my studies."

"Yes, go ahead. And I'll be going out."

"Through the evening?" Therese asked.

"Through the evening, yes."

– 8 –

"Go," he said to Zoltan. "Get moving."

"Yes, master."

The baron leaned back in his seat. The paving stones were well placed and flat, and the landau with its springs cushioned the ride, but even so, the speed was jolting. Yet he was too deep in his colorless thoughts to brace himself, or to notice as he was thrown against the side.

"To where?" Zoltan asked.

"Just drive."

"Yes, master." The whip cracked, lightly, and the matched gray pair of horses lunged forward.

Baron Harsanyi suddenly realized their speed. "Slow down!"

The reins were pulled and the carriage slowed.

"Take time," the baron said. "Take all the time you can. Anything to delay our return." Then he thought. "The Foreign Ministry."

The horses slowed further and with them the city passing. Now they were part of the streaming multitude. They passed the Belvedere Gardens and Palace, and the Schwarzenberg Palace, then swerved smoothly onto the wide promenade of the RingStrasse. The grand façades of the ministries and mansions, brick and marble gray, added to but did not surpass the majesty of the broad boulevard itself. Each straight segment was flanked by its own great edifice: the Opernring and the Opera; the Burgring and the Kunsthistoriches Museum on one side and on the other the Hofburg, the Imperial Palace itself, gleaming white and gold in the white snow and whiter sunlight. Behind it the gardens slept beneath their blanket of snow.

Then the Parliament on the left, then the Burgtheater on the right, and then the University. And Baron Ferdinand Harsanyi returned to his fog of restless agitation. He shifted from side to side on his seat until he forced himself to be still. Even then, nothing in him was still. And finally they reached the Foreign Ministry building.

"Baron Harsanyi." Count Friedrich von Buest slowly raised his head and eyes from his desk. A fringe of white hair circled the head and dove down into extravagant sideburns. When his eyes finally reached the baron's, they were large and watery light blue in a wrinkled face.

"Your Excellency."

"What brings you to Vienna?" His voice was reedy and lethargic, like an old organ that leaked air.

"My wife is ill." By force of will, he kept his eyes straight forward.

"My greatest sympathy," he said with no sympathy at all. "It is fortunate that you are here. I wish you to take instructions back to Prince von Metternich in Paris."

"I am the military attaché," the baron said. "I may not be qualified to—"

"I know who you are. I don't want this to be connected with any official channels in the Foreign Ministry."

"Yes, sir."

"Next month the Archduke Albrecht will visit Paris."

"The emperor's uncle?"

"He must be kept from any communication with Louis Napoleon."

"We will make every effort."

"The archduke is an old, foolish man. He has no understanding of the political realities. He hates the Prussians, and ever since the battle of Koniggratz, he has called for an alliance against them between Austria and France. He may make any outlandish statement or promise to the French government." He looked sharply at Ferdinand. "Are you paying attention?"

Ferdinand tried to. "Yes, sir. The ambassador can make it plain that the archduke does not speak for the Austrian government."

"It must not be plain. The archduke will be insulted and call on Emperor Franz Joseph to intervene here in the Foreign Ministry. That would create a crisis, which we cannot afford. I can't send this message through normal Foreign Ministry dispatches, or the archduke may hear of it."

"I understand, sir."

"And do you have any messages from Prince von Metternich?"

"Concerning the Spanish throne—"

"I don't want to hear it. Whatever he says is just as likely a lie or a trick, coming from him. And he wouldn't listen to anything I said to him, either. But he'll know what to do with Albrecht. In that, he and I will be in complete agreement. And I'll tell you yourself, Baron, don't trust von Metternich. But you know him. You know his wiles."

The baron didn't answer.

"You are dismissed," the foreign minister said.

– 9 –

"Now where?" Zoltan asked.

Ferdinand had just left the office of the General Staff of the Army. It was still only late afternoon.

"Around the Ring. Just keep going. Anywhere."

They returned to the RingStrasse and Zoltan set the gray horses at an easy pace.

The streets and the day passed.

It was dark and had long been, the dark of a crystal Vienna winter night, not the dark of a Paris snowstorm. The streets were still full despite the bone-snapping cold.

"Enough," the baron said finally. "Home."

It was the first that Ferdinand had spoken in all the past hours, and it had taken a burst of strength to say it. As they traversed the wider streets his agitation increased, just as it had in the apartment in Paris, and though there was no place in the carriage to pace, still his unease was apparent. As finally they reached the corner of his own Hegergasse, he spoke out.

"Stop, Zoltan."

Without a word, his servant stopped the carriage and waited.

"I do not want to arrive at my door this evening."

"To a hotel then, master?"

"No. Not that. It has to be done. Go on. I just dread it."

Submitting to his master's mood, Zoltan stirred the horses to walk slowly toward the building halfway down the block. But they did approach, and the house was blazing in light with every window bright, even as they were draped in heavy black curtains.

"The house is in mourning," Zoltan said.

"My wife is dead. Go ahead, go forward."

Chapter Two

BREACH THE
PARISIAN GATE

– 1 –

The arrival of Therese Harsanyi in Paris was the epic arrival of a heroine in a chariot borne on clouds, an iron chariot on clouds of steam, the emblems of the epic of her age. The chariot locomotive came to its conclusive stop, and passengers who were the backdrop cast of the drama billowed forth like the steam. They were the milieu and scenery, and the heroine walked her stage grandly.

Therese Harsanyi's coat was gray and billowing, like the steam and the age. Gray ostrich feathers plumed her hat at the jauntiest angle. A single black mourning armband graced her sleeve. Her cheeks were bright, her eyes even brighter as they swept the platform, the station, the city, and the world. And the crowds noticed her, even in the throng of the Gare de l'Est, even in their hurry; even in Paris they noticed her.

"Father. I am in Paris!"

Baron Ferdinand followed her from the train, familiar with and unimpressed by this Paris.

"Yes, you are," he said. "Zoltan will get porters." He also wore a mourning band on his arm.

And another followed behind the baron and Zoltan and Maria. Unnoticed by the crowds, sweeping the station with wary looks, Rudolph Harsanyi accompanied his family. He carried his own bag, which was heavy. He was dressed in a somber black suit, and his youth was diminished by it.

Nothing diminished Therese. Her undimmed light shone a moment longer as her companions passed her.

"Come along," she was told.

"Yes, Father." But after he had turned away, she herself turned back toward the train. She searched its windows and doors for a moment, and quickly found what she sought. A face in a window, another man, very close, had already found her, and their eyes met. A golden beard half covered the face, but not the joy in his smile. He winked, and she winked back, and no one else saw them.

"Come along!" Baron Harsanyi said again, and Therese came with only one more look back.

– 2 –

Night fell in Paris. As the light faded, Therese's epic grandeur faded, as well.

Even a thousand candles reflected through ten thousand facets of crystal and mirror couldn't lift her above the prosaic company of her father and brother, at the table in the dining room of the Hotel d'Orleans.

"I want to see everything," she said. "What can we do? Is there an opera tonight?"

"Not opera," Rudolph answered, jolted from his morose reverie.

"We have to go out."

Baron Harsanyi awoke from his own thoughts. "You'll stay in your room."

"But I want to see Paris. I want to see what everyone is wearing."

"Overcoats," Rudolph said. He was not seeing the Paris that she was.

"And I'll be at the embassy tonight," her father said.

"My first night, and in prison." Her eyes flashed. "Do you need to go?"

"Yes."

"Why not tomorrow instead?"

"Tomorrow we'll find a house to rent, and you will see more than enough of Paris."

"I'll never see enough of Paris."

Her complaint fell on deaf ears. Baron Harsanyi was finished for the evening, with his dinner and with his family. Rudolph had no desire for either.

"You haven't eaten anything," she said.

"French food," he said. "It's wretched."

"You'll get used to it," the baron said. "And in public, speak French."

He spoke haltingly in that language. "Yes, Father. But I am not French."

"No, we are not French. But you'll need to master the language to attend University here. And besides," he said, lowering his voice, "in Paris, now, it is dangerous to seem too German."

"I'm Austrian."

"I know that. But the French can't always tell the difference."

"I want to be French," Therese said in her very fluent French. "I want to seem French."

"It fits you," Rudolph said. Then, to his father, "What will you do at the embassy?"

"I'll be speaking with the ambassador."

"Father," Therese said, "I want to meet him. And especially his wife, Princess von Metternich. Mother told me about her."

"You will meet her presently." Baron Ferdinand returned his attention to both of them. "Be careful. This is a foreign city and we're aliens here." And then, even more intently, "Don't trust anyone who approaches you. Only trust the people I introduce you to."

"What could be dangerous here?" Therese asked.

"You don't know."

And then the prisoner Therese was escorted by her jailer father and unsympathetic brother to the hotel room cell. Her father left, and she was left with just a window onto Paris.

Therese paced. Rudolph sat.

"Be still," he said finally, in German.

"I can't."

"Then go in your bedroom."

"Rudy, you're inhuman to not be excited."

"Ten days ago, my mother died."

"My mother, too." She sat beside him. She tried to put her arm around his shoulder, but he shrugged it off.

"Are you inhuman?" he asked. "Don't you care?"

"Yes. But everything is so changed now. And we have Father."

"I don't know who he is."

"But now we'll find out!"

"Mother knew him well enough."

"And he knew her well enough," Therese said, but gently. "Rudy. At least be patient. We can't change anything."

"No, Raisy," he said. "Not ever."

Before Therese could say anything else, a knock raised at the door. She reddened. Rudolph began to stand, but she was much faster.

"I'll get it." She flew to the door and opened it, just one inch. In the opening was one inch of the face that had been in the train. "Auguste!" she whispered in French. "I knew it would be you."

"I saw your father leave," the face said.

"Yes, but he told me to stay here in the room."

"Then I'll come in."

"Oh, you can't!"

"Who is it?" Rudolph called from behind.

"The hotel steward. He's just asking if everything is satisfactory."

"Where will you be tomorrow?" the man asked.

"Father is taking us to find a house to rent. His apartment is too small for all of us."

"How can I find you?"

"We will be back here in the evening."

"But he'll be with you."

"I'll get you a message," she said.

"My aunt's house: 28 Rue le Bruyere."

She nodded. "I'm here now, Auguste, in your Paris."

"What are you saying?" Rudolph said. He was standing to come over. "Father said not to talk to anyone."

Therese closed the door quickly. "I'm not. I'm practicing my French."

– 3 –

The next day, Therese did not see enough of Paris. She and her father were driven in a closed carriage, due to the cold, to one house, which her father decided was acceptable for a Hungarian baron with two children and discreet tastes.

"The colors are terrible," Therese told him. "Everything is so old."

But being on the Rue Duroc, it was a twenty-minute walk from the

Austrian Embassy, which was her father's main criterion. And it was certainly respectable with a dignified three-story front and two windows on either side of the door, high enough to look out but not look in. It matched the houses adjoining on either side, and on through the block, to form a long gray and impenetrable wall.

For anyone who did find their way inside, the house had an entrance hall, a sitting room, a parlor and dining areas on the ground floor, three bedrooms on the first floor above, and rooms for two servants in the attic. There was an enclosed garden in the back, all dead at the moment.

"The colors will do." Then he smiled at her, the first time in Paris. "You may have new colors. First we'll move in and then you'll have the task of making the house worthy of us."

Rudolph had declined to accompany them. Therese was handed into his care late in the afternoon while her father returned to his embassy.

"What did you do all day?" she asked him.

"Nothing."

"You just sat here?"

"What else?"

"Oh, Rudy! Did you even leave the room?"

"I ate lunch."

"Would you take me for a walk? Just up and down the boulevard outside?"

"No."

"How will I ever see Paris?"

"You live in it, Raisy." And, not happily, "I do, too."

"It will get better."

"Only God can make it better."

She frowned. "What does that mean?"

"It's what Zoltan says."

"I can't understand his Hungarian."

"It's a saying. When he says 'only God' can do something, he means no one can. It's impossible."

The baron was not late in returning, and they ate again in the hotel dining room. Rudolph's appetite had recovered slightly, but not his attitude. Therese enjoyed the meal thoroughly.

Then their father had an announcement.

"Next week, the Archduke Albrecht is visiting Paris from Vienna. The Austrian Embassy will hold a reception ball for him and we will attend."

"But, Father," Rudolph said, "we're in mourning."

"It's a diplomatic necessity. The Emperor Napoleon will also attend."

Therese had other things on her mind. "What will I wear?"

"Just wear anything!" Rudolph said.

"No," their father answered. "Therese, Princess von Metternich wishes to meet you. She'll decide how to present you properly."

"Oh!"

"We're in mourning, but it would be undiplomatic to make a display in front of the emperor. We will wear armbands," he said to Rudolph. And to Therese, "And you will be instructed by the princess. You'll both accompany me tomorrow to the embassy for your introduction."

"Do I need to go?" Rudolph said.

"You're a baron in your own right and you're the son of one of Hungary's oldest families," Ferdinand said. "Yes. Protocol requires that you be presented to the ambassador."

They were all three in the hotel suite that evening after dinner; Therese's father seemed restless.

"Tell me more about the von Metternichs," Therese asked him. "They're legendary! The princess was in Vienna last month, but Mother didn't let me see her. Is she really a princess?"

"It's their family title. Richard inherited it from his father, Prince Klemens, who received it from the Austrian emperor."

"And Richard and Pauline are also cousins?" Therese asked.

"Princess Pauline is both Richard's wife and his half niece. They've been in Paris for nearly ten years."

"Paris loves them. In Vienna, they say the French empress loves them. Princess Pauline and the Empress Eugenie are almost inseparable."

"Empress Eugenie and Princess Pauline are very close."

Rudolph had taken an interest. "What influence does Prince Richard have with the Emperor Napoleon?"

"There is a great deal of influence both ways. One might even wonder exactly where Prince Richard's loyalties lie." Her father smiled briefly. "But that isn't for us to question. The ambassador is highly respected in Paris and Vienna, and the princess is at the height of Paris society."

"They should be," Therese said. "France and Austria have always been close friends."

"Are you joking?" Rudolph said.

"No. Why?"

"You don't know?" Rudolph had taken more than an interest. Now he was engaged. "Prince Richard's father, Klemens, was Napoleon Bonaparte's worst enemy. He kept all the other countries in Europe at war against France for years. And now that Napoleon's nephew is the emperor in France, Prince von Metternich the son is the Austrian ambassador." He shook his head. "It's ironic."

"That's forever ago. It doesn't mean anything now."

"History is everything."

"But for the present," their father said, looking at Therese, "the princess has decided that you will be her latest jewel."

"A jewel?" Rudolph said. "She's never met Therese."

"Your mother befriended her when she was young, and helped her navigate Vienna society. They have always been friends, and now the princess wishes to repeat the favor back to you. She is anxious to meet the daughter of her old friend."

"But Mother never let me meet her when she came to Vienna."

"I don't know why," the baron said. "But now you will."

"Is that the only reason?" Rudolph said. "Just because she was friends with Mother?"

"She may have other reasons. Therese," he said, looking at her more tenderly than he had, "be very careful."

"Oh, Father. There's nothing to worry about."

– 4 –

"Princess von Metternich." Therese's father bowed and kissed the gloved hand.

"My dear Baron."

"Allow me to introduce my daughter. This is Therese."

The room dazzled—white and palest blue and deepest green, and everything silk, gold, crystal, and light. It was all Parisian in its flowered patterns and the graceful curves of the chairs and tables and in the geometries of the gardens in the landscapes on the walls. And, too, it was all Viennese in the intimacy of the heavy curtains and filtered sun in its windows. The room was all so like the Princess Pauline von Metternich.

She had met them standing, in a white blue-striped afternoon gown, with her long dark tresses in a careless cascade to the side of her pale cheek and astute dark eyes.

"Dear Therese," she said.

"Princess," Therese said, curtsying and, in the presence of the second most powerful woman in France, made to feel very secure and welcome.

"I beg you for your leave," her father said with another bow. "Rudolph is to have an audience with the ambassador."

"Of course I am so saddened," Pauline said when they were alone. "Your mother seemed nearly a mother to me. At least an older sister, the way she took me under her wing. I was such an awkward young girl." The image was hardly credible.

"What was she like then?" In just moments, Therese had been wrapped in intimacy and confidence.

"She never changed. She was strong-willed and brilliant and fierce. Was that how you knew her?"

Therese paused. "Well . . . yes."

Pauline seemed to hear every fiber of the fabric of Therese's words. "And are you like that, too?" she asked.

"I don't think I'm at all fierce. Or brilliant . . . as brilliant as she was."

"Not in the same way," the princess said. "But close enough alike to not be close?"

"We weren't close. Not close friends, at least."

"No? It might have been easier to be friends with her from a distance, instead of close-by. One had to surrender somewhat to her command in order to get along."

"Then tell me about my father," Therese said, not changing the subject. "Did you know him back then, too?"

"Oh, yes, everyone did. They were married when I was just a little girl. Ten years old? Yes, I think so. Almost twenty-five years ago. So I only knew a little what a stir it caused."

"My father?" Therese said, surprised.

"Irene was already such a force in Vienna. She wasn't beautiful— you're prettier than she was—but she was striking, and of course she was a wealthy heiress. Everyone was falling over her. She must have been receiving proposals every week, and with her own father dead she was able to make her own decisions about them. There were dozens of young men, and some not so young. I would almost have felt sorry for most of those suitors if they'd actually married her. But Ferdinand was a poor noble from the hinterlands of Hungary, and he came to Vienna to make his fortune in the world, and Irene saw a kindred spirit."

"I've never heard any of this!" Therese said.

"Everyone was talking. What a dashing couple they were! And they were alike, but not alike. She was mercury and he was iron, and I think they never mixed."

"He was never home."

"They were always together at first, then less and less. But I didn't know exactly. I only had her letters, and after all the years we've been away in Paris, I'm not sure I knew her anymore. Even when I was visiting last month, I saw her much less than I would have wanted."

"Do you know Father very well?"

"No one knows your father, dear."

"We don't."

"We? . . . Oh, of course, your brother. Rudolph! What is he like? How old is he?"

"Eighteen. Mother wanted him to be in the foreign service, but Father doesn't approve. He was going to be at the Institute in Vienna, but now that we're in Paris, he'll enter the Sorbonne."

"Your mother did have plans for him. She mentioned that in her letters."

"He's terribly sad about her. They were so close." Therese thought for a moment. "I think because he did surrender."

"Well. I want to meet him, of course."

"He's being introduced to the ambassador right now."

"It's a formality. They won't have any time to talk. We'll have a more informal occasion sometime later. And now, dear, I'm sure your father has mentioned our little reception for the archduke."

"Yes! I don't know at all what to wear."

"We'll take care of that. I've already decided that you are to make a grand entrance to Paris society, so the costume for your part must be perfect. You shall be the talk of Paris. We'll visit my dressmaker in the morning. I want you to make a very good impression for Austria, and I want Paris to make a good impression on you."

"Oh, it has already! But I don't think Paris cares much what I think."

"It might, dear. You might be more important than you think." The princess smiled dazzlingly. "So, off to see Mr. Worth in the morning. He's English, but he's the most sought-after dressmaker in Paris, and he'll be so excited to meet you."

"It's all a dream," Therese said. "A new dress, a ball. How could it be happening to me?"

Princess von Metternich smiled kindly. "Don't even wonder why, dear. Just enjoy it."

– 5 –

The balance of Therese's day was spent supervising the settlement of their new home. They didn't have many of their own possessions to move in, but the furniture already in the house required a great deal of rearranging. Rudolph pushed and carried, despite that they had laborers hired to do the work. He didn't let them into his own room but just took it and its furniture as he found it.

Their father mostly stayed in his study. He ventured out a few times, once to place a large, heavy, glistening shard of vermillion and scarlet mineral on a stand in the parlor. Otherwise he had no comments on the arrangements.

Therese had no such lack of opinion. She commanded and positioned like a general over an army, and by evening she had the house somewhat more to her taste.

And one other task had been completed. In a foray outside, she'd found a boy idling at the closest corner, sweeping the street for gentlefolk crossing it and collecting *centimes* from them.

"Boy," she said, collecting him and handing him a message. "Take this to 28 Rue le Bruyere."

"Yes, *mademoiselle!*"

And later, when he returned, he collected a whole sou for the reply, *Tomorrow afternoon.*

— 6 —

From the moment her father left the next morning, Therese began haunting the front windows. By the afternoon she couldn't make herself leave them, watching from the upstairs hall, from the entrance hall, from the front parlor.

"What's out there?" Rudolph was watching her.

"Nothing," she said. It was the truth, and her despair.

"What, do you want to be out there?"

She didn't answer but just dropped into a chair. Rudolph was amused for the first time in Paris. And in just that moment, with her attention taken from the watch, a visitor had arrived. The doorbell rang and she hadn't seen who it was. But she knew.

"Maria will get it," Rudolph said.

"No, I will." She flew to the door and in her hand it flew open. And then she flew back in surprise.

Exceptional blue sparkling eyes confronted her, although from a height. The man was very tall and slender, except for a more rotund middle. He had a broad jaw and expansive brow. His suit was dark gray but his smile was bright, and his hair was part silver gray and part sunny yellow, with a shining bare circle in the crown. This would not have been evident to Therese except that he swept off his hat and bowed.

"Good afternoon," she said in German. She was still startled by the unexpected appearance.

"Good afternoon," the man replied in German. Therese, and beside her Rudolph, stiffened. The accent was undeniably Prussian. "I am here to see Baron Harsanyi."

"He isn't here," Therese said. Then she had recovered herself and she smiled. "He is at the Austrian Embassy. He'll be home this evening."

"We had planned to meet." The man took a small watch from his vest pocket. "Yes, two o'clock."

"Then please come in, Herr . . ." She paused.

"Von Stieff."

"Please come in. Perhaps you could wait in the parlor."

"That would be a pleasure." Again he tipped his hat and bowed. It was a very Teutonic bow, with his feet together and a turn of his head. "Fraulein . . . ?"

"Therese Harsanyi. The baron is my father."

"I thought it must be so." He stepped over the threshold.

"And I am Rudolph Harsanyi. May I ask what business you have with my father?"

The Prussian stopped. He bowed again at the introduction and replied deferentially. "I apologize that I am not at liberty to say. But please be assured, I am here at his request and because of my great respect for him. It is an honor to be in his house."

At that moment the baron himself was on the front steps behind the visitor. "Herr von Stieff," he said. "Please pardon my delay."

"It was unavoidable, I am sure. And I had the opportunity for a moment of pleasant conversation."

"Of course," the baron said, not pleased. "We will talk in my study."

Herr von Stieff gave Therese another very courteous bow, and a deferential nod to Rudolph, and followed his host into his private study, the door closing behind them.

Therese and Rudolph were alone again.

"What does he want?" her brother said.

"You shouldn't have asked. It wasn't polite."

"He's Prussian. Straight from Berlin."

"He seemed very nice." And then she remembered who she had been waiting for and darted to the front window. The street was empty again.

She watched Rudolph frown at the closed study door. Then he stalked up the stairs, and she heard his own door shut.

She returned to the parlor window but without the joy she'd had just minutes before. And suddenly, she saw the man in full that she'd seen only moments of in all her time in Paris.

He was all gold, in the gleaming hair and brilliant beard of his uncovered head, shoulders above anyone else he passed; and in his magnificent aura and the power of his movements; and the command with which he surveyed the world. His brown suit would have made anyone else disappear into a crowd of upper-class bourgeoisie, but on him the clothing was flamboyant, because he was. Joy and fear were evenly matched in Therese's heart as she saw him, and as she could hear her father's voice murmuring behind the closed door.

She had the front door open before he could ring, and the look on her face warned him that all was not well.

"Therese!" he said in a voice that was like gold bells ringing, but quietly.

"Auguste." She stepped outside onto the steps and started to close the door behind her. But now, of course, the street was busy and eyes began to turn her way. "Come inside."

She pulled him in, and he let her, and also let himself be pushed into the front parlor, where they were hidden from the hall. No one could have pushed him unless he allowed them.

"What is it?" he asked, half laughing at her caution. He was fully at ease and unafraid, and his beard reflected the sunlight from the window. He put his hand on the vermillion rock on its stand; it was sparkling in the light as much as he was.

"Father is home."

"Now?" He still wasn't worried, though he did lower his voice.

"He came home early. He's in his study, talking to a man."

"Then I must leave." He took hold of her shoulders, gently. "But when can I see you? To be in Paris with you and not see you every moment, that is madness for me!"

"I don't know . . ."

"Tomorrow? I will not accept any later than that!"

"No . . . tomorrow I'm shopping with the princess."

"A princess?"

"Princess von Metternich. Oh, Auguste, I'm going to a wonderful ball next week at the embassy. The French emperor will be there! And Princess von Metternich is getting me a dress. She wants me to be the most beautiful woman there."

Auguste's eyes glowed with hers, and he swelled with pride for her. "In the plainest clothes, you still would be the most beautiful." Absently, he ran his hand across the red mineral. He looked at it more closely. "What is this?"

"Cinnabar."

"Cinnabar? The ore of mercury?"

"It's from our mines in Idria."

But then there was a rattle, and the knob of the closed study door across the hall turned and the door began to open. Therese jumped close to Auguste, both of them out of sight in the parlor.

"It is an interesting proposal, Baron." Herr von Stieff's voice filled the hall. "Indeed, the demand for mercury fulminate has become intense. At the moment the Prussian stockpiles are very adequate. But the General

Staff in Berlin is discussing large orders. And so . . . it is too soon to say. Perhaps I will be in the market soon. But not yet."

Therese was very close to Auguste, and his arm found its way protectively around her. She couldn't have moved away if she had wanted to.

"My apology, then, for your unnecessary trip to Paris," the baron said.

"Not at all. I had been planning to come. I have several other meetings. There is another supplier with whom I would also negotiate. You know who I mean?"

"Yes, of course."

"And," von Stieff said, as the discussion apparently was not over, "may I ask if Herr Sarroche of the French government has spoken with you?"

"Yes, he has."

"And even Mr. Whistler, the Englishman?"

Therese heard her father answer, "Yes, of course."

"Then if Prussia chooses not to purchase cinnabar ore, you will have other customers."

"Possibly, Herr von Stieff."

"Very good, *Auf Wiedersehen.*"

The front door closed. Therese held her breath, but after a moment the study door closed, as well. She looked out; the hall was empty.

"Go now, quickly," she said.

But Auguste seemed very distracted by the questions and statements they'd overheard. His eyes were on the study door, and only slowly came back to Therese.

"I'll wait until that man is gone from the street. His name was von Stieff?"

"Yes. He introduced himself to me when he came."

"And has your father had other such conversations?"

"Oh, I don't know, Auguste. He must spend his whole day at the embassy talking."

Auguste smiled at her. "It is nothing. So, I will leave. But, my dearest, I will not allow you to put me off forever."

"I won't put you off." She tried to say it convincingly, but she was still shaken by the close encounter with her father. "Not for much longer. I'll think of some way to introduce you to Father. But he can't find out about you until he's met you properly, and he's introduced you to me. If he were to know I've been seeing you without his permission, he'd never let me see you again."

They had waited too long, standing by the window. The door hiding them was pulled away and they were revealed. Therese spun, surprised and guilty. Auguste's turn was more regal.

Rudolph was staring at them. For a moment they were frozen, Rudolph in surprise, Auguste in bemusement, and Therese in annoyance and impatience.

"Auguste?" Rudolph said. "What are you doing in Paris?"

"I am French," he said. "It is my home. Where else would I be?"

"Vienna. That's where you've been the last six months. Did you know he was here?" he asked his sister.

"Of course I did. But Father doesn't know, yet."

All three sets of eyes involuntarily moved toward the study door.

"Then you better go," Rudolph said.

"He is going. We were waiting for the street to be clear."

The street was clear, and Therese pulled Rudolph and Auguste to the front door.

"I'll send you a message when I can," she said. "After the ball."

"But that will be next week!"

"It won't be long. Now go, quickly. Rudolph, attend him at the door, so if anyone sees him leaving, they'll think he was here to see you."

Both gentlemen did as they were told. But Auguste had a parting word.

"Next time we meet, I will not be dismissed." Then, to reinforce his point, "I will be undeniable!"

Therese might have been considered to be fully flustered, but she had no time to recover. The study door opened. "Therese."

"Yes, Father?"

"This evening we will have a guest for dinner. Please inform Maria."

"Who is it, sir?" Rudolph asked.

The baron smiled, oddly. "His name is Pock."

– 7 –

The duty of a hostess was to greet guests on their arrival, and then appear again to announce when dinner was served; the duty of a child was to remain unseen until called. Therese chose the child's part. She heard the bell, and Maria's answering, from her room above.

Then she heard the voices. There was her father's low murmur, of course. There was also Zoltan's growl; this was unusual, especially as he sounded informal, as if he was a part of the greeting.

The third voice, the new voice, was stronger, forcing itself through the hall and filling the whole house. She couldn't make out the words but she sensed its vitality.

So she crept out onto the balcony, just as Rudolph's door opened and he came, also. The puzzled, anticipatory look on his face must have matched her own. They crouched like children, stepping very quietly, and moved forward to see through banisters. The whole movement was a reflex from her childhood. Something about the voice made her remember being small.

But they were too slow and only saw a moment of a tall man's back disappearing into the parlor. Yet for the first time in Paris, or almost since she'd seen her father at all, his voice had an element of peace and comfort.

"Do we know who he is?" Rudolph asked.

"I've never heard of him."

"I think he's familiar."

"He reminds you of someone else," Therese said, straining her own memory. "Someone a long time ago."

Before they could concentrate, Maria appeared in the hallway to announce dinner. They saw her bow in the parlor door, and then she turned to the stairs. But before she started up, she saw Therese and her brother spying down, and waved them to the dining room as she would have for little children.

They came, drawn by the smell of the food and the lightness in their father's voice.

In the dining room, they met Pock.

He was tall and straight and regal. He was older than their father, at least sixty, with deep-sunk eyes and a tall forehead that flowed back into the shining blackness of his hair, perfectly straight over his skull. It must have been dyed; no one's hair was so black.

"Pock," their father said, "these are Rudolph and Therese."

"Harsanyi," the voice like an oak said. "They've grown." Then he turned to them and bowed, an old-fashioned, waist-deep, vigorous bow.

Rudolph clipped his heels together and nodded, while Therese curtsied, both very properly.

"Herr Pock," Rudolph said, a young man greeting his elder.

The old man laughed. "You once called me Uncle Arpad."

"Oh!" Therese clapped her hand to her mouth. "I remember!" All the formality fled, and she and Rudolph unconsciously moved closer. "I thought you were familiar when I heard your voice. Do you remember, Rudy?"

"A bit," he said eagerly.

"You were very little!" Arpad Pock said to him, and then to Therese, "And you not much bigger. What a welcome, Harsanyi!"

"We'll call it a homecoming for you," Ferdinand said.

"She was the best horse I ever had," Pock was saying, twenty minutes into the meal and a nonstop discourse. Therese and her brother were spellbound. "Nothing could disturb her peace. Every Prussian field piece was aimed at her at Koniggratz, and she never flinched."

"You were at the battle of Koniggratz?" Rudolph said. "Father was!"

"Of course he was. He was my second in command." Pock shook his head. "Hasn't he told you?"

"We knew he was there."

"But not what he did? Not the whole story?"

"No . . ." Rudolph faltered. "Never."

"It wouldn't be necessary even now," Baron Ferdinand said.

"Bah. Of course I'll tell them. Have you even seen your children in the four years since Koniggratz?"

"On occasion."

"On occasion? Your own children?" Pock shook his head indulgently. "Then I will tell you. Imagine the scene of the battle!" And they did. "Seventy cannon on the Schwartzberg heights, protecting the whole of the Austrian left flank. For the whole afternoon, von Albensleben had sixty of his own guns trained on us."

"Von Albensleben?" Rudolph asked. "He was Prussian?"

"General von Albensleben. Yes! He is very, very Prussian. And we were the thorn in his side, holding up his whole attack. I think we had put him behind his schedule!" He laughed, and they had to, with him. "The Prussians, everything must be on schedule. But we couldn't stop them forever."

The story went on, and it almost seemed that the cannon and smoke and screaming shells were with them in the small dining room, and Pock's voice rose and fell like the tides of the battle, like the trumpets calling advance and retreat.

"But finally, by six o'clock, our lines had been broken. And then—and then!—the final onslaught. You remember it, Harsanyi?"

Rudolph was mesmerized, Therese amazed, and Ferdinand was amused and tolerant. He tapped his fingers on the table. "I remember. So does Zoltan."

Zoltan was with them. He had even been invited to sit. "Only four years ago," he said.

"I'd remember if it were four hundred years! In all our battles, was there anything like it?"

"It was just a battle, Pock," Ferdinand said. "They're all remarkably the same."

"Just a battle!" He spoke again to the children. "It was only minutes. Almost before we knew the lines had broken, six companies of Prussian infantry were on our hill, charging us with bayonets! They were two hundred meters below, coming like wild men. We only had a few moments.

"I called for retreat, the ones of us who were still left. Your father was commanding the forward batteries and in an instant he had the gunners capping the guns. He did two of them himself!"

"Capping the guns?" Therese asked. "What does that mean?"

"You plug them," Rudolph said. "Then you fire them, and they explode themselves. It's so the enemy can't turn them on you."

"And they did explode," Pock said. "But your father's genius was to explode them just as the Prussians came over the crest. What an explosion it was! The devastation was immense. It singlehandedly stopped the advance for at least ten minutes, enough for us to make our escape."

"Singlehanded?" Ferdinand laughed. "It was twenty men doing it, and it was no genius. You ordered them exploded at the moment of the Prussian approach. I think, my friend, you've added a few details, and taken some others out."

"Every tale grows in the telling. And who is to say that your story is fact and mine isn't?"

"That is a contest I won't wage. But it was a narrow moment. The Prussians were closer than I realized. It was Zoltan who was the hero of the tale."

"Without him, you would not be here!" Pock said it with a laugh, but Rudolph's mouth dropped.

"What do you mean?" he asked.

"You could tell it," Pock said to Zoltan. "Can't you, old friend?"

"I remember" was all Zoltan answered.

"Then I'll tell," Pock said, but Ferdinand stopped him.

"Enough. It is time to return to the present. Do either of you have any questions for Herr Pock? And I mean questions with short answers."

"Yes, sir," Therese asked. "How long have you known Father?"

"Forever, and longer. Through three wars, eight battles, a dozen postings in a dozen lands, and even one rivalry."

"A rivalry?"

"An uneven one. I had designs on the fair Irene—"

"Mother?" Therese tried to not laugh and succeeded. Her father scowled, but good-naturedly.

"A very uneven rivalry, and I was only one of the hundreds who lost. And with no hard feelings, let me assure you."

"What brings you to Paris, sir?" Rudolph asked.

"Paris is my home," Pock said.

"With the embassy?" he asked, surprised.

"Pock is on the faculty of the Paris École Militaire," Ferdinand said. "For the last three years."

"I am in exile," their visitor said, and now he was less well-humored. "After we lost the war with Prussia, my recommendations for reforms weren't heeded. I chose to bring my wisdom elsewhere."

"The French army will surely profit from your wisdom," Rudolph said.

"And you, as well," their father said to Rudolph. He paused, very briefly. "I have made arrangements for you to attend the École."

"The École Militaire? But, Father, I was to attend the Sorbonne—" He stopped in confusion. "Father . . ."

Suddenly the mood had changed. The close familial feeling had fallen away. Therese felt her brother's dismay almost as her own.

"The decision has been made," Ferdinand said.

"I'd expected to be a diplomat," Rudolph said in one last attempt.

"I have decided that would not be suitable. Professor Pock," Ferdinand said, suddenly formal, "please describe the course of study at the École."

"Of course." Pock nodded, kindly and embarrassed, showing his sympathy for Rudolph's disappointment. "We study the tactics of infantry, cavalry and artillery, and strategy and logistics, the mathematic sciences of geometry and logic, and the physical sciences of physics and chemistry. It is the finest course in Europe in the military arts. Our best cadets proceed to the Saint Cyr Academy."

Rudolph had recovered enough to speak. "And would I have the honor of attending your lectures, Herr Professor?" he asked, politely but still with difficulty.

"Yes, of course. I instruct on the tactics and procedures of artillery."

"Then I will look forward to your instruction. Father, I beg for your leave now. I wish to return to my room."

When Rudolph was gone, Therese pleaded for him. "Father. Might you have asked him first?"

"My decision is in the best interests of our family, and for his best interests, as well. His opinion would not have been useful."

"He'll accustom himself to it," Pock said. "But it is a reverse for him."

– 8 –

"Has Rudolph accustomed himself to it?" Princess Pauline asked. Her voice came through the curtain from outside the changing closet.

"He doesn't say anything. But he's been gloomy since we came to Paris." Therese was standing as still as she could while Pauline's maid pulled the last ties and buttoned the last buttons.

"When does he start his lectures?"

"He's already started. I've hardly seen him."

"Mademoiselle?" The maid stepped back.

"Am I done?" Therese asked.

"Yes, yes! Come, please!"

The curtain opened and Therese stepped out into the princess's bed-chamber.

"Oh!" Pauline clapped her hands. "Perfect! Therese, my dearest, you are beautiful."

Certainly she was. In a sweeping gown of pale candlelight yellow, with her white skin and black hair, she was the moon and night sky above the golden lit boulevards of Paris.

"I am!" she said, hardly even meaning herself but the mirror reflection before her. "Oh, my! It's beyond my imaginings!" She laughed. "What will I dream about now?"

"What will you dream about? This is only the beginning!"

"It can't be!" Therese said. "Look at me!"

"I am, dear, and you are just how I imagined. Now, do you want something new to dream about?"

"What could there be?"

"Come with me!" Pauline threw open the door to the hall.

"Like this?"

"Yes, yes. You need practice walking in it anyway. Come, come!"

"I don't have shoes!"

"No one can see."

Suddenly they were scurrying through the hall, away from the princess's apartments and into the formal wing of the embassy, to the great entry hall. Therese could barely keep up, scampering in her stocking feet, as the princess ran ahead.

Then they stopped at a heavy double door. The floor was polished granite, and the pillars were veined marble.

"Are you ready?" Pauline said. Therese nodded, not knowing at all for what. Pauline opened the doors.

The room was vast and grand. The lighting was dim, coming in from closed windows, but this only increased its depth and volume. Everything in it was rich: the lustrous tiles in the floor, the crystal and hangings on the walls, the circuit of columns around the edge, and the massive chandelier.

"Now, imagine it," Princess Pauline said, "filled with the most beautiful women and most noble men in Paris. And you, dearest Therese, as its brightest sun."

Therese was speechless as Pauline's words, like perfume, floated around her.

"In just another day they'll all come. All the lights of Paris."

– 9 –

Black night.

Outside, the winter winds blew, the night was bitter cold. The gaslights and unshuttered windows were the city's claim against the dark, and carriages traveled the pavement in defiance, on streets that, on that night, lead from all of Paris toward one brilliant blazing light.

The Embassy of the Austrian Empire was aglow with light. Coaches clogged the street in every direction, and steam rose from half a thousand horses. Each carriage in turn entered the gate and halted at the grand doorway beneath the imperial crest.

The embassy was magnificent. The bright windows were no false advertisement, but only a tiny overflow of the splendor inside. On entering, guests stood for a moment in the foyer as overcoats and hats were taken. Then they progressed, between granite pillars, the length of the entry hall to a doorway where the double doors were wide open, and paused again. Through the doors, the marble floor itself swept majestically down three wide steps to the level of the ballroom.

The guest might have been a bearded diplomat in a dark satin coat, his brocaded wife on his arm; or a grizzled matron of ancient lineage in black and pearls; or a dashing officer in a scarlet uniform dripping braid and brass; or a Hungarian baron in somber gray. And at the baron's side, a young woman of notable beauty.

On the stage three steps above all the society of Paris, Therese stood and was seen.

Behind her father was her brother. His hair was just as black, the same color as his suit and his gaze at the room, and despite his absence of light, he was also noticed.

Their names were read out by a suitably resonant voice, and then they descended the stairs, melting into the sea of colors, like the wax of a brilliant-hued candle dripping into the hundred colors still on the bottle from the previous candles.

But Therese did not melt in any more subtly than a streak of sunlight in a dim room. Her father handed her into the waiting possession of Princess Pauline herself, and then he backed away into anonymity.

Rudolph disappeared completely.

An orchestra was playing the newest Strauss waltz. The music was part of the atmosphere, with the chandeliers' light, and the scents of lavender, roses, and wine, and the rustling of silk and the growing roar of conversations and laughter. More guests arrived to take their turn on the entry stage and the room filled. The dancing commenced, and all the bright color and sound began to move and swirl.

Princess von Metternich was the center of, and above, this world of light, in a white dress adorned with dozens of yellow roses. She took Therese into her presence, and Therese began her ascent.

High ministers, dukes, admirals, ambassadors, bankers, and marquis, and more specifically their wives, all made her acquaintance. Therese tried at first to hold all the names, like a bouquet in her hand with stem after new stem thrust at her, but soon she threw them to the wind and followed.

"It isn't important if you remember their names," Pauline told her. "It's just important that they remember yours."

They arrived at a crinkled, antique assortment of sideburns, epau-lettes, red cheeks, and blue uniform, sagging from the weight of medals and buttons.

"Your eminence, allow me to introduce an Austrian subject. I present you Therese Harsanyi, who has just arrived in Paris to join her father the baron, who is at our embassy. Therese, the Archduke Albrecht, the uncle of Franz Joseph, the emperor of Austria, himself."

Therese couldn't understand the mumbled greeting, but she answered politely and then was off again.

A sudden hush blanketed the room; the orchestra went quiet. The French emperor had arrived. Louis Napoleon Bonaparte and his Empress Eugenie descended to the floor. Therese was left behind for a moment as Prince Richard and Princess Pauline met the Imperial couple and wel-comed them.

Then she was brought forward and was introduced as the entire hall watched.

"Charming," the empress said, and the emperor of France kissed her hand.

"Rudy," she said. "I've been introduced to the empress."

He was by himself in the shadow of a pillar. It was almost the only dark place in the room. "She looks old. And Napoleon walks with a limp."

"You're awful."

"Somehow you would think that an emperor is somehow different, but he's just a little man. He's almost silly looking."

"But he's very nice," Therese said. "He talked with me. And the empress said I should come visit her with Princess Pauline."

"Why?" he asked. "Isn't there anyone else they could invite? Why you?"

"Why not? And you won't meet anyone, sulking in the shadows. Are you just standing here forever?"

"Forever."

"Come meet someone."

"Who? There's no one here I want to know."

She turned to look at all the noble grandeur, the hundreds of men and women, the jewels and light and colors and faces and luxury and heights and richness, and then she froze. Another hush had fallen on the room, and the orchestra's music seemed to vanish into the air. Eyes were turning to the doorway. Her mouth fell open. And Rudolph smiled.

The newest arrival was standing at the entrance, at the top of the steps, commanding the room, shining like a battalion's colors flying above the battlefield, in his perfect uniform of a captain of the Imperial Guards Cavalry.

"Oh, it's Auguste!" Therese said.

She started toward him, but Rudolph held her back.

"It's Father," he said.

And Baron Ferdinand, in conversation with Prince von Metternich, had turned and was watching the entrance, as well.

The majordomo read the card that was handed to him, "Captain Roman Cesar Auguste de l'Imperator."

"That's his name?" Rudolph said.

"Yes, that's his name! Oh, what's he doing here? He wasn't invited."

"He's about to talk to your princess."

A swift convergence took place. Auguste descended the three steps slowly. Pauline swept toward him. Prince von Metternich and Therese's father, who were already close-by, turned to watch. Therese also moved quickly, but then slowed as she got nearer, with Rudolph just behind her.

"Captain de l'Imperator?" Pauline said. "How magnificent!"

"Madame," he said as he bowed. When he straightened, he and his voice towered over her, and everyone. From that height he saw Therese, and for a single instant their eyes met.

In the next instant Therese looked at the princess and knew their glance had been seen. Pauline was amused.

"I am so pleased that you would add yourself to our gathering," Pauline said to Auguste.

"Thank you so much," he answered. "I accept that as an invitation to be here, because otherwise I have none."

"Oh, indeed!" Pauline stole a look at Therese, who was blushing. "Please accept our hospitality. Richard."

Prince Richard had become interested and moved closer, with Therese's father beside him. "Captain . . . ?"

"De l'Imperator," Auguste answered.

"And this is Baron Harsanyi," Pauline said. "Baron, meet this wonderful man."

"My pleasure," the baron said.

"Now, with officers like this," she said, "how could anyone ever doubt that France would sweep her enemies away?"

"There could be no doubt," the baron said. "Therese? Come let me introduce you to Captain de l'Imperator."

Chapter Three

THE STUDY OF WAR

– 1 –

Like grains of sand sifting through the narrow waist of an hourglass before falling to their place, the students of the École Militaire filled the steeply banked lecture hall. They wore black coats and white collars, but their sober garb and their solemn room with tarnished brass railings, smoothed tile steps, dingy walls and grimed ceiling, did not diminish the exuberant, muscular elation of the students' youth. Their conversations were lively, their movements quick, and their faces cheerful as they found seats. Then abruptly the conversations ceased and the entire hundred, only just seated, stood with a respectful clatter and were silent.

The stage door had opened. Straight, tall, severe Arpad Pock stepped to the podium.

"Be seated."

Rudolph Harsanyi sat with his fellows. He opened his notebook and held his pencil ready.

"Today," the professor said, in a very German-sounding French, "we will consider the correct placement of artillery in preparation for an infantry action. We will use examples of three battles. To illustrate defensive uses, we will discuss Sebastopol in the Crimea; for sieges uses, we will discuss Petersburg and Richmond in America; and for offensive uses, we will discuss Koniggratz."

"An Austrian lectures us on Koniggratz?" The remark was just loud enough to be heard. A ripple of nervous laughter spread through the room.

"A Prussian teacher would be better," another voice said.

"Perhaps," Professor Pock said, and suddenly the room was quiet, cowed by the anger and force in his voice. "Perhaps a Prussian will teach you." He was looking directly at a student in the second row. "A Prussian army. They are very good teachers."

A stronger ripple, of pride and indignation, shook the air. But it quickly faded under the withering stare.

And then, Pock smiled. "Or perhaps you will teach them. That would be much better, wouldn't it?" The room laughed, suddenly won over. "I would be pleased to assist you. Austria was not successful in its lessons, but you will do much better. Also, the opportunity is perhaps not far off. And now, to begin our study, we will refer to Clausewitz."

The cadet beside Rudolph shook his head at the impudence from the second row. "Only an idiot would ask such a question. Professor Pock fought at Koniggratz."

"He fought there with my father," Rudolph said.

"Your father?" The young man heard Rudolph's accented French, and looked more closely. "You're Austrian?"

"Harsanyi."

"Gravert."

With their introduction complete, they returned to the lecture.

"Harsanyi."

In the hallway outside the lecture room, Rudolph turned to see his new acquaintance Gravert calling him.

"Are you really Austrian?"

"Hungarian. My father is with the embassy."

"A diplomat? But you said he fought the Prussians?"

Rudolph stepped away. "I'm not lying."

"Then it must be the truth." The young man had a strange intensity. He was plain, with short, light brown hair, a round face and wide cheeks, almost nondescript except for his eyes. They were green, intent and unwavering. It was hard to look away from them.

"My father is an officer," Rudolph said.

"Where do you live?"

"A few blocks from here."

"I live in Belleville."

Rudolph was unfamiliar with the place. "Is that near Paris?"

"In Paris. The farthest from here, east, in the Twentieth Arrondissement.

I walk six kilometers each day to the École, and then back again. How did you get into the École?"

The questions kept coming, and Rudolph backed further.

"My father arranged it."

"I won my place by examination. It was very difficult. I live with my mother, at home. Is your mother in Paris?"

Rudolph turned angrily on this inquisitor. "My mother is dead."

Gravert was not deterred. "My father is dead. He was killed the year I was born, in the December uprising."

"What December uprising?"

"You don't know. You're Austrian. The coup! When the tyrant Louis Napoleon seized the government. Don't you know that?"

"I don't know French history very well. I've only studied Austria."

"I can tell you about France and its tyrants," Gravert said. When he smiled, he had wide dimples in his round cheeks.

– 2 –

"What was the December uprising?" Rudolph asked.

"Which one? What year?" his father answered.

"About twenty years ago."

"A Paris uprising," his father said. "One of very, very many. It was mediocre, compared to most."

The family was at dinner. The days had become routine, as if it had always been the three of them in Paris. Rudolph spent his days at the École, Therese out with her growing circle of friends, and their father at the embassy. The greatest variation was the time dinner was served, as they only sat at the table when Ferdinand returned in the evening, which would be anywhere between five and ten at night.

"It was when the Emperor Napoleon took power?"

"Yes, the current Emperor Napoleon. It was more than eighteen years ago, and most uprisings are far more bloody. There were only a few hundred shot down in the streets."

"There is a cadet whose father was one of them."

"Every family in Paris has been touched by some revolt. The people of the city rise every few years and barricade the streets. Sometimes they are put down, sometimes the government is overthrown."

"But not other capitals? What about Vienna?"

"Paris is much more practiced."

"Does Louis Napoleon have a legitimate right to be emperor?" Rudolph asked.

"He was elected president of France in 1848, when the previous king was overthrown. Then in 1851 he overthrew his own republic and proclaimed himself emperor."

"So he isn't legitimate?"

"After the coup, he held a plebiscite. Ninety percent of the votes were in his favor. So, yes, he is as legitimate as anyone could be in France. Who is this cadet in your class? Are these questions he's put in your head?"

"I only met him today. He lives in Belleville."

"Red Paris."

"Red?"

"Radical and socialist. Stay away from him."

"But—"

"Stay away from him."

Rudolph nodded. "Yes, sir," he said.

Their father had other things to discuss. "Prince von Metternich has requested a meeting with you."

"With me?" Rudolph showed his uncertainty.

"With you. You should be pleased."

"Of course I am, sir."

"I expect you to be. It is traditional for Austrian nobles attending the École to receive a sword from the ambassador."

"A sword." Rudolph was interested. "And I may keep it?"

"It will be yours."

"What will you do with a sword, Rudy?" Therese asked.

"Defend myself from my sister."

"It'll take more than a sword."

"We have cannons at the École."

"And," their father said to Therese, "I've also received a request concerning you. Do you remember, at the embassy reception, the French captain of cavalry? His name was de l'Imperator."

Rudolph coughed.

"Yes . . . I remember," Therese said.

"He called at the house this evening, before dinner," Ferdinand said, "and I spoke with him. We spoke of his military career and the campaigns in which he has fought."

"He seemed very dashing," Therese said.

Rudolph's cough had turned nearly to a fit, and Therese herself had gone very pale.

"He also recognized the cinnabar stone in the parlor, and we discussed where it had come from. He was very interested."

"Had he come to meet you?" Therese asked. "He must think you're very interesting."

"That was not the reason he came. His purpose was to ask my permission to call on you," their father said.

"Yes? What did you say?"

"I gave him my permission. Therefore, you may expect communication from him."

"Yes, Father." Instead of being white, she was blushing, and trying to hide it.

"Father," Rudolph said, drawing away his attention. "Will you tell me more about Herr Pock sometime? All of the cadets seem to have strong opinions about him."

"What type of opinions?"

"Some of them don't think well of him because he is Austrian."

"He is Hungarian, as I am," Ferdinand said.

"Yes, sir. I know he is, but the French don't seem to care about the difference. He is the only lecturer who isn't French."

"And what are other opinions?"

"Other students think very highly of him," Rudolph said. "He's the only lecturer who's actually been in battle, and he also fraternizes with the cadets. He meets them in the taverns and has them to his apartment."

"Yes," his father said. "I'll tell you about him, some other time."

"Was he really one of Mother's suitors?" Therese asked.

"She was receiving proposals for marriage every week. Every day."

"But he's so old!"

"He wasn't so old back then."

– 3 –

Twenty students stood beside their horses. They were each in riding clothes: loose jackets and long boots over tight-fitted breeches.

"Mount!"

Twenty boots were set to stirrups, twenty saddles were grasped, and the twenty young men swung their weight onto their horses. The slaps of cloth on leather were not in unison, as some riders dropped smoothly onto their mounts, and some did not, even on the second attempt.

Perched easily on his horse, Rudolph watched the struggles around him.

But then they were all astride and the horses back into line.

"Forward!"

With a touch to his rein, Rudolph set his horse to a walk. He had to pull back to slow as others caught up. The ragged line never straightened.

The length of the Champ de Mars, the Field of Mars, was before them. At first they were in the shadow of the dome of the École Militaire, but soon they came out into the sun with a kilometer of green grass ahead.

"Wheel right!"

The line was meant to pivot on its right end, but the maneuver was too difficult when the horses were already in disarray.

"Wheel left!" After a fourth of the circle, the pivot end reversed, and they were now meant to come back to their original position, only one rank length to the right. Except for the horses on the far end of the turn, most of the riders were able to come back into line as it moved slowly into its new position.

"Advance!"

Rudolph shook the rein and the horse responded with a canter. Some of his fellows had also mastered the speed, and a part of the rank stayed organized. The kilometer passed under their hooves and the horses, even under inexperienced riders, knew enough to form their line. Rudolph's horse was new to him, but they had already learned to respect each other. The horse understood what Rudolph wanted, and he let the animal do what it knew to do. And the animals, more than the humans, knew what was about to come.

In two minutes they reached the end of the field. The *quai* and the Seine were below them, and the Pont d'Iena with its statues of Greek and Arab warriors standing next to their horses.

"Reverse!"

On command they each turned their own mount to face back toward the dome and façade of the École, the whole field away. The sun was just above it, and very bright.

And everything was still.

"Charge!"

It began like distant thunder as the first hooves beat the ground. The great weight of the horses took long seconds to accelerate as the charge took on the weight and sound, combined into a single unending crash the riders both felt and heard.

They pulled the field beneath them, and the city past them, and the dome toward them.

They pulled the sky and the sun. They felt their strength and power and the violence they were formed of. They were strong young men unstoppable, relentless, inexorable, and inescapable. They were above the earth but still pounding on it, in the sky but still ruling beneath it.

And then it ended.

The horses were pulled short at the end of the parade ground and turned individually, broken from their one mass into single riders, and the charge dissipated into empty space. The cadets babbled, euphoric at the new sense they had of themselves, congratulating each other and themselves.

As Rudolph breathed still air again, he looked back. Some momentary, peripheral image had surfaced among his thoughts as the sense of the ride faded. Back, about a third of the way to the river, a man was standing on the field, near its edge. He was slight with long brown hair and dark clothes.

As they led the horses into the stables, the instructor stopped Rudolph.

"Monsieur Austrian. You are very good with a horse."

"I learned on my mother's estate."

"You have a natural form. France knows that Austria will be with us in the coming war. Won't you ride with us?"

"Yes, ride with us, Attila," another cadet said. But Rudolph was watching the thin, small man, who had come closer and seemed to be watching him.

– 4 –

"This artillery shell," Professor Pock instructed his class, presenting them with a specimen mounted on a cart in the well of the lecture hall, "is used against cavalry, spreading its shrapnel and fragments in a circle thirty meters in radius. It is this type that was used against the British light cavalry at Sebastopol. Of the six hundred in the brigade, two hundred survived the charge."

He opened the pointed tin cylinder the size of a wine bottle, which was hinged for internal inspection.

"There are different methods employed to initiate the detonation. In modern shells a fuse is lit as the shell is launched from the cannon. The length of the fuse is chosen by the commander of the artillery battery depending on the position of the enemy. Field artillery on horse-drawn caissons are able to fire five kilogram shells over two kilometers. A cannon mounted on railway cars is able to fire ten or even twenty kilogram shells a distance of over five kilometers."

He removed a small package from the shell, under intense observation by the silent cadets.

"Two stages of explosive are used. The secondary explosive, making up the majority of the shell along with shrapnel fragments, is a black gunpowder, the same as has been used for more than a century. But this"—he held the package up—"is the small amount of primary explosive, which is first ignited by the fuse and in turn ignites the main, secondary charge."

He carefully unwound the string holding the paper package intact and revealed a white powder.

"It is pure mercury fulminate, and is the crucial element of modern artillery. It requires a special manufacture to produce, and materials that are not easy to obtain. But without it, an army is without its strongest weapons."

Rudolph knocked at the door.

"Enter."

"Herr Professor?"

Professor Pock's office was small and thick with books, papers, and artifacts: *objets de guerre*, both small-scale models and actual pieces.

"Come. Ah, Harsanyi. You have a question?"

"I want to ask about mercury fulminate."

Pock smiled. "I believe that would be of great interest to you."

"Yes, sir. How is it made from the cinnabar ore?"

"The ore that is produced in such abundance at your mother's mines in Idria? Come, my young friend, and I will show you."

They crossed the main square of the École, empty except for the wind. In the sciences building they took a narrow stair down, below ground, to a dim hall and to a closed door.

"This is the laboratory used for preparing demonstrations for chemistry lectures." Professor Pock opened the door. "Cadets are usually not permitted to come in."

The main light was a small window, high on the far wall, which must have been just at the ground outside. By its illumination the room was a chaos of shapes and reflections. Some objects were solid black silhouettes, and some were glass, refracting the light into bent images on the walls and ceiling. After a moment, Rudolph could see a long bench the length of the room with shelves mounted above it, and cabinets against the walls.

A match flared in Pock's hand. He lit gas lamps on the bench and the walls, and the room grew brighter as he did.

"Is mercury fulminate kept here?" Rudolph asked.

"No, we will produce some ourselves."

With more light, the room was still chaos in its shapes, but ordered in its beakers, flasks, bottles, and pipes so that everything was in a right place. After making sense of what he was seeing, Rudolph's nose caught the miasma of vapors and odors.

Pock chose a cabinet near the window and searched inside. "Here!" He took a tray that held several vermillion stones of different sizes. "You recognize them?"

"Cinnabar," Rudolph said. "I've seen it all my life."

"The sample in your parlor is the most impressive I've seen. But these may have come from Idria, as well. Cinnabar is the sulfide of mercury. And have you seen it smelted?"

"Yes. There's a smelter at the mines. The stone is crushed and the kilns heat them red-hot."

"We will not be able to create such temperatures here. But the heated ore gives off a thick vapor, and when the vapor is condensed, it is pure mercury."

He had replaced the tray of minerals in the cabinet and removed an iron bottle. It was small but apparently very heavy.

"And inside this is that very mercury."

He handed the flask to Rudolph.

"We don't keep this at the mine," Rudolph said. "Father says it's too dangerous."

"The mercury itself is inert," Pock said. "But as your father knows well, the vapors are very poisonous. I think we'll be quite safe, though. We'll only have it open a few moments." From another cabinet he took a glass bottle with a glass stopper. "This is nitric acid, very concentrated."

"An acid. It's dangerous?"

"Oh, yes. Most of the materials and procedures in the creation of the fulminate are dangerous. You will be beset by danger as we do this."

"Good."

He took a glass flask from a shelf, with a wide bottom and narrow neck, and filled the bottom with the acid. "See the brown haze? It reacts with the air. And then, we add the mercury." Even more carefully, he took the iron bottle from Rudolph and unscrewed its lid.

Tilted over the flask, the bottle released a large, silver, molten drop of metal. It fell into the acid with a hollow splash.

"Swirl it," Herr Pock said. "Gently."

As Pock closed the bottle and returned it to the cabinet, Rudolph stirred the mixture of acid and mercury. At first the metal was a globule rolling through the clear liquid, but it began to disappear. Brown bubbles formed around it and filled the flask with their dark gas.

"The acid dissolves it. The proportions must be very exact to achieve the best yield." Pock observed while Rudolph swirled. "But for our purpose, this will do. Beware the fumes! They are nitrous oxide, one of the many hazards associated with this production. And observe the reacted solution."

In the bottom of the glass rolled a cloudy, gray-green liquid.

"Next." Another bottle was produced. "This is common wood ethanol. Any farmer is familiar with it! They make it in their stills, from grains, from anything. But this is again highly concentrated. It is added to the acid." He did so, in drops, slightly increasing the volume of the mixture. "And now, carefully, we will heat it."

He lit a burner with another match. The glass was set above the burner. "It will take a few moments to begin, and then the reaction will produce its own heat." The liquid began to bubble, then boil. Pock removed the flask with tongs and set it on the wooden bench.

The boiling only increased as dense white fumes, like mist from a river, rose from the surface and flowed over the top of the flask.

"Step back."

Rudolph was more than willing to. His nostrils burned from just a slight breath of the vapors.

"It will take a few moments," Pock said, and they waited as the boiling went on and the liquid decreased. As it did, something solid appeared and agitated in the violence of the liquid.

For minutes the boiling continued, until finally what remained was a murky brown liquid with crystals settled at the bottom. "These," Professor Pock said, "are the mercury fulminate. We must separate them from the acid solution."

Rudolph was instructed to decant the liquid through filtering papers, and then rinse the crystals with water. It was twenty minutes after they started that the few grams of yellow-gray powder were mounded in a small pile on the table.

"The product is still impure. Further purification is done by dissolving this powder in ammonium hydroxide, which takes many more steps. But for us, this is quite adequate."

"May I touch it?"

Pock laughed. "Very, very carefully."

Rudolph put his finger into the pile. It felt like any dust, somewhat gritty, the clumps crumbling as he rubbed it between his finger and thumb.

"It must be handled, of course," Pock said, "in order to package it for shells."

"Would it explode here?"

"Yes, very easily."

"Does it need a fuse?"

"A fuse or spark will do. Even a simple percussion will ignite it."

"Just hitting it?"

"With a hammer. But we'll use a flame."

Pock lit the Bunsen burner. He scraped a few grains of the powder onto a scrap of the filtering paper and folded the paper. With tongs, he held the paper toward the flame. The white flash was brighter than all the lamps in the room. Rudolph jerked back from the bursting light, the cracking snap, and the immediate bitter smell. And then it had all vanished except the smell. Even the paper was gone without a trace.

"The chemical process is well-known," Pock said. "It has been used for more than fifty years by every army in Europe, in every artillery shell. Even in many bullets; it's preferred over other powders if it is available."

"That would be hundreds of tonnes," Rudolph said.

"Thousands of tonnes. There are large production factories where this process is carried out in immense vessels."

"Where?" Rudolph asked.

"An interesting question," Pock answered. "America had the largest facilities in the world during their Civil War. But now the three largest manufacturers are in Europe." He counted them off. "Partington and Manchester are in England. The French government has large works in Lyon. And there is a factory in Stuttgart that is owned by the von Stieff firm."

"Von Stieff?" Rudolph asked.

"Theirs is now the world's largest fulminate works. And besides Krupp and Dreyse, they are the richest manufacturing family in Germany. They're Prussian, although most of their factories are in the south of Germany."

"There was a man who visited Father." He said it more to himself.

But Pock was looking at the cluttered bench. "And now, to clean up the mess!"

"What should I do?"

"Nothing. I have some other tasks in here for my next lecture, and it is time you returned to your schedule."

"Thank you, then," Rudolph said. "Would there be any reason that my father would discuss cinnabar with a Prussian?"

"Not your father! No one could force him to sell to Prussia. That would be impossible!"

"Only God could force him."

"Only God . . . ? Oh, you've been speaking with Zoltan, haven't you? He uses that expression."

"He said every Hungarian does."

"We are a fatalistic race," Professor Pock said and smiled. "We are comfortable with impossibility. It makes it easier to accept the difficulties of life. And who knows? Perhaps someday, God will do something that we say only He can do."

The hall was windowless and dark. Rudolph paused outside the laboratory door.

He had his finger and thumb together, feeling the powder that still clung to them; an innocent gray powder.

Then he pushed his thumb against his finger and rubbed hard and fast. The white flash was the same, just smaller, and his hand was forced open by the tiny but potent blast. It was several seconds before he was aware of the smell and could feel that his skin was burned.

"Will this meeting be formal like the other one?" Rudolph asked. He was in his dress cadet uniform of red trousers and blue coat, beside his father in the carriage. Zoltan had the reins as they pulled away from their front door.

"The ambassador may choose to engage in conversation. His schedule did not allow him to be at your first meeting. But take care."

"Yes, sir?"

"If he does allow informality, it will be to observe you. And if you go beyond pleasantries, he'll look for an opening to test you. There will be swords out beside the one you are being given."

"What is my position?"

"Your position?"

"I'm meeting a prince ambassador. Who am I?"

"Any male descendant of a baron is a baron himself in full right," his father answered.

"Do I inherit any position from Mother?"

"No. Her family was noble, but the titles are not passed through women."

"But her estates were."

"They weren't estates tied to her family's titles. Her father accumulated them personally."

"Do I have any rights in them?"

"Didn't your mother explain this?"

"I never asked," Rudolph said.

Ferdinand was silent for several moments. The wheels and horses' hooves clattered over the paving stones.

"You will inherit all of her estates when you reach your majority in five years, at the age of twenty-three."

"I will?"

"Hadn't you thought you would?"

"I only thought I would after your own death, sir."

"That's when you will receive my estates in Hungary."

"But . . ." Rudolph was still uncertain. "But you're in possession . . . aren't you managing the mines? And the cinnabar production?"

"I have guardianship over all the estates in your name as I previously had them in your mother's name. It is my responsibility to manage them prudently and exercise all rights until you gain your adulthood."

"But Mother always made her own decisions."

"We always acted in agreement. You aren't yet old enough to have a responsible comprehension regarding your estates." His father's voice had become sharp, hostile to more questions.

"But—"

"Do you understand?"

"Yes, sir."

The silence continued until they reached the embassy. As the iron gate was opened, his father said, "I suggest you begin to consider the significance of this information. As you can see, a great deal has changed for you since your mother died."

"And how do you find your new life?" Prince von Metternich had received them in his parlor between the two fireplaces. "I am referring to living in Paris, of course."

"There have been many changes, Your Excellency."

"But some, at least, to your liking?"

"Yes, sir," Rudolph answered. "Although Vienna will always be my home."

"As it will be for us all," the prince answered breezily. "And your studies?"

"They are going very well, sir."

"I'm pleased to hear. The French system is very modern, but it may have value anyway."

Rudolph smiled politely at the ambassador's joke.

The ambassador did, as well. "The military life is straightforward and un-complex. I presume you have little interest in the concerns I and your father struggle with here at the embassy."

Rudolph answered immediately. "I do have interest in them, sir."

"Oh, you do?" There was a bite to the ambassador's tone, and Baron Ferdinand folded his arms.

"I had considered diplomacy before accepting a military career."

"How very precocious."

Rudolph didn't react to the mocking. He only said, "I still try to follow European events, sir."

"Very well! What do you think of the current Spanish monarch?"

"They have none, sir. Spain deposed its monarch two years ago."

"Oh? He must have been quite bad."

"She, Your Excellency, Queen Isabella the Second. She is in exile here in Paris."

The ambassador smiled. "Yes. In fact, I just spoke with her a few weeks ago. And, young man, what will Spain do for a new king?" This time the question was pointed instead of flippant.

"The most recent proposal was that Prince Leopold of Sigmaringen would be offered the throne."

"Surely he would be a suitable candidate?"

"It would present a European crisis," Rudolph answered.

"Why? Explain." The unobservant demeanor was gone. Rudolph was now under intense observation.

"The former queen was an ally to France. Prince Leopold is a cousin of the Prussian Hohenzollern king. His position on the throne of Spain would extend Prussia's influence, encircling France."

"Then what would France do?"

"France would possibly declare war on Prussia."

"Spain is a weak, minor country. Surely it wouldn't cause a war between the two greatest armies of Europe?"

"I can't answer that, sir."

"And what was Prince Leopold's decision, with such consequences threatened?"

"The matter was settled peacefully. He declined the offer."

"As far as is publicly known, he has," Prince von Metternich said.

Rudolph frowned at the statement. "Sir?"

"Nothing in diplomacy is ever final."

The test was over. The prince moved to a table in the center of the room, on which was a dark wood case, narrow but a meter long. Rudolph straightened to attention.

"So, as we speak of war," the ambassador said in a new tone, reciting a formula speech, "it is customary for Austrians of your rank who study the military arts abroad to receive a token from the Austrian emperor, of whom I am an emissary. The token is to remind your hosts and yourself that your own loyalty must always lie with your own Imperial master, the dual monarch Franz Joseph, emperor of my Austria, and king of your Hungary." He opened the case.

The sword inside, shining, resting on velvet, took immediate captive of Rudolph's eyes and thoughts. He inhaled sharply, but then regained his composure.

"I am honored, Your Excellency."

"It's pretty, isn't it?" the ambassador said. "War isn't fought with these anymore. This is only its symbol."

"You did well." The carriage was retracing its path.

"Thank you, sir."

"You were well-informed and confident. But remember that your main concern is your studies at the École, not politics."

"Yes, sir."

"While you are young, you shouldn't become involved in things that don't concern you."

"Raisy. Come."

Therese was in the sitting room as Rudolph arrived home from the embassy. Without a word, their father closed himself into his study; Rudolph was left in the hall with the long wood case under his arm.

"Is that it?" she said.

"I'll show you. Upstairs."

He led her to his room and closed the door. While she watched, he set the case on his bed and opened it.

"Oh!"

It was just as beautiful in his small bedroom as it had been in a prince's formal parlor. But now he could close his fingers on the handle, lift the sword and feel its weight, and hold it.

He stood, then slowly rotated the blade, then held it still and vertical.

"What?" he said. Therese was staring up at him.

"You're so tall . . ." she said. "You look like . . ."

He and the sword were straight and upright. He was still in uniform and the sword gleamed: they were both sharp-edged and strong and fine.

"You look like a man."

"I am a man."

"But you weren't before."

"It doesn't matter what I was," he said. "Just what I am."

"Father," Rudolph said at the dinner table. "You never speak of Koniggratz."

"Defeats make poor conversation."

"But I want to hear about the battle."

"You'll hear enough of battles in your lectures. And in the long history of European wars, the defeat of an Austrian army is hardly noteworthy. Paris mobs have their uprisings, Austrian armies have their defeats."

"But we want to hear about your experience," Therese said. "It's important to us because you were there."

"All battles are terrible things. That's all you need to hear."

Rudolph gathered his courage. "Then why are you having me study them? Why not be a diplomat and prevent wars?"

"Prevent them? That isn't the purpose of diplomacy."

"But surely—"

"There is only war, Rudolph. Whether by arms or by words, there is only war. What does Clausewitz say about war and politics?"

"War is only politics by other means."

"Politics is only war by other means. They're the same. The study of war is the only true study of man."

"That isn't right!" Therese was indignant. "He's also a creature of love. At least, a woman is. And some men."

"Love and war, those are the same, too," Rudolph said.

"Mistress?" Maria was at the door, a letter in her hand. "This has just come for you."

Therese was on her feet to see to grab it. Rudolph watched her tear open the envelope.

"Father? It's from Captain de l'Imperator. He's asking when he can call on me."

"I'll be busy tomorrow," their father answered. "Tell him the following afternoon."

"Yes, sir."

As soon as the baron had stood from the table, Therese went straight for the kitchen. Rudolph followed.

"Maria?" she was saying. "Father just said that Auguste could come to call on me."

"The captain?" Maria said. "Is he here in Paris?"

"He is, and he's just met Father. Maria?" Therese's voice took on a begging tone. "Father doesn't know that Auguste was in Vienna, and he doesn't know we've already met." She took a deep breath. "We need to keep it a secret."

"A secret? From the master?"

"Please, Maria," Therese said. "It won't hurt. If Father finds out that Auguste was calling on me without his permission in Vienna, he'll throw him out."

"It's all right," Rudolph said. "You don't have to keep a secret, Maria. Just don't say anything about it unless Father asks."

"What if the master does ask me about him?"

"He won't," Rudolph said. "Why would he?"

– 6 –

From his bedroom, after dinner, Rudolph heard the bell ring and his father answering the front door, and the dull knife rasping of English in the hall. Then his father's study door closed. For a moment he returned to his reading.

But Clausewitz was suddenly tedious and lost his attention. Rudolph stood and stepped into the upstairs hall. His sister's door was closed. He listened closely to the air and heard the wisps of conversation from his father's study below.

He descended to the main floor, but he kept his steps very light. For a moment he stood near the door and listened to the voices inside. He heard his father's voice. He put his ear against the door and made out the words. They were speaking German.

"No, Mr. Whistler, your terms will have to improve greatly. I have other offers."

"I know your other offers, my dear Baron, and they're no better than mine."

"The French are offering twenty percent more."

"Sarroche will pay you twenty percent more, but you have to deliver the cinnabar to them at your expense. I will arrange my own transportation. I know every detail of their offer."

"Then you have an agent in the Bureau of Armaments?"

"A minor functionary," Mr. Whistler's voice said. "The French don't pay their officials enough. The poor little people have to live off bribes. But you can see, Baron, that whatever Sarroche is prepared to offer, I will know how to better it."

"At what prices would you sell the final fulminate to him?"

"That wouldn't be your concern."

"I don't want the French overcharged. I want to know what they would pay."

"If you want information from the Bureau of Armaments, you'll need to do your own bribery. And don't pretend you're so concerned for the French. I know you've met with von Stieff. Although I'll admit I don't know his offer. Do you even have a firm offer from him?"

Rudolph pressed his ear closer to hear.

"That will not be your concern," the baron's voice said.

"He's got Almaden in Spain as a source, you know."

"That isn't assured."

"From what I hear, it might well be. It would depend on Prince Leopold."

"He has declined the Spanish throne."

"I expect you aren't fooled by that any more than I am. Partington and Manchester have quite a few sources for information."

"How do you get these sources, Mr. Whistler?"

"We pay them, we bribe them, we threaten them, we blackmail them."

"Is there anything you would not do?"

"Oh, come, Baron. I know you're not squeamish. And the French are as bad as we are. They have even nastier methods, and even more agents."

"Who was the French agent in Vienna who approached my wife?"

The Englishman answered. "I don't see any advantage for me in telling you that."

"But do you know who it was?"

"Why do you ask? Are you afraid Sarroche has found out what happened to your wife? Don't worry about that, Baron. He won't hold it against you. In fact, it might make him respect you more."

"Rudy?"

He jumped. Therese was behind him, on the stairs.

He put his finger to his mouth and backed away from the door.

"What are you doing?" she said.

He shook his head. But before he could say anything, the doorknob rattled and the door began to open.

As quickly as he could, Rudolph got himself to the bottom of the stairs. When his father looked out from the study, Rudolph was leaning on the banister and speaking to his sister as if he had been for minutes.

"So when is that Captain de l'Imprater coming to see you?"

"De l'Imperator! Rudy, what are you—?"

"I think I want to meet him. He seemed interesting." Rudolph turned to see his father and had a moment's glimpse of a red-faced, mustached man in the back corner of the study. His father looked at him a moment, then closed the door.

But in the moment the man had seen him, as well. Their eyes had met, and Rudolph recoiled.

He pushed past Therese on the stairs, ignoring her questions, and hid in his room.

"Maria?"

"Yes, Master Rudolph?"

Night had passed and Rudolph was finishing breakfast. As early as it was, his father had left before Rudolph had seen him, and Therese had still not appeared for the day. Maria was collecting Rudolph's plate.

"Tell me about the day that Mother died."

"You were there, master!"

"But I was out when Father arrived. Had you seen Mother before he came?"

"It had been a few minutes. Not long."

"What did he say after he was with her?"

"That she was sleeping well."

"That was all?"

Maria paused. "And that I didn't need to disturb her."

"When did you go in again?"

"Only after Therese went in and found her in the afternoon. The master had said to not disturb her."

"And he'd left by then."

– 7 –

Twenty cadets stood in the yard behind the main building of the École in long leather coats, but not against the cold. Each held a sword, and each faced a mannequin: a torso of leather-wrapped wood mounted on a post, with no arms, legs, or head.

"Later you will learn more handling of the weapon," the instructor told them. "Now, only rehearse the lethal blow. Raise the swords. Both hands."

Rudolph, like the others, wrapped his hands around the handle of the dull, nicked sword used for practice. The instructor walked behind them, inspecting, correcting the stance and the angle of the arms.

"Continue to hold. Now prepare. Only a powerful blow will be sufficient. All the force of the arms and shoulders will be brought down onto the target, magnified a hundred times by the sharpness of the edge. Now gather your will and determination. Consider your enemy, who deserves this stroke, and your right to deliver it to him. Now, strike."

Twenty blades fell, propelled by all the strength in young muscle and mind. The total sound of it was a single blurred blast of the twenty impacts. Some swords glanced aside, many bit in, and some deeply.

Rudolph's swing had been too much downward and not enough sideways, and hadn't bit into the leather.

"Again," the instructor said.

Gravert was beside Rudolph, and as they lifted the swords together, Rudolph heard him mutter, "To the tyrant!" Then, to Rudolph, "Who are you striking against?"

"No one."

"It's better to choose someone. The blow comes much easier when you know who you're attacking."

"Strike!"

Rudolph's sword went deeply in. He had difficulty removing it.

"What if the other person is better with his sword than you?" Therese asked.

"We don't fight against other people with swords," Rudolph said. He was at his desk in his room, and Therese was sitting on his bed. His sword was in its open case beside her.

"Who do you fight?"

"It's for the cavalry. You use it from your horse as you ride past." He lifted the blade and drew it across an imaginary opponent. "Like this." Then back again. "And that. We haven't used it from the horse yet. We've only practiced while we're standing."

With the sword in his hand, he tried other motions, slicing slowly through the air.

"Why are you moving so slowly?" Therese asked.

"I'm practicing. And I don't want to cut you in pieces by accident." Suddenly he moved quickly, pulling the sword down as fast and hard as he could, checking just before it touched the floor. Therese pulled back.

But Rudolph felt other eyes on him and he turned toward the bedroom door.

"Zoltan . . ." he said.

His father's valet was silent there, watching. He nodded slowly in acknowledgment.

Rudolph raised the sword from its position, nearly touching the floor, and turned to put it back in its case. But as he did, he kept his eyes on Zoltan, and saw that Zoltan was watching his hand.

"That's not the way," Zoltan said in his deep, grinding voice.

"What?"

"The wrist." Zoltan came into the room and took hold of the handle; Rudolph surrendered it to him. "The wrist," he said again, "and the shoulder. The wrist bent and the shoulder loose. If you strike rigid, the shock comes to you. Blow after blow, you become tired and sore."

Rudolph took a breath and asked, "Would you show me how?"

"I will show you. Not today."

"Zoltan?"

He had turned to leave, but he looked back.

Rudolph said, "Can you tell me about Koniggratz?"

"There is nothing to tell," he said.

"Professor Pock said that without you, Father wouldn't be here."

Zoltan shrugged. "But he is here."

"Please tell me what happened."

"He waited too long."

"He was waiting for the Prussians to get there so they'd be killed by the explosion."

"But they came too fast and were there before we could leave."

"What did you do?" Therese asked.

Zoltan held up the sword. "Three men I killed with one of these and that was enough."

– 8 –

Cold wind scoured the land, roaring from the north, over the fields and villages and down onto Paris. The cadets trudged up a steep hillside path toward high gray walls.

"A government that rules by force over its people is illegitimate,"

Gravert said, huffing from exertion. "The emperor has killed thousands. He should be overthrown."

"But he is the emperor!" another cadet argued.

"He is a usurper. He is a tyrant. He is incompetent. And he is a buffoon."

"And who should take his place?"

"The people must rule."

"How do they do that?"

"With justice! With equality!"

"How do you overthrow an emperor?"

"Blood must flow! But the people will rise!"

"Those are just slogans," Rudolph said to Gravert, rejoining the conversation. "I don't think you really mean them."

"I do mean them."

"My father says I should stay away from you."

"He is bourgeois and reactionary."

Rudolph looked sharply at Gravert, but he didn't seem to have meant an insult.

"It is not his fault," Gravert explained. "It's from his birth and position. This is why noble titles must be abolished."

"But I was born the same," Rudolph said.

"Proceed to the ramparts!" The command came from the second-year cadet who was leading them, and they followed silently.

"Sixteen fortresses circle Paris," Professor Pock instructed the cadets. "D'Issy in the south, then de Vanues . . ." he listed them, name after name. ". . . and finally Mont Valerian, where we stand at this moment, which commands the west side of the city."

They stood on the summit of the barbican wall, high above the city that sprawled out of sight toward the east.

"Together, the walls of these forts hold more than two hundred cannon and are stocked with one hundred thousand artillery shells. It is presumed that no enemy force could ever break through their ring. Paris is the most strongly fortified city in Europe. But even one hundred thousand shells would not last more than a few weeks, which shows the importance of the vast amounts of explosive required in modern war."

As Pock lectured, Rudolph noticed a man standing on the wall above them, watching. Rudolph stared at him, trying to make out whether he was the same man who had watched the cavalry practice.

The cadets stood in circles about the five cannon of the foremost battery, facing west away from the city. The villages of Rueil and Nanterre were close at hand to the northwest. Before them lay a long empty plain.

"Load!"

A cadet in each group lifted a heavy shell into the breech of their cannon.

"Aim!"

Two other cadets for each cannon cranked a gear wheel, sighting through a mounted cross hair. An officer of the fort's garrison watched, verifying the aim.

"Prepare!"

Five lit sticks were held ready.

"Fire!"

Unison crashes broke the air; thrown flames became hanging smoke; the cannon recoiled. Then five eruptions lifted points of the plain a thousand meters from them.

A flock of goats scattered, and a white-bearded man shook his fist at them from far below as he chased his flock.

A cheer rose from the wall in answer.

"Professor Pock?" Rudolph was standing on the west wall afterward, looking down on Paris. "Who is that man?"

Pock followed his stare. "Come, I will introduce you. That is Monsieur Sarroche."

Rudolph was startled by the name. The man had been watching them, and as they approached, he came to meet them. He was short and thin; his nose was long and sharp, and his hair even longer, as if to make up for his small stature.

"Monsieur Pock," the man said. "I am observing you and Monsieur Harsanyi."

"And you have been observed. Cadet Harsanyi, this is Monsieur Sarroche of the Bureau of Armaments. Apparently, he already knows you! I think, monsieur, you must know his father at the Austrian Embassy?"

"Yes, of course. We have spoken often in recent weeks."

"And," Professor Pock said, "you are here to ensure we do not deplete your precious stock of artillery shells?"

"I said I am observing you and Cadet Harsanyi. And now, I have other matters to attend." And with that, he walked past them both and left them behind.

"Who is he?" Rudolph asked, but Pock seemed not to hear him. The professor was staring after the disappearing figure. He was pale, and seemed shaken. "I saw him at cavalry practice, too."

Pock attempted to regain his usual confident manner. "He is a very important official of the French government. And he seems to be somewhat out of sorts. And I . . ." Pock shrugged. "I am an insignificant foreigner who does not want important officials displeased with me." His smile showed that he was exaggerating his trepidation for dramatic effect, except that the trepidation was real. "I hope that I didn't use too many of his artillery shells! But every class of cadets is shown how to fire the cannon."

"Would he be responsible for buying cinnabar from my father?"

"Sarroche? I presume he is. That would be the reason for his frequent discussions."

"He said he was observing me?"

"I don't know at all why that would be."

"What was the English manufacturer of mercury fulminate?"

"The English? They are Partington and Manchester."

"An Englishman came to my house to speak with Father. His name was Whistler."

"That is their agent in Paris. He would offer your father a very substantial sum for your cinnabar ore. I expect he and Monsieur Sarroche would not be the best of friends."

"He mentioned 'Sarroche.' "

As Rudolph stood thinking, looking out over Paris, Cadet Gravert joined them. He was studying the construction of the fortress. "The walls are as high facing toward Paris as away," he said, "and the ramparts are just as wide." Paris was an easy target, just beyond the Longchamps race course and the woods of the Bois de Boulogne.

"What do you mean?" Rudolph asked.

"With a moment's effort, the guns could be turned from an enemy outside to fire on the city itself. And why do they need a fortress on the west anyway? The Prussians are to the east."

But Professor Pock said, "Firing on their own city would be like a father betraying his own children!"

"He was here!" Therese said before Rudolph had even closed the front door.

"Who?"

"Auguste!"

"Oh." Rudolph trudged past toward the stairs.

"He was right here in the front room, and we talked together. Father was there so we couldn't really talk, but we'll be able to now. Rudy! Don't you care?"

"I'm happy for you, Raisy."

"That's all?"

"That's enough." And he left her behind.

– 9 –

The Boulevard de Magenta was not convenient to Rudolph's house on the Rue Duroc. He had the whole of Paris to cross, a ride of three kilometers, to reach that boulevard, and then the Rue de Valenciennes. He rode it quickly.

On the boulevard, between the two stations, was an office between other offices. The inconspicuous sign, a plain brass plaque, said only *Partington and Manchester.*

He rang the bell and waited. A pale, flabby clerk soon opened the door, and then took a moment to decide if the young man on the steps was a serious visitor.

"Yes? What do you want?" Even Rudolph could hear the English accent in his French.

"I wish to speak with Mr. Henry Whistler."

"Who are you, please?"

"My name is Rudolph Harsanyi."

The name might have meant something to the clerk. "Please step in."

Inside the door, Rudolph waited again. The office directly to the right was the clerk's. A door on the left was closed. The clerk knocked and disappeared inside.

Reappearing, he nodded to Rudolph, who crossed the threshold into the office.

The brief moment that their eyes had met before was immediately resumed, and even more strongly Rudolph fell back before that gaze. He was being searched, and Mr. Whistler seemed to find something of interest.

"Master Harsanyi," he said. "We meet again. Could it be that you wish to have your own conversation rather than listening in to someone else's?"

"I came to ask what you were discussing with my father."

"How old are you?"

"Eighteen."

"Then you should come back in five years. That's Austrian law, isn't it? You have to be twenty-three before you can take charge of your affairs. Before you even have any affairs."

"You want to produce mercury fulminate to sell to the French army. You're trying to purchase cinnabar ore from the mines in Idria."

Whistler looked at him with more interest. The grand, bushy mustache seemed designed to hide whatever was going on behind it. "That certainly is what I want to do. You must have deduced that by yourself. I doubt very much that your father would have given you that information. But . . ." Rudolph was searched again by the penetrating eyes. "What is it to you? Why are you here?"

"I want to know what is being discussed," he said again.

"Is that all? You just want to be kept informed?" Mr. Whistler had lost interest. "Then you've come to the wrong half of the conversation. Or . . ." Suddenly the interest returned. "Is it that you don't trust the baron? You think I'm more likely to tell you the truth? You know, it might be wise to not trust him. There's a growing circle of us who don't."

Rudolph was at a loss to answer. "That doesn't—"

"If you only want to know what we're discussing, I've told you all I'm going to. So please leave, and come back when you have any legal control over the mercury. The currently brewing war will be over, but I'm sure there will be another by then. Five years is a long time. There might have been two or three wars by then."

The man had hold of Rudolph's eyes, and it seemed, his soul. He could look away, and the words continued to roll out at the Englishman's slow pace, and in his disagreeably accented German.

"Or," he continued, "perhaps five years is too long. Perhaps you have some idea of gaining control from your father sooner."

"I don't—"

"Because that might be possible." The corners of a terrible smile appeared from behind the gray mustache. "He got tired of waiting for your mother."

"What do you mean?"

"What do you think I mean?"

"You said Sarroche had found out what happened to her. What did you mean by that?"

"You've met little Sarroche, too? You have been busy."

"What would he know about my mother?"

"Don't ask me what other people know. Ask them yourself. But . . ." He paused. "If Sarroche makes some type of offer, come back. I'll talk with you about it. And if you decide you don't want to wait five years, maybe something can be arranged. As I said, your father got tired of waiting for your mother. You might get tired of waiting for him."

"Are you saying that my . . . my father . . ." He couldn't finish the sentence.

"I just hope he doesn't get tired of you for some reason. Who will be cleverer than the other? You or your father? Between the two of you, I think I'd bet on the baron." He purposefully looked back at his desk. Rudolph had been dismissed. "Now, run along. I'm busy. Come back when you have something more interesting to say."

Chapter Four

MESSENGERS

– 1 –

The crowded streets of Paris were always empty as Baron Ferdinand Harsanyi walked them. He passed alone through teeming throngs, fashionable women, grimed street children, working men, self-important officials, ponderous businessmen, laundresses, coaches, landaus, open and closed carriages, top hats, caps, bare heads, ostrich feathers, all unseen in his solitude.

His stare was fixed on something far away, not on the city around him. Even Paris was daunted, slightly, by his closed face and made way for his long strides, so that as he moved he was like a jutting rock that waves broke against. And he walked a great deal.

"I've spoken with the leaders of the Assemblee Nationale," Prince von Metternich said to him on an early spring day as they were both in the ambassador's office, studying maps of the Rhine frontier between France and Prussia. "This will be in my dispatch to Vienna today."

Ferdinand read the short message: *Radicals, Moderates, and Imperialists all accept war as an all but accomplished fact.*

"Yes," he said. "They all do expect war, whether they want it or not."

"It's a direct quote from the speaker of the Assemblee. Have we reached the point where war is inevitable?"

"Surely, Your Excellency, you know better than I."

"All the kindling needs is a match," the ambassador said.

– 2 –

Late one afternoon, Ferdinand made his way through the center of Paris, across the river to an alley remote from the Austrian Embassy, to a small café, where he took a table deep inside, invisible from the street. Soon he was joined by the tall, blond, fringed Karl von Stieff.

"Thank you for seeing me," the Prussian said, bowing affably as he sat opposite the baron.

"Thank you for agreeing to this location."

"I understand fully. And I think even here we should be brief."

"That would be wise," Baron Ferdinand said.

They sat a moment in silence, searching for a rapport, choosing how much to reveal, locating their position between enemy and friend. Von Stieff spoke first.

"Herr Baron," he said. "At our last conversation I said we had no short-age of cinnabar and mercury, but that the government had been discussing larger orders." He lowered his voice. "The orders have now been placed. They are very large. I find myself in need of cinnabar."

Ferdinand nodded. "How great a need?"

Despite their caution, von Stieff smiled his gracious, genuine smile. "The answer to that question is the answer to many other questions. At our last meeting you said that your mines could produce perhaps five thousand kilograms of cinnabar ore each month."

"That would be possible."

"And also that you had several months' stockpiled already."

"All of the production of the last four months."

"And the production of the months before? Has it been sold some-where else?"

"All of last year's production was sold to the Austrian government."

"I see. Where is your stockpile?"

"In Idria."

"Eight hundred kilometers from the factory in Stuttgart. But an empire away and a very hostile border in between!" Von Stieff frowned thought-fully. "The ore has been extracted from the mine, but now it would need to be extracted from Austrian territory."

"Idria is only fifty kilometers from the port of Trieste on the Adriatic," the baron said. "We would need an intermediary to purchase the ore. An Italian would be best. For the government in Vienna, Italy would be an acceptable customer. There must be no hint that Prussia is involved. If it is discovered, the sale would immediately be blocked, and my own position would be deeply compromised."

"Of course," von Stieff said. "I could consult with my embassy about the possibilities and agents in Italy."

"How much do you wish to purchase?" Baron Ferdinand asked again.

"All of it. All that is stored, and all that can be produced. Perhaps."

The baron considered. "That suggests a very large production of armaments."

"As I said, the answer to your question of how much cinnabar we need is the answer to many other questions, as well: how large the armies will be and how they will be armed. But certainly, the General Staff expects to use a vast amount of armaments in the very near future."

"When do you need the ore?"

"Immediately. But, only perhaps. You see, there is the other source that I may have access to instead."

"When would you know?"

"Two weeks. Although there is now a great urgency, I can't answer until then."

"Then I'll wait for your next communication," Baron Harsanyi said.

"I've been thinking," Pock said. He was with Ferdinand that same evening in the parlor of the house on Rue Duroc. "About mercury."

"You aren't also trying to buy cinnabar ore, are you?"

Pock laughed. "Ha! Exactly what I'd been thinking."

"You are?"

"No! Only that you must be very greatly in demand by those who are."

"There have been requests."

"The French?"

"Do you know Monsieur Sarroche?"

"Very well," Pock said. "He's very unpleasant. And the British?"

"Do you know Mr. Henry Whistler?"

"Not as well, but he seems just as unpleasant. The English aren't planning to participate in the upcoming war, are they?"

"No," the baron said. "They just want to produce the fulminate themselves and sell it to the French. The largest profit is in the production."

"And between Whistler and Sarroche, do you have a preference?"

"As you said, they are equally unpleasant."

"Surely there would be more to a decision than just their dispositions!"

"Neither has been able to outbid the other."

"And anyone else?" He paused. "The Prussians?"

As Pock asked, they heard the front door of the house open. Rudolph appeared at the entrance to the parlor. "Father," he said. "Professor Pock."

"Yes, good evening," Ferdinand said.

"I have a friend with me," Rudolph said. "A cadet from the École. We'll be in my room."

"Very well. Who is it?"

"This is Cadet Gravert." A young man with a wide face and intense green eyes stood for a moment beside Rudolph, and then they both left the parlor.

"Do you know him?" Ferdinand asked.

"I know him. A radical."

"Radical? I told Rudolph to stay away from them."

Pock smiled. "In this case, I think it more likely that Rudolph will talk sense into Gravert, instead of Gravert corrupting Rudolph."

"Well . . ."

"Your son is a very sensible fellow. We had a long discussion about mercury fulminate."

"That is another subject I have instructed him to avoid."

"You have? Then I will from now on. He wanted to know how fulminate is produced."

"Don't encourage him, old friend," Ferdinand said. "I want him to attend to his studies without distractions." He glanced at the newspaper on a side table. "Prussia is investing in the railway through Switzerland to Italy."

"That will give von Bismarck control of the new tunnels through the Alps."

"And more influence in Italy, at the expense of the French. There is only one end to this rivalry, Pock."

"There have been many other crises and no war yet."

"The only end to 'no war yet' is war."

– 3 –

Henry Whistler looked up from his chair and desk. "Well, well, Baron. It's always so nice when a Harsanyi visits!"

The baron paused. "What do you mean by 'a Harsanyi,' Mr. Whistler? Is there more than one?"

"Oh, I don't mean anything at all. Please, sit down."

Ferdinand sat in the chair offered to him. "I presume that you've talked with your office in Manchester?"

"Yes. Yes, I have. Your delays and prevarications are really quite maddening, but they have convinced my superiors to increase our offer. There would, however, be some additional conditions."

"What are those conditions?"

"First, that you would agree to an exclusive contract to sell only to Partington and Manchester and no one else, even if we didn't purchase your entire stock."

"How much would you purchase, Mr. Whistler?"

"I know you've told Sarroche you could sell him twenty thousand kilograms. I think I'd take all of that, so you wouldn't have any left over anyway. Our second condition is that you would remove your requirement that we not sell our production to Prussia."

"That would be a requirement of the Austrian government."

"It hasn't kept you from negotiating directly with von Stieff. You met with him just a few days ago. But I don't care about your little games. You can claim restrictions concerning Prussia to keep your own government satisfied, but I will not be bound by them."

"Is Prussia willing to buy finished mercury fulminate from you?"

"I prefer to keep my options open."

"And for these conditions, what are you offering for the cinnabar?"

"Seven thousand pounds per thousand kilograms."

"It is not significantly higher."

"It's as high as I want to go. One hundred forty thousand pounds? That's nearly two million *francs*. So you have my offer, and von Stieff's, if he wants your cinnabar at all, which I'm beginning to doubt, and you can get Sarroche's final offer, which I already know, and compare them all."

"There have been other discussions."

"The Russians? The Italians? They've all told you they aren't interested. The Americans have their own mines, the Swedes can't afford your prices, and your own Austrian government still has to build its own fulminate works. We manufactured their last stocks for them. No, it's just the three of us left. You have the whole market to compare. You should be careful that you don't price yourself out of it, Baron."

"The French still have no other source."

"At the moment." Whistler rubbed his eyes, which were bloodshot. He blinked them and shook his head, as if he were fighting weariness. "These negotiations are going on too long. I'm not as young as I used to be." His voice had lost none of its bite, though. "If von Stieff gets the source he wants, your own mines will lose quite a bit of their value."

"But they are still my mines."

"For the present."

"What do you mean?"

"That you may not have as exclusive a control over your own mines as you think. You don't know? How humorous. Monsieur Sarroche's agent may not have been successful with your wife, but he never gives up. There are other members of your family, you know. Or maybe you've forgotten that, in the press of so many other responsibilities."

"What are you talking about?" Ferdinand said. Whistler's sarcasm had finally driven him past frustration to anger.

But Whistler shook his head. "When we sign our deal, I'll tell you everything I know. A little added incentive. But now you'll forgive me as I think I'm done with our meeting today. I'm not feeling completely well. I'll give you a few days to consider our offer, but time is running out quickly, Baron Harsanyi. Once the war starts, it might drag out or it might end quickly, and if it does, the market for mercury fulminate will collapse."

"I understand, Mr. Whistler. And . . . please answer one other question."

"I'm already out of patience."

"When you went to Vienna last winter," the baron said, ignoring his comment, "you said a new wind was blowing."

"I had heard that."

"From your agent in Sarroche's Bureau of Armaments?"

"I've told you before that you should get your own sneak. I don't want to share mine."

"Did Sarroche get his information from his agent in Vienna? Or did he send his agent after he'd gotten the information?"

"I think that I will say again that answers like those only come with a signed contract for cinnabar. Now, please leave. Or stay if you want, but I'm leaving. Good afternoon."

Baron Ferdinand stepped out onto the Rue de Valenciennes. Zoltan was waiting in the carriage.

"Home," the baron said, and after they'd started he asked, "Zoltan, do you see much of Rudolph?"

"In the house. I will teach him how to use his sword."

"At least that's useful, somewhat. If you see that Whistler or Sarroche or any of the others are communicating with him, tell me immediately."

"Maria." Ferdinand found her in the kitchen.

"Yes, master?"

"I want you to think back to Vienna. Particularly about visitors to the house."

Maria seemed suddenly worried. "Yes, master? All of them?"

"Those who called on my wife in the weeks before she died."

She was relieved. "Her friends."

"Besides her regular friends. There was an Englishman, Henry Whistler?"

"Yes. I remember him. He came once."

"Was there anyone else like him? Not necessarily English? Anyone French?"

"No."

"Did she go out to meet anyone?"

"Her friends. I wouldn't know who she was seeing."

"I know there was someone, even if you never saw them. If you remember anything at all, I need to know. How often did she go out to meet friends?"

"Every few days."

"Did she have many friends that she went to visit?"

"No, master, she didn't. And the same ones would also come to visit her. But . . ."

"Yes?"

"She did mention an old friend, once."

"When?"

"In December."

Ferdinand considered. "It may have been Princess von Metternich."

– 4 –

"Describe to me," Prince von Metternich said, "the French and Prussian armies."

Baron Ferdinand considered how to answer. "Surely . . ."

"Yes, yes, I've read the newspapers and heard the briefings, and none of it made sense. I'm not interested in armies. You've told me how many divisions and how many horses and cannons, but what I want to know is which army is going to win."

The baron nodded. "The armies are very different. The French army is professional. It's all long-serving officers and enlisted men. Many of them have been in the service ten or twenty years, and some even fought in the Crimea and in Italy and in North Africa. They are an isolated body in France, living in their own barracks and their own world. They are at least two hundred thousand strong, and many consider them the strongest army in the world."

"And they're ready to move at a moment's notice? That's what I've been told over and over."

"That is their plan."

"But is it the truth?"

Ferdinand took a long, deep breath. "Most likely not, Your Excellency."

"Why?"

"There are two reasons. First, my observations have been that they actually aren't a disciplined force."

"In other words," the prince said, "they are French."

"They are very French. They'll fight bravely, but they have no general staff, and none of the highest generals and marshals is experienced. The men aren't used to hardship. Their drilling is perfunctory or ignored because they consider it unnecessary. They believe that because they're French, they must win."

"And the other reason?"

"They have only three train lines to the front, and they're all single track. They won't be able to mobilize with trains going only one direction at a time."

"No one has mentioned that," the prince said. "Is it really that important? Don't armies march?"

"It will be crucial," Ferdinand said. "Armies march, but they ride much faster."

"All right. And the Prussian army?"

"Prussia is a smaller country, but together with its allies it is larger than France. Its army is also much smaller, but every Prussian man has been through military training. When the order to mobilize goes out, they will eventually reach a strength at least twice that of the French, or even greater. But it will take longer."

"How much longer? The newspapers say it could be months. They say that a French attack at the beginning would face no opposition."

"That is the main question," Ferdinand said. "But it will be less than months, and the Prussians have four train lines to the front, all of them double-tracked. That alone might compensate for their slower mobilization. Then also, the south German states will only take part if France is the first power to declare war. They would represent a fourth of the total German army."

"Which is why I'm trying to keep the French from declaring war first. But, Baron, tell me again. Who will win?"

"I don't know."

"Who is more likely to win?"

"Perhaps the Prussians."

"And, Baron, I've had another request from the Bureau of Armaments, concerning cinnabar."

"Yes, Your Excellency?"

"It would be very useful for you to come to an understanding with Monsieur Sarroche."

"I will remember that, Your Excellency."

Captain Auguste de l'Imperator was at dinner that evening, which now occurred at least weekly.

"Do you think war is unavoidable?" Ferdinand asked him.

"All of France does! The nation is united behind the emperor. It is an extraordinary time."

All French strength and French overconfidence was embodied in the man. He was about thirty, or slightly younger, and magnificent in appearance. He had only dressed in ordinary city clothing the several times he'd now called at the Harsanyis, but his military bearing was more impressive than many officers in full uniform. His beard was fashioned after the emperor's goatee and mustache, but in gold it actually seemed imperial.

"Even Paris?"

"Paris!" The captain dismissed the city with a shake of his head. "The Parisians are unworthy of their city. I speak of course of the common people, the Jacobins who rise against any government at a whim. Their opposition to war is indeed the final proof that war is the most advantageous of all possibilities."

"Do you want war, Captain?" Therese asked.

"By all means. The Prussian upstarts will be crushed, and France's glory will be brightened beyond all the many glories of her past."

"What if France loses?" Rudolph said. His plain French was in stark contrast to de l'Imperator's ornate sentences.

"It is impossible. To whom? To farmhands and shop clerks? It is more than impossible. It is inconceivable."

"What would you do if there was war?" Therese asked.

"I would rejoin my regiment."

"You'd leave Paris?"

"Of course he would," Rudolph said. "They won't fight battles here. Which regiment?" he asked.

"The First Cuirassiers of the Imperial Guards Cavalry," the captain said. "We are at the command of the emperor himself and we are his guard and his fiercest defenders. In every battle we have achieved the highest honor through the fiercest fighting."

"How many times have you charged enemy lines?" Rudolph asked.

"I have been in four full charges, and a dozen or more other actions."

"Were they ever against artillery?"

"Cannon? Perhaps. I am not aware."

"Father?" Rudolph stood in the doorway, looking into the study.

"Yes?"

"This just came to the front door."

It was an envelope with no address or marking except Ferdinand's own name. Inside was a single page, with the words *Tomorrow afternoon at 4, Gare Montparnasse. vS.*

Ferdinand studied the message for a moment, and then noticed that his son was still watching.

"That's all," he said to Rudolph.

"Yes, sir."

Rudolph left. Ferdinand looked more closely at the envelope. It had apparently not been sealed.

— 5 —

"My greatest apologies," von Stieff said, "to bring you here, but I am on a very tight schedule."

The train station was loud and crowded; they might have been under observation, or they might have been completely anonymous. They stood in a corner, at least somewhat out of sight of the platforms and main hall.

"It was no trouble," the baron said.

"And I fear I have bad news for you."

"Concerning cinnabar ore?"

"Yes," von Stieff said. "I will not need your supplies. My deepest apologies. I considered simply sending you that message and sparing you this trip, but I wanted to personally express my gratitude for your patience in our discussions."

"No apologies are necessary," the baron said. "You have been quite plain in all our dealings. I presume you have access to other sources?"

"That information I will need to keep confidential."

"Of course. But this means that I will have to sell my ore to the French, or to the English."

"Yes," von Stieff said, "and that is unfortunate. Do you suggest that I might purchase your mercury simply to keep it from the French?"

"It would be to your advantage."

"Yes, it would. To Prussia's advantage, certainly, and Prime Minister von Bismarck would certainly reimburse me for my expense. But . . ."

"Yes?"

"You must know something of the German spirit, Baron Harsanyi? I know you are Hungarian, but you know us Germans well."

"My wife was Austrian German."

"And you must know that we are not all Prussian aristocrats. We are also the race of Beethoven and Goethe."

"Romantics and philosophers?"

"I am from the villages of the Rhineland. My ancestors were clockmakers, simply Stieff before we were given the *von*. I am no enemy of war, but I believe it is to be fought on the battlefield, not in the factory."

"French shells will be falling on the villages of the Rhineland, and on their sons," the baron said.

"So, then, why are you selling the mercury to the French? For revenge of Koniggratz? If so, then why would you have sold it to me at all?"

The baron only answered, "It seems I will not."

"Yes. You will not. And whatever we do, shells will still fall, and the blood will be on our heads and on our hands. *Adieu*, Baron. I do not expect to be back in Paris. I expect the French authorities will no longer allow it."

"After the war, perhaps," Baron Ferdinand said.

"Perhaps."

The baron watched as the Prussian disappeared into the crowd. Then he consulted the train schedules before he began his short walk home.

"Von Stieff has no interest in purchasing cinnabar ore," Ferdinand said to Pock as they sat in the baron's front parlor.

"Don't tell me you would really have sold cinnabar to the Prussians."

"I was at least interested to know if they would have bought it."

"You were speaking with von Stieff himself?"

"In person."

"And in Paris! So that leaves the French and the English?"

"I dislike them both, very strongly. They spy on each other, they lie to me about each other, and they send agents after me and my family."

"The stakes are very high," Pock said. "Surely you're not surprised. Do you have any idea who the agents might be?"

"Whistler claims he knows who the French agents are. I'm waiting for Sarroche to claim he knows the English agents."

– 6 –

"Herr Baron?" The ambassador's secretary met Ferdinand at the front door of the embassy the next morning.

"Yes?"

The secretary was named von Karlstein, and he seemed to have been chosen to provide the greatest contrast with the ambassador himself, in his old-fashioned dress and precise manner.

"His Excellency wishes to see you immediately."

"Baron," the prince said. "Monsieur Sarroche has made a charge against you."

"Yes?"

"And you will not deny it!" Sarroche broke in. "Again you have met with the Prussian von Stieff. Do you deny it? You cannot!"

"Does the French government keep the staff of the Austrian Embassy under observation?" Prince von Metternich asked, coldly.

"It was von Stieff who was being observed. But surely you see I would have great interest in this conversation between the baron and a Prussian arms manufacturer."

"Is this true, Baron? Did you meet with von Stieff?" the ambassador asked.

"Yes, sir. I have met with him several times to discuss the sale of mercury ore from my estates at Idria to the von Stieff factory."

"The factory that produces mercury fulminate!" Sarroche exploded. "For artillery to be used against France! Ambassador, this is an act of war! He is plotting against France."

"Was that why you were talking with Herr von Steiff, Baron Harsanyi?" Von Metternich was annoyed, and grim.

"I wasn't plotting against France, Your Excellency."

"But you were!" Sarroche accused. "You would sell armaments to our enemy. I demand that he be expelled from France immediately!"

"Would you really have sold your cinnabar to the Prussians?"

"No, sir," the baron said. "I would not have sold it to them."

"Then what is the reason for your secretive meetings if not for that?" Sarroche demanded. "Only to pressure the French government to pay a higher price? There is treachery in this."

"What were you doing, then, Baron?" the ambassador asked.

"I was waiting for Herr von Stieff to inform me that he wouldn't buy my ore."

"For what reason?" Sarroche was beginning to lose his anger in his confusion.

"Then I would know he had gained sure access to the only other source in Europe large enough for his requirements. The mines of Almaden."

"Almaden?" von Metternich asked.

"In Spain, Your Excellency."

"Prussia is buying Spanish mercury?" the ambassador was suddenly alarmed.

"Spain? But that would mean the Spanish government . . ." Sarroche came to a stop.

"Exactly. It would mean Prince Leopold has decided to accept the Spanish throne."

"I met with von Stieff yesterday, as you know," Ferdinand said, "at the Gare Montparnasse. He was boarding a train to Madrid. I watched."

"I will confer immediately with the Foreign Ministry," Sarroche answered. "We will instruct our ambassador in Madrid to put an end to this fantasy at once."

Even after Sarroche had left the room, the heat of his presence was slow to recede. Prince von Metternich's own annoyance remained.

"And so, Baron," he said, "what do you plan to do with your cinnabar?"

"What do you think I should do?"

"Sell it to the French, of course, as quickly as possible. Austria's interests are entirely with Paris and entirely against Berlin. We need them to win this war."

"Cinnabar won't win it for them."

"What are you really trying to do, Baron? Whose interests are you pursuing?"

He answered respectfully, "My own, Your Excellency."

Later in the early afternoon, Baron Ferdinand stepped down the sidewalk in his near military march, turning the corner and leaving the Austrian Embassy behind him. He held to his usual direct route from the embassy toward his house on the Rue Duroc.

Along his way he passed an alley entrance under a high arch. As he crossed its shadow, another shadow approached him.

"Monsieur Baron Harsanyi."

He stopped.

"Monsieur Sarroche."

"I wish to have a word with you," Sarroche said. The baron stepped into the alley, out of sight of the road.

"This is a strange place to have a meeting," the baron said.

"It is a mockery for you to say such things, who have met armaments dealers in cafés and train stations far from your usual habitations. But I have chosen to continue this matter without the ambassador."

"What matter?"

"I am not taken in by your ruse concerning Spain," Sarroche said. "I am still convinced of your intent to sell cinnabar to Prussia."

"Then perhaps we should involve the ambassador."

"No. You have failed in your attempt, whatever its purpose. What is much more important is that now you have no other choices: You must sell your cinnabar to France."

"I could refuse to sell it at all."

"Then you would be a fool, which you are not."

"I could sell the cinnabar to Partington and Manchester."

"I advise that you do not. Your deceits concerning Prussia have brought your position in Paris into question."

"Again," the baron said, "I believe we should take this up with Prince von Metternich."

"One word from me," Sarroche said, "and your residence in Paris would be terminated."

"As would be our cinnabar negotiations. And I don't believe France should be affronting Austria just now."

"And when France defeats Prussia, Austria may wish to appease the victor. Do not sell to Monsieur Whistler, Baron."

"Then offer me more than he has," Ferdinand said. "He says that you can't."

"He does not know what I can offer."

"He has an agent in your bureau who gives him information."

"I know his agent and I decide what information is given to him."

"And I knew you would make that claim. And you accuse me of deceit?" Ferdinand shook his head in anger. "All any of you do is deceive."

"We advance our policies."

"And your policies are war by other means. I'll sell my cinnabar to Whistler just so the two of you will be forced to negotiate with each other. You both deserve it."

Sarroche only shrugged off the sarcasm. "You will not sell to the English. I will prevent it."

"I will sell to whom I wish."

"I said I will prevent it! I will have my way. Have you even spoken with the Englishman in recent days? It may not be possible to conclude a contract. Surely you know that he is ill."

Ferdinand paused. "What do you mean?"

"It is what I have been told. And if his recovery is protracted, the time for negotiations will have passed before he is able to speak again with you."

"What do you know about his illness?"

"I might ask you the same, Baron. I will give you time to consider my offer, but be assured I will not let any obstacle stand between me and my objective."

"Yes," Baron Ferdinand said. "I believe that."

"I am your only choice! And you are my only obstacle! Not von Stieff, not Whistler, and not your wife."

"Zoltan!" Ferdinand didn't pause as he entered the house. "Quickly. I need to go out. Bring the carriage." And then, a moment later as Zoltan was snapping the whip and the horse was lunging forward, "To Rue Valenciennes, by the Gare de l'Est. You know the place."

The clerk seemed even whiter and more worried than usual.

"Mr. Whistler," the baron demanded.

"I'm sorry, sir . . ."

"I am Baron Harsanyi. You know me. It is important."

"He's not in, sir."

"When will he be in?"

"I don't know, sir. He didn't come in this morning."

Baron Harsanyi paused. "What is your name?"

"Wadsworth, sir."

"Where is he, Wadsworth?"

"He . . . he hasn't sent any message that he wouldn't be in. He has a schedule for tomorrow." The poor man was wilting under the baron's stern stare. "I won't know what to do. You could leave him a message?"

"I want to see him now. Where does he live?"

"Oh! I couldn't, sir."

"You will. Take me there immediately."

"But . . . well . . ."

"I said immediately."

The face disappeared, then reappeared under a hat and jacket. He let himself out of the building, locking the door behind him.

"This way, Mr. Harsanyi. I know he won't be pleased."

They climbed into the carriage. "The Hotel Calais," Wadsworth said to Zoltan. "It's beside the Gare du Nord."

The hotel was small and exclusive, more a residence than a way station for travelers. Wadsworth took them through the lobby and up one floor.

At the door, Ferdinand knocked authoritatively while Wadsworth cringed. But there was no answer.

"He's not in, sir."

Baron Ferdinand didn't even answer. He looked in the keyhole.

"The key is in the lock on the other side. He must be in the room." He looked at the door, and seemed to be looking through it. "Bring up my driver."

Wadsworth protested, but obeyed. It took several minutes, and all the while the baron stood still, staring at the locked door. He was still in the same position when Zoltan came, Wadsworth again following.

"I want this door opened," Ferdinand said.

Zoltan looked at it, at its size and weight, and put his eye to the keyhole.

"Break it?"

"If you have to."

"Sir!" Wadsworth said.

But Zoltan had knelt to look at the bottom of the door.

"Is there room?" Baron Harsanyi asked.

"If the key isn't too big."

"Mr. Wadsworth. We want to write a note. Ask at the desk for some stationery and a pen."

"Yes, sir." This request seemed much more reasonable to the clerk. Again there was a wait of several minutes, but Wadsworth finally returned with the requested articles and also a bottle of ink.

But Zoltan had no use for the ink. He slid the sheet of paper partway under the door, just beneath the knob. Then he inserted the quill into the keyhole and began working the key free, pushing it out the other side.

"Sir!" Wadsworth finally realized what they were doing. "Sir, please! You can't!"

A *clank* sounded on the floor inside the room as the key fell from its hole. "I believe we can."

Zoltan was on his knees, carefully tugging the paper under the door. And then he had the key in his hand.

He handed it to his master, but first the baron stooped to look through the hole.

He saw a narrow field of the room. The foot of a bed was in the center, and beyond, against a far wall, a high bureau with a candle, still burning but nearly used up, in a porcelain candlestick.

The baron put the key in the hole and turned. The door opened.

The room was quiet; the one sound was the very slow, rasping breath.

The bed was the largest piece of furniture in the room, which served as bedroom, dining room, and parlor. It was high-posted and the covers were thick and dark green.

Henry Whistler was in the bed. Ferdinand came to stand next to him, with Wadsworth close behind, and Zoltan remaining in the hall.

The bedclothes rose and fell slowly, and Whistler's breath could be heard when they were close-by. Ferdinand put his hand on the man's brow.

Wadsworth was nearly in a panic. "He's sleeping, Mr. Harsanyi! You'll wake him!"

The baron ignored the comment and put his finger on the sleeping man's temple, and then, to the clerk's horror, slowly opened the eyelid. But Whistler gave no sign of being disturbed.

"No, Mr. Wadsworth, I will not wake him."

"But, sir—"

The baron looked around the room. It was well-appointed, with two quality armchairs and matching couch, and a carved wooden bureau. Landscape and garden paintings hung on the walls. Even the silver service and crystal decanters on the central table were appropriate to the expense of the chamber. The walls were green, as were the upholstery and bed covering. There was one low, sputtering dark red candle still in flame, and three others burned out.

"Only God will ever wake him."

"I don't take your meaning, sir?"

Baron Harsanyi had uncovered the man's arm and hand and looked closely at his fingers. There was still no reaction.

"When did you last see him?"

"When he went home early yesterday, sir."

"He wasn't well?"

"He complained of a headache. But he expected to be back in the office today."

"When he went to bed last night, he was immediately unconscious. See that he didn't even extinguish his candles? Now look closely, Wadsworth. Look at his hand. Do you see the pink coloring of the fingers and cheeks? And very closely, see that the fingers are not still, but tremble."

"Well, yes? Perhaps they are symptoms of cholera? We were warned of an outbreak. Or influenza?"

"They are early symptoms of severe hydrargyria."

"I've never heard of such a disease!" The clerk was near to panic.

"It is mercury poisoning, Mr. Wadsworth."

"Poisoning? But how?"

"I don't know." He stepped away from the bed, suddenly angry. "But I can tell you that he will not survive."

"Baron Harsanyi! Surely you're mistaken!"

"Mistaken?" Ferdinand Harsanyi's eyes flashed, and he turned to face the unfortunate clerk. "No. As much as I wish I were, I am not mistaken. And you will see for yourself that I'm not. This is what you will see: He will begin to have seizures. His breathing will become difficult. The pinkness of his skin will progress to the point of eruptions and even peeling. As the brain is more deeply affected, the convulsions will become constant. The pain would be intolerable, except that he'll never know. His only good fortune is that he won't regain consciousness. Finally, in a few days, he'll die."

"But . . ."

"There is no *but*."

"An antidote?"

"There is nothing to do but wait." Ferdinand turned back to the bed, and his voice changed as the anger drained away. "Unless you choose to perform an act of mercy."

"Mercy! What do you mean?"

"A bullet."

"No!"

The baron was still speaking aloud, but he was speaking to himself. "Or, with his lungs already weakened, it's easy enough to suffocate him. In fact . . ." He spoke more specifically to Wadsworth. "It's a proof of the poisoning that he'd die quickly, without struggling."

"Never! I couldn't do such a thing."

"A doctor might. Find a doctor and tell him it is hydrargyria. The name is the same in English and French. By tomorrow the symptoms will be very obvious."

"Then what should I do?" Wadsworth was realizing what this meant for himself.

"You could try to find who has murdered your employer."

"Oh, my!"

"Who'll profit from his death? What dealer in mercury and arms gains the most? It shouldn't be hard to find that out. I've already covered the field and there aren't many possibilities left. Only one, even, now that Whistler has himself been eliminated."

The clerk was shivering, thoroughly terrified. "What will the police do?"

"Whatever they want. They might even decide that you seem suspicious to them. Maybe you shouldn't call them. Or maybe you'll wake up yourself in a few moments and it will all have been a dream. But they'll ask who has come to see Mr. Whistler lately. Who has?"

"Only his normal visitors."

"Who else? Who has been out of the ordinary?"

"Well, sir . . ."

"What?"

"Your son, sir."

"Rudolph?"

"I presumed he was your son. From his name—"

"When?"

"A few weeks ago. Three weeks."

Ferdinand turned to Zoltan, still at the door, watching and listening. "We'll leave now."

"Yes, master."

They waited several minutes for Wadsworth, but he didn't follow them.

After they'd started, Zoltan spoke.

"The baroness died in bed, of illness."

Ferdinand turned at him. "Yes." The streets of Paris passed by, in a bright, sunlit fog. The crowds in their spring colors were gray and invisible. "Yes, she did."

Zoltan was silent, staring at him.

"We'll talk later," the baron said.

"But we are made for war!" Auguste de l'Imperator's voice was flowing from the parlor as Ferdinand came in the front door. "It is past any doubt. In every nation, in every age, man has always practiced war."

"The people don't want war, only the elites." This was another voice, which he didn't recognize.

"In noble nations, the people value the glory they gain from their victories!"

"I don't think war is good." That was Rudolph. Ferdinand looked into the room.

The unknown voice was the friend from the École, Gravert. He and Rudolph were in chairs, and Captain de l'Imperator was standing at the mantel. Therese was sitting close-by, on the couch.

"Oh, Father!" she said. "You're home."

He nodded to her, and to the others.

"Of course, the baron is greatly knowledgeable concerning man and war," de l'Imperator said. "Do you not agree, sir, that war is honorable and displays the greatness in man's character—?"

"I don't want to talk about war," Therese interrupted. "Father, have you had a pleasant afternoon? Maria has dinner."

"The second-year students received their orders today," Rudolph said. "They were all talking about where they'll be posted after their graduations."

"I don't want to talk about war!" Therese said.

"That isn't war."

"But everything is war!" the captain said. "What isn't war?"

"All of normal life," Therese said. "All the things we do every day. Everything!"

"It is man's nature to approach life as if it is war."

"What is war, then, anyway?" Gravert asked.

Rudolph answered. "War is the rejection of moderation in attaining our goals. That's what Clausewitz says."

"Indeed!" De l'Imperator gestured in approval. "And to moderate is to be weak. If a goal is to be achieved, all other considerations must be discarded."

Ferdinand left them.

"How is it done?" Zoltan was with his master in the bedroom later that evening, laying out clothes for the next day.

"How is what done?" Ferdinand asked.

"The mercury poisoning," Zoltan's deep growl answered.

"There are several ways," the baron said, slowly and wearily. "The easiest is to breathe in the mercury vapors. We put ventilation shafts in the mines to bring in fresh air. Before that, too many of the workers died."

"They died this way?"

"No. They breathed thin vapors over years, and then went mad. This today was from a very dense vapor of mercury. The lethal dose had already been inhaled before the first symptoms even appeared."

"How does the mercury get in the air?"

"If there is a large pool of the liquid, it will evaporate. But it's very slow, and there was no such pool in that bedroom. I don't know how it was done."

"How long does it take breathing it?"

"A day." He had to turn away, looking out the window but not seeing. "A day of breathing it continually when the air is saturated. And it can't be sensed. There's no odor or color to the vapor."

Zoltan sat in his master's presence, and his master faced him again.

"And this is how the baroness died." It wasn't a question.

"The clerk today was a coward." Ferdinand took a handkerchief from his pocket to wipe the sweat from his brow. "He will have run and left the Englishman to all the horror of his death alone."

"You did not let the baroness die alone."

"I didn't." His hands shook as he looked at them, even at that moment with the cloth in them, just as it had been. "I couldn't. She was too dear to me. Far, far too dear. I suddenly knew that night, when the telegram came, as I came home from the embassy. I knew something had happened. But I don't know how I knew. I only knew something would be wrong when we reached Vienna."

Zoltan waited until the hands stopped trembling. Then he said, "Now this one is in Paris."

"This one? Yes. This evil one. Be wary, Zoltan." Ferdinand looked his servant direct in the eyes.

Zoltan nodded, and waited again, then finally asked, "Who?"

"I don't know. It must be for the mercury. I've talked with a dozen of the arms dealers, but I believe only two are possible. Von Stieff and Sarroche. And not von Stieff."

Zoltan shook his head. "Only for the mercury?"

"What do you mean?"

"To kill this way. It is an evil way to kill."

"To kill for mercury, they kill with mercury. How we defeat an evil?"

"Only God can defeat evil."

"Is there a God, Zoltan?"

"I know there is evil."

– 7 –

Three days later, it was Pock sitting in the chair and Ferdinand on the couch, on a stormy evening after dinner.

"I see an interesting account in the newspaper," Pock said.

"Not more politics," Ferdinand said.

"Not quite. A mysterious death on the Rue Magenta."

The baron turned from the front window. "Mysterious?"

"A man died in his bed." He looked up from the paper. "Henry Whistler."

"What does the paper say?"

"You don't sound surprised." He looked back to the words. " 'No marks of violence in the room, but the bedclothes were in disarray, as if he'd thrown them off. The body itself was convulsed, and the skin—' "

"That's enough." He returned to the window. "Does it suggest a cause?"

"Cholera, perhaps, or influenza. But his clerk is missing from the office and has not been seen for several days. The French police have asked Scotland Yard for assistance." Pock folded the paper. "Although it would seem that a certain Frenchman would be helped very much by his death."

"Sarroche. Yes, the British will send a new man, but time is too short and Whistler's knowledge can't be replaced. The field is cleared, and Monsieur Sarroche alone is still standing." He sighed, deep in thought.

"He's an energetic little man," Pock said, "and he takes his job very seriously."

"Much too seriously. He is an evil man. I think that in pursuit of his goals, he's done terrible harm."

"Are you saying he might be responsible for Whistler's death?"

"What do you think, Pock? Would Sarroche kill a person?"

"He might. He is in the business of war."

"And he understands what war is. Do you think he would destroy a person?"

Pock hesitated. "*Destroy* is different than to kill?"

"A dead man isn't useful. He needs live men to be his agents, and it's them that I pity most. They would be the men he's destroyed."

"But they'd be willing tools?"

"I think not," Ferdinand said. "I think he must gain power over them, and compromise them, and then use them; and that finally destroys them. I know he has agents, and at least one of them tried somehow to influence my wife."

"When?"

"Just before she died."

"Do you know this for fact, Harsanyi, or are you just imagining it?"

"As a fact, but it is also easy to imagine. Too easy. Pock, I've seen so many ways that men are evil. This agent that I imagine, he must have had a point where he made a choice to accept Sarroche's bargain, or refuse it, no matter what the consequence."

"The consequence might be devastating."

"The acceptance would be devastating. I would not accept a bargain with the devil."

"But should you have contempt for someone who would?"

"I would. I do."

"I am more forgiving," Pock said, and tried to lighten the dark mood. "Besides evil, you must also have seen the many ways men are weak and that they need . . . well, some light to help them along their way."

Ferdinand stared out the window. "When I look out, I see a dark world. I begin to think that there's no light anywhere."

Chapter Five

DARK IN THE
CITY OF LIGHT

– 1 –

On a morning in April they met, at a café in the Boulevard St. Germaine, near the twisted, ancient streets of the Quartier Latin, nearly in the shadow of Notre Dame. She saw him first, reflecting a brilliant light. He saw her, glowing.

They called each other's name and embraced, and said a few words, which were unnecessary, and a few more words, which were meaningless. Their whole conversation was in their eyes.

Paris lent itself to them. Its spring and gray buildings and immortal streets observed them with indulgence. For their part, they were startled at how being in Paris and in love were so much the same thing.

"I'm so happy," Therese said when they were seated and could hear again.

"Of course, my love." He caressed her hands. "How could it be otherwise? To be together, that is everything. For you to have me, so close, could only be happiness for you."

"It is." She blushed and dropped her eyes. "Could anyone have ever . . . ?"

"Ever known this joy before? That is in no way possible! It is ours alone. For me, Therese, it is as new and astonishing as for you. Even Paris has never seen a love like ours."

"I believe you, Auguste."

And she did, for a few more moments. Then she said, "Now, you promised to take me for a drive."

"Because this is our day to see the countryside, it is perfect." Auguste guided the horse around the Arc de Triomphe on the way to the Neuilly gate.

"Where are we going?"

"Argenteuil."

"Is it as beautiful as everyone says?"

"It is very beautiful, but it is only the setting for the jewel."

"What jewel, Auguste?"

"You, my love."

Outside the city walls, the fields were Elysian beside the Champs-Elysees. Neuilly, a kilometer from the gate, was picaresque and noble, and the groves of the Bois de Boulogne were vital with unfurling leaves.

As a setting, the countryside was overwhelmed with jewels. The fields were grassy emeralds surrounding the sapphire Seine, and the wild flowers rioted everywhere, in colors fashionable and not, in combinations that proved the jeweler's skill was undeniable and his taste perhaps questionable.

"It is beautiful," Therese said. "Just how I knew it would be."

They crossed the river to Courbevoie, and then across the narrow neck of the long peninsula between loops of the Seine toward the village of Argenteuil three kilometers ahead.

Halfway they were stopped at the railroad crossing as a steaming black iron locomotive and its cars raced past.

"Where is it going?" Therese asked. The cars were full.

"To Saint Germain, beyond the hill."

Therese followed his outstretched arm. "Auguste, what is that?"

The hill was as verdant as all its surroundings, with a few trees and cottages and streaks of poppies, cornflowers, and daises, but harsh gray stone walls circled its brow in two ranks.

"The Fortress du Mount Valerien."

"Rudolph told me about that. He practiced firing its cannon. It's so ugly!"

"It is not built for beauty, that is true. But it is to guard the beauty, and all Paris."

"From what?"

"From whoever would assault it." He smiled at her and shook the reins to urge the horse forward.

"Auguste," she said, "when the . . . if the war comes, will you leave me?"

"It will only be for a short time."

"Is it weakness to love?"

He frowned at her indulgently. "Love is no weakness."

"A few days ago, you said that to be moderate was to be weak. You said that you'd discard everything unimportant to reach a goal. But isn't love moderate? Would you discard me if you had to because of a war?"

"But, my love, you are my goal."

"What would you do to win me?"

"Is it not said of love and war, those two, that no rules can apply?"

"And which am I?" she asked.

Auguste lifted his golden head. "For me, you are both."

They lunched in a pavilion beside Argenteuil and watched punts and rowboats on the Seine. Violins played and the sun played along. On the far bank, artists with their canvases reflected the flowers and bridge and boats just as the river did.

"Will you dance?" Auguste said as other couples waltzed.

"No," Therese answered, overwhelmed by the day.

"We should take a boat onto the Seine?" The houses of Argenteuil were aged white, and all red and green roofed, and the flowers in their gardens were uncontrollable, and the river took all the colors and shook them together like petals in the wind. The bridge stepped daintily across the water in arch after arch. Above, the sky was a perfect blue. A hawk was circling.

"No."

The hawk suddenly dove, toward some exposed prey.

"Then will you marry me?"

"Oh!" She dropped her cup. "Oh, Auguste! I couldn't."

"Why not?"

"Father would never allow it."

"That is the only reason?"

"No . . ."

"It is not that you do not love me?"

"I do love you. Of course I do."

He spoke so earnestly. "Then nothing must stand in our way." His eyes were as blue as the sky.

The hawk had resumed its place high overhead.

"Not even a war?"

"I would defeat the enemy all the faster, to return to you."

Therese laughed and clapped her hands. "And what would we do if we were married?"

"We would have paradise." He was surprised at her doubt. "Therese. Why ask such questions?" His eyes clouded with reproach. "It would all come. And would it matter? You would have me. What else would be necessary?"

"Besides you?"

"Every need, I would provide for you. You would lack nothing."

"Auguste . . . why didn't you ever say this in Vienna?"

"That was so long ago."

"Only months."

"But forever. A different world, and we had different lives. I ask you because now we are in Paris."

"You make me light-headed!" she said. "But we can't. Not now."

"Then when?" He frowned. "Oh, of course. So soon after your mother's passing. How insensitive of me!"

"Yes, Auguste." She had to laugh again, at his passionate penitence. "Yes, that can be the reason."

"Then tell me how long I must wait."

"A few more months."

"In the summer. I must warn you, the flowers in Argenteuil are even more immense in July. When I bring you back then, you will find them irresistible."

"And you will be, also?"

"Even more."

They walked beside the river. The boats were flowers of the water in all their colors. The red and dark green roofs held up the rippling, milk-colored houses mirrored on the surface.

They sat on a bench, looking out on the river. The sky was now filled with hawks and falcons, some so high they could only be guessed at, and some very close.

"It is most beautiful, mademoiselle, is it not?"

The voice came from behind them. Therese turned. The speaker was an extraordinary-looking man in too many jackets and scarves, all too loose, wearing a wide-brimmed hat, an easel and canvas planted beside him. The palette in his hand was smeared with all the colors they were seeing.

"Most beautiful," she answered, a bit startled but amused.

But then she realized that Auguste beside her was much more than startled.

"Good afternoon, monsieur," the painter said to him, with an odd humor in his words.

"What are you doing here?" Auguste said.

"Argenteuil in the spring? Where else for an artist?"

"Auguste," Therese said, "you know this man?"

"Yes, we are acquainted."

"I am Pierre Beaubien," the painter said. "No doubt you have heard my name? I introduce myself, as my friend Captain de l'Imperator has perhaps forgotten."

"I have not forgotten." Auguste seemed much less than pleased at the man's appearance, even suspicious, but also intrigued. "As you have not forgotten me. And why have you sought me out?"

"Sought you out? It is nothing. Simply a greeting on a most beautiful day, to a most beautiful couple."

"An implausible response! I repeat, Beaubien, what is it that you want?"

Beaubien shrugged. "Perhaps to request that the mademoiselle might wish her portrait painted?"

"Me?" Therese laughed. "What a strange thought!"

"Hardly!" He bowed deeply to her. "There are many women in Paris who would beg to have a portrait by the greatest artist in France at the current time, or even at any—"

Auguste guffawed. "The greatest fraud! How can you say such things about yourself?"

"It is true!"

"Please," Therese said, trying to stop laughing. "Auguste, how did you ever meet Monsieur Beaubien?"

Auguste frowned, pausing to choose his words. "It is not of conse-quence. And I must state frankly that it is not advisable to sit for a portrait with him."

"But surely," Beaubien said, "it is the mademoiselle's choice?"

"I would have to ask my father," Therese said.

"Say to him my name, Pierre Beaubien, and he will grant your request. I am sure of it."

"I am not," Auguste said. "For he will either have heard of you and not wish to be associated, or more likely he will not know of you at all."

The painter shrugged off Auguste's judgment. "And you, Captain? What of you, now that you have returned to Paris?"

"I am fully engaged. I have no time for additional pursuits."

"Of course," Beaubien said. "I see that indeed your current pursuit is very adequate."

"What do you—?" Auguste rose to his feet as his anger rose, but then thought better and shrugged off his irritation. "Come, Therese, let us visit the shops in the village."

"All right," she said, and followed Auguste, who was already moving away. The painter stayed behind.

But he called to her as they strolled away. "Mademoiselle! Remember me!"

"Father," Therese said, "have you ever heard of an artist named Pierre Beaubien?"

"No."

"I met him today in Argenteuil. Auguste took me out to see the flowers and the river."

"He paints flowers?"

"Father, he asked to paint me."

Rudolph looked up from his plate. "What color?"

"Rudy!"

"Tell him green."

"And what did you do today?" Therese asked, her jaw set. "Did you ride horses, or play with swords?"

"We were instructed that attack must only be attempted if success can be assured."

"You were told that?" their father asked sharply.

"Yes, sir."

"Do you believe it?"

"I don't think success of an attack can ever be assured."

"You are correct."

"Our subject today," Rudolph recited, "was that the French grand strategy for the coming war is based on impregnable defense. Therefore, the Prussians will be unable to attack successfully, and will be unable to gain any victory."

Ferdinand shook his head. "And do you believe that?"

"Cadet Gravert asked the lecturer if the Prussians had been instructed as to their assigned role. He was reprimanded for insolence. The Prussians will have no choice but to act precisely as the French strategists wish them to."

"Does that seem likely to you?"

"No, sir. I've been reading in Clausewitz about the error of symmetry, where the strategist assumes that the opponent will act the same way that the strategist himself would in the same situation."

"Then how do you defeat an enemy?"

"One must be prepared for any possibility. I would watch for his weaknesses and take advantage of them. I would move as quickly as possible and always be ready to change my plans in light of new information."

"How do you gain your information?"

Therese was uninterested in the conversation, but she suddenly noticed a sharpness in her father's questions.

"I would use cavalry scouts and—"

"No. I mean you."

"Me, Father?" Rudolph said.

"How do you gather information?"

"I'm not at war."

"Are you sure?"

"I don't understand, sir."

Somehow, though, he sounded like he did. But Therese didn't understand, nor the abrupt silence that followed. But it was uncomfortable and she quickly broke it.

"Father, may I sit for a portrait with Monsieur Beaubien?"

"It is not suitable."

"But, Father—"

"Would the portrait be publicly displayed?"

"I don't know. I'd thought we would hang it here. Like Mother's."

Her father frowned, still irritated by Rudolph. "You may ask Princess von Metternich for her advice. She would know whether the man is respectable."

And Rudolph had excused himself and left.

"Your dear father," Pauline said. "Lately he's been so grim."

The princess's parlor was filled with both guests and furniture, all beautifully arrayed. Guests were still arriving, mostly women but a few men, as well.

"You know he's always that way," Therese said.

"But more since . . . well, since January, of course, but he seemed to be coming out of it. Then last week I saw him at the embassy and I almost ran and hid, for the look on his face. We need to draw him out more."

"How would you do that?"

"I've already started thinking who he should marry."

"Oh, my!" Therese couldn't help her surprise. "But it's only been a few months since Mother died."

"Yes, but these things take time, and we need to start working on it. And besides . . ." She paused. "We all know they weren't happy. It can be a new start for him." Pauline put her hand on Therese's arm. "I think you've put the best face on it, dear. You've become such a part of Paris since you came."

"Thanks very much to you, Princess.

"You and Auguste."

An hour had passed and the salon was at its crescendo. Dozens of conversations swirled through the air. An art critic next to Therese was extolling the emperor's new portrait.

"Oh, that reminds me," Therese said. "Princess, do you know the painter Pierre Beaubien?"

"Of course, dear! Everyone does."

"Is he reputable? My father said you'd know."

"He has a reputation," the critic smirked.

"Not a good one?" Therese asked.

"He's very fashionable," the princess said. "He has a very good reputation for his portraits."

"He wants to paint my portrait."

"Have you met him?" She was very interested. "Did you go to him?"

"He approached me. In Argenteuil."

"Go ahead and sit for him, dear," Pauline said. "And take your Captain de l'Imperator with you for protection."

"Auguste warned me against him."

"Then he'll be even better protection. It will make your name in Paris, Therese."

Therese put her hand to her throat. "But what will I wear?"

— 3 —

"This is the man's studio," Auguste said.

They were in the north of the city, in the neighborhood of Montmartre on the slopes of a great hill that commanded all of Paris. Just as Montmartre was visible anywhere in Paris, all of Paris was visible from Montmartre.

"Have you been here before?"

"My family has lived on these streets from before they were part of Paris. Even my aunt's house on Rue la Bruyere is only a few blocks from the base of the hill. And beyond the slopes in that direction"—he pointed toward the northwest—"is the cemetery where my father is buried."

"Oh, I want to see it."

"It is not a joyous place. But sometime, you will see it."

Auguste had taken them directly to a grand old manor house, slightly revived from the decay of age. It had a garden with flowers and bushes as mixed as the neighborhood, and a white fence at the street. Auguste didn't pause at the gate, but opened it and walked right through the yard and pulled impatiently on the bell.

A woman answered. She was a piece with the house, disheveled and shabby but lively with motion as the house was with color.

"What is it?" she asked, annoyed at the interruption.

"Monsieur Beaubien?" Therese asked. "He is expecting me."

"Oh, you!" she wailed, not at Therese or Auguste, but back into the house. "There is a woman here!"

"What woman?" the house asked back.

"You ask her yourself!" But then the woman had seen Auguste. "And a man, too! One of them! What have you done this time to have them come after you?" She looked at Auguste again. "It's one who's been here before."

The house's voice had arrived. "Shoo! Back to your sweeping, old woman!" And Pierre Beaubien waved the woman away. She had to evade his hand, or it would have hit her.

"Mademoiselle," he said and bowed. "And Monsieur. Please come in."

There must have been walls in the room, but they were invisible behind dozens or hundreds of canvases. A few were hung and the rest were stacked, leaned, stuffed, and stuck against the unseen wall and on shelves, bureaus, tables, and chairs. All of them were covered with color, and an effort was required to look just at any single one to see that the colors were a landscape, a garden, a parlor, a waterfall, a battle, a castle, a duchess, a carriage, a street, a general, a fruit bowl, a tree, a child, a Greek myth, or a saint's uplifted face. None were blank, except one.

The one was on an easel in the somewhat empty center of the room. "Now. Sit."

Therese put herself on the sofa. The painter was beside it, in as many loose clothes as he'd worn when they met in Argenteuil. "Let us see," he said, "how you shall be."

Its previous occupants, books, papers, supplies, and more canvases were still in a pile from where they'd been cleared off. A blue curtain was hung behind her from two poles.

She sat properly upright. "Like this?"

Beaubien considered. "It is very straight. Is this how you imagine yourself to be?"

"I haven't imagined myself."

"Then do so. And first, become comfortable. A little lean to the right? The hands apart, one on the cushion beside you, the other resting on the folds of the dress."

"Bah!" Auguste had watched silently, a dark blot in a far corner. "It is absurd! You make her careless, as if she was simply sitting in her own room." He could ignore the action no longer, and placed himself on the stage.

"How do you think I should be?" she asked.

"A portrait should be noble. A heroine, a goddess, an empress. You should at least stand."

"My mother is standing in her portrait."

Beaubien shook his head thoughtfully. "Standing? It could be done. It is archaic according to the style of the moment, but done well, it could set a new style."

"Then you must stand," Auguste said. "Only the highest of art is worthy of you."

"But, Auguste," she said, "you didn't even want me to come here."

"But as you are here," he said, "I will guard you from the foolishness of tastes and styles."

She listened, but despite the talk of standing, she was still in the seated pose Beaubien had arranged her in. "I think standing would make me feel more like a statue than a person. Do you really think I should be so formal?"

"It is how I see you."

"Monsieur Beaubien?"

The painter had listened, amused. "Mademoiselle, how do you see yourself?"

"I don't know."

"Because it is not how another sees you, but how you imagine yourself, that I wish to see and place on this canvas."

"Well . . ."

"Indeed," he said, stepping forward, and incidentally coming between her and Auguste, "who are you, mademoiselle?"

Therese looked down, away from him, at her own hand still resting on a cushion. "Please, monsieur, paint me how you think I would look best."

"Yes. Then. Simply sit as you are."

Her seated, relaxed position was certainly comfortable enough for her to remain nearly motionless for over an hour as Pierre Beaubien, in a frenzy of motion, scraped and brushed and daubed onto the canvas. Auguste was simply impatient, but he had been ejected from the stage and had no possibility of influencing its action.

Finally, he exploded. "How long will this continue? It is impossible! You are demanding too much of her!"

Therese kept her pose. "Will it be much longer, monsieur?"

Beaubien dropped his palette. "No. It is enough. For now, it will be enough."

"May I see?"

"Stand, mademoiselle. Stretch your limbs and restore their vigor. Then come and see."

She stood, and she did need to stretch out her arms to feel them move. But she did it quickly and came around the canvas.

"It's beautiful," she said. "Is it really me?"

"It is fully you," Beaubien said.

"It is only a shadow," Auguste said.

It was her. The details were still vague; the essence was already complete, and it was her. She was drawn in mostly to the eyes, her own eyes, facing herself but not in a mirror. This was a separate Therese, that she could study, and perhaps even come to understand.

"Tell me how you know Monsieur Beaubien," Therese said. They were in the front parlor of her house. Rudolph was lounging in a corner with a book, but too bored to read.

"I hardly believe that I know him," Auguste said, "so casual is our acquaintance."

"Please, though, tell me how you met."

"Very well." He shook his head, making every effort to dismiss the event as unimportant. "When I was graduated from Saint Cyr, I was assigned to the Imperial Guards Cavalry, which was my highest aspiration. In my regiment I met a lieutenant who was three years my senior, and to him I was particularly drawn, as he had a stately bearing and a dignified manner, and this was how I perceived myself. But this man was Honore Beaubien, and he is indeed an honorable man and officer."

"Honore? But I thought his name was Pierre."

"This painter is the cousin of Honore."

"Lieutenant Beaubien introduced you?"

"I was young and not experienced in the ways of the world. Pierre at first seemed a sociable character, and I was intrigued by his unconventional ways."

"He does seem to be unconventional."

Auguste frowned. "But then as I gained maturity, I soon saw through his childishness."

"Where is the cousin now?" Therese asked.

"He is still in the Guards Cavalry, now as a captain."

The inert Rudolph spoke. "Why aren't you, Auguste?"

"Why . . . what?" He was startled by the question.

"Why aren't you still in the army?"

"Why? But I am still an officer."

"But you aren't with them. What were you doing in Vienna?"

Auguste only smiled. "Seeking my treasure," he said, turning his back on Rudolph and giving his full attention to Therese.

"Mademoiselle, you are finished." Pierre Beaubien stepped back from his easel.

"It's done?" Therese asked.

"The portion that is you."

She hurried to see, at the same time stretching to undo the stiffness in her joints from another motionless hour. Auguste had been sitting in his same corner and he also came, but much more slowly.

Her first impression was of herself floating in a white cloud. She was on the canvas complete, but the background was still only a few pencil lines.

Then she focused on her completed self.

"It is better than before," Auguste admitted. But she could hardly speak.

She was seated as she had been, at rest, at peace. Her face was the same that she saw in her mirror, but it had a peace that she hadn't seen.

"Who is it?" she said.

"It is you."

"It's my face. But who is inside?"

"A painting is only of the outside," Auguste said. "What else can you see?"

"I don't know. Pierre, who do you see?"

"I see a woman who is wise, and who thinks deeply."

"I see her, too!" Therese said. "But who is she? She isn't me."

"It must be that I see more than you," the painter answered. "But what you do not see is not necessarily absent."

As she tried to understand what he'd said, Auguste asked a more practical question. "And it is still unfinished. What is the rest of it to be?"

"What would you like?" Pierre asked her. "Where do you want to be?"

"In a palace," Auguste said. "Versailles, perhaps."

"Sitting like that?" she said. "That isn't how a person sits in a palace."

"With a vista behind, outside a window."

"Maybe a parlor?" Therese asked Beaubien.

"It could be an intimate sitting room," he answered.

But she wasn't convinced. "I don't know. Or a garden?"

"A garden bench, yes."

"No!" Auguste protested. "It is too trivial."

"Pierre, I want you to decide. You know better than I do."

Beaubien nodded, not in agreement but in acceptance. "Mademoiselle, I will choose the place."

"When will it be done?" Auguste asked.

"Another week. And then shall I bring it to you?"

"Father said we would come to get it."

– 5 –

"Here," Therese said.

"Stop." Once Zoltan had brought the carriage to a halt, Ferdinand stepped out and held the door for Therese. She saw him studying the tended but disordered garden and the sturdy but disheveled old house.

"The mind of the artist," Auguste said, getting out of the carriage beside her, "is not disciplined. His household reflects this."

"Oh, you!" The housekeeper's voice wailed loud enough to be heard at the street, even if she wasn't seen. "They are here!" The door opened. The woman had been cleaning and her broom was still in her hands. She pointed with it back into the house. "Go in. I've told him you're here."

And so they were swept into the studio of Pierre Beaubien.

"Mademoiselle," Pierre Beaubien greeted them. "Monsieur Baron. Monsieur Captain."

Facing them was the canvas, on its easel, but hidden beneath a draped white cloth. All three of them were impatient: Therese to see the painting, her father to be back to his work, and Auguste, apparently, to be away from Beaubien.

The painter was not in a hurry. His dramatic pause seemed to be fed by their impatience as a flower is by the rain, and the opening of its bud was eternally slow.

"Would you be seated?"

No one wished to sit.

"Mademoiselle informs me, sir, that you are a diplomat with the Austrian Embassy."

Ferdinand agreed that he was.

No further attempts at informal conversation were any more successful.

"Then without further ado," he said, and with much more ado, finally he pulled the curtain off.

Therese was astounded. Even though she had seen her own image already, and she had seemed complete, now she was truly complete.

She was still in the same seated pose, of course, but seated in a café. Her chair was elegant wrought iron and her elbow, instead of resting on the arm of the sofa, shared a small round table on a Paris sidewalk with a cup and saucer. Behind her was the café's dark window.

She was alone, or she thought so at first, until she saw in the window the reflection of someone, a man, who must be standing where the viewer of the painting would be. He was only a shadow.

"Who is it?" she asked.

"You, of course." Beaubien laughed. "As I said at our last sitting."

"No. The man."

Auguste had seen the reflection, also, and came up close to the canvas to see. But the image wasn't clear enough to recognize.

"Mademoiselle, you know."

"But I don't."

"But look at yourself. You must. See the expression on your face? You are joyful."

"Is it Auguste?" she asked.

"It must be!" Auguste said. "How can you ask, if it is with joy that you greet the man? Who else could it be?"

"It is you, Auguste," she concluded.

Chapter Six

DECLARATION

– 1 –

For a millennium young men had made the left bank of the Seine their own. Whether scholars or courtiers, artists or ruffians, poets or lords, they have sought their own in the warrens of the Quartier Latin.

Rudolph had learned the area as well as any of his other studies, and his feet led him to certain streets more and more often. One evening in May, after his father had eaten with them and then disappeared into his study, and Therese into her own room, Rudolph followed his well-known paths.

The sky still light, and with time on his hands, he wandered east and about and through a familiar doorway under a sign that showed, roughly, three soldiers with rifles forward and a billow of smoke, and the name *Café du Fusillade.*

In ancient times it had been a cellar. The walls were massively thick and arched low over a stone floor. There were lanterns hung from brackets that had surely once held torches, and three vast barrels behind the bar counter.

The lanterns did very little to dispel the murky gloom. It was the spirit of the young soldiers who were its constant patrons that kept the place bright.

There was the usual knot of cadets, and they hailed Rudolph and welcomed him to their tables. His French blended with theirs, not nearly as accented as it had been.

Later, Professor Pock looked in the low door and joined the group, and here he was received in exactly the opposite way that he was in the lecture hall, with familiar greetings and jest, yet he was still respected.

As his classmates became boisterous, Rudolph ended up at a corner table with Pock, away from the others. The French cadets boasted and railed as their wine bottles emptied.

"You never drink wine," Professor Pock said in German.

"Only coffee," Rudolph answered. "I'm not French yet."

"It would be best to remain not French."

"I don't understand them. They only live to have crises."

A newspaper on the table had the headline, *L'Affaire Hispano-Prussian.* "The Spanish Throne, you mean? The news has come out that Prince Leopold has been invited again."

"They don't have to be offended," Rudolph said. "That's all it is. Just an insult."

"*Just* an insult?"

"Spain isn't worth anything. They don't have an army. They're poor and backward. The French should just ignore it."

"You know they can't," Pock said.

"Because they're French."

Pock smiled. "The French aren't the only people who take offense at insults."

"But they've made it an art."

"The French make everything an art."

A new voice spoke. "Revenge, as well." It was Gravert. He pulled his chair to Rudolph's table. "We are expert at it."

"The people will take revenge on the tyrants?" Rudolph said, yawning.

"In the end, they will. But revenge on Prussia will come first."

"Revenge for what?" Pock asked.

"They have always insulted us. They treat us like children. They command us to do their bidding. We have tried to treat them with respect, and they answer with derision."

"The Prussians might say the same thing about the French," Pock said.

"Then they would be lying."

"Would you fight for your hated Emperor Louis Napoleon in a war against Prussia?" Rudolph asked.

"I wouldn't be fighting for him. I would be fighting for France. And what about you, Harsanyi? Will you fight with us? Austria hates Prussia."

"Your father wouldn't allow it," Professor Pock said.

"He treats you like a child!" Gravert said. "He commands and you obey!"

"But he's my father . . ."

"But you are a man!"

Rudolph stood. "I have to leave."

"To where?"

"Home."

Outside on the street, Pock caught up with him.

"Rudolph."

"Excuse me, Herr Professor, but I need to be home. My father doesn't want me out late." He spoke bitterly.

"Do you want to fight in this war?"

"My own preference is unimportant," he said stiffly.

"But your father would be right. It isn't your war."

"No. My war must be somewhere else."

With a fast, shuddering blow, Rudolph's broomstick was torn from his hands. It struck the ceiling of the stable above him and dropped into a hay-filled manger.

"How do you do that?"

Zoltan held his own wood sword at his side while Rudolph retrieved his.

"I am faster than you and stronger, and you hold your sword like a milk pitcher."

"That's how they told us to hold it." He had it in his hand again. "Just like this."

"At your side?" With one quick motion, Zoltan knocked it from his hand once more. "I would cut your throat next."

"We hold it that way to use it from horseback."

"You are on a horse? Then I would shoot you with a rifle."

"No. You'd shoot me with a cannon. Me and ten others, all with one canister of grapeshot." He picked up his sword. "I want to use my sword the way you do. I want to be able to fight another man with a sword, not just cut them down from the saddle."

"Then hold your sword right."

"Where did you learn?" Rudolph asked, holding it as closely as he could to how Zoltan was. "Only officers have swords."

"In armies, only officers. In the village, you have what you have."

"The village where you're from."

"On the plain, with no shelter. The Poles, the Cossacks, the Turks, in a year any of them might come. Only the village will defend the village."

They faced each other and raised the wooden poles, ready to begin.

"Have you ever cut someone's throat?" Rudolph asked.

"Yes."

"Why?"

"So he wouldn't cut mine."

The poles met in midair between them. Rudolph was knocked back by the force, but pushed in again.

"You killed three Prussians at Koniggratz."

"So they wouldn't kill me."

Zoltan let him try different attacks, parrying each one, and Rudolph learned from each. It was hard to tell the man's age. His black hair and mustache, both of which swept straight down, had no gray, but he must have been nearly as old as his master the baron, or older, and he was very strong.

"Have you ever killed someone who wasn't trying to kill you?"

"I would never do that. Killing is an evil thing."

"But sometimes you have to. Is it evil then?"

"Only God could keep a man from never having to do evil."

They had only a few more minutes before Therese came looking in the stables for Rudolph.

"What are you doing?" she asked impatiently.

"Zoltan and I are practicing."

"Father wants us ready to leave."

"For what?"

"Don't you remember?"

"No," Rudolph said. "Or I wouldn't have asked."

"Today is Franz Joseph's birthday."

Rudolph only looked puzzled.

"The embassy is having the emperor of Austria's birthday reception. We're all supposed to go."

"Do I have to?"

"Yes, Rudy, and Father says you have to wear your sword."

"Oh." He smiled. "All right, I'll come."

With only a few hundred guests, the reception for the emperor's birthday was a far smaller affair than the January reception for his uncle, but of course Albrecht had been present in person, and the emperor was present only in the person of his portrait hanging grandly on the wall.

Still, the ballroom was pleasantly filled. The orchestra was quieter, and the conversations much more intimate.

"Is it really his birthday?" Rudolph asked Therese as she curtsied and nodded at her father's side. Rudolph was a step or two behind.

"No. It's in August. This is the official celebration."

"Then why do we celebrate it now?"

"It's too hot in the summer."

But theirs was one of the few conversations about the emperor personally. Most were about his policies.

"Austria and France are natural allies," the French foreign minister was emphasizing to Prince von Metternich as the Harsanyi family reached the center of the reception.

"Austria is very sympathetic to France's complaints with Prussia," the ambassador said. His sympathy had only a trace of his usual mocking, which the minister apparently chose to ignore.

"And Austria could influence Russia, as well."

"Our influence in Saint Petersburg is limited."

"I'm sure it isn't."

Von Metternich only smiled.

"Why does Prussia want war with France?" Therese asked Rudolph quietly.

"It's simple. Prussia wants to take over all of Germany and make it one country under their control. But all the other Powers don't want them to. Germany would be too powerful. Prussia has already defeated Austria twice in the last seven years. England is a naval power, but their army isn't large enough to do anything. Russia is so big, they don't worry about Germany as much, and they'd like Prussian help against Austria in the Balkans. So there's only France."

"Could France stop Prussia?"

"That's what everyone's talking about. Whether they could or not."

"And is that the only reason France would want a war? To stop Prussia?"

"The country is getting tired of Napoleon. He could use the war to make himself more popular. If he wins."

"The country isn't tired of the emperor!" Therese said.

"The people at his parties aren't. The people on the streets are."

"The whole country is loyal to him."

"He's having a plebiscite next month."

"A what?"

"A plebiscite. A vote of confidence. The whole country will vote whether they want him to stay in control, or whether he should give more power to the Assemblee."

"I'm sure he'll win."

"He will because no one trusts the Assemblee, either, and only the middle class and the rich can vote. He's just trying to prove that he's still legitimate."

"The emperor and empress of France!"

The crowds parted as Princess Pauline guided Louis Napoleon and Eugenie toward her husband. All other sounds hushed, and everyone could hear the emperor and his Austrian friend greet each other in the friendliest way. The music started again as all the planets in the room began to circle and draw in toward the sun.

"The French strategy is straightforward and elegant." The French emperor was elegant, as well, as he discoursed for the highest-level diplomats who were favored to be close to him. But despite his charm, he was certainly worn and tired. Rudolph, standing beside his father, listened closely.

"The armies will be concentrated in Strasbourg and Metz. Together, they will thrust quickly and sharply across the Rhine and join in the vicinity of Stuttgart. Then, as Bavaria and her sisters in the south repudiate their alliance with Prussia, the French Grand Army will march on Berlin. The campaign would take perhaps three months." He stroked his goatee beard and then patted his forehead with a cream-colored silk handkerchief. "And at the end of the three months the Prussian army will just be completing its mobilization." He beamed, like a magician just completing a trick and waiting for applause.

The applause was granted.

"An offensive campaign?" Prince von Metternich asked politely.

"The French spirit and nature demand it."

"The French public demands it," von Metternich said to Ferdinand moments later, after the emperor had drifted to another circle. "He has to give them quick victories. He'll lose their support if he doesn't. They'll never be patient enough for a slow, defensive war."

"It's a complete change of plans," Ferdinand said. "They had meant to maintain an impregnable defensive line. The Prussians would attack it at the cost of immense casualties and finally give up."

"But surely it isn't hard to change a few plans?"

Rudolph was as close as he could be to the conversation, listening even more closely than he had to the emperor.

"It will be a disaster," Ferdinand answered. "They haven't planned specific invasion routes. They don't have the supplies they'd need for a campaign in enemy territory. They don't even know what supplies they'd need. They don't have the carts and horses to transport the supplies. And that's just the beginning."

"Are you sure they don't?"

"Completely. And even more, as I've described before, the French have built their entire army around a defensive strategy."

"I was told they would mobilize two hundred and fifty thousand men."

"A hundred thousand men at Strasbourg and a hundred fifty thousand at Metz. But they're too far apart to support each other, and they're separated by the Vosges Mountains. They'll have to fight two separate campaigns. Then the reserve of fifty thousand at Chalons exists only in the plans. There are no battalions yet assigned to it. Their only hope will be to push back a Prussian invasion. They might be able to do that. But if the French invade Germany, they're lost."

Von Metternich leaned closer. "I was told the French have a new weapon. They're keeping a secret."

Rudolph leaned closer, as discreetly as he could.

"I've heard of it," his father said.

"What is it?"

"They call it a *Mitrailleuse*."

"But what does it do?"

"No one outside the Bureau of Armaments knows. It's some new type of gun."

Louis Napoleon and his wife were dancing. The orchestra was playing a Strauss waltz, but in deference to French tastes, much more slowly than it would have been in Vienna. The French foreign minister was again beside Prince von Metternich.

"It would stop Bismarck completely. A grand alliance of France, Austria, and Russia."

"I will pass your suggestion to Vienna," Prince Richard von Metternich answered.

"An alliance of Europe's three emperors. It is, as I say, natural."

As close as he had been to all the conversations and whisperings, Rudolph had been silent and nearly unnoticed. But suddenly he spoke to the foreign minister.

"Sir, Europe has four emperors."

All eyes in the group turned on him: the minister, von Metternich, other officials, and his own father; a dozen senior officials of Austria and France.

"Four?" the Frenchman asked, clearly shocked at the young man's impertinence.

"Lord Gramont, this is my son, Rudolph," Baron Harsanyi said, introducing him but not defending him. He seemed interested in what might come of Rudolph's intrusion. Prince von Metternich smiled like a spectator at a prize fight.

"Europe has three emperors," the minister, Lord Gramont, said to Rudolph. "Your Franz Joseph, the tsar in Russia, and the gracious Louis Napoleon, who is before you. Surely you do not refer to the Turkish Sultan?"

"No, sir."

"Then who—?"

"Karlstein!" Suddenly, von Metternich's predatory pleasure had turned to confusion, and then alarm. He called for his senior aide, interrupting the foreign minister. "Karlstein! Come here."

The bald and fussy von Karlstein was quickly beside him.

"What is the news from Frankfurt?" von Metternich asked. "Don't tell me they've done it?"

"I have placed the dispatches on your desk. The North German alliance has offered the title of Kaiser to the Prussian king, and Wilhelm has accepted. It is a nominal honor, as it is a title only, but . . ."

The rest of his comments were lost in a babble of offended anger and belligerence as the French officials swiftly concluded that the entire reason was to insult France.

"How did you know?" Ferdinand asked in the carriage on the ride home.

"I saw a newspaper on the way to the embassy," Rudolph said.

"You made an impression on several important people. But it was most likely forgotten in the passions afterward."

"And why did you have to say it?" Therese asked. "Everyone was looking at you, and then afterward they were all so mad."

"I was getting bored," Rudolph said.

"It put the emperor himself in a bad mood," Therese said. "Why was it so important?"

"It shows that Prussia is becoming ever more dominant in Germany," their father answered. "It's one more step toward a united Germany."

"Is it really an insult to France?"

"That's not the reason they did it," Rudolph said. "France is just insulted by anything."

The next that Rudolph saw his father was at dinner that evening.

"Princess Pauline took me to the Italian ambassador's this afternoon," Therese said, and Rudolph didn't listen as she described dresses and flowers and music, and he didn't listen further as she went on to tell them about the next ball the princess would take her to at the Tuileries Palace.

When she finally finished, Rudolph said, "That sounds so dull."

"It's delightful."

"And Auguste goes with you?"

"Everywhere."

"They must want something," Rudolph said. "Both of them: him and the princess."

"We're friends. Don't you have any friends?"

"My classmates." Then he added, "The cadets all received orders today. The old orders for the second-year class have been cancelled. At the end of the term, all the cadets will be sent to barracks for training. Even the first-year cadets."

"Are you going?"

"I'm not in the French army." He looked at his father. "I could be. It could be arranged. Would I ever be?"

The baron had finished his meal and stood up. "No."

"But—"

"And I will be leaving Paris," he announced.

"When?" Therese asked, surprised.

"Tomorrow. For at least two weeks. I'll be inspecting the French fortifications at the border. And be careful while I'm gone." He looked sternly at both his children. "Next week the government is holding its plebiscite. Stay off the streets. There will be unrest."

– 2 –

Rudolph was fitted into a narrow corner of a sitting room, and Gravert squeezed beside him and three other cadets. Every wall was filled—with bookshelves, papers, color prints of battle scenes, a saber, tankards, tobacco pipes, a violin, oil lamps and candles, a cuckoo clock. And the corners were stuffed with stuffed chairs, an old sofa, and tables.

Arpad Pock, their host, set a japanned tray on the table with bread and cheese and beer and coffee, and the eating and drinking of it commenced with no interruption of the argument.

"Manassas? Chancellorsville? He was a genius."

"Gettysburg."

"One battle! Only one loss! Lee was far superior to the Union generals."

"And Gettysburg was decided by a grain of sand in a balance. It could have been a great victory."

"But Lee lost the war. What do you say, Harsanyi?"

"He was the brilliant battle general of the war."

"See! Austria agrees!"

"But he lost the war!"

"Be calm." Pock was still standing, amused at the passions.

"Professor! Who was the great general? Lee or Grant?"

"I have met them both." Pock settled into his own old chair. "Lee was noble, and Grant was common."

"That tells it! It is in the blood!"

"That is not an insult to Grant," the professor said. "It was part of his strength."

"But he could only defeat Lee when he had vast superiority. With even armies, he was inferior."

"And so he created vast superiority. And then he won his battles and his war. It isn't battles that win wars, not in this modern age. It's the might of the nation."

"No, it is for the elite. Only the tyrant oppressors profit from war, and they profit handsomely."

"Then I will be an oppressor, if that's where the profits are."

"The profiteers don't start the war. There are always vultures, but great wars are for great purposes, for the nations and their glory."

"What glory? It's only blood!"

"French glory! The French soul knows what war is and why it must be fought!"

"The French soul knows only oppression and poverty—"

"Hold, hold!" Professor Pock laughed. "Before the walls crack. Young men know little but passion, and that too well."

"When age cools the fire," one of the young men said, "the blood thickens and the heart slows."

"And life is more comfortable," Pock said, and they all laughed, even Gravert. "But your chance for war will come."

"We'll be in Berlin in two months."

"One month!"

"No," Pock said, "I think it will be much more difficult."

"What do you think, Austrian?" the cadets asked Rudolph.

"He's not Austrian. He's a Hun!"

"Attila, will you ride with us against Prussia?"

Rudolph shrugged. "It won't be my war."

"But you want to ride with us?"

"My father would never allow it." He couldn't hide his frustration.

"His father," Gravert said. "He's only a tyrant, like them all."

"You don't even know what a father is," Rudolph said, and abruptly the room was quiet.

Gravert answered slowly. "My father died for a great cause."

"Resisting our emperor!" another cadet answered into the suddenly knife-sharp tension.

"The false emperor! He thinks his plebiscite vote will show that the people are behind him, but Paris will rise! I promise it!"

"Traitor!"

"We must allow for our passions," Pock said, dulling the blades. "And not inflame them! There will be enough war soon without seeking even more of it among your own countrymen."

"It's just because they're French," Rudolph said after the others had left. They were standing in the street in front of Pock's apartment building. "It's all about insult and defending their honor."

The Rue Serpente in front of them was on the edge of the Quartier Latin. It was narrow, shadowed by high buildings of questionable character and structural soundness, but very full of character.

"What do you think of Gravert?" Pock asked. "Do you take offense when he insults your father?"

"Not too much. I like Gravert."

"But you still get very angry."

"Not at Gravert."

"He only rubs the salt?"

"Herr Pock, would my father ever let me go to the war? He only says no, and he won't even talk about it."

"He would never approve. But I think you could ask him to explain his reasons."

"He's away. He's at the Rhine, looking at the French defenses."

"Do you want to be part of this war?"

"All the other cadets will go. It's all they talk about."

"Why would you want to? For the glory?"

"I'm not French."

"Then why?" Pock asked. "You didn't even want to be in the army."

"I think a man has to show that he's brave," Rudolph said.

"No. I know you better. There is that reason, but there is more."

"My father was in his first battle when he was eighteen."

"Do you know that he still has a bullet in his side from that battle?"

"In him?"

"If it had been a little closer to his heart, he would not have survived. And you, Rudolph, would not be living."

"But he did survive, and I'm still not living. Professor Pock, I have . . . my father . . ." Rudolph struggled for words. "And when my mother died . . ."

"Yes? What?"

"I don't know who I am." He shook his head. "I'm sorry. It's nothing. My apologies."

– 3 –

"What's happening?" Therese was panicked.

Rudolph was home early from his classes and his sister was at the front window, staring out at the street.

"What have you seen?" He was eager for news.

"I went out and there were people, crowds. They were angry and I was afraid!"

"The plebiscite. They announced the results. The emperor won and the people are rising up against it."

"But . . ." Therese was confused. "Why are there crowds?"

"He won in the provinces, but not in Paris. Paris hates him. It's the only thing they can do, Raisy!" He removed his jacket, pulled off his necktie. "When the authority won't listen to you talk, you have to shout."

"What do they want?"

But he was too impatient to explain. "I'm going out. I want to see."

"But Father said to stay off the streets—"

Not looking at her, he said, "When authority won't listen, it has to be ignored."

Rudolph was back out as quickly as he could be, on his horse, searching Paris for the uprising. A whole army regiment was creating a camp on the Champ de Mars, just outside the windows of the École. More troops were patrolling outside the Assemblee Nationale and, across the river, at the Palais de Justice. The Tuileries gardens were only rows of tents among the trees. The Tuileries Palace, with the emperor and his family locked inside, was heavily guarded. There would be no violence with such an impressive show of force. So Rudolph continued east, searching for violence, or the threat of it.

Beyond the central city, crossing the Boulevard Voltaire, he found what he was looking for. Whatever numbers the army had in the center, the eastern arrondissements equaled with their crowded, angry streets. He went farther east into the city than he'd ever been before, crossing the Boulevard de la Villette, and coming to the squalor and dirt of Belleville.

He'd seen these people before, sweeping the streets, in the stables of the wealthy, tending the hot ovens in the bakeries and shoveling coal into furnaces in the cellars of the palaces. And all the while, the palaces had been shoving coal into the furnaces of the mob's discontent, and here it was overheating and flaming out.

The men and women, and also the children, looked up at him, high on his horse, all with the same expression. It was a sullen and affronted resentment. But today, with the furnace stoked hot, the outrage behind the brooding was close to breaking through.

He paused at the intersection of the Rue des Pyrenees and the Rue de Belleville, in the district's heart. There were other horses, pulling loads, but none other with a rider. He was above them all.

A cabbage whistled by his head, missing only by centimeters, and only because he had jerked away. He turned his horse and started off at a trot, then a canter, then a gallop, swerving in the crowded street to avoid carts and children, and then he was back in the gray, beautiful streets of his Paris.

– 4 –

At the beginning of the first lecture after the unrest, the chair beside Rudolph was empty. Because the city was only returning to normal, he wasn't concerned, though he did ask, "Where is Gravert?"

That day, there was no response among the cadets but shrugs. The next day Gravert was still absent, and there was a darker shade to the answers: "We knew it would happen," "He had it coming," and "He should have been more careful. He talked too much."

"What happened to Gravert?" Rudolph asked Pock behind the closed door of his professor's office.

"He has been dismissed from the École."

"But he was harmless!"

Pock shook his head. "Most likely he wasn't. You don't know whether he was part of any organizations, or whether he was influencing anyone else. Paris takes revolutionaries seriously. He has been under observation."

"Did you know?"

"I only assumed."

"Why didn't you warn him?"

"He hasn't been imprisoned, only dismissed from his appointment. In truth, I think it's best for him."

"What will happen to him?"

"The police will decide, and I think there are more important things for them to worry about for now."

"He used no restraint!" The talk at the Café du Fusillade concerning Gravert also used no restraint. "He would say anything! To anyone."

"What purpose did he have at the École, if he only wanted to over-throw the emperor?"

"He's poor, and he wanted a career."

Rudolph only leaned his chair farther back into his corner. It was after ten o'clock, but the street outside was still haunted by a ghost of late spring sunlight. That sunlight didn't reach the back corners of the tavern, and when he saw the small man come in the front door, the man had to search shadows to see within.

Rudolph watched as he made his way between the tables, completely unnoticed by the boisterous cadets and other patrons. He found his way to Rudolph.

"Monsieur Harsanyi," the man said, and Rudolph recognized him.

"Monsieur Sarroche?" Rudolph moved his chair forward again.

"Yes. I see that you remember me." With a little more light, Sarroche would have stood out in any tavern for the incongruity of his fussy appear-ance and long hair, and in the Fusillade even more for his nonmilitary expression. But he was ignored. "I will take a moment of your time."

"What do you want?"

"I will be blunt. I wish to purchase cinnabar from you, and I will pay you very well."

Rudolph started in surprise. Again he looked closer, but it was almost as if doing so only made him see less. "What do you mean?" he asked.

"I wish to purchase mercury from you. You have estates in Slovenia, and large mercury mines. I have an urgent need for your mercury."

"But . . . they're my father's . . ." He stopped and forced himself to think. "I know you've talked with my father."

"Yes. He has so far only delayed, and I have no more time."

"I can't sell you anything."

"These mines are your inheritance. By right they are yours." Sarroche was already speaking quietly, but now he came much closer and was almost whispering. "Your father has attempted to betray Austria and France for his own enrichment. It is your duty to overthrow his treachery."

"But I have to be twenty-three before I inherit."

Even in the dark, Sarroche's eyes searched him as they had searched the shadows of the room when he arrived, and just as they had found Rudolph at his table, they seemed now to find in him what they were looking for.

"It is not necessary for you to wait," Sarroche said.

"I won't inherit—"

"I have instructed the French ambassador in Vienna to intervene. It is possible to have your father's guardianship removed. For the sake of the French and Austrian alliance, the Austrian government would do this."

Rudolph tried to think clearly. "You want me to break with my father. You want me to oppose him."

"Surely," Sarroche said, "that would not be a difficulty." Then he leaned closer to Rudolph and whispered, "You would even welcome that, wouldn't you?"

Sarroche pulled back then and was silent. Rudolph's breath was short and sharp, gasping of panic until he regained control and answered, "I can't."

"You must! Time is critical. The decision cannot be delayed." But then, pausing, he relented. "Two days. That is all that is possible. After that, it will be too late. Do you know that Monsieur Whistler is dead?"

Like one of Zoltan's thrusts, this threw Rudolph back. "He's dead?"

"Yes. He was ill and he died in his bed. Your father was the last person to visit him." Sarroche bobbed his head in a short, formal bow. "Please be careful, monsieur. As I have said, it is very urgent we move quickly." And then, the final thrust, as he was already standing. "And you would gain vengeance for your mother's death."

He was gone before Rudolph could reply.

"It's all absurd!" Pock said. "How could he claim such things?" They were in the professor's small sitting room, amidst the books and papers and clutter.

"How would he know so much?" Rudolph said.

"He employs agents, I'm sure, and he has the police to assist him. He said your father was the last to see the man Whistler?"

"Yes. But why would he think I'd do what he wanted?"

"Perhaps for the money?"

"He said that. But he just assumed that I would betray Father. He seemed to think I'd do it willingly."

Pock sighed. "Rudolph, I know that your father has made decisions against your wishes. I know that you are frustrated even now. But surely that would be a drastic action."

"No! I can't."

"Of course not. I'm sure you wouldn't."

Rudolph was perplexed. "Should I tell Father what this Sarroche said?"

"It's hard to say what would come of it. If Sarroche truly has such a plot against your father, then your father should know. But Sarroche might be bluffing."

"Why would he do that?"

"I don't know. But you must be firm in your own mind before you open this subject with him."

"What do you mean?"

"Think carefully. Would you truly consider accepting Monsieur Sarroche's offer?"

Rudolph opened his mouth to deny the possibility. But somehow, to his dismay, the words stuck in his throat. "I wouldn't," was all he could manage.

"If you would," Pock said, "your father would see it in you. I suggest you do not tell him."

- 5 -

"Come outside with me," Rudolph said to Therese the next evening. The somnolent, late May air was as warm as summer.

"Where?"

"Out of this house."

On the doorstep he turned left as he always did.

"Where are we going?"

"Some or other way," he said.

Therese followed and he set off at a fast pace, almost leaving her behind.

"Slow down!"

"Hurry up."

But he wasn't going anywhere, only going quickly. Therese ran and caught up with him.

In minutes, he had come to the gate of the École Militaire, but he stopped himself from going through it. "Around this way," he said.

"Why am I coming with you?" Therese said. "You haven't even said anything to me."

"Go home if you want."

"I'll come."

Around the side of the École, past its buildings, they came to the corner of the Champ de Mars, a kilometer long and a half kilometer wide, spreading out from the grand façade of the main hall of the École down to the Seine.

"This is where we drill," he said.

"What do you do?"

"I charge my horse forward and wave my sword and practice cutting down the enemy."

"Cutting them down?" Therese grimaced.

"It's enjoyable. Everyone's together, and it's loud. Like fifty heavy guns all firing."

"Is the enemy firing at you?"

"We don't practice that. It wouldn't be enjoyable."

"Rudy! It sounds terrible."

"That's what your Auguste does."

"Just in battles."

"Come onto the field."

He led her through the corner gate and out into the wide grass. They walked for more than a minute toward its center. Except for them, the field was empty. The brilliance of spring was ending, and the light had begun its fade, so that the grass was dull green and gray. There were many areas of torn brown soil where the hooves and boots had scarred the grass or trampled it.

"Napoleon graduated from the École in just one year," Rudolph said.

"The emperor was here?"

"No," Rudolph said in disgust. "The real Napoleon. The first one. Not this one. It usually takes two years. There was an observatory on the roof of the main building." He pointed at the dome in the distance. "When the Russians took Paris in 1814, the Cossacks smashed it and sold the parts for tobacco. They used the manuscripts in the astronomers' library to light their pipes. For the riots two weeks ago, the army bivouacked five thousand troops on this field. You should have come to see it. And they did the same in 1848 and 1852, too. And in 1830. All the uprisings."

"Did they put down all those other uprisings like they did this one?"

"No, it depends. Sometimes the troops overthrew the government instead. Whichever side the generals think will do better for them."

"They're so heartless."

"Everyone is. That's what they teach us. War is all about winning and nothing else matters."

"But not everyone is like that."

He shook his head. "I think they are. Who do you think Father should sell our mercury to?"

"What? I don't know anything about mercury! How do you even know what Father's trying to do?"

But Rudolph didn't answer. He started walking again, but slowly, and Therese stayed beside him.

"What do you think happened to Mother?" he asked.

"Rudy, I don't understand! What are you saying?"

"She didn't want to sell to anyone. But now that she's dead, Father can sell to whoever he wants. He'll make lots of money."

"Don't say that!"

"But he's being too slow. The French are getting impatient. They might do something."

"Stop."

Therese did as she said it, and Rudolph stopped beside her.

"I know that about the French," he said. "It's certain."

"I don't want to hear this."

"Why not? Because you just want to think about Auguste? And the princess, and dances and dresses?"

"I'd rather think about dancing with Auguste than hear you say all these things about Father. What's wrong with you, Rudy?"

"I'm thinking too much."

"Don't think."

"They teach us to always be thinking. Most of the cadets only want to race their horses and fire their guns, but some of us listen to the professors." He kicked a stone and it tumbled a few feet and stopped. "I knew how everything was going to be in Vienna, and then it was kicked away and now I don't know anything. I think I'm on strings like a puppet, and Father has them in his hand. I don't know what he's really doing."

"He's doing what's best for the family."

"Do you think that? You don't. You still haven't told him that you knew Auguste for months before you came to Paris. You don't trust him."

"That's different."

"It's all the same. Everything is war. If you listen to what they say about war at the École, you can get very upset about who man is."

"I'm not upset. When you're in love," Therese said, "you get very proud of who man is."

"If you study war, you can do that, too. I think . . ." he paused. "I think God is at war with man."

"That doesn't sound right."

"We're at war with everything. Why not with Him?" Then he was finished, and they walked home in silence.

– 6 –

The next day, Rudolph was met at the door by Maria as he returned from the École.

"A man is here to speak with you, Master Rudolph," she said.

He knew, but still he asked, "Who is it?"

"He wouldn't say. He's in the front room, waiting."

"When did he arrive?"

"Just a moment ago. He said you were already on your way home."

Rudolph was frozen in the front hall. He heard the creak of a chair in the parlor. He asked her, "Is Father here? He hasn't come today, has he?"

"Of course not, master. It will be another week at least."

"His name is Sarroche. I won't talk to him."

"But, master—"

Rudolph was already on the stairs, fleeing to his room.

With only one week of lectures remaining before the end of the term, Rudolph walked the back alleys to the École, kept to the shadows, and watched for watchers.

"I won't be home at all tomorrow," Therese said to Maria at breakfast.

Rudolph turned to her. "Are you coming to the École?"

Therese looked at him blankly. "Coming where?"

"The last day of the term. The commissioning. The second-year cadets are commissioned, and the first-year cadets are advanced. Father won't be here—aren't you coming?"

"I forgot!" Therese was plainly distressed. "I'm sorry, Rudy, but I can't. Auguste is leaving Paris. It's his last day. I'm sorry . . ."

"It doesn't matter."

"He's going back into the army."

"The Imperial Guards Cavalry?"

"No. It's a different cavalry. It's under General LeGrand."

The cadets, in their long rows, in dark blue jackets and red trousers, stood silent on the Champ de Mars as the commander of the École finished his address. Commands were given and the troops fell into parade lines and marched past, saluting the grandstand.

The second-year cadets, freshly commissioned into the regular army, marched first. Rudolph and his class followed, taking their places as the senior cadets of the school.

But it was only a ritual, because they were also joining the army.

Rudolph marched with them. Afterward, in the milling crowds of family and well-wishers, he stood alone, and then he left as soon as he was able.

He chose not to join any of his fellows at the taverns or cafés for their last night and revels before reporting to barracks. He walked the short blocks to his house, still alone.

When he opened the front door, he was startled by the commotion.

"Zoltan!" he said.

Zoltan nodded, and continued toward the stairs with a trunk on his back.

"Father?" Rudolph called. "Are you here?"

"Here."

He was in his office, at his desk, with papers spread across its surface. His head was down, reading, with a pen in his hand. He scratched a note on the top paper and looked up.

Rudolph stood in the doorway. He was still in his dress uniform with his sword at his side and his high hat under his arm.

His father frowned. "Why are you dressed this way?"

Rudolph swallowed. "Today was our commissioning ceremony."

"Today?" The baron set his pen down. "But I thought Pock said it was next week. I must have been mistaken. Why didn't you tell me?"

"You weren't here, sir."

"You could have written."

"I apologize."

"No! Rudolph." His father stood, staring at him. "Don't apologize. It was my fault. I should have found out myself." They faced each other, but Rudolph only waited. "Congratulations," his father said.

"Thank you, sir."

"I have to go to the embassy. It's urgent. But be here when I get home tonight. We'll celebrate as a family."

After six o'clock, the front door opened and Rudolph looked out of his room. But it wasn't his father; he saw his sister coming up the stairs.

Her face was white, except where it was streaked from tears.

"What's wrong?" he asked.

"He's gone."

"Auguste?"

"We said good-bye."

"He'll be back, Raisy."

"I know he will!" she said, and laid her head on his shoulder.

"Father's home."

She lifted her head, suddenly hopeful. "Where?"

"He's at the embassy. He'll be back soon."

"Oh, Rudy. Why are there wars?"

"Because hate is stronger than anything else," Rudolph said.

The dinner table was set, but still unused, as the evening passed. Rudolph stayed downstairs, near the front door just as Therese used to do waiting for Auguste. Finally, he opened the door himself and stood on the step, looking to the end of the block, watching for his father's hard, long stride to come into view. Then he took a few strides of his own toward the corner. As he reached the last house on their block, he prepared himself to look out onto the Boulevard des Invalides, where he could see several more blocks, almost half the way to the embassy. Looking into the distance, he missed what was close at hand, and as he turned the corner he collided with someone else.

"Monsieur, the very one I seek." It was Sarroche.

Rudolph stepped back. "I'm waiting for my father."

"He will be delayed. I have just come from the Austrian Embassy, and he will be there for many more hours."

"What is he doing?" Despite his distaste at begging information from this man, Rudolph still wanted to know.

"He is briefing all the senior officials of the embassy on the state of the border defenses. And I have come to seek you, and here I find you, and you will not be able to escape to your bedroom this time. Unless you consider turning and running from me?"

"I won't run."

"Then instead you must come with me, while your father is inaccessible, and we will attend to the papers to complete the sale of cinnabar ore to France."

"Now?"

"It is the last moment. Even tomorrow might be too late."

"But . . . it still isn't mine."

"That would also be quickly resolved. I have charges ready to file against the baron, and officers who will arrest him as he leaves the embassy."

"You can't arrest him!"

"It would only be for a brief internment, until the embassy protests and he is then released but disgraced. A single telegram from me to the French Embassy in Vienna will initiate the necessary proceedings with the government of Austria."

"No," Rudolph said.

"Everything is in readiness!" Sarroche's manner changed from urging to threatening. "It must be done tonight!"

"I won't."

"And why? Because of a foolish fealty to a man who ignores you and cares nothing for you?"

"That's not true!"

"Tonight, in my presence, he ridiculed you."

"I don't believe you."

"As he jested and scorned the heroic young men who will soon fight for the glory of France, I asked him if his own son would fight with his fellow cadets for France. He made mockery of your own natural desire to seek honor. He said his own son was too fragile and weak for such an arduous task."

"He wouldn't say that."

"And then he laughed."

"Who are you?" Rudolph shouted it, in desperate anger, overwhelmed by the attack.

But the thin little man replied quietly, forcefully, "I am your friend. And if you will not do this thing for the sake of France, then do it for the sake of your mother."

"You're lying!"

"You know it to be true. I wish retribution for his betrayal of France; you wish it for his betrayal of your family. Together these make for a double reason that he be stripped of his power and privileges over you." Sarroche paused, then added, "Whether you believe it or not, I am telling you the truth, and you must come with me immediately."

Rudolph's eyes lifted for a moment above the thin face, searching down the street, and then he saw, close and quickly coming closer, his father.

The baron had seen them. Sarroche saw the change in Rudolph's face and spun around.

Baron Ferdinand Harsanyi was a black storm cloud in the dusk, and his eyes were lightning. In seconds he was on them.

"What are you doing?" he asked harshly, to them both.

Sarroche was faster and answered, "We are simply discussing the cinnabar mines in Idria. What else would you expect, Baron?"

"Go!" Ferdinand's words exploded. "Go, and leave him alone!"

Sarroche was at last intimidated, and shrank back. But as he left, he fired back, "It is not always for you to command! You have enemies, Baron, strong enemies who will defeat you!"

But Rudolph was now the target of his father's glare. "What were you doing? What were you saying?"

"He wanted me to sell him cinnabar—"

"You? Why were you talking to him? What did you agree to?" The baron's voice was full of suspicion and anger, all trained on his son. "Answer me! What are you doing?"

Rudolph returned the anger and suspicion. "Nothing, sir!" And then, "What are you doing? What have you been agreeing to? Why have you been talking to him?"

The baron's rage hardened, visibly and slowly, in his features. "Home," he said, and Rudolph turned, and without any more words spoken they walked the block to their front door.

Inside the door, Therese was waiting. She buried her face in her father's shoulder while Rudolph escaped to his room.

– 7 –

The day after dawned as a sullen and rain-swept morning, slowly passing through cloud and wind and sodden air. Rudolph Harsanyi left his house on horseback before the unseen sun had nearly risen.

He rode out of the city, to the southwest, past Issy and Vanves.

Across a train track, and in the empty fields between those villages and

Clamart farther south, he stopped in a shaft of sunlight that had fought its way through the clouds. Two of the southern forts were less than a kilometer on either side of him, both still in shadow and rain while he was in his momentary fastness of light.

The light came from a sun low in the sky, still far away east. The cloud opening the light had found drifted south, and Rudolph was soon in shadow again as he watched the brightness advance across the fields, and he followed it.

Within a few hundred meters he topped a ridge. Below, in a wide, shallow stream valley, were at least three hundred men unloading crates and bags from a train, loading everything onto horse carts that were pulling them toward the Fort at Issy. He rode closer to see what they were carrying.

The crates that were open revealed rifles and artillery shells.

At noon, on the southeast corner of Paris at Charenton, he saw a train of flatcars pass by, each with a single bronze cannon barrel. Later, near St. Denis, another train was headed east carrying cattle.

And in the evening, having circled the city entirely, he saw soldiers drilling in the Bois de Boulogne. They weren't regular army; they were Gardes Mobiles, the new national guard of citizen volunteers.

He was home late, and his father and Therese had already finished dinner. He ate in the kitchen.

"Where have you been?" his father asked as he was walking up the stairs afterward.

"Riding."

"Did you speak with anyone?"

"No, sir."

They stood for a moment. Rudolph waited for the next question.

"Tell me if you do."

Ferdinand didn't wait for an answer. Rudolph watched him disappear into his study.

All he did for the next week was ride, and watch France prepare for war. He saw nothing more of Sarroche.

He only saw his sister and father at dinner sometimes. Beside the barest politeness, he was silent. Like the forts around Paris, he kept his walls strong and high.

But as the next week passed, and nothing else was said, and the tension eased, he slowly rejoined his family. Therese was all the more anxious for his company with Auguste gone.

But it wasn't true peace. It was more a cautious neutrality.

— 8 —

By early July, the languid heat of a French summer had fallen heavily on Paris. All of Europe was cast adrift as statesmen and ministers took leave of baking capitals and settled into mountain and seaside resorts.

"The Emperor Napoleon leaves in two days for Saint Cloud," Ferdinand said. "Half the court is already there." He seemed relieved.

"Princess Pauline said they'll take a house there," Therese said. "Couldn't we? Or in Sevres?"

"I need to stay at the embassy. But maybe we'll go for a day or two each week."

Rudolph ventured a question. "What are you doing at the embassy?"

"Writing dispatches and sending them, and reading the dispatches that are sent to me."

"Maybe there won't be a war," Therese said. "Everyone's out of town."

"Tomorrow von Werther, the Prussian ambassador, will leave for Bad Ems to vacation with the Prussian King Wilhelm," Ferdinand said. "Once he leaves, I think everything will be quiet and safe. There can't be a war; there won't be anyone left to tell."

Rudolph used the next day to walk around Paris. Everywhere was placid, slow, and empty. The boulevards were gray ghosts, and the Seine was the city's unfeeling iron spirit. The air was warm oppression.

For two hours he sat in a café by the Place de la Bastille, a quarter of Paris he didn't know well, but all Paris was the same that day. Then he strolled back across the river and finally back to Rue Duroc.

The baron was not home, and was not home still at dinner, and even the late July sunset came before he did arrive home. When the last red streaks were gone from the sky and the candles were bright, Rudolph heard the front door open and the study door open and close, and he came down the stairs and knocked on it.

"Come," his father said, and when Rudolph saw him, he was far from the cheerful man he had been the night before.

"What's wrong?"

"Today, when von Werther, the Prussian ambassador, stopped at the Foreign Ministry to take his leave for the summer, he was met by Foreign Minister Gramont himself. Gramont was furious."

"Is it about Prince Leopold?"

"Yes. He's formally accepted the kingship of Spain."

"Von Bismarck must have convinced him to," Rudolph said.

"Of course." Ferdinand was frustrated and angry himself. "To insult France. It's all to insult France. It's all to goad and prod and insult. And France has risen to the insult and doubled it back. Gramont gave von Werther an ultimatum to pass to von Bismarck and the kaiser."

"What did he say?"

"He demands that the acceptance be withdrawn immediately."

Rudolph paused. "What will happen?"

"The next move is for Prussia."

"What will I wear tomorrow?" Therese swept into Rudolph's room. "I think white, but everyone in Saint-Cloud will be wearing white."

"I don't think we are going anywhere tomorrow," he said.

"But—"

"Herr von Bismarck has delayed our vacation."

The next morning, Rudolph paced the streets of Paris again, but now the ghosts had fled and living men had taken their places. The Assemblee Nationale was buzzing with activity, called back by the prime minister, and by late afternoon the newspapers were publishing the bellicose speech that Foreign Minister Gramont had given there.

Olympian silence was all that was heard from the emperor's court in Saint-Cloud.

"He's scared," Rudolph told Therese when he returned home. "I think he's afraid of war."

That evening, when Rudolph's father did finally get home, he had an assignment for his son.

"Take your horse, or walk, but go everywhere. Tell me what's happening in the city. I want to know."

"Yes, sir." They had a common cause, to know what Paris was doing and thinking and saying, but for different reasons. Ferdinand said he wanted the information, while Rudolph wanted to be a part of it.

For three days, Paris's fever increased and Rudolph gave his report. "The people hate the Prussians even more than the emperor. If there's no war, there will be an uprising. The only thing they talk about on the streets in Belleville and La Villette is that they want war, and they're afraid the government is too cowardly to fight."

But a week later, Paris was knocked backward in its passion with the news that the crisis was resolved.

"He's withdrawn!" Rudolph said, reading the newspaper his father had brought home. "Prince Leopold says he won't take the Spanish throne."

"There won't be a war?" Therese asked.

"Maybe not. But everyone is so angry. Something will happen."

"France isn't giving up its outrage easily," their father said at dinner that night.

"It's all over," Therese said. "At Princess Pauline's salon this afternoon, everyone said the crisis was over."

"Prussia insulted France. France will want some kind of compensation."

"What?"

"An apology."

"Can't they just accept that it's over?" Therese asked.

"No," Rudolph answered. "This is France and they're furious. Something has to happen."

The fury, now without a direct target, only grew. Prussia was still distrusted for its provocation, and the government for its wavering response. Another four days passed with charges leveled in the Assemblee and answered from the Foreign Ministry, and echoed in every newspaper in Paris. And then, just when even the most impassioned began to consider that July might slip by without war, the headlines suddenly exploded. "The Kaiser himself!" Rudolph threw the papers onto the parlor table in front of Therese. "He's insulted the French ambassador."

"What happened?"

"The Kaiser was vacationing in Ems, and Benedetti, the French ambassador to Prussia walked up to him on the street. The Kaiser said he was happy that the Spanish crisis was over, and then Benedetti said that France still demanded an apology! King Wilhelm was so angry, it says here, that he didn't even answer. He just walked away. Then the Kaiser's secretary sent a telegram back to Berlin that described the encounter, and somehow, all the newspapers got a copy of the telegram."

"Von Bismarck let them have the telegram." They both looked up to see their father in the doorway. "After he changed the wording to make it more insulting."

"What does it say?" Therese asked.

Rudolph read from the newspaper. "It says that the French ambassador demanded that the Kaiser promise that Prussia would never push another candidate for Spain. Then it says, 'His Majesty the King thereupon refused to receive the Ambassador again and that the latter informed that His Majesty had no further communication to make to the Ambassador.' "

"Is that all?" Therese said. "It doesn't seem very offensive."

"It is very offensive," Ferdinand said. "On both sides. On such little words, wars are fought. It is even worse to have it made public in the newspapers. It can only be interpreted as an insult."

The words, and the telegram, and the entire existence of Prussia, were interpreted by Paris as a tremendous insult. Ferdinand was at the embassy from sunrise until after sunset, and Therese was bewildered with each new announcement, every statement confusing her more. Rudolph finally gave up explaining.

"It's just going to be war, Raisy. Nothing can stop it now."

And fundamentally, she only had one question anyway.

"What will happen to Auguste?"

"He'll go to war."

Three days after the telegram, the Assemblee voted for war funding, and the army ordered its mobilization to begin. But peace still hung by one thread, the final debate in the Assemblee over whether to declare war. Until that act was passed, the future still only teetered on the edge of the precipice, and hadn't yet fallen.

– 9 –

The curtains in the front parlor were nearly closed, letting in a thin line of bright light and a wide cloud of diffuse light. Rudolph stood at the door to the hallway and his father by the window, both of them watching quietly and with respect. Even Maria and Zoltan in the hall were at attention.

Therese was seated. Before her, on one knee, Auguste held her hands in his, and her eyes with his.

"I will return," he said quietly. "And every moment I am not with you, I will have you in every thought. Indeed, it cannot be otherwise."

"I wish you wouldn't go," she said.

"I am called by France, for her glory and my own."

"When we heard you were coming through Paris, I was so happy that we'd see you one more time. But it means we have to say good-bye one more time."

"For every parting, there will always be a reuniting."

"What if you don't come back?"

"It is fully impossible. How could I not return?" His voice rose with a shade of anger. "How could these feeble conscript Prussians be of any consequence? Only a short time will be necessary to debilitate them thoroughly. And of even greater potency is our own love, which even whole armies cannot sunder."

"You're everything to me, Auguste."

He answered slowly and passionately. "You are everything to me, dearest Therese, you and France."

"What unit are you in?" Rudolph asked as Auguste's departure paused at the front door. Therese had run to her room to find a token of her affection for Auguste to take with him, and Ferdinand was talking quietly with Zoltan.

"The cavalry of the Thirty-fourth Battalion."

Rudolph said, "But I thought you were in the Imperial Guards Cavalry."

"The Thirty-fourth is a new regiment and in need of experienced and resourceful officers."

"Is your friend Captain Beaubien still in Imperial Guards?"

"He is. Perhaps I will see him on the field of battle."

"Why did you leave the Guards? You never told us."

"It was long ago."

"But—"

But Auguste was annoyed. "What is it to you?" And then, recovering himself, and taking an even nobler tone than usual, he asked, "And what of you? What will you do for this war?"

Rudolph didn't have an answer. "What could I do?"

"Any man who is brave and who, in his heart, knows his purpose, is welcome to fight for France."

"I'm not French."

"But your blood burns for war. I know it does."

"I don't think—"

"No, Rudolph, my friend. I know you, and I know your spirit. You are a man of war."

"My father—"

Auguste interrupted again, with a glance at Ferdinand's study that dismissed the arguments, and the man. Rudolph was surprised at the disregard.

"Your father is a great man, but he has fought his wars. The fire has passed from him." Auguste's eyes were intensely on Rudolph. "The fire has passed from him," he said again. "It is yours now."

Before Rudolph could answer, Therese was back with them. Hanging from her hand on a silver chain was a small red jewel in a silver setting.

"This was my mother's necklace," she said. "I want you to take it."

"Your mother's? But surely it is too precious."

"No. She'd want you to."

"But to take a thing of beauty into war?"

"Even war," she said, trying to smile, "needs something beautiful."

Finally, Auguste was gone.

Rudolph steeled himself to face his father.

"Come," his voice called when Rudolph knocked on his door. "Yes?"

"Father, I can't stay here."

His father looked up from the desk and saw the storm facing him and reflected it back.

"You will stay. You will not be part of this war."

"Why?" Suddenly, all the resentment and frustration boiled to the surface. "Everything you've taught me is for war," he said, his voice raised in anger. "When you were eighteen, you rode against the Turks. Why shouldn't I?"

"You'll be killed," his father answered, as cold as he himself was hot. "One glorious ride into a bank of rifles and cannon and you'll be dead."

"I won't be in the cavalry."

"You won't be in the war at all."

"Then why did you force me into the École Militaire?" He wasn't in control of his own words. They came rushing out by themselves. "Why? I didn't want to. I wanted to go to the Sorbonne. Why didn't you let me do that?"

"You would have hated it."

"I hate where I am now. I've been taught war because you forced me to, and now that war has come, you won't let me be part of it." He tried to find some verbal knife to throw. "I should have done what Mother wanted."

"And been half a man, half alive."

"Then let me live! I don't understand."

"Maybe I should have let you do what your mother wanted."

"Do you hate me because you hated her?"

Ferdinand rose from his desk. "Don't say a word about Irene! Not to me." His voice and his eyes were menacing. But Rudolph was beyond the threat.

"Because you don't want to be reminded! You don't want to think about her when you make your agreements with Sarroche and the others, when you sell her mines for your profit." And then, firing his heaviest shell, he said, "You don't want to think about her dying, do you?"

"What do you mean?" His father's look was murderous.

"Did you kill her, Father?" He waited. "Deny it if you didn't."

And like the detonation of the shell, the one moment lasted forever, but was only a moment.

"Father?" Therese was standing in the hall behind Rudolph, wide-eyed and in shock at what she'd heard. But she had something else she had to say. "There's a messenger here from the embassy. He says he must speak with you immediately."

Ferdinand didn't seem to realize she was there, but he answered, "What?"

The messenger had come with her, a young man in the uniform of an Austrian lieutenant. "Sir," he said. "The ambassador requests that you come at once."

"What has happened?"

"The Assemblee has voted. War has been declared."

"I'll come at once."

Rudolph stood aside as Ferdinand disappeared out the front door. His last view of his father was of the man pulling on his coat with his back turned to his son.

"What were you saying?" Therese asked, still dazed.

"I'm leaving."

"But—"

He didn't stop. He climbed the stairs two at a time, and in his room he opened a small chest and started throwing things into it.

"Rudy."

He ignored her.

"Rudy!"

He didn't look.

A hand took hold of his shoulder and he pushed it off.

"Leave me alone," he said.

"Don't leave."

He reached under his bed and pulled out the long wooden case that held his sword. When he stood back up, Therese was in front of him.

"Don't leave."

"I am leaving."

"When will you come back?"

"Never."

"Rudy!"

He heard her behind him going down the stairs, out the door, onto the street.

"Rudy!"

But he was running.

Everywhere Paris was enraged, and the rage was in him. The stones of the buildings and the pavement echoed with the tramp of boots and the ring of swords and the weight of horses, not in the reality of the moment, but in ancient truth. He didn't see them but he heard them, the echoes of not just the present but of all Paris' ages: two millennia of going out to war; of Roman legions and Frankish hordes and Vikings and crusaders' armored knights and troop after troop after troop of marching men; under Charlemagne and Caesar and Clovis of the Franks and Joan of Arc; and under Louis the Fourteenth the Sun King and Philip the Fair and Henry of Navarre; and Napoleon, the great Napoleon who reordered Europe from his Tuileries palace; and Rudolph heard them all, the trumpets and drums all echoing; and they rang in his ears, the echoes that had always been there for him and he finally opened himself to them.

Chapter Seven

THE PRACTICE
OF WAR

— 1 —

Hatred like straw and dry wood covered France, an old orchard of arid trees bearing acid fruit, multiplied by generations, tended by willing hands, and now at last receiving the thrust torches. The fire was immediate and furious and unstoppable.

Baron Harsanyi watched from the carriage as the streets, the heart of Paris, pulsed with the flames. Flags hung from windows: the eagle and tricolor of the emperor, and ominously the old tricolor of the republic, and even more ominously, the red flag of the radicals. The streets were full, which only happened in July if there was war or revolution.

All of Paris was rising before his eyes; for once, though, not against its own government but against the kaiser and everything Prussian. A crowd was gathered at the gate of the Austrian Embassy, France's most likely ally. Baron Ferdinand was taken through to the courtyard, and in.

"I've just come from the French Foreign Ministry," Prince von Metternich said to him without ceremony, before he had even crossed the room to the ambassador's desk.

Ferdinand reached the desk and waited.

"The fools," the ambassador said.

Ferdinand still waited.

"Foreign Minister Gramont is shocked that Austria is not joining France against Prussia. Shocked that Austria is not leaping into war the moment blundering France stumbles into this foolhardy declaration."

"There is no public alliance," Ferdinand said.

"No public alliance, no private alliance, no secret treaty, no assurance of any type. There has been only the strongest assurance to the contrary, that France must not depend on Austria in a war. That has been stated in public and private. Repeatedly! And Gramont—what does he say? He throws Archduke Albrecht's wild pronouncements at me, which I told him at the time were not official or even rational. And now he says France is betrayed at its moment of need. The fools."

Ferdinand waited, but the flood was over. Prince von Metternich was simply staring at him.

"Should Austria go to war?" the baron asked.

The ambassador sighed. "Perhaps."

"France and Austria together might finally stop von Bismarck."

"Yes, yes. Foreign Minister von Buest is wavering. And now I'll have to telegraph him to describe how forcefully France is demanding that we do."

"Yet if Austria begins to mobilize," Ferdinand said, "Prussia will take that as an act of aggression. Prussia might even attack Austria preemptively."

"So we must roll the dice. This might be the best opportunity to defeat Prussia, or our chance for another grand defeat of our own . . . Baron?"

"Yes, Your Excellency?"

"In light of these circumstances, you will understand the importance of the assignment I will now give you."

"Of course."

"At the invitation of the French Foreign Ministry, and the French High Command, you will accompany the French general staff to the front, immediately. You will be our official observer. The French wish you to see the strength of their arms and their overwhelming superiority in the field. Such as it is."

"Yes, sir. We had planned that I would observe at the front."

"Oh, yes. But this invitation will weight your observations much more heavily."

"Vienna wouldn't make a decision based on one observer's judgment," Ferdinand said.

"No, of course not. And whatever we say may make no difference to Vienna anyway. But I will forward your dispatches to the Austrian Foreign

Ministry, along with my own comments. It will inform their decisions heavily. And, Baron . . ." The prince drew close, and all his manners and mocking airs had vanished. "What I want to know from you . . . what I need to know from you, is whether they are winning, and whether they even can win. We have to know as early as possible."

"Yes, Your Excellency."

"You'll leave at once. A train will depart at ten o'clock tonight from the Gare de l'Est with the first elements of the general staff. You will be an honored guest. They will try very hard to impress you."

"I will make my own observations."

"That is critical. Whatever the French want you to say, I must have the truth."

"But when will you be back?" Therese asked. They were still in the hall; she had been standing there waiting when he got back.

"That depends on the war. Zoltan!"

"But, Father! Rudolph—"

"It may be several weeks. Perhaps I'll know soon."

"Yes, master?" Zoltan arrived from the back rooms.

"We are going to the Rhine front to observe the French campaign. Pack for two weeks. Our train leaves the Gare de l'Est at ten o'clock tonight."

"Yes, sir."

"Tonight?" Therese was shocked. "But, Father . . . what about Rudolph?"

"I need to speak to him."

"But he's gone. I've been trying to tell you."

"Then get him, quickly. I don't have time."

"No, Father, he's gone."

Ferdinand finally gave her his attention. "Where has he gone?"

"I don't know."

"What do you mean? When will he be back?"

"I don't know. He took his things and left. He said he wasn't coming back."

"What things did he take?"

"Some clothes and books. It wasn't much."

"Just that?"

"And his sword."

"His sword." Ferdinand paused, realizing. "Did he go join the French army?"

"I don't know. He wouldn't tell me."

"What did he say?"

"He just said he was leaving. That was all. He said he wouldn't come back! What will we do? We have to find him."

Ferdinand Harsanyi paused for a moment, realizing, then thinking, and then deciding. "You'll have Maria to look after you. Go to the embassy, and tell Princess Pauline that you're alone. And I'll write."

"Don't leave me, too, Father."

"I have to."

"Father! I'm afraid!"

He made himself be gentle, "It won't be for long." He gave her a few minutes, but he didn't have time for more. There was too much to do.

"A perfect example of anarchy," Pock said, seated on a bench in the train station. "The French can create chaos like no other nation." The Gare de l'Est was indeed in chaos. Soldiers and families, officers, tradesmen, sightseers, vagabonds, and a few regular travelers pushed and pulled alongside mountains of luggage and supplies. "It's incredible that the army would use the busiest station in Paris as their depot! The anarchy is more than perfect—it's superlative. Who could have planned this?"

"There is no plan," Ferdinand said.

"I begin to doubt either of us will travel tonight. General Bataille has aksed me to advise him on the use of his artillery. But I see no sign of his Forty-second Battalion. I only see anarchy." Pock looked at him closely. "I believe that your thoughts are in anarchy, as well. I see it in your eyes."

"My thoughts are very confused," Ferdinand admitted.

"Has something happened?"

"Rudolph has left."

Before their eyes, only meters away, a tower of four large, crazily stacked crates began to lean. The motion accelerated. The people beneath sensed the danger and pushed to get away, but the crowd was thick with most of them unaware.

A scream pierced the tumult as the highest crate fell on a man, landing on his leg. Other men tried to move the crate and finally did so, while the pinned man kept screaming. And then he was free, his leg bloodied and bent, and he was still screaming. Even so, the noise of the crowd slowly covered him.

"Isn't there a stretcher?" Pock said. "There must be someone to help."

"There are no stretchers," Ferdinand said. "None were ordered for the army."

The man had been lifted by some soldiers and was being carried out of the station.

"No stretchers?"

"And no ambulances, and all medical supplies are to be kept in the rear, away from the lines where they might be captured."

Zoltan was pushing through the crowds. "Master. The train is ready, outside the station. A long walk."

Then Pock remembered what they'd been saying. "Rudolph has left? Where?"

"I don't know. He left the house. He took his possessions with him."

"But he must have gone somewhere."

"I don't know where."

"Has he joined the army?"

"It's possible."

Pock was aghast. "You have to find him!"

"That isn't possible. I will be at the front for weeks."

"Therese? Does she know anything?"

"I had to say good-bye to her at the same time she was telling me about Rudolph."

"She'll look for him."

"Yes," Ferdinand said. "I know she will. I hope she finds him."

"What a way to begin the war."

"Another war," Ferdinand said as the train began moving, after midnight.

"I like this way," Zoltan answered, meaning the general staff's comfortable train.

"And when we arrive, we only watch. So we'll live through it."

"We lived through the others."

"But I wonder . . ." He looked out the window. "I wonder where Rudolph is." In the window, he only saw his own reflection. "Is he out there? I remember my first battle, when I was eighteen. It was the Turks."

"I know all your battles."

"Somehow, I thought I'd be with him the first time he'd be under fire."

"He'll learn, like you did."

"I hope I can talk with him about it afterward."

"He might be in Paris for the entire war."

"It will be on my mind, Zoltan."

"You have other things to do. It's not good to think about too many other things when there is a war."

– 2 –

Three days later, Baron Harsanyi sat in his hotel room in Metz, writing a morning dispatch.

The French mobilization continues to be pure disorder. Men are delivered to the station with no instructions on where their battalions are being constituted. Equipment arrives with no information as to which battalion it belongs to, so men take what they want whether it is meant for them or not. I have also not seen any material associated with field hospitals. The trains are irregular because the main lines are only single tracks, so trains must first all come east and be unloaded and wait, and then all the trains are returned to the west for reloading.

However, I estimate that already 70,000 men have arrived and are more or less armed and organized, and many more are arriving. Also, the armies being organized around Strasbourg are growing rapidly, and are already more than 50,000.

There is no information about the forces of Prussia or her allies. The high command does not yet have any reconnaissance of even the whereabouts of enemy forces, let alone their size or composition.

He set the report aside and took out another sheet of paper.

Therese,

I hope my other letters have reached you. The mails are the lowest priority and may take days to reach Paris from here. I have not received any from you yet, so I believe they must be delayed.

My days have become somewhat regular. They are mostly spent inspecting the forces that have gathered so far. What I have seen worries me greatly. These are said to be France's best soldiers. Some units are ready and disciplined, but many are not.

I have a guide who tries to keep my eyes away from the poorest examples and the worst disorder, but those things are difficult to hide. His name is Major Bourget.

He is very energetic and earnest, but I doubt he has ever seen a battle. At any moment he will knock on my door to begin today's travels.

His writing was interrupted by a knock on his door.

"It is I, Major Bourget."

"One moment."

The baron folded the official dispatch and inserted it in an envelope. From his desk drawer he took a stick of sealing wax, and using his candle he melted the wax and sealed it with a brass seal from his pocket. Then he stood to open the door.

Major Bourget was there, and not alone.

"Monsieur Sarroche," Ferdinand said. "This is a surprise."

Sarroche wasted no time with pleasantries.

"Monsieur le Baron. I have come on important business."

"Not to buy mercury," the baron said. "Not at this late hour."

"No." Sarroche was already bothered, apparently at this interruption to his duties. The mention of mercury caused him even greater anger. "It is too late for that and we will use the stocks we have, which will be sufficient. This is an entirely different matter."

"Then please come in."

Sarroche stepped inside the door but did not sit. Major Bourget, always smiling, did sit down.

"Monsieur Sarroche has come in his official capacity with the Bureau of Armaments," the major said. "We have been instructed to demonstrate to you our Mitrailleuse."

Nine men stood in an open field. Baron Harsanyi and Zoltan were accompanied by Major Bourget and Sarroche. Four more were the crew of a mechanical beast of some species related to a small cannon but with two particular differences. The first was the muzzle. Instead of a round hole, the end of the cannon was covered by a plate with twenty-five small holes in a square. The other difference was the breech, which did not open for the loading of a single shell, but had a slot for the insertion of a large block loaded with twenty-five bullets, and a long-handled crank beside it.

"They are thirteen millimeter," Bourget described. "Far greater in power and range than infantry rifle bullets. Monsieur Sarroche?"

"The Mitrailleuse has not been demonstrated to officers outside the French army," Sarroche huffed. "It is deemed an important secret of the French government."

"However," Bourget said, still smiling, "we have been instructed to demonstrate it to the baron."

"Whom I do not trust."

"But we are instructed."

Sarroche gave up. "The bullets leave the chamber at five hundred meters per second, more than three times the velocity of the Chassepot rifle, which itself has a far higher velocity than Prussian rifles. Each bullet contains fifty grams of black powder. The entire block of twenty-five bullets can be fired in five seconds. A new block can be inserted within ten seconds. This guarantees one hundred bullets each minute. It is a machine of guns."

"What is the range?" Baron Harsanyi asked.

"From one to two thousand meters. The weight of the barrel and housing ensure that no recoil is encountered and therefore no re-sighting is required." Sarroche lifted his hand to shield his eyes from the sun, looking out into the field. "Now, a demonstration."

The ninth man was a mannequin 500 meters away, standing at the far end of the field. The crew of four took their places.

"Begin," Major Bourget said.

The crew sprang to action. The first block was pressed into the gun's breech while the officer sighted the barrel. He nodded, and the loader placed his hand on the crank and turned, one long revolution.

The sound was horrific; loud but more terrible from its deep, snarling rasp that carried and echoed over the field. Even before the crank was complete, while the beast was still growling, the mannequin shook and trembled, but they could see little more at such a great distance.

"It is not a perfect aim," the officer said and bent over the sight, making an adjustment as the spent block was retrieved and a new block inserted. Again the officer nodded and the crank turned.

This time the aim was perfect. The mannequin splintered and then disintegrated.

The baron put a field glass to his eye. All that was visible was the mannequin's lower legs, still upright as stumps in the grass of the field. There were no other parts large enough to be visible.

"Enough," Sarroche said, before a third ammunition block was inserted.

"It is very impressive," the baron said. "I will inform the Austrian Embassy of its effectiveness." Zoltan, beside him the whole time, shrugged.

"You were not impressed," Ferdinand said as they walked back to the carriages.

"What does it do? Less than a cannon, and it is just as slow to load."

"But a machine of guns. It tears a man to pieces."

"One man. How dead can one man be?"

"What would you do with it?"

"Put it on a pivot," Zoltan said. "So it will turn."

"The machine seemed easy enough to turn when they corrected its aim."

"Turn it while it is firing. Like the hose on a fire truck."

"It would be like one man firing twenty-five rifles," Ferdinand said. "Then it would be terrible."

"Monsieur Sarroche." The carriage bumped and swayed on the rough road back to Metz. The baron was in the rear of the two seats, while Zoltan and the major were in front.

"Yes, monsieur?"

"Now that the war has begun, do you have enough shells for your artillery?"

"Surely you are not again trying to sell your mercury."

The baron shook his head. "No. I want to know if France will run short of critical supplies. The Austrian Embassy has requested this information."

"The Austrian Embassy may report to Vienna that the French supply of artillery shells is entirely adequate."

"You seemed less sure when you were trying to buy my mercury."

"I was energetically ensuring we had every advantage possible."

The baron nodded. "Very energetically." He paused. "How energetically, Monsieur Sarroche?"

"The embassy has also requested that information?" Sarroche replied.

"You had conversations with my son."

"That is not your concern."

"My own son is not my concern?" Ferdinand barely held back his anger. "You've threatened me, and made accusations, and intruded into my family."

Sarroche shrugged. "What can you do to me? It is simply the consequence of your own duplicity. I have only one concern and one interest, and that is France."

"And if a man's life stands against the position of France, do you have any concern for his death?"

"That is an ironic question for you to ask," Sarroche said.

"In what way?"

"In weeks or days, tens of thousands of men will die who oppose France. One or two lives more would be insignificant."

— 3 —

"Pock!" Baron Ferdinand said. "You're returning to Paris, as well?"

The Metz train station, as it had been since the baron's arrival, was loud and full and very confused.

"Yes, and for good."

"But there's not even been a battle yet."

"Oh yes, there has been. A seven-day battle between General Bataille and myself on his use of artillery, and I am in full retreat."

"He didn't appreciate your advice?"

"He didn't," Pock said. "Not at all. And why should a French general listen to an Austrian anyway? We lost our war. So now the French will lose theirs. And what have you been doing for the past week?"

"Inspecting and observing."

"I hope you've been more encouraged than I have?"

Ferdinand shrugged. "There is good and bad, but much more bad. If they can hold to their original strategy of defense, they might do well. They have very strong positions at Forbach and Wissembourg. But they'll be incapable of an open field battle."

"And are you also being dismissed?"

"No. This will be a brief visit to Paris and then a return to Metz."

"To see your daughter?"

"I hope to. But I am being sent back to watch the grand spectacle. The Emperor Napoleon himself will march victoriously through the streets of Paris to take his place at its head."

"He'll march all the way to the army?"

"No," Ferdinand said. "He'll take his carriage from Saint-Cloud to

Neuilly, march down the Champs-Elysees to the Place de la Concorde, and then return to his carriage to be driven to the train station."

"Somewhat less than inspiring."

"Somewhat."

"Does Therese know you're coming?"

"I've written to her, but there have been no replies, and the telegraph is for military use only."

"So Rudolph might be home and you wouldn't know it."

"I'm hoping he will be."

"You'll go straight to your house?"

"There won't be time. I will be taken from the station directly to the reviewing stands." He looked out again at the confusion. "Napoleon and Paris must come first."

Few men or women were old enough to remember the great Napoleon marching to war at the head of his armies. But Paris remembered, in its collective mind, the echoing of thousands of hooves on cobblestones, of soldiers, veterans of many triumphs, shouting, and of the people's passion answering and breathing the glory of France that was the very air of those years.

The echoes. Paris was the city Napoleon had ridden from and returned to, and the echoes still rang, immutable whispers, part of the essence of the city.

Louis Napoleon, the nephew of the great Napoleon and in his shadow, now led his army to war. He was ten years older than his uncle had been when he died, and he was not in much better health.

A second horse was beside his and on it was the hope of France's future, his son, fourteen years old and small for his age.

Behind them were ranks of cavalry and men. But times had changed; the horses would be loaded on trains, as real warhorses were now made of iron. The parade was only for show, but it was indeed a spectacle, and Ferdinand, seated behind the Ambassador of Austria in the row of military attachés, at least appreciated it for that.

"Welcome back to Paris," Prince von Metternich shouted as drums and bugles blared and blasted by.

"It's quieter at the front," Ferdinand shouted back.

"Not for long. Now you're getting the emperor and all his noise."

"Have you been receiving my reports?"

"Yes." It was nearly impossible to talk. "You'll come to the embassy to discuss them?"

"As soon as I'm able."

The echoes from the boots and hooves and wheels had hardly died before Ferdinand and Zoltan were hurrying through the city, across the river toward the Rue Duroc.

The street was as always, and the house, also. He was up the steps with his hand on the door, but it didn't yield; it was locked against an uncertain city. He knocked loudly.

It was a few moments before it opened. Maria fell back into the hall.

"Master! You've come! I knew you would."

"Where is Therese?"

"Therese is in her bed."

He started up the stairs, then stopped.

"In her bed?"

"Yes, master. But she's doing well. Better than the last few days."

"What do you mean?" He nearly grabbed Maria's collar to shake her, but stopped himself.

"Well . . . she's ill, master. Didn't you get the letters?"

"I've received no letters."

"Oh! Oh, master! She's ill. She's been in bed for most of the week."

"No!" He flew up the stairs and threw the door open.

The room was dim with the windows curtained and only a single white candle burning. He was quickly beside the bed, above the pale face and feeling the quick, shallow breaths. He put his hand on her forehead; there was a slight fever.

"The doctor says it's cholera," Maria said from the door. "But she's through the worst of it."

And even then, Therese's eyes opened.

"Father."

"Yes, dear. Yes, I'm here."

"You came."

"Just rest. Maria said you are getting better."

"She's been wonderful, Father. She's been here every minute."

"Yes, she is wonderful. And Rudolph?"

Her eyes had closed, but they opened again.

"I don't know," she said. "We haven't seen him at all."

"No word?"

"Nothing."

"Rest, then."

"Yes, Father. Are you back to stay?"

"No. I'll leave again in the morning."

In the hall, he asked, "Where is the doctor?"

"He's gone. He looked at her before he left for the front."

"Are there any doctors left in Paris?"

"No. But, master, I know how to take care of her. There's nothing a doctor could do."

"I know. Take very good care of her. Don't let anyone else in to see her."

"Yes, master."

"Not anyone."

"Baron," said Prince Richard. At the parade, he had seemed in somewhat good spirits. Now, in his office, his spirits were much darker, as if the whole war were being fought to personally annoy him. "What is happening?"

"Nothing so far, Your Excellency."

"How many thousands of men, and still nothing?"

The large map of the Rhine frontier was open on the same side table where it had resided for months. Ferdinand pointed to the towns and camps. "Fourth Corps under Ladmirault, Second Corps under Frossard, and Third Corps under the emperor are stretched from Metz to Forbach. The First Corps under MacMahon is in Strasbourg. The Fifth Corps under Failly is near Froeschwiller to support either side of the Vosges Mountains. The Seventh Corps under Douay is in the south, at Belfort, near the Swiss border. The Imperial Guard under Bourbaki is in Metz, where the emperor will meet them this evening. And General Canrobert is forming the Sixth Corps in Chalons as the strategic reserve."

"That looks proper to me. What do you make of the dispositions?"

"MacMahon is isolated by the Vosges. He's been ordered to the north, toward Wissembourg, but Fifth Corps isn't enough support. Otherwise, the forces are in a strong defensive position."

"But are they going to invade? Isn't that what the emperor told us?"

"They are very poorly placed for an invasion into Prussia."

"Then what are they doing?" the ambassador asked angrily. Then he relented. "I know it is not your responsibility to decipher the minds of French generals. But Vienna needs to know. How long will the war last?"

"I hope not long."

"That would be to the advantage of France?"

"It would be to minimize the number of men killed," Ferdinand said.

"But that's what wars are for," the ambassador said gloomily. "To kill as many men as possible. As many of the enemy, and of your own troublemakers. What would happen if the French did invade?"

"They'd outrun their supplies within thirty kilometers."

"And if Prussia invades France?"

"They'd reach French strongholds within five kilometers."

"I hate war." The annoyance had returned. "There are no answers. At least I know your reports are truthful, and very little else is. If I showed them to the French Foreign Ministry, they'd have you banned from the front in an instant."

Ferdinand said, slowly, "I would rather be home."

Von Metternich looked at him. "Stay at the front until something happens." He stared at the map. "I'm sending Pauline away."

"Out of Paris?"

"To Calais at least. Most likely to England."

"Then you don't have confidence in the French, either."

"I'm just being careful." He looked back at Ferdinand. "You might consider your own children. Therese could accompany Pauline."

"I'll consider it."

"And your son? What are your plans for him if the war goes poorly?"

"I have no plans."

"He could travel with them, as well. Pauline would be more than happy for their company."

– 4 –

On the last day of July, settled back in Metz at the front, Ferdinand Harsanyi was collected by Major Bourget.

"Monsieur Baron, I invite you and your servant to accompany the Imperial staff to the front. Orders were given this morning for a general advance into Prussian territory, to take place tomorrow."

"Have you located the Prussian armies?"

Bourget dismissed the question. "It is impossible that they could be near. It is less than two weeks since the war began, and the Germans will not be mobilized."

"How can you know for sure?"

"The reports in the newspapers for the whole past year are all in agreement that it will take a month at least. Besides, the emperor himself will participate in the action."

The charming village of Forbach, two kilometers from the border, had fewer, and far more primitive, accommodations than the city of Metz. Much of what was available was reserved for the emperor and his personal staff and General Frossard, who was commanding the armies under the emperor's direction. Mere Austrian observers, despite the honor of their position, were only able to be provided with tents. They were not even in the Forbach itself, but in the neighboring village of Spicheren.

But Ferdinand preferred the location. It was barely a kilometer from the border, at least as shown on the maps. But it was a magnificent kilometer, almost as much vertical as horizontal. The village was on a commanding height, and the French were strongly dug in.

Zoltan approved of the tent, as well. "Tonight I will sleep," Zoltan said.

In the cot beside him, Baron Ferdinand answered, "On the edge of battle, I prefer a tent. Even if it isn't our battle."

At noon the following day, the baron wrote a dispatch to the embassy in Paris.

The advance began this morning when the soldiers felt themselves ready, which occurred at about ten o'clock. The reports are that there was slight resistance by one platoon of Prussian infantry and that the French troops covered themselves with glory at their overcoming of this enemy. This afternoon the emperor and his staff will ride forward to observe the French occupation of the Prussian city of Saarbrucken, which is two kilometers beyond the frontier.

In the afternoon, the staff moved forward from Forbach, through Spicheren, across the frontier and Saarbrucken.

But there were difficulties. The road was cluttered with packs, blankets, mess kits, and all the other equipment the soldiers would have been carrying.

"It is abandoned by the enemy?" Major Bourget said, or asked.

"Abandoned, but it's all French," Zoltan said.

"It's very heavy to carry," Ferdinand said, "and it's a warm day. They must mean to pick it up on the way back."

"This is proper?" Bourget said hopefully.

"No."

The emperor stopped in the town square of Saarbrucken. Foreign observers and newspaper reporters surrounded him. His son, the Prince Imperial, played on the ground in front of him with a few bullets he'd picked up from the road.

"See how easy it will be?" Major Bourget encouraged again. "And this shows unquestionably that the Prussian mobilization is still far from complete. Now, Monsieur Baron, we will return to Forbach for the night."

By the following day, the rest of the French had withdrawn back over the border, as well. No explanation was given.

The French command had no plans for exploiting their success, Baron Ferdinand wrote. *They had also realized that all their supplies were still back in their camp. Additionally, they may have gained some information concerning the approach of enemy forces. Therefore they prefer to claim their victory and then extricate themselves safely.*

At noon, one day later, Ferdinand was in his official chair in General Frossard's briefing room. The staff and highest officers were debating plans, as they had at all the other noon meetings that Ferdinand had attended. The emperor was slumped in a chair in the corner of the room, ignoring, and ignored by, the arguing generals.

"General MacMahon has been attacked!" A newly arrived messenger had been unable to gain anyone's attention and had finally just shouted out his message.

"Where?"

"Wissembourg."

"Impossible!"

The arguments resumed until additional details arrived. Even then, it was deemed that it couldn't be a serious battle.

"Is anyone going to go support him?" the baron asked Major Bourget.

"I will determine the answer." And in a moment, he had. "No. It would not be possible to cross the Vosges. He will be able to withstand any German forces. The Prussians will not have been able to pull any kind of army together yet."

Late in the evening, the report came that MacMahon had been heavily defeated, and First Corps had been pushed back fifteen kilometers, and orders were sent to Fifth Corp to move forward to assist. But later reports said that it was only a small portion of First Corps that had actually been involved in the battle.

"It was a strategic movement. It is hardly to be considered a defeat."

Orders were issued to spend the next day building even stronger defenses into the hillsides below Spicheren and Forbach.

Back in the tent that night, Ferdinand told Zoltan, "Two thousand casualties out of eight thousand men. MacMahon was already abandoning the town before the Prussians attacked. He knew he was too exposed and too far from any help. At least he saved two-thirds of his army." He was quiet for a few minutes. They weren't far from the French camps, and he could hear digging, and horses, and singing. "I watch for Rudolph."

"You will not see him. There are too many camps and too many armies."

"It's possible that I would see him." He sighed, wistfully, then smiled. "God might find him for me. It isn't impossible."

"There are many things God might do," Zoltan said. "He does none."

"Someday He might. And I will keep watching for Rudolph."

– 5 –

As the victory at Saarbrucken, in hindsight, became greater and greater, and the defeat at Wissembourg became lesser and lesser, the mood of the French staff grew bright and brighter; not any less for also successfully extricating themselves from both their victory and their defeat. The morning after their withdrawal, the headquarters buzzed with activity. The discussion was not about the individual battles but the still-undecided grand strategy.

The mobilization was nearly complete: French armies were gathered and ready. The generals continued to consider what to do with them.

Baron Harsanyi continued to be an honored observer of their deliberations.

General Frossard sat at a long table in the town hall in Forbach, slumped far to his side and leaning on his arm. The question was raised of where the enemy might be, but this was still dismissed; there had been no sign of his troops in Saarbrucken.

While discussing the location of the enemy, Ferdinand watched the generals completely ignore the battle of the day before. They decided it was impossible that the Prussians could have gathered conscripts from their villages and towns into an army in such a short time. Surely, every initiative still lay with the French.

It was the same discussion he had heard the day before, and the days before that. Lunch was served and the debate ended. But then lunch was interrupted.

"General Frossard?" A major was at the door. "We have been attacked."

"Where?"

"At Spicheren. General Laveaucoupet is asking for support."

Frossard smiled. "That is perfect. It could not be better. There is no more impregnable position in our line. I will come immediately." Everyone else in the room followed.

"What strength is the enemy?" General Frossard was standing on the edge of the plateau, looking down on the valley. There was little to see except a thin haze of smoke in the trees below them.

"It is possibly two divisions." General Laveaucoupet was commander of a single regiment. He was showing the strain of trying to hold back a much larger force.

"And their method of attack?"

"At first, they approached straight on, against our strongest points. They were easily repulsed."

"And then?"

"Sir, I have ordered two counterattacks."

"With what result?"

"The Prussian artillery fire was too strong. We retired to our positions. And now there has been no substantial action for the last hour."

Frossard turned to his aide. "Bring up the entire corps. Reinforce the line." Then he addressed the entire assembly. "We will see what the Prussian conscripts and peasants make of our little hillside." He laughed. "And of our French soldiers! It will be an entertainment for us all!"

Ferdinand abandoned the command post to make his own judgments of the lines and the troops; Zoltan was with him, along with a very alarmed Major Bourget.

"Is this wise?" the French officer asked. "I think it would be advisable to return to General Frossard's position."

"We will soon," Ferdinand said.

"Perhaps I will immediately. I will inform them that you—"

"No, stay with me. I don't want French soldiers to start shooting at me."

The three of them moved quickly through the lines. The hillside was very steep, in some places so much that it was difficult to move across it. It was lightly wooded with a few large trees, and more small trees and scrub growth, and about half was open grass. The French emplacements were well engineered, deep with high earthen walls and good fields of fire.

Soon they came to the sections of the line that had been involved in the morning action. There were craters from artillery fire, some still smoldering, and damage to the trees, but not so much to the defensive positions. Even the morale seemed good; the men were talking and joking with one another.

And while he studied the lines, Ferdinand studied the men, especially any who appeared young and had black curling hair.

When they finally acquiesced to Major Bourget's panic and returned to General Frossard's forward observation post, they encountered a new battle.

"We must attack!" General Laveaucoupet and several others of the regimental and divisional generals were pushing the corps commander. But General Frossard was holding firm, and with him his entire army.

"We will not attack. We have the strongest position. There is no need!"

"But the entire corps is now on the line! Twenty-five thousand men! We can crush the Prussians."

Frossard began to waver. He was beginning to be persuaded when the deliberations were doubly interrupted.

The first interruption was by the Prussians. Very close at hand, at the far left end of the French line, a sudden thunder of artillery broke the afternoon quiet. And above the low, heavy detonations was the higher staccato of rifle fire.

Even as they froze in shock, the ground under them shook from a shell landing less than fifty meters away.

"Return fire!" Laveaucoupet bellowed, running toward the attack. "Turn the guns! To the left!" All of the lines that had such command of the valley were less suited to defend against an attack from the sides.

"They've been flanked!" Ferdinand said to Bourget. "All the talking and arguing, and the Prussians marched around your side."

And at that moment, the second interruption occurred. A messenger on horseback galloped right into the command post. The man jumped from his saddle directly in front of General Frossard.

"Sir. From MacMahon."

"Yes? What is it?"

"The First Corps has been attacked."

"Yes, yes, we know. Two days ago at Wissembourg."

"No, sir, this morning. Froeschwiller. He begs you to send reinforcements."

"He has Failly and the Fifth Corps!"

"Both Corps are in danger of being overrun. He begs for reinforcements."

"It is impossible. Do you not see that we ourselves are in contact with the enemy? And Froeschwiller is fifty kilometers from here."

"But, sir—"

"And French generals do not beg."

While Frossard was speaking, the generals under him were acting. Already the French artillery was answering the Prussian guns. Ferdinand watched as at least two regiments were running to the left, shifting from their forward-facing emplacements to the new battle line.

The smoke was thickening in the valley, but he could see enemy movements. A long front of gray-coated Prussians was advancing to the base of the hill, and on the left flank, the hillside was much shallower.

But the French were laying a murderous fire on them and the advance quickly stalled.

Then, over all the other roaring, he heard the grinding, tearing sound of the Mitrailleuse. Just down the slope from him, one hundred or more meters away, a company of many machines had settled and were firing at a horrible pace, loading and firing twice and three times a minute. It was impossible to see their targets; perhaps they couldn't see them, either.

Then there was a new sound, of men screaming. The Prussian artillery was too accurate. Even the well-built fortifications were crumbling under the cannonade, even more now that they were enfiladed from the side. The same paths on which men had been running to the left to face the enemy were at the moment in use carrying the wounded and dying to the rear.

All the ones who were carried close enough received a moment of Ferdinand's attention. But they were only dozens out of thousands.

Despite their losses, the French were pressing forward. They still had the high ground and their own artillery, and they must have been inflicting as many casualties as they were suffering. But then their center and right, weakened to reinforce the left, were suddenly attacked.

The whole line, at least five kilometers long, gave over to individual combat as men, in fives and twos and ones, became no longer part of a large battle, but were in their own personal battles, with rifles in split-second and at point-blank life-and-death moments, and with bayonets, and knives, and bare hands.

"It's time to leave," Zoltan said. "Too dangerous."

Ferdinand nodded and turned his back on the battle. "Who'll win?"

"It could still be either."

Chapter Eight

CRY HAVOC, PANDORA!

– 1 –

Delight had filled Paris like the August sunlight filling the air. Each day had been warmer, and the sun higher, and Paris more heated. France had invaded Prussia in magnificent headlines and glowing adjectives.

But the joy of Saarbrucken was ephemeral thunder, shaking the earth, then gone. Paris wanted more: more victory, more action, at least more news. The froth of jubilation evaporated in the early August warmth. Suddenly, from the front, every word was smoke, solid at a distance but indefinite close, and insubstantial when touched.

The day before, all the news had been about the French advance, but now there was nothing.

Therese wanted something. A week in bed had starved her of more than food; now she had an intense hunger for light, for conversation, and even more, for news. A war involving Auguste was taking place and she knew nothing.

Maria knew less. "There's nothing good in the market, and it costs everything. That's enough trouble for me."

"It isn't enough trouble for me," Therese said. "So I'll go out and find some."

"There's no one to go with you!"

"I'll go alone."

A newspaper stand was close-by in the Place de Breteuil. She read and read, but the more words there were, the less was said.

"Isn't there any more news this morning?" she asked. "What's happened yesterday?"

"Go to the Bourse," the man behind the newspapers told her.

"The stock market?"

"The official government dispatches are announced to the public there."

"Why at the Bourse?"

"So the stock traders can hear it all first. The stock exchange always knows before anyone else. That's where to go for anything official."

"When do they make announcements?"

"Whenever they come. You just have to wait."

The Paris streets were filled with unofficial news, all as vaporous as anything official. Victory and defeat had both already occurred, both overwhelming. A brother in the army, a son, a husband, had gotten word to his home, and to all Paris; and as fog spreads, the news did, as well, with the same bewildering result. The August sun couldn't burn off this fog. Instead, it heated it and baked it.

Therese struck north toward the city center, toward the thickest of the rumorous fog. She passed the Assemblee Nationale, which was silent, and crossed the Seine to the Place de la Concorde, which was very full. She crossed the Concorde to the Rue Royale.

The spire of the Madeleine was ahead. Here, in the heart of bourgeois, wealthy Paris, she stopped for a pastry at a café.

"Is there any news?" she asked, and everyone at the other tables answered. But it was all useless!

"A battle two days ago, on the Rhine. Fought to a draw."

"No, the Prussians were pushed back!"

"Then why is there nothing in the newspapers? It must be bad news if they haven't announced it."

"Because there is no news! If there were any battle, we'd know."

"Has anything been announced at the Bourse?" Therese asked.

"Not today, not yet."

Therese left the café and turned on the Boulevard de la Madeleine, passing the construction pile that was meant one day to be the Palais Garnier Opera.

The Palais de la Bourse was only a few more blocks, and she could already see a large crowd gathered. She came to the edge of it. It held as many women as men; the men wanted news of the war, and the women wanted news of their men, and they had been hours waiting for it. She pushed through the swarms, all the way to the front steps, and the people made way for her in her upper-class dress.

As she moved farther into the crowd, she saw that it was immense, densely filling the square between the building's wings and stretching down the streets in every direction.

A platform had been built at the front door for the government messengers to make their announcements. The crowd was impenetrably close to it.

The walls of the Bourse were fronted with large columns all around the building, and Therese found a spot behind one.

A thin, old man in a black suit came out of the building and stood beside her to watch. "Do you know if there will be any announcements soon?" she asked.

"There might be," he said in a high, staccato voice. "There just might! There's a rumor inside there might be something coming."

A few other black suits had edged out of the door. The crowd noticed and slowly began pushing in against the already solid center around the platform.

"From the front?"

"Had better be! Terrible morning. The market's terrible. A sullen temper to it! Everything's down."

The same sullen temper inhabited the crowd on the street, and even more as they saw the black suits filling the spaces between the columns. The brokers and bankers and speculators of the Bourse were unpopular, and the government's preference for them in announcing its news at their den added to the bitter air.

But then their attention was diverted. An official had appeared! He made his way to the platform. He climbed the steps.

"A dispatch has arrived! The horse has already passed the east gate at Vincennes!"

The effect was vast and instant. All sound stopped for a moment, and then it doubled. The minutes passed, and everyone's imagination was following the messenger through the streets toward them.

The silence struck again, harder. The courier, on a sweating, exhausted horse, was pushing through. In the sudden immeasurable quiet, the courier dismounted and walked solemnly the last few meters to the platform. He handed the dispatch to the official. And as he turned back to his horse, those who were close saw, for one instant, a jubilant smile quickly suppressed.

The official opened the dispatch, read it quickly to himself, and proclaimed, "There has been a great battle. A great French victory! Twenty-five thousand Prussians have been captured. And forty guns." His voice rose. "Even the Crown Prince of Prussia is captured!"

There was surely more. It was not to be heard at that moment, though. The crowd seemed ten times as great as it had just been. Its great roar was the exultation of all Paris, and all Paris knew in moments what had happened. Therese Harsanyi stepped back as the crowd grew and filled the streets, waving flags, singing in deafening chorus, reaching the heavens with their celebration.

The man beside Therese had disappeared. All the traders and bankers had run back to the exchange floor, jostling each other in their eagerness as the market shot upward.

The prime minister's residence was in the Place Vendome, and the crowd began to surge toward it. A victory of this magnitude would demand a speech, which would be the capstone to the jubilation. Therese was part of the crowd and moved with it the several blocks to the Place.

But after twenty minutes, the balcony of the prime minister's residence was empty, and stubbornly it stayed so. The crowds waited.

And then, like a dull, featureless sunset, darkness began to overshadow the people, spreading from side to side of the Place.

"A fake."

The story suddenly was wildfire. The official, the courier, both were swindlers. They had driven the stock market up for a profit, to sell their shares at the highest price.

Now the crowds shouted for the prime minister, demanding him to tell them something about this war that they had been led into and now was being hidden from them. And finally the balcony door opened and he appeared, tiny above the great crowds. The people screamed their hatred, and he quickly disappeared without speaking a word.

Therese had followed the crowd willingly, but now she was done with them and wanted to leave. The press was too great, though. The square was still filling, and she was in the center where the density and force were greatest.

Then, from the direction of the Palais Royale, they heard drums. A shiver ran through the crowd. The sound of marching boots came next— Guard troops arriving to clear the Place and rescue the prime minister. The crowd was so thick that many individuals couldn't move, and Therese was pushed harder by the crowd's motion.

The motion turned to panic. The government troops were at the south entrance of the square.

A gun was fired over the heads of the masses. Those near the north entrance could leave, but most only forced themselves harder against the dead walls. Another gun fired, and the bullet chipped the Vendome Column high above them and ricocheted into the crowd.

Therese tried to kneel, but there was no room, and the chance of suffocation was too great.

Some of the crowd seemed to be pushing back toward the troops to threaten them. At least the troops did seem to feel threatened and lowered their rifles toward the crowd.

Therese wasn't strong enough to push against the men pushing her. She was about ten meters from the front rows facing the soldiers, close enough to see what was going to happen.

Then there was an even more violent motion close-by. The man beside her was shoved roughly aside by someone strong enough to move him. A hand closed around her wrist and pulled.

"Come on, Raisy. Now!"

A crash of rifle fire overwhelmed all the other sound in the square.

Before she could answer, her arm was pulled, hard, and she was snatched out of the pocket that had held her. Then she was moving. The grip on her wrist was tight, but she managed to bend her hand to grasp the hand that was holding hers, and hold as tightly as she could.

It seemed forever, with the people running and pushing, and more rifle thunder, but then they were out of the square and in the streets, which were crowded but moving.

They stopped near the Madeleine, and finally Therese could breathe.

"Rudy," she said with her first breath.

"What were you doing in there?" he asked.

"Where have you been?"

"With a friend."

She held her questions while he took her the length of the Tuileries gardens, empty except for Guards troops, around the Place de la Concorde, and finally to the Seine at the Pont des Invalides. But here, on the edge of their own neighborhood and less than a kilometer from the Rue Duroc, Rudolph was going no farther.

"You're safe now," he said.

"You are, too. Come home!"

"I've left home," he said.

She stared at him, trying to see what was different. His hair was longer, the curls over his ears now. His jaw was a few days unshaven. It was his eyes, though, that hardly seemed to be her brother's. "Then I'll come with you."

"No."

"Father's gone."

Rudolph shook his head. "It doesn't matter."

"Yes, it does. I'm alone."

"I am, too."

Therese paused enough to see him and his dark stare. "What's happened to you, Rudy?"

"Nothing." Then, "Everything. I don't know."

"Where are you living?"

"With a friend."

"Everyone from your class has gone to the army."

"It's Gravert."

"Where does he live?"

"I won't tell you."

"You have to. I won't let you go until you tell me."

He looked at her, a little curious. "How can you keep me from going?"

"I'll scream."

He shrugged. "Go ahead." Arguing with her, he seemed more normal.

"I can't scream right here in the middle of the street!" She looked at him closely. "And you look thin."

"They're poor. They don't have much food."

"We have food! At least come get some to take back."

"No. I don't even want to see the house." He was so stubborn. "Who's taking care of the horses?"

"I am. Tell me where you live," she insisted.

"It's a ghetto."

"A ghetto?"

"It's where the uprising's going to start. All the ghettos, all over Paris."

"What uprising?"

"When France loses the war."

"How do you know they're going to lose?"

"They already lost one battle at Wissembourg, two days ago. And there are two more happening right now, at Spicheren and Froeschwiller. All around Metz. They're not going well."

"How do you know?"

"We have a man in the government. We get the real news."

"A man . . . we? What do you mean, *we*?"

But Rudolph had a different question. "Where is Father?"

"At the front. He's there to report back to the embassy."

"And you look thin, too."

"I was ill. I—"

"Ill?" Rudolph grew more intense. "Did Father know? Was he with you when you were ill? When you were sleeping?"

"It was cholera. I'm better now. Today's the first day I'm out. And he came back for one day, last week, and we talked."

"I don't want him alone with you."

"What? Rudy, what do you mean?"

"Nothing. Do you have money?"

"Forty francs. Do you need some?"

"Give it to me."

"Here. Rudy . . . would Auguste be in the battles?"

"I don't know. It's likely."

"Where is he? Can you find out what's happened with him?"

"Why should I?"

"Because I want to know."

"I can't. He can take care of himself." The mention of Auguste had turned Rudolph back to the hard man he had been before. "Go across the bridge. I won't leave until you do. And don't tell Father anything about me. Don't tell him you've seen me."

"I have to tell him."

"Promise me that you won't."

"Why?"

"I don't want him to find me."

"But why?"

"Just promise!"

"All right. I promise."

That was all. She crossed the bridge, and from the other side of the river, she watched him until he waved once, and then the city took him from her.

– 2 –

Therese was home, which seemed very safe and not at all confining after he morning outing. She was at the writing desk in the front parlor, with pen and paper and ink.

My dearest Auguste, she wrote. *All Paris is desperate for news of the armies, but no one is more desperate than I for news of you. I know you are bravely leading your men and I am sure that no harm could possibly come to you, but still my heart trembles at every mention of battle.*

I saw Rudolph this morning, but he has refused to return home. Father is still at the front, perhaps very close to you. But I am far from everyone. I am so alone! I need someone to be with me. I feel so very unprotected and vulnerable. How I wish someone were here with me.

Her pen came to a stop, and her eyes drifted up toward the painting on the wall, of a beautiful and intriguing woman sitting in a café.

The next morning, she sat for a long time staring at the picture.

"It's just like you," Maria said, dusting the mantel.

"I don't know. She seems better than I think I must be."

"No! You're even more beautiful than that painting."

"She seems to know something that I don't. I'm going out for a ride, Maria."

There was no Zoltan or Rudolph or even her father to hitch the horse to the carriage. Therese was satisfied to do it herself, and she was on friendly terms with the horses from tending them while Zoltan and Rudolph were gone.

"Mademoiselle!" Pierre Beaubien was taken aback. "What an honor! How have I deserved this?" He was actually in his yard, cutting back summer flowers.

"I just wanted to get out," she said. "The views are so nice from up here."

"Incomparable. But are you alone?"

"I came out today alone."

"And the captain? I know that he is at the front."

"Yes, he left weeks ago."

"And your father? And brother?"

She answered, "They're very busy."

"They must be. I was greatly impressed by them. May I presume, mademoiselle . . ."

"What, Pierre?"

"To call on you? At your home?"

"Oh . . . no, I don't think so."

"I could call on your father? I feel that our brief meeting was sufficient to consider him an acquaintance."

"No, Pierre. You shouldn't. I was just out for a ride and I wanted to say hello."

"Tell me at least where you live."

"I don't think Father would want me to."

A messenger had come while she was gone with an invitation for Therese to come out of the city for the afternoon; but it wasn't from a painter, a cavalry officer, a baron, or a cadet-revolutionary. It was from a princess.

Therese, dear, come and lift my spirits and say good-bye. Pauline.

A groom at the embassy door took her carriage away as a maid took Therese away into the princess's private apartments. Therese had come to know the rooms so well.

"Madame will come soon," the maid said, then left Therese in the usual small sitting room.

All the day's newspapers were scattered across the tables and chairs. Therese read the accounts and descriptions of battles.

Just as Rudolph had said, there had been three battles in three days, all in small villages close-by the German border: Wissembourg, Froeschwiller, and Spicheren. They seemed insignificant names for such heavy things as battles.

The newspapers called them victories and painted wild pictures of valor and glory. She read every description of cavalry actions and tried to recognize any detail about General Ladmirault or General Legrand or the Fourth Corps. But the more she read, the more the reports seemed to contradict each other.

It even seemed uncertain which army had the field after the battle. A single sentence near the end of one account simply said, *"The emperor and General Frossard have now moved to consolidate the army in the fortress city of Metz, which will be impossible for the enemy to take."*

Frossard. Ladmirault and Legrand were both under Frossard.

"It's all so frightening, isn't it?" The princess stood watching Therese look at the papers.

"I don't know if knowing or not knowing is worse."

"I don't want to know!" the princess said. "I don't want to know anything about this war!"

Therese was noticing the princess's plain dress. "Your note said to come and say good-bye."

"I'm leaving Paris. Richard is sending me to Calais, and he says to be ready to leave for England at any moment."

"But why?"

The princess seemed near collapse. "Oh, Therese. I don't want to know anything, but Richard knows everything. He doesn't tell me, but they must be losing the war. That's why he wants me to leave Paris."

"But there's no war here."

"Madame?" The maid was at the door.

"Yes, Annette?"

"There are two ladies here. From the empress."

"From the empress?"

"They said they have to see you at once."

"Then bring them, Annette! Quickly!"

"Should I leave?" Therese asked.

"No! No, stay, dear. Something else terrible must have happened."

They waited for only a moment before the maid returned, and with her two other young women. They were maidservants themselves, from the way they curtsied to Pauline and to Therese.

"Rosa?" the princess said. "What's wrong?"

One of the girls had a wood chest in her hands, almost too large for her to carry, though it didn't appear to be heavy.

"Madame," she said, in a high-pitched voice. "Her Highness sends this. She says you are the only one!"

"What is it?" But Pauline seemed to already guess.

In answer, the girl set the chest on the table near Pauline's chair and opened it. At first, all they could see was tissue paper wrapped around dozens of smaller packages. Almost fearfully, Pauline lifted one from the pile and opened the paper.

Both she and Therese drew back from the open paper and its contents exposed. In Pauline's hand was a diamond and ruby bracelet.

"Her jewels!" Pauline said. "Has it come to this?"

"She asks you to take them to the embassy in London," Rosa said. "She is afraid, madame. She fears the people will rise against the dynasty if the war goes any worse."

"Everything is breaking, Therese," Pauline said once the chest had been safely hidden among the princess's baggage. "Everything good and beautiful is breaking apart. It will all be underfoot and trampled."

– 3 –

In the days that followed, Therese stayed mostly at home, alone with just Maria. Twice a day she went out to find newspapers, but the streets were surly and she stayed away from even the smallest crowds.

She did not return to Montmartre, or the studio of Pierre Beaubien, although she often found herself staring at the portrait he had painted of her.

Maria went with her in the morning and they stopped at the markets. At least there was still plenty of food.

But there was no hope. The wall about Paris, built to keep out news of the battles, had been breached. Therese went through every word.

The reeling French army on the front had stumbled back toward its historic strongpoint, the city of Metz. Paris read in breathless suspense the daily reports of the moves and countermoves, marches and cross marches, as the new hope of France, Marshall Achille Bazaine, replacing the disgraced Frossard, tried to regroup and reorganize.

But the Prussians were moving faster around Metz. While the French plodded in and through the ancient city on the banks of the Moselle, the Prussians had raced around, north and south. Bazaine had only reached the village of Mars-la-Tour behind Metz when he met the advancing Prussians.

Then Paris read how he had been thrown back in a swift, sharp battle. Two tense days later the worst news so far arrived. In a set-piece clash of the entire armies at Gravelotte, France had again been defeated. The army had been encircled in Metz, the Prussian siege lines were thrown up, and that new wall cut off any communication between France and its most precious army. Now there was no obstacle facing the Prussians.

Only the emperor and his guard had escaped Metz. In defeat, he chose not to return to Paris. Instead, he announced he would establish himself in Reims and gather a new army.

The next day, as Therese and Maria went to the market, they had to hide twice in side alleys as furious mobs filled the streets. The people of Paris were making it plain that the emperor had chosen wisely to stay away from his angry capital.

– 4 –

As before, the only announcement of her father's return was when Therese saw his face as she woke. It was late night and he had just lit a candle at her bedside.

"Father?"

"Yes. I'm back." The statement was final.

"You won't leave again?"

"I'll not be returning to the front."

She was still too sleepy to read any meaning in his words. "Thank you for waking me," she said. "I'll sleep better now knowing you're home."

"I wanted to be sure you were all right."

"Yes, Father. I am."

He paused, looking at her. "And Rudolph?"

She paused longer; her hope of better sleep was gone.

"Has there been a message?" he asked.

"No message," she said.

The next morning she came to breakfast, anticipating an end to her solitary meals. Besides her father, she found another visitor.

"Uncle Arpad!"

"Dear Therese," he said. "What a pleasure to see you, and Paris, so unchanged."

"Paris has changed," she said.

"And it will change more," her father said.

"Have you heard of the siege?" she asked. "The whole French army is in Metz."

"I've just come from Metz."

"Father! You were in Metz? But you're here. Is the siege over?"

"No, and it won't be anytime soon. I was given safe conduct passes to leave."

"Did you see Auguste?"

"I did not see Auguste," Ferdinand said. "There are over a hundred thousand French soldiers in Metz. But if he survived the battles up until then, I expect he is now in Metz."

"I know he must be there. Could he get a pass to leave?"

Pock laughed. "That is not likely, my dear! Your father is Austrian, and the Prussians are glad to be rid of him. They would prefer the French to stay."

"I'm very glad you're back, Father," she said. "And Zoltan, too?"

"Yes, Zoltan, too." He pulled a leather wallet from his coat and showed her a vellum sheet, inscribed in German in perfect script.

To all present, be it commanded to the armies of the Kaiser Wilhelm of Prussia and all German allies, that this safe conduct pass allows the Austrian Baron Ferdinand Harsanyi and his servant to pass without challenge through all points of occupied France. Gustav, Count von Albensleben-Erxleben.

"General von Albensleben himself was pleased to sign it. He remembered me from Koniggratz."

"I believe you should put it in a frame," Pock said.

"I'll put it in my desk," Ferdinand said.

"Will you stay home now?" Therese asked.

"I will be at the embassy."

"Even today? You're only just back."

"Even today," her father said. "I will accompany Prince von Metternich to the Tuileries Palace to inform the empress that Austria categorically refuses to come to France's aid."

"The emperor is raising a new army," Therese said. "The newspapers say it will be two hundred thousand men."

"Untrained conscripts," Pock said. "None has ever held a rifle. It won't be much of an army."

After breakfast, and the departure of her father and Herr Pock, Therese was alone again, and again she found some comfort looking at her portrait.

Then, impetuously, she wrote a short note. "I'm going out for a walk. I think I'll find a café on the Rue Royale and watch Paris," she said to Maria. But first she stopped at a newspaper stand at the Place de Breteuil, where there were always street children waiting for the chance to earn a few sous. "Take this," she said. "See the address? It's in Montmartre."

The café on Rue Royale was full, yet even the most casual observer would have noticed that fear and anger rendered the scene less than what Paris usually afforded. Therese had a table to herself in the bright sunshine; most of the other tables had the luxury of shade under the wide awning over the sidewalk.

"Mademoiselle Therese?"

She looked up to see a dark, smiling face, and the billows of jackets in the slight cool of the late August afternoon.

"Oh, Pierre! I was hoping you would come."

Pierre Beaubien took a chair beside her. "My unease torments me and drives me to the streets. Only moving seems to satisfy the moment."

"Everyone is uneasy."

"Even you?"

She smiled. "Of course. I'm worried for Auguste."

"Oh, yes! The brave Auguste. And is there still no word?"

"No word. Father thinks he's in Metz."

"Then he will be as safe as anyone."

"I just wish I knew he was safe."

"But, for the moment, he is absent," Beaubien said. "So I hope that I might console you."

"I want to ask you about my painting," she said in answer.

"Of course!"

"What did you . . . who . . . ?" She tried to ask. "Who did you see when you painted it?"

"You, mademoiselle."

"But I don't think it's me."

He frowned. "Certainly it is you."

"Then who is the *me* that you see?"

His next comment was delayed, first by his confusion at the question, but then more because Therese had noticed a woman running on the sidewalk, her skirts hitched up.

"Maria?" She stood and waved. "Maria!"

"Mistress," she wheezed. "Oh, mistress, I had to come. You said you'd be on the Rue Royale and I ran all the way."

"What's happened?"

"Look what's come!" She held out an envelope, and Therese's mouth dropped open as she saw the handwriting.

"It's from Auguste!"

"It came by post, but they brought it special by courier. They said it was from Metz, by balloon."

"Balloon?" She looked at Pierre Beaubien. "What does that mean?"

"They have begun floating balloons out of the city with mail like this," Pierre Beaubien said. "The Prussians shoot some down, and some get out."

Therese took the letter, trembling, and forced herself to sit back down. Beaubien watched on with great interest, and some slight annoyance.

She opened the envelope and took out the single half page.

My dearest Therese,

It is from the dangers and cares of the siege lines that I write to you, without any knowledge that you will ever receive these words, or that I will ever know that you have. For the uncertainties are great and would fill many hearts with trepidation, but for the steadfast bravery and nobility of the men with whom I live and might die, who will never surrender their bodies or their minds to the affronts and threats of the enemy. I may not write any word of our situation for fear of it falling into the hands of the enemy, yet you must know that hazard accompanies my every step, and peril is my constant companion. But it is the never dimming thoughts I have of you, and of the glory of France, that lead me on unwearied and unafraid. That I may one day pass through the hazards that beset me, and that I may cheat death, and come to you once again in happier times! But even more, that I may know for all the balance of my life, whether it is measured in years or days, that my honor was earned by every action.

Your most dear and true, Auguste

"Oh." Therese sighed, melting into her chair. Then the accumulation of the words, of danger, cares, and peril reached her heart. "Oh, Pierre! What can I do?"

"What can you do? Why, there is nothing to do!"

"No! There must be something. He says he might only be days from his death!"

"He is in a great army, in a besieged city. What can anyone do?"

"I have to rescue him."

"Rescue him? But it is for him and his army to rescue us!"

"We aren't in danger."

"Mademoiselle, it is not for a lady, be she even as beautiful as you, to fight through many thousands of Prussian soldiers and open a road for the French army to march out. Please be assured, if it were possible, that army would open its own road."

"You're afraid," Therese said.

"Afraid! Afraid? Never. Only reasonable."

But Therese was in turmoil, until she finally came to a decision. "Maria, thank you. Go back home now. I'll be late getting back." Then, to her painter companion, "Thank you, Pierre, for coming. I have to go now."

"To where?"

"To see a friend."

"I would come with you?"

"Oh . . . no. No, I have to go alone."

"But is it far? I have a carriage."

She paused only a moment. "Yes, then, thank you. I'm in a hurry, and that would be a great help."

"This place?" Pierre Beaubien asked. "I will come with you. It does not seem suitable for a woman to visit alone."

They were stopped outside the old apartment on the Rue Serpente in the Quartier Latin, where Arpad Pock lived. Beaubien's concerns were well justified by the bohemian raggedness of the building and street.

"No, it's fine. My friend lives here. That window up there."

"Then I will wait for you."

"No. Please go on now, Pierre. I'll be all right."

He sighed and flicked the rein and the carriage started away.

Therese knocked on the old, shabby front door and was let into a shabby hall and climbed shabby stairs to knock on Pock's door.

The door opened and the familiar face and voice greeted her.

"Therese! What are you doing here?"

"Uncle Arpad. Please help me!"

"But of course. Come in, come in. What can I do?"

She stepped in, but she was in a hurry. "I need to find one of the cadets from the École."

"Which one?"

"Gravert. I have to know where he lives."

"Gravert?" Pock frowned, then sat, leaving her standing. "Why Gravert?"

She couldn't answer; she only shook her head. "Just please tell me."

Pock's frown deepened and he answered slowly. "That is a difficult thing to tell you."

"Do you know where he lives?"

"Yes, I know. But it isn't a safe place, and he isn't a safe person."

"But I have to know."

"All right, then. He lives in the Rue Soleillet, in the twentieth arrondissement, near to the Pere Lachaise cemetery. Have you heard of Belleville?"

"I've heard of it."

"It's the nineteenth and twentieth arrondissements. They call it Red Paris. It's the radical heart of the city. It might be very dangerous, especially after the defeats."

She shook off his warning. "Thank you, Uncle Arpad."

"Do you really mean to go there?"

"Yes. I have to."

"Then I will come with you."

She hesitated. "Is it really that dangerous?"

"It is. Go home, Therese. The whole city is dangerous."

She found a cab close-by, and true to her word, gave the driver the address on Rue Duroc. But she told him to wait, and after less than a minute inside, she came and seated herself again in the carriage.

"Belleville," she said.

"Oh, no," the driver answered. "Not there."

"Then as close as you can."

He left her on the Boulevard Voltaire and she started walking. Soon the streets were all dirt. The buildings were mostly new, but cheap and poorly built, and they looked more ruinous that any of the older apartments in the other parts of the city.

The streets were very full, and Therese had to walk in the dirt because the sidewalks were crowded. The best people were working class, and the worst were just beggars and street children.

Therese was mostly unnoticed. She had on a long gray cloak that blended with the drab clothing of the neighborhood, and she kept her eyes down.

She finally reached the cemetery. Inside its walls, she saw trees and bushes tightly packed between hundreds, or thousands, of mausoleums and graves and statues. They were all stone, angled from age and crowding, like a fantasy city; and the only living green in all the streets from the river was inside the walls, and the green trees were all that was living inside the walls.

She turned north on the Boulevard de Memilmontant, and then into the narrow, smelling streets of the Belleville itself.

They were mud and dirt, with rubbish crushed in as if it were part of the surface. Here the buildings had no order in height or width. They were like the rubbish beneath her feet: random, broken, and stinking.

She quickly came to the Rue Soleillet. It was as bad as the other streets, and just two blocks long. She started at the midpoint of the street, asking at every porter's window for Gravert.

At the fourth building, a scrawny, old, unkempt woman stared at her with hostility in her eyes.

"Three floors up, then left. But you won't find him there," the old woman said. "Him or his foreigner friend." She pointed her arm in a different direction. "You'll find them over there."

Therese looked. On the corner was a ramshackle café with grimy windows, unmatched tables, and chairs on the dirt street outside.

She walked toward the corner.

The café was like a cave. The men at the tables outside watched her with the same hostility she now saw in every face. Some were old, some young, but all were angry.

She went to the door and peered in, but the dark was impenetrable.

"Raisy! What are you doing here?"
She had to follow the voice in the dim light to find him.
"Looking for you."
He came forward from his table. No one was with him. "Go back home."
"No."

"Then come back here. Don't stand in the middle of the room."

She followed him and sat beside him at the table.

But he wasn't unfriendly to her once they were alone and hidden back in the shadows. He was only wary.

"What are you doing here?" Rudolph asked again.

"I want you to help me. What are you doing here?"

"I live here."

"So you just sit here all day?"

"No." He was annoyed, but it was his usual impatience with her, not the anger that everyone else had. "I work in a stable."

"You work with horses?"

"That's what's in stables, Raisy. I'm a stable hand. What do you think I'd do there? Milk cows?"

"I don't know."

"And I like it."

"But why? You don't have to work. What's happened to you, Rudy?"

"I'm one of the people now."

"No, you aren't."

"Be quiet! Don't talk so loud. Yes, I am."

"Why?"

"What else is there to be? I'm not a diplomat, and I'm not a soldier. I don't want to be a baron."

"But you're not a worker. What would Father say if he knew?"

"I don't care what he thinks."

"He's back again. I can tell him I've seen you—"

"No! You promised you wouldn't."

"I won't, then. I wish I could."

"No."

Therese changed the subject. "Why do you work in a stable?"

"Gravert's cousin used to do it, but he's in the army. No work, no eat. That's the rule. I clean the stalls and feed the horses. I like it better than artillery."

"No, you don't! I know you don't. You don't want any of this."

"You don't know what I want."

"I know you better than anyone."

"I'm different now."

"You're still my brother."

Rudolph looked up. Someone was standing, blocking the small amount of light that was reaching them. Therese turned to see.

It was Gravert. She recognized him, but he wasn't the earnest cadet she'd known in her own parlor. This Gravert was unshaven and in the old clothes of the neighborhood, and with its anger.

"She's all right," Rudolph said.

"There's a meeting tonight," Gravert said.

"I'll be there."

Gravert gave Therese one more look, not hostile but not friendly, just a close study. Then he jerked his head in a barely polite bow, and left.

"I want you to do something, Rudy," she said.

"What?"

"I want you to find Auguste and bring him back."

"Auguste!" He was so surprised that he almost shouted. Then, more quietly, "What are you talking about?"

"He's in Metz."

"The whole French army is in Metz."

"I want you to go get him out and bring him back here."

"Are you crazy? How do you know he's even alive?" He'd lost his hardness and working-class manners. He was just her brother, arguing.

"A letter came. They said the letters got out by balloon."

"Raisy. I can't get him out of Metz."

"Please!"

"It's impossible. The whole Prussian army is around Metz. Even God couldn't get him out! I couldn't even get in!"

"Yes, you could."

"How? Should I ride the balloon?"

"No. I have this."

From inside her cloak, she took out a folded parchment and opened it on the table in front of him.

Rudolph looked at her, and then read the words.

To all present, be it commanded to the armies of the Kaiser Wilhelm of Prussia and all German allies, that this safe conduct pass allows the Austrian Baron Ferdinand Harsanyi . . .

"Baron Ferdinand Harsanyi! This is Father's!"

"He was in Metz and they let him out."

"But . . . but I can't use this!"

"Yes, you can!" She leaned closer to him. "You can, Rudy. You can take this and go through the Prussian lines into Metz and find Auguste, and then use this to get back out. See? It says Baron Harsanyi and his servant. Auguste could be your servant. And you're Baron Harsanyi. You are!"

"I won't use Father's pass."

"You have to."

"Why do you have to get Auguste out, anyway?"

"I just do! I want him!"

He stared at her, now suspicious. "Why?"

"I love him. And he's in danger. His letter says he might die any day." She waited while Rudolph thought.

"Does he really love you?"

"He does."

"How do you know?"

"I know!" She pressed her argument. "He's in General Legrand's cavalry, in the Fourth Corps under General Ladmirault. I know you can find him."

He considered, the suspicion in his eyes getting stronger. "You're in his power."

"Yes. I am. And I want to be."

"What does he want from you?" Abruptly, he took the paper and folded it, and put it in his own pocket. "I'll get him. I'll leave tomorrow."

It was Therese's turn to be surprised. "You'll get him?"

"I will."

"Why?"

"I have a reason."

Chapter Nine

BONE UNDER
MUSCLE

— 1 —

The road to Metz was a road to war.

Rudolph traveled east toward war. It was an easy road. The weather was fine after earlier rains, and the countryside idyllic with beautiful ancient villages scattered like grain among the hills. It was still dark, but there was enough early light to see that the land was well watered and green. East from Paris, by Vincennes and Montreuil, and then a long view down to the Marne River from the high hill of Rosny. Houses and a church and market square held the side of the hill, and above them the high-walled, black double fortress crowned with cannon was on its crest, the easternmost of the ring of forts guarding the capital.

But the Marne was at peace with the hills and itself. Rudolph rode into the red sunrise, down into the Marne valley, and the ride's illusion at first was of peace. Too much peace; the fields were quiet but abandoned, and the roads had a trickle of carts and horses and people, but all going west to Paris.

Rudolph alone traveled east. The carts he passed that should have held vegetables, bread, and cheese for Paris instead carried refugees for Paris. Some of the walking men he passed still wore uniforms, while others had thrown theirs away.

Rudolph wore a gentleman's black coat and tan leather breeches for riding, studiously unmilitary. He had an old but sturdy horse, a brown mare. He kept her at a leisurely pace, not because his errand wasn't urgent but to keep her strength for a 300-kilometer ride. His saddlebag was as light a burden as he could make it.

At midmorning he came to Meaux, twenty-five kilometers from Paris, and he stopped at an inn and stable for water, wine, hay, and bread. He kept his conversation minimal to hide the German in his French, and because he wanted more to listen.

Prussia was a hammer striking blow after blow against France, the people said. The emperor, France's brittle hope, was still in Reims with his new, last army, still 100 kilometers ahead, 200,000 strong, and everyone knew Metz would be free in a week. It would be a real victory. The people were still waiting for their first of those.

Someone else said he had already advanced to Chalons. A stable hand argued that the army had left Chalons a week ago, retreating to Reims. And a traveler said he'd just come from Reims and no army was there; they'd left days ago, and it had only been 100,000.

"There were supplies gathered for 250,000 at Chalons," the stable boy said. "My uncle saw the orders."

Rudolph slipped away.

The ride turned longer under a hot sun. The road stayed by the Marne, sometimes in view and sometimes hidden behind the growing hills and thickening trees. The river traveled through a valley a few miles wide and banked in the near distance by steep bluffs. It became rare to meet anyone, as if a bottle had been stopped and the people he'd seen in the morning had been the last drop wiped from its mouth. He passed the turn to Reims without taking it and stayed with the river. There were no signs of any armies.

He was deeper in the countryside of Champagne, less thickly settled. Still in the valley, he came to a place where the road was muddy, the grass still wet, and his horse's steady dry tramp changed to a thick sound like cannon muffled and distant.

Black clouds were jostling the sky above him now and finally one struck. He rode in the rain, his horse trudging through the mire. The thunder was like cannon fire, sharp and close-by. Then the clouds and rain passed and the sun came back into view and he and his horse steamed in the hot afternoon. The Marne climbed from its valley to a wide plain and the town of Epernay, and there were people on the roads again.

In dark evening he came to Chalons, and here he saw real evidence of a real army. The fields to the north were trampled and filled with the detritus of a huge army camp; the soldiers had left these fields for Reims only a few days before. There could be no disagreement about that, or also that the army had not returned. A faint smell of burning hung in the air. Rudolph foraged a few minutes in the field and found a hatchet, a writing case, a pair of gloves, a coffeepot, and more. So much had been left behind that even a town the size of Chalons hadn't been able to scavenge the fields clean. But he had no need for most of the items and left them, just keeping the hatchet for its usefulness, and the writing case because he liked it.

At the edge of the field, the burnt smell was much stronger. He came to a huge black scar hundreds of meters square where a fire had raged. There were no signs of battle, just hectares of blackness, large piles of charred and unrecognizable debris, and a suffocating smell.

In the town, two taverns were deserted, a third let him in but had no one to care for his horse or watch the stable, and finally he fed his own horse in an empty stall. But he did hear about the fire.

"It was the supplies they gathered," an old man outside the tavern door told him. "They piled them up and burned them."

"The Prussians?"

"No, the emperor himself gave the order."

"Why?"

"It was too much. Supplies for two hundred thousand, but the army only half that size. So they burned everything that was left. Didn't want the Prussians to get their hands on it."

Rudolph left the town, by now in moonless black night, and went on to a thicket of young fir trees. Deep in their cover he laid his cloak on a dry bed of needles and slept.

He was awakened early, before the light, by men marching on the road. In the disorientation of the dark and hard ground and tree branches it took a moment to realize the voices were German.

His horse was still close. They waited together for the infantry to go by, and then the supply train. The dawn had begun and the column was still passing, into Chalons, when Rudolph chose to move, rather than waiting for full light.

In the gray he pushed out the back of the trees to a small stream and then a field. The sky was fast brightening, but he was across the field without being noticed, where he found a narrow path, mounted his horse, and went on.

Now he was on the wide, white plain of Champagne. From Chalons, the road to Verdun and Metz left the Marne valley and its more fertile fields. The land away from the river was chalky, bare of nearly all trees. The horizon became a distant, flat, indistinct intersection with the sky. There was no cover for a single man traveling.

He kept away from the road; after the passing of the German column, any encounter would be unpredictable and likely dangerous. His progress was slower than the day before. Twice, he saw mounted figures riding swiftly in small groups, but too far away to make them out. And once, it seemed, much farther, he might have seen a dark line of troops or wagons, just on the edge of sight.

Finally, by early afternoon of his second day he came to the hills and forests of the Argonne, the sylvan, broken opposite of the empty plain that stretched to the north. He returned to the road and descended with it through the jagged country into the valley of the Meuse.

Back on the road, his solitude ended. He was never out of sight of a cart or a pedestrian, all leaving toward the west. Later, as evening began, he reached the river and the city of Verdun, still very full of people, and shaking from the passage of the Prussian army the day before. Most of the people who had left had gone south; the few Rudolph had passed were hoping to reach Paris, which everyone knew would never fall. No one had any word of the emperor's French army; it seemed to have disappeared.

The inns were open and he could have found an empty room easily, but any town seemed like a trap to him now, so Rudolph chose again to take his German accent away, and he slept in the woods. He slept soundly. If another army had passed, he would never have heard it.

The next morning, the third day, he climbed back through the Argonne hills. The forest was thick and smelled damp and old, and streams appeared beside the road and disappeared back into the trees. Before noon he came out on the far side of the forest onto the wide, rich plain of Lorraine. Metz was forty kilometers beyond on the Moselle, and the pickets of the Prussian army would be much closer. An easy two hours ahead, 300,000 men, half German and half French, were locked in the largest siege Europe had ever seen.

Lorraine was the opposite of Champagne. It was fertile country, dense with farms and villages. Its fields cultivated every rationale for peace: quiet domestic life, tranquil lanes and verdant land, ages of worship in its churches and their lovely altars. But storms from beyond its borders had always swept it. Lorraine was again shorn of its peace and stained with blood.

As he surveyed the land ahead, he saw in the distance several small groups of fast horsemen. One was only a kilometer away, close enough to see their black cloaks and hats; they were Uhlans, the Prussian horse patrols, swarming over the whole French countryside.

Rudolph urged his horse on. Uhlan, picket or sentry, he knew the first Prussian would be near, and now the sooner, the better.

Rudolph waited. He was in the large farmhouse of what would have been a prosperous farm. A sentry, Bavarian by his way of speaking, stood next to him while he sat at a rustic kitchen table. His horse and two other soldiers were outside in the farmyard. The Germans were courteous; he had been given a lunch of stew and bread.

An officer arrived from another room. He was an old colonel, bald with a white mustache and a round, red face. "What is it?"

The sentry answered, "This man. He presented himself on the road from Verdun. He says he's Austrian."

The colonel turned to face Rudolph. "What is your business?"

"I have a safe conduct signed by General . . ." He took his pouch from under his jacket and removed the pass and unfolded it. "General von Albensleben."

"General von Albensleben?" The man was shocked. "I will see it." As he looked, doubt increased. "Baron Harsanyi? You?"

"I am Baron Harsanyi," Rudolph said.

"And a servant? Where is he?"

"He had to turn back."

"What is your business?" the man asked again.

"It's diplomatic."

"Improbable." The white mustache frowned. "How did you get this?"

"The Austrian Embassy arranged it with the Prussian General Staff." Rudolph folded his hands, patient with the colonel's slowness. "Von Albensleben. You know who that is, don't you?"

"Of course I do! He is commanding this entire army."

"Then ask him personally about me, if you won't honor his signature on this pass."

"I will not bother him with a minor matter." He shrugged, as much as his rigid bearing allowed. "Lieutenant. Take this man under white flag to the crossing. Give him to the French. Let them do as they want with him."

Rudolph waited. He was in the large farmhouse of what would have been another prosperous farm. A sentry, this time Gascon by his way of speaking, stood next to him while he sat at another rustic kitchen table. Again, his horse, and this time a dozen other soldiers, were outside in the yard. The food was much better than the Germans'.

"For what reason have you entered this sector?" a French major asked. He was quite different from the colonel, especially that his mustache was black and waxed to perfection.

"I'm trying to reach General Legrand's cavalry division."

"But for what reason? I must know the reason."

"I have a message for a man there."

"Show me this message."

"It isn't written down."

"Then tell me what it is!"

"It's from an important person in the Austrian Embassy."

"Austria . . . you are Austrian?"

"Yes, sir."

"How did you get through the Prussian lines?"

"I have a diplomatic safe conduct pass."

The major's eyes opened wide. "A diplomat, from Austria . . . yes, go. General Ladmirault's Fourth Corps is camped on the other side of Metz, in Saint Julien. General Legrand's division will be close-by. I will send an escort with you."

"No, please," Rudolph said. "I don't want to be noticed."

"It will be for your protection."

The siege of Metz was two weeks old, enough time for the French army to settle very comfortably around the well-stocked storehouses and hospitable inns of the old city. Metz itself, a garrison town for centuries, was happy to host a siege as long as officers were receiving pay and soldiers were kept controlled. Over 140,000 men, in addition to the city's population of 40,000, made a grand market for overpriced food, as well as for boots, coats, blankets, and anything else the army quartermasters had neglected to provide or the men had lost from their heavy packs in the course of several battles and many long marches.

Rudolph rode, with his two attendant French lieutenants, through a vast bivouac of tents and campfires. The Metz pocket was large enough, four kilometers by five, to accommodate even a large army easily, with space to spare. Most of the fires were surrounded by men sitting and standing, talking, at ease and enjoying their life of free food and minimal duties.

At first, still near the front lines, he heard occasional stray shots and disturbances; but deeper into the heart of the encampment it seemed more that the men were simply being warehoused. At least they would be well rested and prepared if the commander, Marshall Bazaine, ever decided on action.

In the center was Metz itself. Built on the banks and islands of the Moselle, closer to the Rhine than the Seine, its spires and grand halls had more than a hint of German bulk to their French grace. Rudolph was taken across three bridges to reach the center, as the river was split between large and small islands, each with its portion of the city. The buildings were all rich golden limestone so that even at sunset the feel of the sun was still warm in the old, narrow streets.

Just at sundown they reached the city center. The windows were bright yellow, and the doors of the taverns sounded with laughter and even the clink of glasses and dice. The streets weren't lit, but the doors spilled light as well as sound into them; in the dim above, though, he could see the heights and colors of the buildings. The impression was of a strong and lovely place, easy to enjoy and not easy to defeat.

And even as the streets became dark, the last rays of sunset still lit the towers and buttresses and spires of the cathedral, solid and strong as a fortress.

Rudolph noticed the signs on the road: They were on the Rue des Allemands, the Street of the Germans. Then they came to one more river and a huge medieval tower bridge.

"The Porte des Allemands," one of his companions said. "Those towers are six hundred years old, and those four hundred."

"They look strong," Rudolph said.

"They will never fall."

The horses clattered through the massive, brooding gate and they were outside the city.

Then they were climbing the banks of the river plain, up into the camps on the other side.

It was after nine o'clock when they were challenged by the guards at General Ladmirault's staff headquarters at the village of Saint Julien. The general himself was living in a hotel in the city, but an aide was rousted out to tell them where General Legrand's cavalry divisions were camped. Another half-hour ride, in which they were lost much of the time, brought them through orchards and ravines to a smaller array of staff tents, yet no one of importance could be found.

"I can find him from here," Rudolph said.

This was agreed; whether the escorts were tired and wanted to be back in their cots, or whether they weren't tired and had the lit windows of Metz in their minds, they left him without argument. And then he was alone, in the dark, among the French.

He fought the desire to find an empty corner and sleep. In the dark he could see dozens of campfires over a hillside, and the nearer ones at least ringed by men, sitting, standing, eating, talking. He could even hear the dissonant humming of their conversations, rising and breaking out and falling back like a muffled battle.

By now it was ten o'clock at night. Below and behind him, the bells of the cathedral rang the hour.

– 2 –

It seemed more likely to find Auguste visible in the dark than in the morning light.

So Rudolph stalked the darkness. He left his horse behind and silently hunted in the black sea between the glowing islands. Of all the thousands of men in this one division, it might have been unlikely that he would find the one he was searching for, but Auguste de l'Imperator was an officer and outstanding personality, as noticeable as a gold dagger among steel nails.

Rudolph was never noticed as he walked dark paths. One after another he came close to campfires surrounded by soldiers and officers, talking and eating. It seemed everyone was awake that night, away from their families and farms and work. Their conversations were loud and he heard the boasting, the politics, the memories of home and stories of their families, and, occasionally, the discontent.

And just as twelve heavy notes sounded from Metz, Rudolph heard the ringing voice, and then he saw a glinting gilt reflection of the firelight.

He moved closer but stayed out of the light.

Like the others, this fire was circled by eight or ten men, with a pot heating, voices raised in rough talk. He stood in the shadows and listened and heard the same coarse humor, politics, and war stories from the present war and earlier wars, from Italy and Africa and the Crimea. The men were like half-men, their fronts lit and real, their backs gone in the darkness.

Eventually they would break the circle and go to their tents. Rudolph chose not to wait. He moved as close as he could to the ear he wanted.

"Auguste."

The golden hair turned, and other heads, too.

"Who is it?"

"Come over," Rudolph said, still in the dark.

"Who are you?" Auguste stood, searching the shadow. A few others of his comrades were also staring.

"You know me."

Auguste shrugged and the others returned their attention to the fire, but still half-watching the meeting in the dark. Auguste walked closer.

He started in surprise. "You!"

"Yes," Rudolph said. "Me."

"What are you . . . how . . . ?" And then finally, "Why?"

"I've come to take you back to Paris."

By the flickering light, the shock and surprise in Auguste's face were complete.

"This is astonishing! It cannot be!"

"It is," Rudolph said.

"But how did you even get in?"

"I have a Prussian army pass."

"Incredible!"

"I don't want to wait." Rudolph spoke impatiently. "Get whatever you're going to bring and come."

"But . . . but it is impossible." Auguste was finally understanding. "I can't leave. This is my post, my duty. These are my men! To leave would be desertion!"

"You're being ordered to."

"From whom are these orders?" He was getting angry. "Who sent you?"

Rudolph frowned, puzzled, as if the answer were obvious. "Don't you know?"

Face-to-face, they were side to the fire, and Auguste's face was half lit and half shadowed. "No, of course not!"

Rudolph shook his head, frustrated.

"Sarroche," he said.

The shock was paralyzing. Auguste's mouth dropped open. Finally, he could only say, "But . . . it was finished. It was all finished!"

"It isn't."

Auguste shook his head to clear it. "But why you? What are you to do with Sarroche?"

"There's no one else. I was the only person who could come."

Auguste seemed to accept the answer, but still not the situation. "But what else could he want?"

"I don't know. You'll have to ask him."

"Does my colonel here know?"

"I was only told to bring you back. I haven't talked to anyone else."

"Come with me, then, to discuss it with him."

"I'm not French. He wouldn't listen to me."

Auguste was in despair. "It is too impossible!" He was shaking his head again. "It is more than impossible! How can I leave my men? And how can I pass through 100,000 Germans? And for what? My agreement with Sarroche was finished. What else is to be done?" He breathed deeply in resolve. "I will not come. Tell him I will not . . . that I cannot leave my men." But the resolve broke. "I must know why he has sent for me! To leave here, I must know why!"

"Therese wants you, too," Rudolph said.

"What?" Auguste reacted violently. His eyes grew wide as he realized what that might mean. "What does she know? Does she know of Sarroche? Tell me that she doesn't."

"I'm not going to say anything else until we're out of Metz," Rudolph said. "Come now."

It was too much. Auguste visibly torn, with confusion, anger, fear, remorse.

"Answer one question," he said. "What does Therese think of me?"

"She says she loves you."

Auguste put his hands to his face, sighing and groaning. "It is too terrible. I cannot leave, but I must. There is no choice!"

Rudolph waited patiently for half a minute, then he said, "Choose."

"I will come." And once his choice was made, he acted quickly. "Do you have a horse?"

"I'll have to find where I left her."

"Get her. Meet me here . . . there, down farther, in ten minutes."

"It'll take longer," Rudolph said.

"I will be waiting."

Auguste returned to the fire. Rudolph stayed to hear few words. "Nothing. Simply some orders from the colonel. A short reconnaissance, and then I will return in the afternoon."

After a half hour of stumbling in the dark, Rudolph reached the meeting place, leading his horse. Auguste was waiting with his own.

"I will not be missed before tomorrow night," he said. "Which way?"

"Well . . . to Paris. Back through the city? Is there any other way across the river?"

"No. It is the only way. All the other bridges are in the hands of the enemy."

"Can you get us through the sentries?"

"Of course. But how do we pass the Prussian lines? I can only get us through the French posts, not the Prussians!"

"I can do that," Rudolph said. "Except that you're going to have to change clothes or cover your uniform. The pass is for me and my servant."

Auguste wasn't pleased. "I am a servant?"

"That's the only way."

"What is this pass?"

"It's for me and one servant, and it's signed by General von Albensleben."

"No! That is impossible! It must be a forgery!"

"It isn't. And what difference does it make, anyway?" Rudolph said. "It got me into Metz. It'll get us out."

Metz was darker and quieter, but even after midnight the taverns were still full and their windows were just as bright. The light and sound spilled into the street, laughing and songs and the clanking of heavy beer mugs and the tinkling of wineglasses. Auguste paused to look in.

"I'm leaving them," he said.

"You have to."

He shook his head. "No. The right thing is to stay. But I am choosing the darker path."

"You'll have to lead," Rudolph said. "I don't know the way from here."

They left the lights and crossed the dark Moselle.

After the last bridge and city wall, Auguste turned aside. Now it was after one o'clock and the sky was stubbornly black. At the end of the bridge, the road forked in three directions.

"Now, we must make decisions," Auguste said.

"About what?"

"There are several roads from Metz. You traveled from Verdun?"

"Yes. Through Gravelotte."

"And what did you see as you rode?"

"I saw horsemen."

"Uhlans. The Prussian cavalry scouts."

"And a Prussian column at Chalons." He worked out the days in his mind. "It was two mornings ago. But the emperor is somewhere with an army. No one knew where. And no one knew where the main Prussian armies were."

"They are between here and Paris, I am sure of it," Auguste said. "It was not safe when you first passed through, and it will be doubly danger-ous now. I believe . . ." He paused. "We should go north."

"North? Toward Luxembourg?"

"North toward Thienville, and then west to Charleville, and Laon, and then to Paris."

"That's a hundred kilometers longer."

"An extra day. But Champagne is too open. We must not meet the Prussians in open country. To the north, we will avoid these armies."

"What if the armies have gone north?"

"It is possible. But the Prussians want Paris, and the emperor wants to free Metz. I think the next battle will be on the line between the two."

"Then we should stay off that line," Rudolph said.

"It is not that I am not fleeing danger," Auguste answered. "But I will avoid the delays it brings." He turned his horse to the right and proceeded on the northern road. Rudolph followed. Finally, the half-moon was rising and there was a shade of light.

They rode for a kilometer, through fields and fields of more campfires, tents, and, even so late, of men talking and eating. The road rose; the view expanded and at the top of the hill, Rudolph could briefly see a whole great circle of lights, thousands on thousands, each a universe to itself of dozens of men and their whole lives of the moment; behind him, the lights and towers of Metz as the center of the circle; and beyond the sudden edge of the lights, darkness; but in the darkness, more men, enemies, as many as within the circle, but inhabiting an outer darkness, surrounding the lights and strangling them.

Then the fields ended and the road cut through forest for a short distance. They had come to the French front lines and yet another farmhouse command post.

"I am Captain de l'Imperator," Auguste, in all his golden magnificence, said to the startled lieutenant manning the farmhouse's kitchen table. "I must reach the Prussian lines as quickly as possible, and I require civilian clothes. What do you have? At least an overcoat and shoes. Bring them quickly!" His hair almost sparkled in the candlelight.

"Bring a hat, too," Rudolph said.

"Trade horses," Rudolph said. They were approaching the final French sentries while an escort from the farmhouse rode behind them, just out of sight in the darkness.

"Not that!"

"This will be hard enough. I don't know how you'll ever pass for a servant at all, and on that horse you still look like an officer."

"Then I will ride your mare."

Changing to the warhorse was like the difference between the worn, blunted practice swords at the École and the fine-honed one that he'd received from the ambassador. Rudolph was half a head taller than before, higher than Auguste, and he could feel the power of the animal beneath him. The horse itself was suspicious, but a touch of the rein moved it forward. Auguste held the white flag.

They passed the French line and walked slowly toward the shadows ahead.

"Halt!" the shadows commanded.

The final farmhouse was not a farmhouse but the inn in the village of Semecourt. Auguste stooped as they were escorted in, trying to decrease himself.

At two o'clock in the morning, the Prussians had mustered a major and he was not welcoming.

"Yes? What is it?"

"This man is an Austrian diplomat, he says," said the corporal leading the escort.

"Now? At this hour? What proof does he have?" The major turned to Rudolph. "What proof do you have? And what are you doing in Metz?" Then back to the corporal, "Put him in a cell." He looked up at Auguste, still towering even as he bent forward. "Both of them! I will consider this matter tomorrow." Shaking his head, he turned to leave the room.

"In that case," Rudolph said, "I will appeal to General von Albensleben."

"General von Albensleben? What?" The major returned his attention, sharply. "How dare you—"

"He provided me with a safe conduct," Rudolph said. "Allow me." Again, he took the pouch from his coat and unfolded the page.

The major became even more agitated. "It is a forgery." He looked more closely at the paper, and then the young man holding it. "And you? A diplomat? You are a schoolboy."

But the steel in Rudolph's eyes stopped him. "I am Baron Ferdinand Harsanyi," Rudolph said. "In the name of General von Albensleben, allow me to pass at once. Or else take me to him, and let him vouch for his own signature."

The major was concerned, but not convinced. At least Rudolph's manner had bought him a few more minutes, though.

"Why is the Prussian command providing Austrians with passes in and out of Metz. This is unacceptable."

"Tell that to the general."

The major struggled with the decision. "Harsanyi is not an Austrian name."

"I am Hungarian."

"For whatever that means," the major said, still doubtful. He sighed in dissatisfaction. "You will be allowed to proceed. Escort them as far as Amneville," he said to the corporal.

But just as the major was nearly through the exit, he suddenly said, in French, "Attention!" and spun back into the room, his eyes on the silent Auguste.

Auguste remained motionless.

"Very well." The major was satisfied.

Rudolph shrugged. "Come," he said in German, and Auguste followed him from the room out into the village street, with the corporal close behind.

After Amneville, they were again alone. Metz and its armies were behind them. In twelve hours, Rudolph had passed the lines in and out, and now had Auguste at his side free of Metz.

"My horse," Auguste said, and Rudolph dropped from his height and returned to his plodding brown mare.

The moon was more than halfway to the height of the sky. They rode thirty minutes on an empty road toward Thienville. Just past a village called Uckange, Auguste stopped at a crossroads.

"Toward Longuyon next."

"How far is that?"

"Forty or fifty kilometers."

"I need to sleep somewhere," Rudolph said. "I've been sitting in command posts and riding back and forth since Verdun."

"A little farther. Then we will stop."

Rudolph obediently followed behind his servant.

Three kilometers on, the road came to a stream and tracked its narrow valley between higher hills. Auguste found a place on the water's bank, shielded by the trees and terrain, and they dismounted.

"I have no tent," Auguste said. "Of necessity, I left all my equipment behind."

"I don't need a tent," Rudolph said as he sat on a soft patch of the grass.

"We'll take turns watching."

Rudolph rolled his coat into a pillow. "No one will see us here." And moments later, his eyes were closed.

- 3 -

It seemed just minutes later that Rudolph awoke, but the sky was bright.

Some sound had awakened him. As he tried to think what it was, he heard it again, and shoved Auguste beside him.

"Wake up. You're snoring."

The shadows were still long, and a thin mist was rising from the stream beside them.

"What time is it?" Auguste said, mists rising in his foggy expression.

"About seven o'clock." Rudolph watched Auguste stand and stretch. "Did you get any news from outside when you were in Metz?"

"No. We were told nothing."

"And I haven't heard anything in two days. We should try to find out what's happening. Someone must know where Napoleon is."

"What provisions do we have?"

"I don't have much left," Rudolph said.

"There will be another village soon."

The next village was called Fontoy. A café in its center was already open, and they ate beneath an arbor dripping with grapes.

The old man who served them was as complacent and unmoving as any and all Frenchmen had ever been.

"What is the news?" Auguste asked. "Where are the Prussians?"

"In Metz!" he said.

"No. The other armies."

"Not here," he answered. "Nor French army, either."

"Do you know where they are?"

"The barber's daughter, she says they are in Troyes."

"See?" Auguste said to Rudolph. "Two hundred kilometers to the south. They are moving toward Paris. And the emperor will be there to meet them."

"I don't think the barber's daughter would know," Rudolph said.

"But there is no news to the contrary."

Then they were on their way again. The stream had climbed to the top of a plateau, and a wide land of ever more farms and villages stretched ahead of them. Church steeples marked the towns from afar.

"On to Longuyon," Auguste said. "We will be there by well before sunset."

As they rode toward the wide horizon, the sun rose above them. But before noon, the sky had filled with clouds and long before Longuyon they had twice been soaked. They met few people on the road, and after noon there was no one. The rain and mud slowed them considerably.

"The safe conduct pass," Auguste said, "it was written for Baron Ferdinand Harsanyi?"

"Yes. My father."

"How did Sarroche obtain it for you?"

Metz was long behind them now.

"He didn't," Rudolph said.

"No? But who did?"

"Therese."

"Therese?" Auguste exploded. "She . . . how could this be? What are you saying?"

"The pass was my father's. She stole it from him and gave it to me."

"But what about Sarroche?"

"He didn't send me."

Auguste pulled his horse to a stop and Rudolph halted beside him. The lightning in the earlier rains had been nothing to this thunderbolt.

"But—"

"Sarroche didn't send me," Rudolph repeated.

"Then why did you come?"

"Therese sent me."

"You lied to me!"

"You lied to her."

Rudolph started moving again, his horse walking at an even rate down the dirt road.

He kept his eyes forward. Within a moment, Auguste was beside him, furious. "Why did you lie?"

"I didn't think you'd come if I just said Therese wanted you back."

"That was the only reason? To deceive me into abandoning my troops, my friends?"

"I also wanted to know if you really were working for Sarroche."

"You were guessing? You didn't even know?"

"I do now."

There was still no change to their forward motion. Auguste's fury increased, but so did his confusion. "How did you even guess?"

"It wasn't hard. Sarroche came to me, too."

"And now I've deserted! What am I to do?"

"Come to Paris. Therese still wants you back."

"She doesn't know?"

"She doesn't know about Sarroche. I didn't tell her."

"But will you?"

"I don't know." He turned to face Auguste. "Why did you lie to her? She thinks you love her."

"I do love her!"

"Because Sarroche paid you?"

"No!"

"Then what did he pay you to do?"

"He didn't pay me anything."

"What did he do? What were you doing in Vienna? Why did you leave the army?" Then, strongly, "Tell me, Auguste."

"I was in Vienna because I was unable to return to Paris."

"Why?"

"I had difficulties."

"And Sarroche fixed them for you."

"Yes. What of it? It was an understanding between me and him."

"And your part was to deceive Therese, until she fell in love with you."

"I said that I love her, as well!"

"You just want the cinnabar mines."

In response, Auguste spurred his horse forward to a trot. Rudolph let him get ahead, then urged his own horse to match the same pace, a dozen meters behind.

Eventually, they slowed again to a walk.

Thirty minutes later, and still ten meters apart, Rudolph said, "Auguste."

Auguste had seen the same thing. "Uhlans," he said, slowing for Rudolph to catch up.

The three black-coated Prussian horsemen were far across fields to their left, not even on the same road, moving at a fast canter.

"Are they scouting?" Rudolph said.

"At that speed, they're carrying a message."

"That means there are Prussian commanders around."

"That could not be," Auguste said, "unless they are small companies in isolation."

They continued on in silence, side by side again.

The road descended, and a bank on their left blocked their view of the open country and whatever horsemen were crossing it. Above, dark clouds were galloping across the sky, one line against another.

"How long were you in Vienna?" Rudolph asked.

"Nine months."

"Three months before you met Therese?"

"Yes, it was three months."

They saw the rain coming, like a cavalry charge directly toward them. There was no shelter. They hunched their shoulders against the onslaught and kept riding.

"Then Sarroche told you to meet her."

"You have no right to question me!"

"I'm her brother. What were your difficulties?"

"Do not question me!"

"Why did you have to leave the Imperial Guards Cavalry? Why couldn't you rejoin them?"

Auguste answered with silence and Rudolph gave up his questions. They rode on in the pouring rain.

They heard the Uhlans first. The rain had passed, and the road was a muddy mess winding through a small forest. The trees were close in on both sides.

"Quickly," Auguste said, his first word since their argument. There was little undergrowth but the shadows were enough. Twenty meters from the road they stopped and watched a troop of thirty Prussian cavalry pass by.

"As if it were their own country!" Auguste said.

"We're in the middle of something," Rudolph said.

"Yes, I agree. We must be. Longuyon will be close ahead. Perhaps there will be news."

"I don't think we should go into Longuyon."

"We will find a path around."

Once they were clear of the forest, they reached a crossroads. From the distance they saw it was guarded, so they turned north across a field. After a kilometer they turned west. They soon crossed the road leading north from the crossroads, but they continued on west across open country.

They came to a steep valley, carved by a swift stream. It took an hour to climb down one side and then back up the steeper far side, often on foot and leading the horses, and they were drenched once again by another heavy shower.

On the opposite heights, they had a long flat vista with the lowering sun ahead.

Looking back into the valley, Auguste pointed. Six horsemen were at the streambed below, where they themselves had been only thirty minutes earlier. He and Rudolph pushed their horses faster.

The next five kilometers went quick with no sign of the horsemen, and then the same valley appeared again at their feet. Here it was wider, but the sides were still steep, and it was nearly dark at the bottom.

Beside the stream, in the base of the valley, ran a railroad track.

"That will go to Montmedy," Auguste said. "We will follow it through the night." The light was fading quickly.

The climb down was as difficult as the last had been, but beside the water and the iron rails the ground was flat. It was fairly dark in the valley now, and they passed two small villages unseen. Their warm, hospitable lights were beacons in the damp dark, but were also untouchable in the unknown of the night.

They traveled on the left bank of the river, on its southern side. Soon after one of the villages they saw different lights on the north bank, brighter and concentrated in a single building. Auguste studied them for a moment.

"A check post. This river must be the frontier with Belgium, at least for a short way."

Two kilometers later they passed another guard building, and then saw no other sign of the border.

It seemed at least midnight and Rudolph finally said, "I'm ready to stop."

"Yes. For several hours, but not more."

A distance from the road, beside the river, they found an area where the bank cut into a low rise, creating a sheltered spot. On the horizon, a white glow showed the moon was nearing.

Rudolph dropped from his horse and found a grassy place. It was very dark. He heard, more than saw, Auguste searching his saddlebag for a blanket and the horses drinking from the water.

"Did you ever ask Therese about the mines?"

"There is no purpose for such a discussion now. When we reach Paris, we will resolve these questions."

"But I'm trying to understand," Rudolph said. "Therese would never have been able to sell cinnabar to the French while Father or I were alive. Was there some way to get control away from our father?"

"I know nothing of Monsieur Sarroche's plans."

"You must know something. He must have given you some instructions." Rudolph wrinkled his nose. "Do you smell something?"

Auguste paused. "Stand up. Feel around. There is something here."

Rudolph stood and began walking slowly, feeling with his feet. His boot touched something and he tripped, falling forward. His hand touched something cool, firm but yielding, and he leaped back with a cry of fear and dismay.

Even then, the moon cleared the horizon, its cold light spilling into the hollow.

A man was with them, less than two meters from Rudolph's seat. He was on his back, his white face upward, his eyes and mouth open. Auguste approached him.

"It was as he lay," he said.

"Is he dead?" It was a foolish question.

"Yes, very much. Not in flight, with no struggle. He was simply executed."

Rudolph fought to master his panic. "Who is he?"

"A simple soldier, no more. Hiding perhaps from an Uhlan patrol, or perhaps caught unaware." He sensed Rudolph's shock. "My apology, that I am not distressed as you are. I am afraid I have seen many other dead in these few weeks of war, and also in my other campaigns."

"But he was just shot? Why?"

"The country is at war." But then Auguste's reserve did break. "Oh, France! What has become of you? Your enemies roam your countryside at will, shedding your blood!"

They stood quietly, then Rudolph said, "We'll keep going. I won't stay here."

Past Montmedy, the road left the river valley to drive straight across fields. They rode in silence as the moon rose higher. Then, after an hour, the river joined them again, it and its valley both broad. The night was cold, and mists were rising from the water.

"What will you do in Paris?" Auguste asked.

"Go back to where I was staying."

"Will you see your father? Therese wrote that you are no longer at home."

"I won't see him."

"But you will see Therese?"

"I don't know."

The fog blotted the moon for a moment.

"What will you say to her about me?"

"In Paris, we will resolve these questions," Rudolph said, mimicking Auguste's answer from before. "I should tell her everything."

There was a longer silence as the vapors tugged at them. All sound was killed by the heavy air.

"I will assure you," Auguste said, "that for whatever reason I pursued her in Vienna, all my heart toward her now is pure and selfless."

"Then you should tell her about Sarroche."

"There is no need!" Suddenly, he reined his horse and stopped. "What was that?"

"What?" Rudolph stopped beside him.

"The sound. Wait." They both were still. "There, that."

"I didn't hear anything."

"Stay here."

"Auguste—"

But Auguste was gone, into the fog. For a few seconds, Rudolph could hear his horse walking over stones and through mud, but then the sound died.

Silent minutes passed, although it was hard to judge the time. Rudolph stayed quiet, but his impatience grew. Finally, he said aloud, "Auguste! Where are you?"

In answer, a bullet tore through the mist a meter from his head. Before he could react, his horse suddenly reared, high on its hind legs.

A second bullet cut the air; in the moment Rudolph heard it, he also felt his horse, in panic and arched high, shudder from the bullet's impact.

The horse screamed. Rudolph fell from the saddle, tumbling, thrown to the ground.

Chapter Ten

WHAT WAS POSSIBLE, WHAT IS CERTAIN

— 1 —

"Where is the emperor?"

It was possible that the month of August could hold no more disasters for France, because, it was nearly September.

"What is he doing?"

But it was not certain. August was not quite over.

All eyes were on the city of Reims, where the emperor was commanding his newly gathered army, soon to march forward and break the Prussian ring around Metz. Then, together, the two armies would end the disgrace of German armies on French soil.

"He is no longer in Reims."

The army of national salvation had marched forward into the fog of war and disappeared.

"Where is he going?" Prince von Metternich asked, confounded by the map on his desk.

"There are several roads to Metz," Baron Harsanyi said.

"Which one would the French emperor take? The latest reports are that the Germans have gone south, to Bar-le-Dux."

"Then he will take the road north, toward Sedan."

"And elude the Germans," the ambassador said.

"Only if they want to be eluded."

"Is there any news about Metz?" Therese asked at the dinner table that night as she did each night.

"The same news," Ferdinand said. "There are 140,000 French in Metz, and 150,000 Prussians around them."

"Is it possible the new army will rescue them?"

"Another 200,000 French trying to slip around another 150,000 Germans. Nothing is certain."

"An extremely interesting situation," Pock said, sitting in the baron's front parlor. "Blind man's bluff, and the blind men are the two largest armies in the world."

"It's all guessing," the baron said. "It all depends who can best guess the other's mind and trap him with the guess."

– 2 –

"They've met," Prince von Metternich said. "There's a dispatch to the empress. A battle at Beaumont. Forward units of the two armies."

"Here," the baron said with his finger on the map. "Fifteen kilometers south of Sedan."

"So the emperor did choose the northern road."

"And the Prussians guessed that he did. The French are in a trap now, between the Belgian border and Prussian army. We'll see if it is possible for them to get out."

"If Auguste did escape Metz . . ." Therese said.

"He couldn't," the baron said. "And he wouldn't leave his fellows."

"But if he did . . . if he was out of Metz, trying to get back to Paris . . . what would he do?"

"A single man in the countryside? If he was lucky, he might get through. But if he were to get caught between the armies, then . . . then only God could save him."

"I like to imagine him escaping and getting back home."

"Then imagine him staying very far from Sedan."

– 3 –

The month of August did finally end, along with all its woes, and September began with word of a new battle, at Sedan, with the emperor himself fighting for the life of France.

All day crowds wandered Paris like leaves in the wind, tossed and caught aimlessly, waiting. Ferdinand bowed to his daughter's pleas to be released from the house, and took her out to see the city. But everything was dull and colorless beneath lead skies, and finally they both escaped the dead tension and returned home.

And once home, they immediately wanted to be out again, just like everyone in Paris who was waiting and waiting and waiting.

A French victory would mean it was possible that the war could still be won; a French defeat would mean it was certain that the war would be lost.

"The war is lost," Pock said, coming in the front door after ten at night with a late-printed newspaper.

"What happened?" Therese was white as she stood from her chair.

"Defeated. The emperor's entire army has been surrendered. Two hundred divisions."

"And the emperor?" Ferdinand hadn't stood.

"Captured with his army."

"Is the war over?" Therese asked.

"It must be," Pock said. "The Prussians have the emperor."

– 4 –

"It's the worst outcome possible," Prince von Metternich said. "There is now no way for the war to end. France can't surrender."

"Who would sign the surrender treaty?" Ferdinand asked.

"That's the point. There's no one. As weakened as he was, the emperor was the only legitimate government leader. Now there's no one with the authority or the stature to negotiate."

"And so, the war will go on?"

"The war will go on, because no one in France can stop it. France will have to keep fighting until a new leader can negotiate the surrender of the country, and who wants to take that role?"

"Who might?"

"There's talk of Adolphe Thiers. He was prime minister twenty years ago before Napoleon, and he's always been opposed to the empire. But what about the Prussians? What will the kaiser and von Bismarck do next? What are their military plans?"

"That is certain," Ferdinand said. "After Sedan, Paris."

"And what will happen when he and his hordes come to Paris?"

"A siege. The city can hold out if it chooses."

"How long?"

"It would either starve, surrender, or be destroyed by Prussian artillery."

"Marshall Bazaine could save Paris. Could he break out of Metz?"

"It isn't possible."

Even as Ferdinand answered, a sudden roar sounded from the courtyard outside. He looked out at the heavy, abrupt downpour. In just seconds the courtyard was filled and the gutters became streams.

Von Metternich joined him. "These rains. They're the only thing keeping the empire alive. As soon as they stop, the mobs will take to the street and the Imperial government will be overthrown."

− 5 −

The next day the torrents continued to fall on Paris. Throughout the morning, Ferdinand stayed close to home, watching the streets. Twice he saw mobs passing: men and women stalking angrily, holding iron bars and butcher-shop knives, soaked in the downpours and marching toward the Assemblee Nationale.

"Therese."

She was asleep, napping on the sofa in the parlor, and the baron waited while she woke.

"Yes, Father?"

"I'm going out."

"Where? What time is it?"

"It is two o'clock in the afternoon. The rain has stopped and I'm going to the embassy, and from there to the Tuileries Palace."

"The Tuileries?"

"Yes. Prince von Metternich has been summoned to the Empress Eugenie. I will accompany him."

"What does she want?"

"Help. The empire will be overthrown tomorrow. The Assemblee is meeting and the mobs are gathering."

"Tomorrow," she repeated.

"If not for the rain, it would have happened today."

Zoltan drove him to the embassy, and the ambassador met him at the gate. "We'll take your carriage," he said. "It would be dangerous to be recognized by the crowds."

And when they reached the palace, the crowds were angry and large. The baron's plain black carriage was ignored, and they managed to get into the palace unnoticed through a side door.

"The emperor has abdicated." Eugenie, the Empress and Regent of France, sat on a bare wooden chair in a spare, small room in a corner of the Tuileries palace. The chamber had been a guardroom in centuries past, guards would have been very welcome at the present, but there were none. "My husband sent the telegram this morning. No one else knows yet."

"They will know very soon, Madame," Richard said. "You must leave Paris immediately, before the news gets out. Where is your son?"

"He is the new emperor." She didn't seem to understand her danger. "I will remain regent," She buried her face in her hands. "Oh, how can I? The burden is terrible."

"Madame." Prince von Metternich spoke as gently as he could. "Do not allow your son to accept the title."

"Abandon the empire? No. He must accept it."

"The empire is over. You must leave Paris."

"Flee?" She could hardly speak.

"As quickly as you can."

"Tomorrow . . . I'll consider it tomorrow."

"Flee now."

"I'll send Rosa to pack some things." Her gaze had been on the floor the whole time, but now she lifted her head. "What was that?"

They all heard the dull, snarling roar. "It is the crowds, Madame. Where is your son?" von Metternich asked.

For her answer, Eugenie stood and opened a small closet, or even just a cupboard, built into the woodwork. Inside, the small prince crouched, shivering, blinking in the sudden light. "Come, dearest," she said, and the boy, looking much younger then fourteen, crawled out into the room. He seemed even tinier than when Ferdinand had seen him at Saarbrucken, or at the parade leaving Paris with his father only a month before.

"There is no time to pack," von Metternich said. "This way."

He led them to a low, narrow corridor; he seemed to know the palace as well as the empress. The empress still seemed dazed. At the end of the corridor was a small door.

Only the young prince Napoleon didn't have to lean down to get through the doorway, and they found themselves in a wood-paneled office. Von Metternich closed the door behind them, and it blended in to the wall almost invisibly. "We're in the Louvre now," he said. "I believe if we can reach the far end, we'll be safe from the mobs."

They walked and ran through the museum gallery for minutes, parallel to the Rue de Rivoli, which they could see occasionally outside the windows. At first it had been full of people, but eventually they were beyond the edge of the mob. They kept going, past artifacts of Egypt, Greece and Rome, past dozens of memorials to ancient fallen empires and statues of long dead emperors and kings.

At the far end of the Louvre, through another side door, they came back out onto the nearly empty Rue de Rivoli. Far in the distance they could see the mob surrounding the Tuileries; but so far, they themselves were unseen.

Almost miraculously, a cab was standing just meters away. "I'll come with you out of the city," von Metternich said to the empress.

"My maids . . ."

"They can join you in England."

"England!" The word seemed to finally bring home to her the enormity of her situation. "I'm fleeing to England?"

"Of course, Madame. That is where all Bonapartes go when they flee France."

"Go west," Ferdinand said to Zoltan as he slipped into the carriage. The streets were still filled, but less than they had been. "We won't be able to cross the bridges here."

"The Pont de l'Alma?"

"Yes, make for that."

Halfway to the bridge, they were brought to a stop. A government building stood twenty meters ahead of them, imposing enough, but only some minor, anonymous bureau. But it was a target, and fifty or more men and women were trying to force open the front door. Some official above, unwisely, threw a heavy box out a window in very ineffective defense of his office.

The reaction was swift, angry, and violent. The door was torn off the wall and the mob went pouring in.

"This is happening all over Paris," Ferdinand said. "Everything to do with the Imperial government is being sacked. Get around them if you can, Zoltan. Just find a way home."

They did reach the Rue Duroc, and home, safely. Zoltan left Ferdinand at the front door. As the baron unlocked the door, watching the carriage turn the corner at the end of the street on its way to the stables in the alley beyond, he heard a quiet voice.

"Monsieur Baron."

The whisper came from directly behind him. He spun in surprise.

"Monsieur Sarroche," he said. The man had appeared as if from nowhere.

"I must have a word with you." Sarroche's manner was the opposite of his usual bluntness.

"Of course. Please come inside."

He opened his door, and Sarroche walked slowly and unsteadily up the front steps. As he waited, Ferdinand noticed a shadow in an alcove of the house next door, where a man might have waited without being too easily seen.

Inside, Sarroche stood paused in the hall. His breath was hurried and irregular. "I find myself in a difficult position."

"Because of the change in government?"

"Not that. I will quickly establish my position with the new government. I must make a request."

"Of the Austrian Embassy?"

"Of you. You, personally." He leaned closer. "Please."

The Frenchman removed his coat, gingerly, and showed that the sleeve of his shirt underneath was stained red.

"You're wounded. What happened to you?"

"I will not discuss it here." He staggered and the baron caught him. "It is not that I refuse. It is that I am not able."

"Please be seated."

The request was a polite formality, as Sarroche was obviously unable to stand much longer. His face was white and his eyes not quite focused.

"Thank you."

Ferdinand supported him into the parlor and helped him to a chair. Then he left him and went back into the kitchen.

"Zoltan!" When he had come, Ferdinand instructed him. "There is a man in the parlor who's been injured. He has several wounds, and his arm may be fractured."

Zoltan needed no other information. He returned in less than a minute with a black satchel and followed his master into the parlor.

At Sarroche's side, he probed with his fingers, feeling the length of the arm bones. Sarroche grimaced as Ferdinand filled a large glass with brandy.

"How is it?" Ferdinand asked Zoltan in Hungarian while handing the glass to Sarroche.

"Maybe it's broken, but not bad. The bone is still in place." With a knife he cut the sleeve from shoulder to cuff, leaving its red-stained tatters hanging loose. "These are injuries by a street mob. This is from the edge of a shovel or a pike."

"What is he saying?" Sarroche asked. The brandy was reviving him.

"He says it might be broken," Ferdinand answered. "Tell me what happened."

"An accident." Sarroche's speech jerked from the pain. "Nothing else."

"Then why did you come to me?" Ferdinand didn't wait for Sarroche to fabricate an answer. "Zoltan will do as well as a hospital. He's very skilled." He watched as Zoltan scrubbed the blood from Sarroche's arm; the Frenchman shuddered in pain. "He's just not gentle."

"Then you will enjoy this opportunity . . ." Sarroche had to pause a moment as Zoltan moved the arm. "This opportunity to see me in pain."

"I do not find it enjoyable. Only satisfying."

Sarroche's arm was thin and white, contrasting with the dry brown blood that Zoltan had now mostly cleaned, and with the fresher red blood that still oozed from the several wounds, and also with the blue and dun bruises growing beneath the skin from elbow to shoulder.

Ferdinand said again, "Why did you come to me?" And again he didn't wait. "Because there is no one French that you trust."

Sarroche had to pause to swallow, to collect his thoughts. "I do not trust you, either."

"But you know I won't hand you over to the mobs attacking the Bureau of Armaments and all the other government ministries."

"The mobs will be dealt with."

"Yes," Ferdinand said. "They always are. The army will just need more ammunition. Do you have sufficient stockpiles?"

Sarroche reacted to the sarcasm. "Do not trouble yourself, Monsieur Baron. It will only require time for a new government to be formed. This rising will be put down." The effort of the long answer had exhausted him, and he closed his eyes.

"Will you need a safe place to stay until then?" Ferdinand asked.

Sarroche came back to awareness. "You are inviting me to stay here? I will not accept." Despite his refusal, he did look around the room, as if considering the offer. His eyes came to unsteady rest on the portrait above the fireplace. "And this is your wife?"

Zoltan had completed cleaning the wounds and began bandaging them. As he tightened a knot, Sarroche shuddered.

"Yes," Ferdinand said, answering Sarroche's question. "Many years ago."

Zoltan tugged again on another bandage, and Sarroche said angrily, "He should learn gentleness!"

"I'll tell him." Then, in Hungarian, he said, *"Be more painful. Hurt him."* Zoltan complied.

"Imbecile!" Sarroche yelped. "What is he doing?"

"He isn't harming you," Ferdinand said. "The bone is broken. It will be painful until it heals." He offered Sarroche another half glass of brandy.

"It was my mistake to come here."

"Anyone else would cause you as much pain." He paused. "Did you ever meet my wife?"

"Meet her? I never have. How would I have met her?" Sarroche's anger had changed from its usual arrogant haughtiness to a hotter, less manageable type.

"I was very fortunate to have married her," Ferdinand said. He waited while Zoltan tied another knot in the bandage. "She was very wealthy. And once we were married, I had control of it all. You were very mistaken to approach her."

"Your control is not so complete!" Between the brandy and Zoltan's incessant wrenching, Sarroche had finally lost his temper. "Do you think she was so weak as to yield to you? No, she was not! She was fully aware of your callous attitude and was very willing to work against you!"

"She was not."

"But she was! She knew she had been cruelly betrayed! What had been possible in your marriage to her, what she had hoped for, became only certain disillusionment."

"You're foolishly mistaken," Ferdinand said.

"I am not! I have it on good authority! It is certain—" And then he stopped, red-faced and furious. He pushed Zoltan aside and stood, unsteadily but with determination, and stumbled from the room.

Ferdinand and Zoltan stayed where they were and watched his exit.

"Did you understand what he said?"

"No," Zoltan said.

"Someone has been lying to him."

"Paris is no longer a safe place," Pock said, sitting in the chair that Sarroche had occupied earlier in the afternoon.

"It's safe enough for me."

"The police are only barely keeping control, and now the Prussians have an open road right to it. You should consider sending Therese away."

"I am considering it. Pauline von Metternich is in England."

"Of course. She would be just the one to watch out for Therese." Pock opened a newspaper that he'd brought with him. "When the emperor surrenders, he does it magnificently. Not only does he end a dynasty and evaporate an entire government, but he also takes a hundred thousand French soldiers with him."

"What will the Prussians do with them?"

Pock frowned as he continued to read the newspaper. "It's a problem for them. Even the Prussians, who plan for everything, didn't foresee this. There is a loop of the Meuse near Sedan and this says the French army will be kept there. It's known locally as the Iges Peninsula, for a village nearby. They'll transport the prisoners to Prussia when they've built barracks for them."

"At least the French have their own supplies."

"Surely the Prussians will let them keep their supply train."

"A hundred forty thousand men in Metz and a hundred thousand in Sedan," Ferdinand said.

"I know what you're thinking."

"Yes, that is what I'm thinking."

"Two hundred and forty thousand men locked up one way or another. Surely one of them could be Rudolph."

"It would explain why he hasn't come back. And he would be safe."

"He would be safe," Pock agreed.

"Unless . . ." But Ferdinand couldn't finish the thought.

Far past midnight there seemed to be no chance of sleep. Baron Harsanyi got out of his bed, put on his robe, and looked out into the hall. It was as empty and dark as the street outside. He opened the door next to his own, and looked into Rudolph's room.

It hadn't been touched since his son had left. He stood for minutes looking, with only starlight to see by.

"Only God could bring you back," he said aloud, quietly.

He listened for an answer, waiting as more silent minutes passed, and finally he heard a horse in the street, far off but coming fast, then louder, and stopping somewhere close. Then, a sudden pounding on the locked front door. He ran out into hall before the first volley was over and the second was sounding as he rushed down the stairs, with Therese behind him and Zoltan and Maria coming from their rooms.

He threw the door open onto the night. Zoltan's candle from the far end of the hall flickered on the black rectangle like lightning tethered and led forward, growing but leaping and uncertain. In the open door it illuminated a man in whites and grays and shadows, his beard ashen then silver then gold as the light grew.

"Auguste!" Therese cried.

Behind him his horse stamped and whinnied.

"Come in," the baron said. For a moment the vision beyond the door didn't respond, and he took hold of Auguste's arm and pulled him through the door. Zoltan took the reins from his stiff hands still holding them.

"You came back," Therese said as Auguste slumped into a chair. But Baron Ferdinand shook him.

"You've come from Metz?"

"Yes. From Metz." He still didn't seem to realize his journey was over. "Three . . . four . . ." He shook his head. "I have lost count of the days that have passed since we began."

"We?" Baron Ferdinand said, and Therese went pale.

"Yes, we. Rudolph and I."

"Rudolph!" Both Ferdinand and his daughter said it simultaneously.

Auguste saw the surprise in his eyes, and that seemed to break him from his stupor.

Ferdinand said, "Was he with you in Metz?"

"Yes . . . that was where we met." Auguste's answer was hesitant. Therese seemed panicked still from the shock of Auguste's appearance.

"So he did join the army." The baron sighed. "But he was alive." And then, urgently, "Where is he now?"

"I don't know."

"You separated?"

"Yes."

"Then he will be here soon," Ferdinand said.

"I don't know." Auguste blinked, heavily weary. "Yes, perhaps."

"Bring him to the kitchen," Therese said, and she and Maria took over.

"No," Auguste said. "Just sleep."

"He can sleep in Rudolph's room," the baron said.

– 6 –

The following morning, Ferdinand was awake early and waiting. Therese joined him at the breakfast table.

"Have you slept at all?" she asked.

"I was hoping that Rudolph would also arrive in the night," he said. "At least we know now where he's been. And that he was well."

They returned to silence and waited.

They didn't have to wait long. Despite his exhaustion the night before, Auguste's tread descending the stairs was steady and quick. In the doorway he paused and bowed to his host.

Ferdinand stood as Therese and Auguste embraced.

"And now, Captain," Ferdinand said as they sat and Maria served them, "I hope you are recovered enough to tell us of your journey."

"Yes, sir," he answered. "And I am anxious to do so. For it was arduous and long and not without danger."

"Begin with Rudolph. He was with you in Metz?"

"That was where I saw him." Auguste paused, apparently sorting his memory. "He came to me at night and said he was planning to break through the Prussian lines and escape the city."

"Only then? That was the first you saw him."

"Yes. I had not even known he was in the city."

Ferdinand tried to understand. "How did he find you? And why? Had he fought in any of the battles?"

Auguste sighed. "I am sorry, but I cannot answer your questions fully. It was indeed the first I saw of him since we parted in this house months ago. And as you will hear, there was not opportunity to exchange our histories in the few hours we were together."

"Then please continue."

"Yes, sir. He came to me in the night and called me from my comrades at the fireside. He said he was escaping from Metz and beseeched me to accompany him. I at first refused; it would be desertion."

"Was he deserting?" Ferdinand frowned. "Was he in uniform?"

Auguste paused again. "He was not in uniform."

"Was he enlisted in the French army? Wasn't that why he was in Metz?"

"That is the great misfortune in our separation, that I was not able to ask these questions. That he was not in uniform was in no way astonishing, as in the city of Metz any manner of clothing and supplies were available. And for his plan to leave the city, a military uniform would not be advantageous."

"How did he convince you to go with him?" Therese asked.

"He begged for my help in crossing the enemy lines. And so I told him that I would help him at least that far. I took leave of my commander and told him that I would return soon. But alas, the vicissitudes of war prevented me. We were through the lines before I understood, and then it became impossible to pass through in reverse. I resolved to at least proceed to the emperor's army, to render my services and honor there, in expectation of participating in the ultimate relief of my comrades in Metz."

"And at that moment, that army was surrendering," Baron Ferdinand said. "But what happened to Rudolph?"

"Yes. We were together for barely one day of secretive travel, with no occasion for discussion. If we had known it would be our only chance, we would have availed ourselves of every moment. But as we headed north and west, we came upon the evidences of the passage of the enemy armies. But we were not alert enough, and we were suddenly attacked."

"Just the two of you?"

"It was dark and in deep fog, and as I investigated a noise, we were separated. In the black I could not find him, despite my calls and seeking. But I did find a patrol of Prussian Uhlans and narrowly escaped them, and only by riding hard and fast for some distance. And then there was little hope of rendezvous. So I made my only choice and returned to Paris with all speed."

"Could he have been captured by the Prussians?" Ferdinand asked.

"It is possible. But he could have very possibly eluded them. I have every hope that he will soon join us."

"Where was this?"

"Montmedy. North of Verdun, near Sedan."

"A very bad place to be." All three of them turned to the door. Pock stood there, frowning and listening carefully.

"Pock. You remember Captain de l'Imperator," Ferdinand said.

"Quite well," Pock said. "Your appearance at this moment, sir, is astounding."

"I myself am astounded most of all."

"And Monsieur Pock is as concerned for Rudolph's safety as much as I."

"Even more concerned," Pock said. "You were separated near Sedan?"

"Yes, sir."

"Have you seen the newspapers this morning? I collected a few on my way over. The Prussians are in control of the whole region, and they're collecting every scrap of the French army they can. Anyone wandering there is being captured or shot."

"I was not!" Auguste said.

"Nearly anyone. The reports are terrible."

"But Rudolph isn't French!" Therese said.

"They might not make much distinction," Pock said. "And if he has been part of the French army, he is French. Whoever sent him to Sedan may possibly have sent him to his death. Oh—I'm sorry, I shouldn't have said such a thing."

"It does not matter what is said," Auguste said. "It only matters what has actually happened. And that, we do not know."

"But is there anything else you can tell us?" Ferdinand asked. "You're the only one of us to have seen Rudolph in two months."

"I know it seems that I should be able to. But in truth, I cannot."

"You may remember some other details when you've rested. And you're welcome to stay here as long as you wish."

"Thank you, sir. I had been living with my aunt, but even before the war began, she was planning to leave the city. I fear that her house is closed and empty."

"You'll stay here," Therese said.

– 7 –

Auguste was not the only person on the road to Paris.

With the fall of Sedan, and of the army, and of the empire, all eyes were turned toward the French capital. With no French army left to defeat, and virtually no French governments left to negotiate with, the city was both Prussia's greatest remaining military and political objective. Besides, Prussia was Prussia, and Paris was Paris, and there was no other possibility except that they would meet.

For the next few days, Ferdinand toured the city and the villages, inspecting the city of light for its military capabilities.

Everywhere he went there was some sign that people knew what was coming. The walls were being repaired, the Gardes Mobiles were drilling on the fields outside the walls, and the city's suddenly roused militia drilled in the streets and parks in the city itself.

In the Bois de Boulogne forest on the west side of the city, he saw vast herds of cattle and butchering pens, for when they'd be needed. Whenever he went in or out of the city walls, the gates were clogged with carts bringing in supplies of every kind: food, clothing, coal, candles, bricks, books, pillows, furniture, medicines; both necessities and luxuries.

As the days passed, the flow changed. Fewer carts were coming in, and more began to leave.

And most of all he, and everyone in Paris, was watching the ring of gray, grim fortresses.

From outside the north and west, at first, the reports had been very confused. But as the situation became clear, the progress of the Prussian army was measured by the cities that fell to it. Laon, Reims, and Chalons in the north, and Chatillon in the south, were each occupied in the ten days after the emperor's surrender.

Everyone in grim and anxious Paris was infected by the uncertain fear. Parisians were confronted with the choice: to stay or leave. All motion in the streets became fast and frantic.

"How long will the city hold out?" Prince von Metternich asked.

"If they choose to, at least two months."

"The new government is officially moving to Bordeaux."

"And the embassy?"

"We'll move when they do. They haven't set a date yet. Surely they'll decide before the Prussians have actually besieged Paris." He studied the baron with an odd scrutiny. "And your family?"

"I've decided to send Therese back to Vienna."

"Pauline is in London, but she'll travel to Vienna in a few weeks. And your son?"

"I still have no plan."

"Then I'll expect to see him with you in Bordeaux. Have you had communication with any French officials since you returned to Paris?"

"No. None that was official."

"Your name has been mentioned. But perhaps nothing will come of it."

– 8 –

"You'll have to go through Italy," Ferdinand said. He was sitting in his parlor, facing Therese.

"Switzerland is more direct," Auguste said, standing behind her.

"Dijon is about to fall. Lyon to Turin is the only route."

"Then we will go through Italy. Therese?" Auguste's voice was calm speaking to her. "We will see the splendors of Milan and Venice."

"Will you be all right, Father?" Her voice was full of worry.

"Of course."

"When will we see you again?"

"When it's safe. It won't be long."

"I don't want to go."

"We will make it a holiday," Auguste said.

"It doesn't seem right. We're leaving Paris behind."

"Everyone else is fleeing. It is necessary for your safety."

Ferdinand nodded. "You must, Therese. And thank you, Captain, for going with her and Maria."

"Of course."

"We'll need to be at the Gare de Lyon by ten o'clock tomorrow morning. I don't know how long the trains will keep running."

"I will be there," Auguste said.

Once again, Ferdinand pushed his way back through the frenzied station. "He's still not here." It was after one o'clock.

"What will we do?" Therese said. She was overwhelmed by the crowd and the three hours of waiting.

"You must be on the train in thirty minutes. If Auguste isn't here, you'll have to leave without him."

"I can't leave without him!"

"She won't." Auguste had appeared. "I am here." He put on his most reassuring manner. "My most extreme apologies. The streets of Paris are very difficult to navigate today."

"I have your tickets," Ferdinand said. "The train is at the platform."

"Then let us take our places," Auguste said.

The Gare de Lyon was also difficult to navigate. Together, Zoltan, Auguste, and Ferdinand were able to get themselves, the luggage, Therese, and Maria across the wide room, and then the endless length of the platform to their car.

"In Lyon you can get first class," Ferdinand said. "But second class is all that was left."

"It will be better than walking!" Auguste measured the train's small door and the large crowd trying to get into it. A conductor was trying to allow only passengers with tickets to board.

"Send me word from each stop," Ferdinand said. "I want to know that you're safe."

"When will you leave for Bordeaux?" Auguste asked.

"Within three days. Send telegrams to the Austrian Embassy there. I'll get them."

"Oh, Father." Therese buried her face in his coat. "I don't want to go."

"I don't want you to, either. Auguste will take care of you."

"Home?" Zoltan asked, flipping the reins. The horse started forward.

"No. We'll stop and get Pock. I think I'll want company this evening after saying good-bye." They rode in silence. "Now I'm separated from both my children."

"You were before, at the front."

"But I knew I'd be home. Now I don't know when I'll see either of them again. I want there to be a God, Zoltan. It's so terrible a world they're both living in, and I haven't done well protecting them in it. They need someone better."

"There is something empty looking about it, isn't there?" Pock said as Zoltan brought the carriage to a stop on the Rue Duroc in front of the house.

"It always seemed empty to me."

It was the first either of them had said anything on the ride from the Quartier Latin. Even after picking up his guest to relieve his loneliness, Ferdinand had been lost in thought. Mirroring his silence, Pock had also been subdued.

"We'll make for a rousing afternoon and evening, then. I know you must have food, even if you don't have Maria to cook it."

"Yes, there's plenty. It would go to waste if we don't eat it before I leave."

"Then I'll be the lonely one," Pock said. "Go ahead."

Ferdinand opened the front door and looked into the front hall. He stopped in the doorway, with Pock looking over his shoulder.

"Something wrong?"

"Something seems out of place," Ferdinand said. "The carpet."

The corner of the carpet in the parlor, which was all that could be seen through the door into that room, was at an angle to the wall. He stepped forward to see, and stopped again. Besides more of the carpet, he could also see a hand, open, lying on it.

He took another step and heard Pock's gasp. In the parlor, sprawled on the floor, lay the painter Pierre Beaubien. His head, which was flattened, and the carpet were covered with blood. The heavy stone of cinnabar was on the floor beside him.

Chapter Eleven

EAST INTO
THE SUNRISE

– 1 –

As bookends were identical but exactly opposite, the departure of Therese Harsanyi from Paris mirrored her arrival seven months before. She left to the south, from the Gare de Lyon. She left unnoticed by the crowds. She left with her Auguste at her side, she left her father behind, and she left without her brother entirely. And she left as no unique heroine in victory, but as one of many desperates fleeing defeat.

The steam and smoke cleared; the train was finally beyond the city walls, beyond Charenton, across the Marne. It was beyond Paris. The car was overfull and there was an urgency, even a panic, in the engine's hurry toward the south.

For the first hour they traveled in silence. Then, as the fear of Paris fell behind and the promise of Orleans and the south rose ahead, the passengers began to talk in quiet tones, and the farther they steamed forward, the greater was the relief that worked into their conversation.

Therese was nearly the last to speak. Auguste was pushed close beside her in the crowded compartment, and Maria had a small part of the seat opposite.

"Tell me again about your escape," she said. "Tell me everything about Rudolph. Father isn't here. You can tell the truth."

"Yes, of course," Auguste said, but he was silent until Therese prompted him.

"How did he come to you?"

"Just as I said. I was at the campfire that night. He called my name from the dark."

"Did he say how he found you?"

"He used your father's safe conduct pass to get into Metz. And from there, it would not be difficult as he knew my regiment."

"What did he say?"

"Only that you had sent him to bring me out. In every other detail, the story is as I told your father. There was truly no opportunity for any other discussion."

"You told Father that you didn't plan to leave. You were only going to help him through the enemy lines and then return to your camp. But you really didn't mean to return, did you? You meant to come back to Paris the whole time."

Auguste paused, weighing the difficulty of his answer. "I . . . I faced a terrible decision, dear Therese. On the one side abandoning my men and duty, but on the other possibly never seeing you again. I believe I meant to return to Metz as I promised, but in my heart perhaps I realized I would not. I knew I must at least help Rudolph to escape from Metz. And then, as I described truthfully to your father, the choice was taken from me."

"Tell me about Rudolph. Everything."

"I fervently wish there were more to tell! But in the hazard of the moments, and the difficulties of our travel through enemy territory, there was no opportunity for conversation. Even most of our travel was at night, so I can hardly describe to you what he looked like."

"What do you think happened to him after you were separated?"

"I thought at first that surely we had only been separated, and that he would also quickly return to Paris. And indeed, that may still be the case."

"Father will be waiting for him as long as he can," Therese said.

"What will we do in Vienna?" The evening was advanced and Lyon was not far. Therese could only stare out the window, even though it was only her own reflection.

"You will return to your house," Auguste said.

"But what will I do there? Maria? Will everything be just like we left it?"

"Of course."

"But without Mother or Rudolph."

"It will be only for a month, perhaps. And you have friends there," Auguste said.

"Yes. And Princess Pauline will be there soon."

— 2 —

The travel itself seemed endless. Past Lyon, the next day took them east to the Italian frontier. Two days after Paris they came to Turin.

In Italy, the war was distant and they stayed a day in the city, waiting for the next train and feeling solid ground beneath their feet and calm in the air. They looked into the cathedral and paid a guide to walk them through a few charming streets.

The train to Milan left the station at dusk. Auguste opened a newspaper and read what they had missed experiencing.

"The new French Republican government has said it will not yield to the Prussians. President Thiers says the war will continue."

"What about Paris?"

"The first Prussian troops have already engaged the northern forts. The city will soon be under attack."

Still another night and day passed as they crossed Italy, through Milan and Verona to Padua.

"Venice," Auguste said to the ticket seller, and they left the train at Mestre and took the slow trolley across the lagoon bridge to the island of canals.

"Does it bother you?" Therese asked as they wandered the narrow walks between palazzi and waters. "To be here, when the army is still in Metz?"

"Does it bother you?" Auguste asked in return. "For in fleeing Paris you have also escaped a siege and left behind your father and the many other people you know?"

"No. But I didn't have a duty to stay."

"My duty was to the emperor, and there is no emperor."

"But your men?"

Auguste shrugged. "Fate removed me, and I can no longer help them."

The next train, early in the morning, was to Trieste on the edge of the Austrian Empire. And here, Therese specified their next destination.

"High Laybach," she said. "And telegraph the station there that I will want a carriage to Idria."

High Laybach was small and ornate in a very rustic fashion. The questionable charm of the buildings was easily surpassed by the setting of high hills to its east and low mountains to its west. The carriage and the driver were a part with the rough and close mood of the village; their horse had been walking these roads for many, many years.

"Where is Idria from here?" Auguste asked.

"A half day."

"But how far?"

"It isn't measured in distance," Therese said. "Only in time."

The distance wasn't hard to judge at their slow pace. A gap in the high terrain to the southwest was their first goal, which they met after two kilometers. Then the driver turned to the northwest into a long valley defile, broad for the first five kilometers and narrower for the next five. They stopped in a tiny hamlet called Godovic for a late lunch of hard, dark bread and a strangely bitter cheese.

"I could be walking faster," Auguste grumbled.

"I don't want to walk," Therese answered.

The driver hadn't uttered a word since the start.

From Godovic the track began a wild twisting upward to 200 meters high on either side, covered with dense forest that brushed against the cart and horse. The coils became tighter, where they could sometimes see dust rising directly beside them from their passage of an earlier section far below.

Then the valley narrowed even more but began to drop. A thin rivulet alongside the path grew from a first trickle into a determined stream and then a torrent as they cut lower into the steep valley sides, now many hundreds of meters in height.

"They call it the Zala," Therese said of the water.

"What does that mean?"

"I never thought of it meaning anything. It just means that stream."

When the stream was full, it and its valley joined a larger river in a deeper valley. The track was almost a road now, and it followed the new river directly to the north. Around the next hill, another stream joined and the hills opened into a meeting of rivers and valleys, creating a bowl no more than two kilometers broad in any direction, but broken to the south and north by the river, and to the west by another wide, swift tributary. The mountainsides were thickly covered with dark evergreens.

"This is Idria," Therese said.

The bowl was filled haphazardly with habitations of man, beast, and spirit; the last denoted by four blunt spires above and in the midst of everything else. The town was prosperous and had a number of larger buildings.

"It is strange to have so large a town in so remote an area."

"These are the largest mines in the Austrian Empire," Therese said.

Auguste stood with his hands behind his back in the center of the square. He turned in full circles, once looking forward, and then again with his head pitched back, following the circle of the mountains.

"Isn't it charming?" Therese asked.

"Yes, but my object is to consider the defenses and military prospect of the geography."

"And what do you notice?" Therese was amused.

"The town is utterly defenseless in itself, as any of the heights command it. A few cannon at any point would be unanswerable. But I see that this has been considered." He pointed westward to the crest closest above, capping the steepest slope. "There." The afternoon sun made the entire ridgeline a dark silhouette. But the silhouette at the summit pricked the sky with three sharp towers. Two were symmetric about the higher third. "That stronghold would be impregnable. Holding that fortress, one would be master of all he could see."

"Mistress." Therese laughed.

"Mistress?"

"That is Mother's castle."

Auguste stared. Then he looked at the elderly horse and wagon.

"I think you'll get to walk now," Therese said, still laughing. "You said you wanted to. I don't think that nag can get all of us up this hill."

A strenuous thirty minutes brought them to the castle gate, although it was hidden for most of the climb and only appeared suddenly at the final bend of the road. As they watched, the gate was opened by an ancient, smiling, desiccated porter, and they stepped into the courtyard where the castle was revealed—a long, whitewashed front, with three rows of windows and three steep round towers crowned with spires. The upper windows were small and deep-set, but in the lowest line they were large and inviting.

The heavy door opened to them, and Therese swept through the hall, showing rooms to Auguste. "The banquet hall. And . . . the library. The grand hall."

The rooms were the same whitewashed stone walls as the exterior, with flagstone floors, rough-carved wooden furnishings, and iron chandeliers. Thick tapestries of hunting scenes hung on the walls. On the main floor, the ceilings were high, and every room had a huge fireplace.

The next floor was more compact. Many of the rooms were storerooms, now unused. The bedrooms were small, each with a single tiny window and the same plain style. Every room, except one.

"This is their room," Therese said.

It was three times the size of any of the others, filling one floor of an entire round tower at the end of the building. The bed and dressers and chairs were also rustic but of a much higher quality. The bed was canopied and thickly covered.

"When did they ever come here?" Auguste asked. "You did not visit in the months I knew you in Vienna."

"We all came when we were children. There were no trains then, so we came by carriage and it took days. Auguste?"

"Yes, my love?"

"Why were you in Vienna all those months?"

He was surprised at her question. "But you know, my love. It is as I always told you. I came just to see the world. I had visited Brussels and Amsterdam, and then I came to Vienna. And as delightful as that city is, I would surely have gone on to other lands had I not met you."

"Why did you meet me?"

He was even further taken aback. "But . . . why could I not have? How could I not have? Was it not fated that we would meet? From the moment I saw you in the Stadtpark, I knew that I had found my greatest purpose."

– 3 –

The sun was bright the next morning, and all the brighter outside after the darkness of the castle. The ride from the gate to the town was much easier than the reverse, and from the center they took a different road, along the river, for a kilometer to the south. The houses were squeezed between the road, the river, and the steep slopes of the valley, and soon they straggled to an end. But instead of forest, the edge of the town was marked by a large building of red brick, the only structure not of the native stone. It was capped by a short smokestack.

"This is the smelter," Therese said. "The mine entrance is just beyond."

"Where are the workers?"

"I don't know. We'll find the foreman—that's his house."

The last house was the largest, and even as they approached, a burly gray-headed man was coming to greet them.

"And where are the workers?" Therese asked, after they had been welcomed.

"There are none."

"None? Why? Where have they gone?"

"I dismissed them. That's what the orders said."

"What orders?"

"From the master."

"Father?"

"In February, after the baroness died," he dipped his head in respect, "the master sent orders. He said no more mining, not until he said otherwise."

Auguste was shocked. "Incredible!"

"What's wrong?" Therese asked.

"That there would be no production!" Auguste said. "With war to begin at any moment and both sides offering great profits to him for cinnabar, that your father would have stopped his production completely! Incredible!"

"How do you know anyone was offering to buy Father's cinnabar?"

"It is obvious that they must have been."

"Rudolph said that Father was talking to people about selling it."

"Perhaps your brother mentioned it to me sometime in the months before the war. Where is the entrance to the mine?"

The foreman took them just a few meters farther on the path. A smaller building, the size of a cottage, was built into the side of the mountain. The foreman unlocked the double doors and opened them to a world of darkness.

"It seems very large!" Auguste said. He had stepped to the brink of the blackness. "How deep does it go?"

"More than a kilometer into the mountain." A light flared behind them. The foreman had lit a lantern. "Come along," Therese said.

Auguste took the light and walked with her into the cave. The foreman followed them with a second lantern. "It is all like this?" Auguste asked, as the tunnel bored wide and straight forward.

"This is the new entrance that Father had them build fifteen years ago. The old entrance is up higher on the mountain, and it's narrow. It followed the lode from the surface. This one cuts through to the middle of it."

The walls were gray stone and hard-packed brown soil, held up by heavy wood bracing, almost like the rooms of the castle. Then abruptly the wide road ended as it intersected a rougher, winding passage.

"This is the old mine," Therese said.

"How old?"

"Hundreds of years. No one knows. The first mines were started centuries ago."

"What did they even know of mercury back then?"

"It was the cinnabar. They made vermillion from it. It's beautiful. You've seen the piece we have in Paris."

"Yes. Does all the cinnabar look the same?"

"I think every piece is different. They're every shade of red, from pink to very dark. Some are crystalline, and some are rough so you can hardly tell them from a plain rock."

"Will we see any in here?"

"All of it along here has been mined long ago. Foreman, how far to the seam?"

"Very far, Fraulein. But the cathedral is close."

"Cathedral?" Auguste asked.

"You'll see," Therese said. "Through here."

She turned into a side tunnel that was even narrower. Auguste had to stoop, and then even Therese was squeezing through tight spaces. But abruptly the tunnel widened into a large room.

The walls seemed to be on fire. The firelight was absorbed in their blackness, but then was yielded back in strange, garish flashes and glistenings.

"The master said to leave this room alone," the foreman said.

Auguste held his lantern close to the stone. It threw back the bright-

ness at him in indefinable colors and pinpoint lights that reacted to the
fire's motion with their own.

"In the sun, it's red," Therese said. "But here it's something else."

"Its darkness had been disturbed," Auguste said. And suddenly the
lanterns flickered in a cold draft. "A wind?" Auguste asked. "Where does
it come from?"

"There are two ventilation shafts," Therese said. "They keep air moving through."

"Would the men stifle?"

"No. They would die from the mercury vapors."

Auguste jerked back from the wall. "The vapors? Is the miasma present here? Is there danger in it now?"

Therese laughed. "No. The vapors are never very strong. It takes
years for it to poison a worker. Father brought doctors here to study the
poisoning, and help the workers, but once the mercury is in their body, it
doesn't ever seem to go away."

"The poisoning takes years?"

"It does in the mines. But I think it can be much faster if the vapors
are heavier."

"It is an evil place here," Auguste said, "with the dark and the poison."

"It's just a mine," Therese answered.

A sharp draft blew out the lantern in Therese's hand.

"Enough!" Auguste said aloud. "Leave us alone."

"There's no one else here," Therese said.

"No. No one. And yet, I am somehow defeated." Auguste took the
foreman's lantern. "Show us the way back," he said. When finally they
came to the intersection with the new, wide tunnel, he stopped. Then,
suddenly, he lifted the lantern to his face, and with a gust from his own
lips he extinguished the light. "I will be master of this cave by his own
darkness."

"Auguste! How will we see?" Therese asked.

"There is only one way to go," he anwered. The black was total. Even
as they stood and their eyes groped for light, there was none.

"Why did you blow out the lantern?"

"The cave battles me with fear and dark. I fight it back with the same
weapons. Follow me now, by the sound of my feet."

Therese listened. She heard Auguste take a step forward, and she took
her own step in his track. The foreman, without a word, followed her.

Now the way was very slow but as they walked, Auguste's tread became firmer and more sure, until he was walking almost at a regular slow pace. Therese held her hands in front of her, but as long as she followed him through the darkness, she never touched anything but air.

"Has anyone ever been lost in here?" he asked.

"Rudolph was once."

"He was allowed in alone?"

"No, but he came anyway."

"Tell me."

They continued through the underground night.

"He sneaked in and hid. Then the men finished their day's work and left. He went exploring and got lost."

"He had a light?"

"He didn't want one. He told me he didn't want to explore the mine. He wanted to explore the dark."

"How was he found?"

"When we didn't find him at dinner, Father sent everyone searching."

"They knew he was in here?"

"No. It was midnight when Father finally sent searchers to the mine."

"And when he was found? He was panicked?"

"He told me he wasn't."

"So he also fought this battle."

They kept along in the dark, until, far ahead, the outline of the door appeared. In the dim light, Therese saw Auguste ahead of her. His arms were stretched out from his sides to their full length, and on either side they touched the two walls.

"And what did he find in the darkness?" Auguste asked as they reached the doors and the billowing sunlight and sweet, fresh air.

"He said he wouldn't tell me," Therese answered.

– 4 –

Two days later, on a beautiful afternoon on the edge between summer and fall, Therese and Auguste arrived at her home in Vienna.

The autumn colors during the journey from Slovenia through the Carinthian Alps had been vibrant, with the mountains cutting clean white across blue skies. And Vienna was so lively and crisp, with the horses in the streets prancing and arching their necks, and the shops filled with bright confections and brighter fashions, and the coffeehouses bustling, and the green lawns of the Belvedere Gardens and the Stadtpark still emerald green even so late in the year, and all the promenading Viennese enjoying them.

The house on the Hegergasse appeared just as it always had, almost denying that the six months in Paris had really been, just as the Viennese urban exuberance strongly refuted that any grand city could be in a vise of fear or danger. Only the newspaper accounts reminded them that Paris was now besieged, that the city of light had been darkened.

Auguste arranged accommodations in a hotel, while Therese and Maria settled into their familiar rooms. Then, there were all the other familiarities of Vienna: their cafés and shops and friends. Therese looked toward her future in Vienna, whether it would be weeks or months or forever, but saw only her past.

The second morning after her arrival there was nothing left to unpack. When even her breakfast was over, and Auguste was at her side in the morning room, she said, "It's Mother. It isn't at all the same without her. I don't know if I miss her or Rudolph more. Both of them. And now I miss Father, too."

"By this lack, Vienna is greatly diminished," Auguste said. "There is a melancholy for you that all the joys of this city do not cover."

"Come with me upstairs," she said. "I want to look in her bedroom."

The room was just as it had always been. The bed and furniture, pure white and gold, were newly dusted. The cover of the bed even looked as if it had just been laundered. The light was cool and dim, with just the one bright streak between the curtains, falling across the bed. And the bed was empty.

"I wish I'd known her more," Therese said. "I've changed so much this last year. I feel I could know her better now."

"Only by her departure could you have changed as you did," Auguste said.

"This room makes me remember her so vividly."

"Have you opened the drawers? The closets? What has become of her belongings?"

"They're still here." Therese opened the wardrobe, and the thick line of colors and patterns brought her to tears. "I know every one of these."

"Would you wear them yourself?"

"Oh, I don't know! They'd fit. Some of them are out of fashion." She touched a sleeve hanging limply, white and pink. "I couldn't."

"And her jewels?"

"They must still be at the bank. Father took them for safekeeping." She opened the middle drawer of the small armoire. "It's empty. She didn't wear much jewelry." But then Therese noticed the drawer wasn't empty. A white card rested nearly hidden in the back of the padding. Auguste saw her pick it up and read the words with her.

It was not handwritten, but expensively engraved. It said, *May our love always burn as bright.*

"Who is it from?" she said.

"Who could it be from?"

"I don't know! Auguste, who could have sent Mother such a card?"

"Your father, assuredly."

"He wouldn't . . . not a card like this. I don't think he would have . . . I don't know! But what if it wasn't Father?"

"There must be some other explanation. Perhaps it was not sent to her. She obtained it in some other manner."

"That couldn't be." She looked at the card more carefully, but there was no other sign. "Who could have sent it to her?"

There was no answer to the question, and finally she returned it to its place, and they left the room.

Chapter Twelve

ALL WHO THIRST, COME

– 1 –

Rudolph hit the ground, hard. More than seeing, he felt a sharp weight falling toward him and rolled wildly as his horse's front hooves struck where his head had been an instant before.

Another bullet broke the air, and the horse screamed and fell. The ground shook from it and then it was all still.

Rudolph was alone.

For just a few seconds. Then he heard other horses, and men calling, and two shadowy giants were suddenly above him. He heard the horse's excited whinnies and then a voice, in German.

"There he is."

One of the shadows moved and Rudolph, again by feel more than sight, knew a rifle was aimed at him.

"No!" he said, rolling again. The rifle cracked. A soft thump sounded in the dirt just beside him. "No! Don't shoot! I'm not French!"

"Halt." This was the other horseman, speaking both to his fellow and to Rudolph. "Who are you?"

"I am Rudolph Harsanyi, I'm an Austrian—"

"Liar." The rifle was raised again.

"No! Please!"

Something struck him on the forehead, but very lightly, then again, then more. One of the Germans cursed. "More rain."

"I am Austrian." Rudolph struggled to master the hysteria in his voice. "I'm—I'm a diplomat."

He was answered by coarse laughter. "Oh, a joke?"

"No, it's true. My father is in Paris. He's at the Austrian Embassy—"

"Stop your jokes, boy." The men's voices were deep and harsh; they were both twice his age at least, and his own voice did sound like a child. "Take him. Where's your rifle?"

"I don't have a rifle," Rudolph said.

"Already tossed it, hey? Like them all. Take him to Sedan. I'm done with riding in the rain."

Rudolph managed a half run for the first kilometer. His shock and panic wore off in the first few minutes, and he quickly knew his shoulder was hurt from where he'd hit the ground. The Uhlans on their horses walked beside and behind him, pushing him faster. The rain slackened but was still falling.

Just as they came to a crossroad, he tripped headlong, driving his face into the muddy road.

"Shoot him."

"No. He's a prisoner."

Rudolph struggled back to his feet.

"I'm not French. I'm not in the army. I'm Austrian."

"Liar, they all say something. Get moving."

While they were paused, though, the pattering of the rain had been joined by the sound of more horses, and more feet. A whole troop of Prussian scout cavalry were coming up another of the roads, and as they came closer, Rudolph saw dozens of other prisoners.

Most were French soldiers in uniform, and some even with their packs. But at least two were not soldiers at all. One was a farmhand and the other a thick-bellied bald shopkeeper, still with his white apron on, wheezing and puffing from the exertion.

Rudolph was folded into the herd, and his captors joined the herders. The larger group hardly paused, but at least their pace was slower than Rudolph's had been alone.

Rudolph was ignored by the other captives. They were from different regiments, and he listened as they were telling their stories.

He heard how they had been captured hiding or running. The ones running too fast or who made trouble had been shot.

He heard more, as they compared how they'd fought, and Rudolph began to realize there had been a battle. Soon he knew how huge a battle, and how terrible. And these men who'd escaped were being brought back, on their way to Sedan. The name was said over and over. That was where the battle had been, and the French army had surrendered, and it was now being imprisoned.

It had been a vast event, and now he was part of it.

The rain ended, but the fog replaced it, just as wet and cold. Rudolph was lost in fog as his shoulder burned and his body shivered in the damp chill. The horses and the men kept moving and moving, and the night went on.

After some time, Rudolph realized he could see. The night was coming to an end. He also saw buildings, then more streets, filled with Prussian soldiers.

They passed a café. Its tables were overturned in the street, and a heap of broken wine bottles was piled in the doorway. The name of the café was *Le Vin de Sedan*, the Wine of Sedan.

A sudden crash sounded above the café's awning. He looked up to see a second-story window shattering, then a rifle butt, then a head with a Prussian kepi hat.

Across the street, a trio of soldiers was kicking in a door.

Then, in the next block, another German bent over, looking into a sewer hole in the curb.

"Come out," the soldier said.

Then he pointed his rifle into the hole and pulled the trigger. No one paid attention to the muffled crack. The soldier looked back into the sewer and, satisfied, walked away.

And everywhere, converging into the main road, were French prisoners and their captors, all flowing through the city, heading west. Some of them were in uniform; some were as haphazard as he was. Many were wounded, but all had the same dead look and hopeless step.

They crossed a bridge, and Rudolph saw the Meuse beneath him, a source of fog and mist that the rising sun hadn't burned away. The road turned slowly to follow the river, and the sullen parade followed the road out of the city.

A kilometer or two past the river, in a village of farms within sight of the towers of Sedan, the crowds stopped. Ahead, a barricade stood across the road. The prisoners moved forward slowly, stopping and starting. Rudolph saw that a canal cut through the fields and the barricade stood where the road crossed over it.

As he got closer, he saw what was being done. At the barricade the men were being searched; beside the road was a great pile of weapons and gear. No guards went beyond the barricade, but for the whole length of the canal Germans stood with rifles and even artillery. The canal marked the boundary of a prison camp.

Rough hands were laid on him, and he jerked uncontrollably from sudden pain in his shoulder. He hardly saw the men who searched him. Then he was thrown forward to the bridge over the canal.

"Wait," he said, stopping in the road. "I'm not French."

No one even answered. Five rifles were directed at him, straight at his heart. He stumbled quickly forward to get away from them.

In front of him was a broad, open pasture. To his right, fifty meters distant, the canal joined the Meuse, which flowed straight north.

The field was filled with men, most of them standing and walking slowly away from the canal, some of them asking where their units were.

The men were finding their regiments and battalions, regrouping into camps. He moved out of the main flow and stood.

Finally, he was still and he felt the full pain in his shoulder again.

Besides the pain was hunger.

He started walking. First he went toward the river. It was fifty meters wide, and across its water, Prussians were posted in groups every twenty meters. He walked north, following a road that stayed close to the bank. Hundreds of men were sitting, standing, walking, sleeping in small groups or alone.

A hill rose up ahead. The road climbed to its top, and from there Rudolph could see the entire camp.

The Meuse flowed straight north for two kilometers or so from the canal, then bent west for a kilometer, then back south again to where the canal rejoined it. The whole formed a kind of peninsula bounded on three sides by the wide loop of the river and on the south by the canal cutting across its base.

The whole was guarded by Prussian troops on the far banks, and none within.

The French were within. There were thousands, tens of thousands, in the two or so square kilometers, not crowded but very full. There were still large areas that were empty, but still more men were being forced in.

And there were thousands of horses. Some were with specific camps and many were roaming free. But nowhere did he see the wagons of provisions the horses would have been pulling.

As he looked, he didn't see anything like a supply depot. He approached a camp close-by, dozens of men and as many tents in ordered rows, and a good campfire. He realized for the first time how cold it was.

He was hardly noticed.

What he saw when he grew close was that there was no pot on the fire; every campfire in Metz had been heating some kind of stew. Here there was none.

Some of the men were sitting by the fire, others wandering or standing, all of them looking despondent and aimless. The words he overheard between them were all about food, and just as he had pieced together the news of the battle, now he understood that the whole supply train for the army had been seized by the Prussians. Food for 100,000 men for a month was in Sedan. Just the horses had been sent into the prison camp, but none of the rations.

But the Prussians were orderly and punctual. Surely they would issue the meals at the correct times.

Or else they would keep them and give none to the prisoners. The men argued angrily over which it would be, but Rudolph walked away. There was a smell of dead horses too close and he wanted to get away from it.

He went back to the hill; it was still mostly empty. Three trees stood near the top, next to five fresh stumps. The three would certainly also be cut soon and join their fellows in the campfires.

Rudolph sat on a stump, and once he was off his feet and not walking, he found himself desperately tired and painfully hungry.

Everything that had been in his saddlebags was gone. All he had was his coat. He felt to see if there was by chance any food or any supplies. There was only one thing in the pockets: a long, flat leather rectangle a few centimeters thick. It was a writing case, and he stared at it dumbly before he recognized it as the abandoned writing case from the field at Chalons.

He opened it and everything inside was still intact. There were two pens, an unbroken bottle of ink, and a dozen sheets of linen paper. There was even a thin wood shingle that unfolded to make a writing surface.

There was nothing else to be done with it but to open the shingle flat, smooth a sheet of paper open onto it, and fit the ink bottle into its slot. He felt the weight of the pens and touched one to the black ink.

Then he held it over the paper and was confronted by its white blankness. It was all by unthinking reflex, and now he waited, unsure what he was meant to write and waiting to be told.

No one told him, and he was still too dazed to let his reason retake command. Instead, he responded to some interior impulse. His hand moved in obedience to it.

Dear Father,

The words surprised him. He studied them for several minutes, waiting to see what would appear next. Then he wrote again, and the script flowed from his fingers in short bursts, each too fast for him to keep up with, followed by pauses that left him confused.

I am a prisoner.

They threatened to kill me.

I've been terrified.

I'm hungry. There is no food.

Then he stopped. He folded the paper and returned it and the pen and ink to the leather case, and put the case back in his coat pocket.

He sat for a while, then stood and started his wandering again.

The day went on. There was rain at times, and deep mud, dead horse stench, and hunger. He walked. He walked the whole perimeter of the river and canal, about six or seven kilometers. He didn't take part in any conversations and was easily ignored.

As night was falling, he chose a group with a fire and moved cautiously toward them. Close enough to feel the heat, he was still unnoticed. But with the heat he also could smell a pot on the fire, simmering something. He could even guess what it was: horsemeat, and potatoes.

He edged closer and was noticed.

The men at the fire, dirty and ragged, didn't speak. One held up a short, thick splint of wood and another a heavy spoon he'd been using in the stew. Their meaning and threat were plain. But Rudolph stood his ground.

The man with the wood swung it at him, and he dodged and made a grab for the pot on the fire. He caught the handle with his fingers but three men had their hands on him and threw him aside.

The pot fell on its side, and the men rushed to set it upright before it spilled, letting go of him. They didn't follow him as he scrambled, and then walked, away. They only shouted at him.

– 2 –

Rudolph found a low, empty place on the side of the hill above the river to sleep.

Once in the night he woke, his mouth full of water and mud as the rain filled the ditch. He crawled to a higher place and immediately slept again.

Later, though, he found himself awake. From the high moon he knew it was three or four in the morning. He picked himself up from the mud and started his wandering again.

He walked past the camp with the horse stew. It was dark and the men were all asleep, mostly on the bare ground, and a few in a single tent. He lifted the pot from the warm embers and carried it far enough away to be safe. It was heavy.

But when he looked in, it was only rainwater. Anything that had been left was washed away. He left the pot there and began a new search, hunting by moonlight among the dead fires and sleeping camps. He found one potato just centimeters from a man's hand, dropped in his sleep. Back by the canal a fire was still live with a lidded pot on the ground next to it. He got very close and almost had his hand on it.

Someone beside the fire sat up, and the fire reflected a long knife.

Rudolph left the pot and ran.

The potato had already been cooked but was cold as the night. Rudolph sat on his hillside, taking slow bites out of it like an apple, watching the sun come up over the river. Amidst tens of thousands of men, he wrote on his paper.

I am alone here.

I am an outsider.

He waited for the next words, which didn't come. He looked at what he had written and supplied his own next words.

I've always been an outsider and I've always been alone.

The pain in his shoulder had returned. He tried sitting, standing, lying to find any position to relieve it. Finally, he started walking again. He followed the river as he had done the day before. The far bank was still patrolled by Prussian soldiers.

He passed a group of French soldiers, who were pushing dead horses into the river. The carcasses were becoming more numerous. Some of the animals had died from malnourishment, not just from the few days in the prison camp but from weeks of campaigning without proper supplies. Others were being killed so they wouldn't eat whatever food was left in the camp.

But the carcasses didn't float far. As he walked downstream, the river's edge on both banks had begun to accumulate piles of them. Soon, Rudolph had to leave the riverbank completely.

But in abandoning its path, he also abandoned any direction to his wandering. He circled the one large farm complex in the northern half of the camp and then followed the road back south toward the bridge over the canal.

It was early afternoon when he came to it. The flow of new prisoners had mostly ended and the guards were idle. Rudolph approached them, slowly, with his hands carefully at his sides.

He tried to argue that he wasn't French, and that he wasn't in this army.

The guard, warming himself at his well-fueled fire, answered by shrugging.

He went back to writing. There were no trees left to sit under, but there were still empty hillsides to sit on.

Auguste is our enemy and he is betraying all of us. He has been paid by the French official Sarroche to turn Therese away from us. I accused him and he admitted it. Then he betrayed me to the Uhlan patrol.

Then he remembered and dug in his shirt pocket, under his coat, and pulled out the folded parchment. He hadn't felt it before when he was trying to find food in his pockets.

To all present, be it commanded . . .

And the grandiose signature, *Gustav, Count von Albensleben-Erxleben.*

He hurried back toward the guard line at the canal. He had hope, for the first time since his capture. The same sentry who'd shrugged him off before was more annoyed to see him again. Rudolph held out the paper and used his most Viennese-accented German to beg to be let out.

The man glanced at the parchment, then looked more incredulously at it, and at Rudolph.

Then he laughed and threw the page onto his fire. It was gone before Rudolph could react.

Later in the afternoon, he saw a disturbance beside the river. He moved closer to see a crowd of maybe 200 French soldiers forming a group. One of them was shouting over the others' heads, inciting them to break out, promising that a few Prussians couldn't hold in thousands of brave Frenchmen.

Many other men were watching from a distance as the speaker, and others, became more passionate in their provocations. Then a single shot from a Prussian sentry across the river killed the leader and the rest dispersed.

I am in a terrible place, he wrote. *Men are dying around me. I don't know what will come next for me.*

Only God can save me.

He crossed out the last line.

Then, after a long silence, *Father, I want you. I need you. Please help me.*

– 3 –

The second day ended. Despite his hunger and pain, or because of them, Rudolph didn't even try to sleep. The spot he'd slept the night before had been occupied by three other very rough men.

Rudolph just walked. In time he lost track of where he was; he felt hot in the cold night. Even at midnight, most of the other prisoners were still awake with fires burning everywhere.

The island was a city of lights.

There were no roads, no buildings, nothing that made a city, but light, everywhere.

But as he walked and walked and the night went on, the lights became lower and fewer as the last wood was used, and the city went dark.

As he had the night before, Rudolph began his hunt. Besides every camp being bare of food, there was less evidence that there had even been any that day. He found one handful of stew, but it cost him a bruised shin as he ran to get away from the alerted camp.

He wasn't the only nighttime hunter. Most camps had set night watches. He had a fever now, too.

He sat to watch a fiery, violent sunrise.

Father, please come and take me out of this place. I want to come back home. Please forgive me.

Rudolph couldn't stop walking now. His shoulder hurt at times, but less when he was moving. Hunger was the stronger driver. His internal heat was growing, and not everything he saw with his eyes was really there.

He sat to write more, but there were no more words.

But as he sat, he noticed a camp not far away. He'd seen it, and all the encampments, many times, but he watched how this one was well organized, and the men had their horses.

There was even a regimental flag stuck in the ground, and he saw the name of the unit.

He walked, unsteadily, toward the closest men.

"Is there . . . do you know . . . do you have an officer named Beaubien?"

"Beaubien?" one said.

"This is the Imperial Guards Cavalry?"

The man nodded and another. "Captain Beaubien, yes. He's somewhere by those tents."

Rudolph hurried toward the tents.

"My cousin? Pierre?" Captain Honore Beaubien was the first French officer Rudolph had met who was clean-shaven. He had only the slightest resemblance to his cousin, and only externally. His eyes windowed an austere and entirely different soul. He was about thirty-five years old, not impressive but very haughty. "This is a bizarre circumstance." He was also wary.

"I met him through Auguste de l'Imperator," Rudolph said.

The wariness changed to disdain. Captain Beaubien stretched himself to his full height, and his eyes became narrow slits. "For what my cousin did to him," he said, "I will have nothing to say to you."

But Rudolph was too desperate to be put off. "He painted my sister's portrait."

"That is nothing to me. What are you doing here, anyway?" It was an attack, not a question.

"I was with Auguste. We were separated and I was brought here."

"Do you ride in the cavalry? Where is your uniform?"

"I'm not in the army. I'm not French. I'm Austrian. I'm just here because the Prussians brought me here and they won't listen to me."

"And why have you sought me out?"

"I saw this was the Imperial Guards. Auguste told me once that he knew you from the Imperial Guards." He had to catch his breath. It was hard to speak after so long a silence. "I need help."

"Help? Even here, in this miserable place, I am beset by my cousin's corruption. What help is it you want? Does he owe you money? That is nothing to me! I will not assist you in any way!"

"He doesn't—"

"Or you owe him? It is more likely. Even less, then, do I have care for your position. If you say he has cheated you, I will not defend his honor or the honor of the family, for we have disowned him."

Rudolph was swept back by the onslaught. "I don't know what you mean."

"And your association with him? Cards? Dice? To utter his name is to stain your own."

"No." Even more than for food, Rudolph was desperate for some answer that wasn't hostile. "I don't know anything about any of that. I just met him because of Auguste and my sister."

"For any acquaintance of my cousin, I hold no regard," Beaubien said. "But for Captain de l'Imperator, I still hold some regard." He frowned, but his expression was not simply anger. "You said you were traveling with him?"

"He was in Metz, and we left together. We were going back to Paris."

"You left Metz? Is the siege ended?"

"No. We escaped. Then we were attacked by a Prussian patrol and I was captured."

But Beaubien was caught on the first sentence. "Escaped? Without his men?"

"Just the two of us."

"He deserted?"

"No." It was getting too hard to continue. "I told him he had orders from Paris. Do you know how Auguste met your cousin?"

"I introduced them, before I knew the depth of my cousin's corruption."

"What happened?"

"He quickly ensnared Captain de l'Imperator in his gambling and soon had him in debt. Greatly in debt. The captain came to me for help, but I had to refuse."

"What did he do?"

"He was forced to leave France. I only was told of his return some months ago, when he requested reinstatement in the Imperial Guards. Again, it was necessary to refuse. Such a scandal cannot be allowed to touch this regiment. But at least his debts must have been paid if he was able to return to France." Beaubien was getting tired of the conversation. "And so you are here. What help do you want? I see no possibility of helping you."

"Neither do I," Rudolph said. "Do you have any food?"

"The provisions we have cannot be given to anyone outside the Guards."

"I'm starving."

"Speak with the Prussians. Explain that you are Austrian. They will let you out."

Rudolph turned and walked away.

I know more about Auguste, he wrote. *He left France to escape his debts. He has made himself Sarroche's agent in exchange for Sarroche paying his debts. He is only pretending to love Therese. He is really trying to get cinnabar ore for the French.*

Then he had to sit still and think, think very carefully.

What were you doing, Father? Is it the only important thing to you, to sell cinnabar and collect the profits?

There was no chance of the letter ever reaching his father, so he kept writing.

Tell me the truth so that I won't hate you.

The smell of the horses was unspeakable, and he saw two more men shot dead by the guards.

– 4 –

Another night passed in a place that was filled with images and terrors and dreams, where the only fires were in his mind. But the morning light brought some return of reason and a new activity. A few camps were being abandoned and prisoners were moving toward the gate at the canal crossing.

Rudolph ran toward the ragged line of men and got close enough to ask questions and hear what they were saying to each other before Prussian guards forced him away; they were the first guards he'd seen actually enter the prison fields.

There were at least fifty of them, and they were herding the French, by unit, out of the encampment. They were being taken to the train station in Sedan to be transported to prison camps in Germany. The French were in good spirits from the news, because they'd been told they'd be in barracks and be fed.

The Prussian guards told Rudolph to get back to his regiment and wait his own turn. He didn't argue with them. Instead, he went to the gate to argue with the guards there.

Those guards were busy with columns of French marching past and didn't want to be bothered. But after one try, Rudolph waited for a pause and prepared to press his case again.

While he waited, he saw another prisoner with the same argument. It was the bald, fat shopkeeper who had arrived in the same net that had caught Rudolph. Rudolph hadn't seen him in the days that had passed, but the man was still breathless and red-faced. He was also angry. Wherever he'd been in the camp, he hadn't learned enough about Prussian guards. Rudolph watched for a few minutes as the man began to abuse the sentries.

Rudolph turned so he wouldn't have to watch, but he still had to hear the rifle.

There is no way out from here.

He watched the procession from as close as he could, and it was endless. Man after man, row after row, hundreds and thousands as the day went on, and there were still many more waiting and watching. The units were announced and the men gathered.

Rudolph tried twice to join a unit, but he was refused, and the second time beaten, but not badly. He only had a bloody lip and a bruise in his side to show for it.

As the sun began to set, the last unit for the day lined up, and it was the Imperial Guards Cavalry. They had their horses and a dispute quickly started over whether they would be allowed to take them. The train apparently had no room for horses.

The disagreement was sharp, and Rudolph began to fear more shootings. But it was the officers' horses that the guards shot and their resolve was broken. There was confusion, though, as the men tried to take their saddlebags and say good-bye to the animals, all in a short time and under growing impatience from the Prussians.

And in a moment, Rudolph saw Honore Beaubien struggling under the weight of his bags.

"I'll carry them," Rudolph said, running to him. "I'll be your *aide-de-camp*. Let me come!"

"Get away!" Beaubien was too angry to give him any civility.

"I'll carry your bags!"

"I said get away, boy!"

There was no use in begging. But in a last, desperate hope, Rudolph pulled the writing case from his coat.

"Take this!"

"What is it?" Despite his annoyance, Beaubien was a little curious.

The polished leather, lustrous in the sunset light, seemed magnetic to him. Rudolph offered it. "Take it."

"You will not bribe me with such a thing." But Beaubien's eyes were still on it.

"There's a letter in it for my father. Send it to your cousin and ask him to give it to my father."

The case was knocked from Rudolph's hand as a rifle butt hit him from behind. He fell and rolled, avoiding another blow from the Prussian guard.

But as he stood, he saw Captain Beaubien pushing the leather case into his bag.

The line marching out the gate was done, the road was empty, and the sky was dark. The fields were still occupied by many men, but certainly fewer than there had been.

For once, the sky was clear and the stars multitudinous, but the air was cold. Rudolph walked to the river edge. The moon was in the middle of its own wandering above him.

It had been too long since he'd eaten for him to even feel hunger. He was only empty and alone and shivering from the cold and from his own heat inside.

Time and the river flowed by. Later, after the moon was gone, he saw that the stars were also blacking out from the east. The clouds were returning, just as they had every day, and always with rain.

Finally, the storm came and Rudolph didn't even move. It seemed to warm him somehow. Then it passed, but the sky stayed dark.

– 5 –

Later, in another rainstorm, he decided to swim the river.

He stepped into the river, which felt like ice. Only two meters from the bank, it was up to his shoulders and he couldn't keep his footing. He was lifted off the riverbed and started floating along, keeping his head down.

He saw many guards, yet he himself wasn't seen. He was becoming numb.

Then he saw campfires on both sides of the river, and he realized he was passing the mouth of the canal. A freezing minute later he was beyond the camp.

He knew he wouldn't survive much longer in the frigid water. He tried to paddle toward the far shore. The current kept him away from it and his arms weren't moving easily.

Then his foot touched the bottom. He was back toward the left shore, but now he was far enough past the canal and guards that he must be free. He caught his shoe on some rocks and pushed, and the water was shallow enough that he could stand.

It had been so easy.

He started walking through the river toward the bank, but at an angle, still moving as far as he could away from the guards and the canal. The air was a different, stinging cold on his soaked shirt and coat than the deep, heat-robbing water, but more painful. His feet, still under the surface, had no feeling at all.

He was just a meter from the shore, in water only to his knees, bowed low, when he heard the grunting laugh. There was still no light, but he could see in the dark.

He could feel, too. There was a rifle on him, only three meters away. He knew it because he had seen it so many times, and had felt it too many times, and now the feeling was knife-sharp, piercing his deadened nerves and skin to where his heart was still alive and could still feel, and the pain there was enormous. Death like the river had flowed by and around him and frozen him and now was overwhelming him, ready to both lift him from the river bottom and pull him down.

He sprang. The trigger was already pulled and the bullet seeking him, but it missed his heart and only found other muscle and bone to tear.

But he was numb and didn't feel anything at all, in any part of him but his heart, which burned. His hands met rough cloth and hardness behind it, and it yielded. There were sounds of scraping rocks and heavy motion; then there were hands on him, but it was so dark.

He fell back with the hands still on him, and his hands holding their sleeves, and then his head was under the river. He didn't even know it except that he was breathing the water. He pulled harder on the arms and felt their weight shift, and a heavy weight fall on him.

He pushed and the weight fell aside, but he didn't let go. He got his head in the air and pulled on the arms again, and he was above and the other was below. And then he pushed again. As hard as he could, he pushed. The water under him was thrashing and for one moment he saw a face, in the dark water, its eyes wide and screaming while its mouth sucked air before Rudolph pushed it down again and water rushed into the open throat. There was a neck under the chin and he forced his knee onto it and pushed harder and harder.

Long after the last struggles, for minutes and forever, with the flow of the water the only motion or sound, Rudolph stayed and held. His heart slowed and cooled. His hands were bitterly numb, but they stung like needles and hornets.

At last, his muscles loosened and let go, and he stood. He walked away from the river without feeling.

He walked through rain and the dark, through night cold and fever heat, and through a searing pain in his side that finally broke through his consciousness with memory of the bullet that had penetrated him. He stumbled and fell.

But he could see the sun and the morning, still distant but coming. He was on a road, just a dirt track, and there was no sign of rivers or horses or men. Ahead lay a farm and an old house.

He reached the door and pounded on it.

It opened. From the dark behind it, a rifle was pointed at him.

He grabbed it, and shoved, and tried to strike at whoever was in the house, but then he fainted.

– 6 –

When he woke, the room was dim and warm, yellow and red firelight. An old woman was sitting beside the fire, and an old man at a table.

"Where am I?" Rudolph said.

In very broken German, the man answered, "In place of safeness."

"But who are you?" Then he was awake enough to change to French. "Who are you?"

"You speak French?" the man asked. He had a long scab on his forehead.

Rudolph was in a bed under warm covers. "Yes. Who are you? What's happened?"

"You are safe."

"Will he eat?" the woman asked.

"Eat?" Rudolph said. "Yes. Yes, please." He started to get up, but he winced in pain and dropped back down.

"I'll bring it to you," the man said.

Rudolph felt his left side, below his ribs. It was bandaged. A wide strap of cloth was wound around his waist and stomach. Then he realized he was in a long nightshirt.

The man carried a bowl over to the bed and held out a spoon. "Take it?"

Slowly, Rudolph brought himself upright, swinging his legs over the side and sitting. He took the bowl and the spoon, and then his first mouthful.

It was hot. He choked it down. Then another spoonful that he blew on to cool.

It was wonderful. Beef and potatoes and a thick stew broth.

He coughed and lost most of what he'd eaten.

"Slowly," the man said.

"What happened to your head?" Rudolph asked. The bowl was empty, and Rudolph pointed the spoon at the man's wound, which looked to be about a week old.

"You happened to my head!" the man said. "You hit me when I opened the door."

"But you had a gun."

"There is no gun here! It was only a broom."

"Oh."

"I was sweeping!"

"I'm sorry."

They were both dressed in farm clothes as old and worn as themselves. The woman had only spoken once, and her voice was deeper than the man's, but also like a slow song, like an old hound.

"Are you Prussian?" she asked.

"No."

"But you speak German. You talked in your sleep."

Rudolph shook his head. "I'm Austrian."

His answer didn't seem to mean anything to them. "You are a soldier?" the man asked.

"No. I'm not. I'm not any part of the war."

"We thought you were a Prussian soldier."

Rudolph paused. "But you're French," he said.

"Yes!" the man said, as if Rudolph were slow to understand. "We're French."

"But . . ." Rudolph was confused. "But why would you care for a Prussian?"

"But why not?"

"The Prussians are your enemies."

The woman answered. "We take care of you because it the good thing."

Rudolph's clothes were under the bed. He looked for a place to put them on, but the one room was the whole house. It was kitchen, bedroom, and parlor in one. He could only get dressed sitting on the bed with the man and woman present.

He put on his pants, which were dry and clean, and then took the nightshirt off over his head. The cloth strap was the width of a hand, wrapped around him to hold a pad over . . . something. He lifted the bandage off his skin.

The wound was still open. It was a small round hole, disturbed by his movements and oozing a little blood and pus. He settled the pad back onto it and pulled his shirt on. The brown stain that covered a fourth of it was light from washing. He could smell the bleach.

Then he looked at the man's forehead wound again.

"How long have I been here?"

The man looked at the woman uncertainly. They both took some time to count.

"Five days," the woman said.

"Five days!" Rudolph was astounded. "Five days?"

"You were very bad," the man said. "You were hot and bleeding too much. I thought you would die. God said you would not!"

"You thought I was Prussian, and you took care of me for five days. You kept me from dying." Then, to be polite, "You and God."

Neither of them seemed to think this was remarkable.

Their names were Jacob and Jeanette. The couple said they were both about seventy years old, though they didn't know for certain, and they had both lived in the house their entire lives.

"But you lived with your family when you were a child?" Rudolph asked Jeanette. "Before you married?"

This was her parents' house. Jacob had been taken in as a farmhand when his parents died. He didn't remember them.

The first night that he was awake after dark, when they were asleep in the far corner on the floor, he tore off the bandage and its cloth belt and felt the wound. It was closed enough to not bleed anymore. He pushed and prodded with his fingers, trying to feel beneath his skin, and deep inside it seemed there was something small and hard.

They fed him for two more days. It didn't take long to regain his strength. He didn't want to leave, but of course he had to.

"I have to get to Paris," Rudolph said.

"What is there?" Jacob asked. Their slow, rhythmic speech sounded like singing.

"Everything. Haven't you ever been there?"

"No, not to Paris!" They might not have believed it was real.

"My family is there."

They pressed all the supplies they could on him: bread, cheese, apples, and dry, tough beef.

"I can't carry it all!" he said, but they were insistent and so he had to take everything. He needed a horse, but theirs had been stolen. He wouldn't have taken it from them anyway.

"God be over you!" he heard Jeanette call, and he turned one last time to give his thanks to them both.

He left in the morning and walked most of the day, resting a few times. He had no money. When the first night came, he slept in a field, under a hedge, wrapped in his coat.

He knew it was more than 250 kilometers from Sedan to Paris, which was at least a week's walk at his slow pace. Forcing himself, he could do it in maybe five days. He didn't have a map, so he'd have to find main roads.

There weren't many people on the road, and he was reluctant to talk to them. Only once the first day did he see anything military: a patrol of Uhlans that he hid from.

The second day he accepted a ride in a farmer's cart, taking cabbages and potatoes to a place called Rethel. They rounded a line of hills and could see the church steeples of the town ahead of them. Before they came to the first houses, though, a column of troops emerged from the hills behind them.

The farmer pulled off the road and they waited.

The troops were South German, mostly Bavarian, and some from Baden and Wurttemberg. After 5,000 men came over 200 supply wagons. It was two hours before they could get back on the road. When they reached the town, it was garrisoned by hundreds of Germans.

Past Rethel, Rudolph was walking again. He had only reached the edge of the Champagne plain, which was endless in front of him. There had been a train station in Rethel, guarded by the occupying troops. He turned off the road to find the tracks.

They were just a few hundred meters south of the road. He walked beside them about a kilometer until he came to a cutting, where the tracks ran straight while the land rose. He found a place high enough and waited.

It wasn't a long wait. He saw the train from a distance, and he knew immediately that he couldn't jump it in daylight. It was a freight train, and every car had a Prussian posted in the open door.

He waited until night, hoping the trains would still run after dark, and they did. They were running slow. It was frightening to jump onto the roof of a car, but it turned out to be easy. Once he'd settled on the roof for a few minutes, he crawled to the end where there was a ladder, and down into the car. There were no guards there.

He rode the train for two slow days, through Reims and dozens of small villages, only stopping for coal and water. When he thought he must be near Paris, he jumped off at the edge of town.

It was a city, which he quickly realized was Troyes. From Reims, the train had been going south, not toward Paris, and he still had 150 kilometers to go.

Now he was impatient. He found a tavern and asked for rides to Paris.

"You don't want that!" a traveler told him. "The whole Prussian army is heading that way."

"But I need to go anyway," he said.

He did find a ride eventually. An old woman with a carriage full of trunks and boxes wanted someone to be her driver, groom, butler, laborer, and guard as she fought her way to her daughter's home in Corbeil-Essones, thirty kilometers south of Paris.

She was going for a visit and no war was going to delay or alter her plans.

The war didn't intrude on their two-day journey. The woman talked constantly, and Rudolph learned everything about her family and upbringing in Dijon, her schooling at a monastery, her husband who had been a banker, her son-in-law who was a government official, and especially her disgust with Paris.

When he left her at her daughter's house in Corbeil-Essones, she opened a trunk and gave him fifty one-franc coins. He thanked her and fled back into the silence of solitary travel. He had one-day's walk left ahead of him.

Even before Corbeil-Essones, the roads had become crowded, and now they were filled with the flight from Paris. Still twenty kilometers out, Rudolph had to leave the pavement and walk through fields and farm lanes while the main road was choked with carts and carriages, drawn by horses and men. Every imaginable person and belonging passed by.

Eight kilometers south of Paris he encountered the first invaders. The Prussians hadn't cut the road yet, but he saw observers in force, a large troop of cavalry in the fields to his right. He was told that the Prussians were already digging in in the north, starting their perimeter.

Late in the day he came to Vitry, just two kilometers from the Paris walls. He'd been forced to the east by the crush of evacuees on the main south road, and in the village he had a clear view of the Seine, and Charenton where the Marne joined it. He headed toward that way.

The streets of Charenton were blockaded and defended by Gardes Mobiles, the National Guard. While he was watching them, he heard the first heavy booms of the attacking artillery.

And accompanying the thunder came, like lightning, a horseman from the road to the southeast, and the message that that way had now been overrun.

Rudolph left the village and headed for the Charenton gate. He had to push through it, fighting against the current of the panicked, late-leaving families, and then he was inside the city walls, in Paris.

— 7 —

It was still four kilometers across the city to the Rue Duroc. The streets were calm; most of those fleeing were gone, and the majority of the inhabitants left were in their homes, just waiting. This was ominous as two houses, just inside the wall, were burned ruins. Shells had already fallen from artillery at the far end of its range.

He crossed back over the Seine, hurrying toward the low sun in the west, through neighborhoods that were more and more familiar. He turned onto the Rue de Grenelle and passed the Austrian Embassy. It was locked and empty.

Down the Boulevard des Invalides, he came to the corner and then he was on the Rue Duroc. It was in shadow.

But only a few meters into the block, he saw that something was wrong. The house was darker than before, like a black square on the gray wall of the street.

Then, he saw that it wasn't the house that was black, but the shadows left where it and its neighbors had been. The buildings were only a pile of rubble and debris in the street.

He kept walking.

The house had been destroyed. He stopped and stared at it dumbly.

Then he kept walking, past the house and away from the Rue Duroc and the destruction and brokenness that were left of his life there.

As the sun set, the vast parade field of the École was before him. Emptiness flowed from him and filled it. He walked out into the middle of its loneliness, his loneliness. Faint sounds reached him, the cannon of the Prussians on all sides, and answers from the forts. Even more faint, he seemed to feel Paris tremble and shudder as the shells struck and wounded her. She was in the iron grasp of her enemy.

The first stars appeared as the real light of the sky, the sun, already set, surrendered the heavens to the dark. Rudolph fell to his knees.

This was the Champ de Mars, the Field of the god of War, and he was in the center of a universe of war. Its planets orbited a dark sun, held in their course by a gravity of hatred between men which, like gravity, was unchanging. The planets were men and their nations, and the sun was their dark heart.

"O God," he cried to the answering heavens. "Why?"

Chapter Thirteen

PURSUIT

— 1 —

"It is a policeman," Zoltan said.

"Bring him in." Ferdinand stood to greet the official; Pock remained seated, while Monsieur Beaubien remained on the floor.

The detective was young and energetic. His high forehead wrinkled and smoothed with every expression and even with every word as he spoke. His uniform was spotless and well ordered.

"There has been a murder, I have been informed?"

"You have been informed correctly," Ferdinand said. He held out his hand to the body sprawled before them.

"Indeed."

The inspection of the body was brief. The policeman knelt for a moment to examine the crushed head, and then he rolled the body over onto its back.

"Monsieur," the policeman said, standing, "I wish to ask you several questions."

"Please," Ferdinand said.

"First, you will understand, of course, that a full investigation will not be possible."

Pock coughed discreetly. "Because the city is about to be attacked by the Prussian army?"

"Indeed. Can you tell me the latest news?" the policeman asked. "I have been unable to see a newspaper yet this afternoon."

"A report said that Chateau-Thierry had fallen yesterday evening."

The policeman did a quick calculation. "Then still two days before they reach Paris, or at earliest tomorrow evening. Yes. I will institute the proper paper work for this investigation, and it will be continued when normal conditions prevail."

"Please ask your questions," Baron Ferdinand said.

"Does Monsieur Baron know the identity of the person on the floor?"

"He is Pierre Beaubien, a painter. I believe he is well known."

"Beaubien?" The detective looked with new interest at the body. "Beaubien! Yes, of course he is well known! And forgive me, but I have not yet been introduced to Monsieur?"

"I am Baron Ferdinand Harsanyi, of the Austrian Embassy."

"A diplomat? Indeed. I am Detective-Inspector Envienne. And so, can Monsieur Baron inform me of any reason that the painter Pierre Beaubien would have been murdered in your parlor?"

"I know of no reason he would have been alive in my parlor. I am not aware that he knew where we lived."

"But you do have a connection with him?"

"He painted that." Ferdinand gestured to the wall opposite the fireplace.

"Indeed." The policeman drew closer to the portrait of Therese. "Yes, I see. This is a member of your family?"

"My daughter."

"And then he appears again, for no reason, and is murdered. By . . . what is that?" He made a brief attempt to lift the red stone.

"It is the mineral cinnabar."

"Indeed. How would it have come into the room?"

"It is kept here."

"Ah, a curio? Perhaps obtained on your travels as a diplomat. But surely, it would take a strong man to lift it!"

"It isn't heavy." Ferdinand set it back on its table.

"But heavy enough, is it not, to crush a man's skull?" The policeman paused. "And you can shed no light on the reason?"

Ferdinand paused himself. "No. I can shed no light."

"Very tragic. Monsieur?"

"Me?" Pock said. "Not at all. I'd never met the man. I knew of the portrait, though. That was the only reason I'd heard of him."

"Few in Paris have not heard of him. It will be sorrowful news in a year of sorrowful—"

A modest crash and grinding sounded from the street outside. The policeman jumped and turned white, staring at the window.

"The invasion?" he said. "Has it already come?"

Ferdinand looked out the window. "A tradesman's cart has lost a wheel." The cart had fallen sideways and a load of cabbages and potatoes was spilled beside it.

"Of course. Yes." The policeman's manner had become more hurried. "I will complete the paper work. How then did you find the body?"

"I was taking my daughter to the train station and—"

"Are the trains still running?" the policeman interrupted.

"They hope to still have departures tomorrow," Ferdinand said.

"Yes. Good. I will look into it. And is there any indication in the room of anything out of place? Have you searched the house?"

"I have seen nothing out of place."

"Would you know of any enemies of the victim who might have wished him dead?" He was beginning to speak more quickly.

"I know nothing of his associates or business affairs."

"Do you know of any information, anything at all, that may be important?"

The fast pace of the conversation halted. Ferdinand hesitated. "No."

"Indeed." The policeman frowned. "As a routine question, do you plan to leave the area in the near future?"

"Very possibly," Ferdinand said. "The city is about to be attacked."

"In that case, please inform the police of your whereabouts in case your assistance is required for this investigation. That is all. I bid you good day."

"Detective Envienne?"

"All questions may be directed to the police station."

"Will you take the body?"

"Oh. Indeed. I will have someone sent."

"Do you have a carriage?"

"Yes."

"My servant will help you carry the body out to it. Zoltan!" Ferdinand called.

Envienne was not pleased. "Very well," he said.

With no hesitation, Zoltan took hold of the dead man's shoulders and began dragging the body from the room. The policeman assisted by watching.

"I presume that you'll inform the family?" Ferdinand asked.

"Yes, of course, and please be assured that I will proceed to the morgue, and the body will be taken care of there."

"Thank you," Ferdinand said. "I feel entirely assured."

"I don't feel very assured by this investigation," Pock said as Ferdinand watched the policeman's carriage pull away.

"I thought momentarily of mentioning Mr. Whistler's death."

"Why?"

"Yes, why? I doubt this painter was trying to buy cinnabar," Ferdinand said.

"Although it was cinnabar that killed him," Pock answered. "So, is there anything to be done? Or will you leave the whole thing to the police?"

Ferdinand thought for a moment. "Would you accompany me to Montmartre? Bring the carriage," he said to Zoltan. "But I'll drive. You stay and start packing for our evacuation."

"The little I knew of the man," Ferdinand said, "he seemed to have lived wildly enough that someone would want to kill him." He was driving with Pock beside him.

"I know nothing at all of him."

"I am only interested now because he was killed in my own house and I would like to know why, and by whom."

"Is that the only reason? That it was in your house? Or are you more suspicious of Whistler's death than you've said?"

Ferdinand waited before answering. "It's at least worth a trip to Montmartre."

"The Prussians will be at the edge of Paris within a day or two."

"They're not here yet."

"Here," the baron said, bringing the carriage to a halt. They were on the west side of Montmartre, high enough to see a great deal of the city below them. The house was the same as it had been, except for the garden, which was in its autumn decline.

Ferdinand climbed out of the carriage and stood for a moment on the street. The sun was setting, and the Seine reflected a ribbon of it, as if a red line of fire were snaking through Paris. All the rest of the city was violet, umber, and indigo. The gaslights on the main boulevards were on. Their yellow and whiteness made the city seem as free of care as it had always been.

"He's not here."

Ferdinand looked up to see the speaker, the same woman with her sharp peasant accent, leaning from an upper window in the house.

"The painter Beaubien?" Ferdinand shouted back.

"Not here. Gone all day."

"Is he coming back?"

"He'll be back." The window closed and Ferdinand stared at it thoughtfully, as it was not obvious whether that had been the end of the conversation.

It had not been. The front door opened. "Do you want him?" the woman asked.

"Are you sure he hasn't left Paris? Everyone else is leaving."

"He hasn't told me he was."

"Did he say when he was coming back?"

"He never does."

"May I come in?"

"Come in, that won't bother anything."

Ferdinand and an obviously fascinated Pock walked past the flowers and through the door.

Pock was immediately drawn to the anarchy of the studio and its scores of canvases; Ferdinand had to look away from them.

"You want to buy one of them?" the woman asked. "Is that why you're here?" She looked at him again, and he was finally recognized. "Oh, you're the one with the daughter he painted. That was pretty. One that he got right."

"I wanted to see other paintings he's done." The incongruity of such an errand in the moment of the city's crisis seemed lost on the woman. "What do you think of them?"

"I just cook and clean up after him, and not in there. I don't know a thing about his paintings. I wouldn't touch them, and he doesn't want me to."

"Have you worked for him long?"

"Five years."

"And he pays you well?"

"Well enough. The work's not hard, it's him who's hard to get along with."

The woman seemed to have no reluctance to answer questions and gossip about her employer. "Do other people come here?" Ferdinand asked. "Besides people like me who want to buy his pictures?"

"Not here. He always goes out."

"I'm asking because I want to know if he's respectable. His portrait of my daughter is very good, but I want to know more about him before I buy something else. Is he respectable?"

"Oh, his family's good enough, if that's what you mean."

"But himself?"

"Himself?" She smiled slyly. "Maybe not. It depends on what you mean."

"I don't want to be connected with any scandal."

"If you stay with the painting, you'll have no scandal. You wouldn't gamble a bit, would you? He'll find out if you do."

Ferdinand paused. "Well, I've played cards a few times, of course."

"Then he'll be wanting you to play with him. That's his vice, and I'm just speaking the truth. There are some that know him for his art, and there are some that know him for his cards."

He nodded slyly. "And does he make money at it?"

"More than he loses, and by a long ways."

Pock had been listening. "Did he—does he cheat?"

"That's not my place to say," she said, saying *yes* very specifically.

"Indeed," Pock said.

"But he's not miserly with his money," she added. "He spends it as fast as it comes in."

"Or faster?" Ferdinand asked. The woman needed very little encouragement.

"There might be times when he does. I just know I always get paid, or else he doesn't eat."

"His family would help him if he's in debt?"

"Not them. Marseilles merchants, they are. They never come here."

"They've disowned him?"

"Not disowned him quite. He had a letter just this morning, and I noticed it because it was from his cousin. Those two have less use for each other than the rest of the family. That's why I noticed it in particular."

"What does his cousin do?"

"He's in the army."

Ferdinand was more interested. "Do you know which regiment?"

"I don't know. Just that he's cavalry. I saw him once, all in his fancy uniform."

"The blue jacket and red pants?"

"No. Red jacket and gold braids all over it."

"That's the Imperial Guards."

"I wouldn't know. He treated me like I was nothing."

"They are like that," Ferdinand said. "The letter came this morning?"

"I saw it. Then he read it and he was gone not ten minutes later, before he even had his breakfast. And he's still gone! I won't leave him supper. He knows I won't if he comes back late."

"What would you do if he never came back?" Ferdinand asked.

"Why wouldn't he?"

"There's a war. Unforeseen things can happen."

"He'll be back. It might be at three in the morning, but he always comes back."

"I suppose it wasn't our place to tell her," Pock said as they descended the steep side of the hill.

"I didn't want to tell her," Ferdinand said. "There will be enough terrible things to come. I didn't want to be party to her grief."

"That woman? She won't grieve."

"She will." Ferdinand shrugged. "The Imperial Guards would have been with the emperor in Sedan."

"And the letter only came today. I would wonder when it was sent."

"With all the delays, it could have been a month ago, before the campaigns. Or only a few days."

"Since the battle?"

"If the cousin was a prisoner, he might have been allowed to send a letter from Germany. Or he might still be free."

"What could have been in the letter?" Pock asked. "You have no connection with the cousin."

"I believe . . ." Ferdinand searched his memory. "The cousin was a friend of Auguste de l'Imperator."

"Then Auguste might know something. But he is on his way to Vienna."

"He's watching over Therese as she travels."

It was well after dark when Ferdinand reached his own door. He noticed a carriage parked across the street.

Zoltan was waiting. He nodded toward the closed door of the parlor. "The ambassador."

"Here? Has he been waiting long?"

"A half hour."

Ferdinand opened the door and bowed.

"Your Excellency."

"Baron Harsanyi." Prince Richard was standing by the fireplace. Despite the stress of the last weeks and days, his mocking manner had returned.

"My apologies for keeping you waiting."

"It's nothing."

Ferdinand asked, "How may I be of service?"

"We'll leave tomorrow. For Bordeaux."

"I knew it would be very soon. I believe I have everything ready."

"Yes, it's all ready. The French government will have a train for us."

"Surely, you didn't come just to tell me this."

"No." Von Metternich paused, gauging his words. "There has also been a request from the French Foreign Ministry concerning you."

"Me."

"It's the new government." Now he was soothing, even consoling. "They have no experience in diplomacy. They're peremptory. They issue ultimatums as if any other power were just a disobedient child."

"What is their request?"

"Oh, yes." The ambassador sighed. "They request that you be recalled."

"*Request?*"

"Demand."

"Of course," Ferdinand said, "I will resign immediately."

"Oh, no, I don't want that. You're very useful to me, Baron. Even more, it's unacceptable. I can't allow France to dictate to us on who the ministry in Vienna chooses to appoint to its embassy. I only wanted you to know that the request has been made."

"Do they give a reason?"

"Cinnabar. The mercury ore that they say you wouldn't sell to them."

Ferdinand rested his hand on the piece, returned to its stand in the window.

"Monsieur Sarroche made the request?"

"It came through the Foreign Ministry." Von Metternich acted as if the whole affair were a tiresome detail, although his eyes were very closely on the baron. "It might be Sarroche, or it might not. They are completely convinced that Austria has betrayed France. They're looking for someone to blame for the whole disaster of the war, and Austria is convenient." He seemed to be enjoying Ferdinand's position.

"Should I still travel to Bordeaux?"

"Yes, plan to. But you must remain aware that at least some officials of the Republican government are hostile to you."

"I will remain aware."

"And even now, we could regain some standing with the French if you would reconsider. I never did understand why you objected to the sale."

"I had reasons."

The ambassador's heavy coat was lying across a chair, and he moved forward to pick it up. "I will see you in the morning. The train is scheduled to leave at three o'clock in the afternoon."

"I have a few matters to attend to. I'll be at the embassy by eleven."

"That will be good." He paused once more. "And there was an odd occurrence at the embassy this morning. I was only told about it just before I came here."

"Yes?"

"A man came to the gate asking for you."

"Who was it?"

"I don't know. He was allowed in to the front desk and told you weren't in."

"Yes?" Ferdinand was listening very closely.

"Then, apparently, he began to claim that he knew the identity of a French agent somewhere in the embassy. At that point, he was taken to see my senior aide, von Karlstein. He claimed again that there was a French agent in the embassy, and he demanded to talk to you."

"This is very strange. Did he say who the agent was?"

"He offered to sell the information."

"Why did he want me?"

"He didn't say. You might want to ask von Karlstein. He spoke to the man."

"I will ask him. The man wanted money for the information?"

"Quite a bit. He thought it should be very valuable to us. When he was told that you weren't at the embassy, he asked for your address."

"It's interesting," Ferdinand said.

"Do you have any idea what it was all about?"

"I believe I know who the man was."

"You do? And why do you say 'was'?"

The constant mocking and disdain had exasperated him. "Because he's dead."

"Dead?"

"In this room. He was murdered."

"Here?"

"He was struck on the head while he was sitting in that chair."

Prince Richard snatched his coat from the chair. "I don't know what to say!"

"The police have been and gone."

"Whatever happens, I don't want a scandal attached to the embassy."

"I hope none will be."

"We'll leave for Bordeaux tomorrow," he said to Zoltan after Prince von Metternich had left.

"For how long?"

"I don't know. Whenever the Prussian army leaves. I don't know when we'll be back."

"Rudolph . . ." Zoltan said, for both of them.

"Where is he?" Ferdinand said. "Would he come back here? I don't know."

It was late night. Ferdinand sat at his desk in his darkened office with just one candle burning. A sheet of paper lay in front of him. He wrote one word.

Rudolph.

Just as he did, he heard a sound, perhaps thunder, but then again and again, four times, in regular intervals. It was a deep sound, almost below hearing, filled with great weight and hard, heavy movement.

Ferdinand sat silently and still.

Then it sounded again, four times more, just the same.

The first Prussian guns have come. I would stay in Paris to wait for you, but I have been ordered to Bordeaux where the Austrian Embassy to France currently resides. They will know there of any further travels I undertake. Therese is in Vienna.

Again the guns sounded, four times.

He paused again.

The thousand francs I have enclosed will take you wherever you wish to go.

Then he sat. The candle flame wavered from some wisping current, and he watched it until it was unmoving again, and then long after.

An hour or more passed without any sound.

Then the night silence was broken by a terrible white light and a wrenching, crashing sound, and then a sudden onslaught of rain. More lightning and thunder followed as the storm blasted itself against Paris.

God bring you soon, Rudolph, and safely. I pray for our restoration.

And then, after rain and thunder and dark night and finally silence again, he came to be able to write, *I am sorry for the mistakes I have made. I want you back with me. I want this more than anything else I can imagine.*

Your Father

He enclosed the message in an envelope, sealed it, and put Rudolph's name on the front. As he set it on the center of the empty desk, more guns sounded.

– 2 –

The first part of the morning was busy with final packing.

"Take everything valuable," he told Zoltan. "The house might be looted while we're gone."

He himself removed the two portraits, of his wife and his daughter, from their frames and rolled and packed them.

"I'll look in at the house here while you're gone," Pock said.

"Watch for Rudolph."

"Oh, of course. Do you really think he'll come back here?" He was in the parlor chair, Ferdinand watching out the window as Zoltan piled luggage into the rented carriage.

"Where else would he go? If he was in the French army, he won't go back to their barracks. And if he's a prisoner, he'll be released when the rest are."

"And if he does come back? Have you left him a message?"

"It's written and on my desk. There's money to follow me to Bordeaux."

"Do you think he would? Come, Harsanyi, I'll be frank. He left in anger. What will have changed?"

"I hope the letter will cause a change. And you're sure you'll wait until the end of the siege, also? You could come with me."

"Paris is as much of a home as I have. I'll stay with her. And if I see a light in the window here, I'll welcome Rudolph home."

– 3 –

The baron's train arrived the next afternoon in Bordeaux, 500 kilometers from Paris, on the long estuary of the Garonne. Its history of manufacturing and new-world trade were evident in the innumerable warehouses and merchants' houses on the quays, and the grand municipal buildings that now housed the national government.

Housing for the sudden and vast influx of officials was at a premium; Ferdinand found a set of rooms on a back street that was beneath the dignity of many of the newcomers, and he and Zoltan settled into it quickly.

Finding the Austrian Embassy proved more difficult, but finally Ferdinand came upon the ambassador's aide von Karlstein in a corridor of the temporary Assemblee and was directed to an expansive manor in a tree-filled suburb.

Arriving there, he was met by Prince von Metternich.

"If the war is prolonged," the ambassador said, "at least we'll be comfortable."

"Will the war be prolonged?"

"Yes. Every indication is that it will take months for President Thiers to get enough control of his new government to negotiate a surrender. Excuse me," the prince said, smiling cynically. "To negotiate a final treaty. No one is to call it a surrender."

"Will Austria be represented in the negotiations?"

"I believe we'll have an observer. But neither side is much concerned with Austria's interests. I'll tell you again, Baron, that France does not consider Austria to be a friend. The new French government especially doesn't, and they're looking for villains to blame for this catastrophe of a war. Be very careful what you do and say. I've already received another protest at your continued presence."

"I am always prepared to return to Vienna, Your Excellency."

"Not yet, Baron. You are a useful pawn in my game with this new government, and I'm not ready to sacrifice you yet."

– 4 –

Distant from the fronts and battles, and curtailed from discussions with French officials, both by the ambassador's warning, and by the difficulty of finding any particular official in the French confusion, Ferdinand found he had far more time at his disposal than was his preference.

So, on one of many October afternoons, he took the opportunity to sit at a café and read a newspaper. It was from London, brought in by the latest steamship, and the picture it painted was more objective, organized, and dismal, than the French reports. The headlines alone were a diary of defeats.

"It is discouraging," a voice said behind his shoulder. In German.

Ferdinand turned quickly. "What are you doing here?" he said in surprise, though he had the presence of mind to keep his voice low.

Karl von Stieff smiled and sat with him. "Not compromising you as I have before, I hope." Even sitting in the middle of the café patrons, the high dome of his scalp with its yellow and gray fringe was hardly inconspicuous.

"I'm already more than compromised."

"So I've heard. But I believe the French security forces haven't yet put their nets in place here. We should be unobserved."

"You would be in greater danger than me."

"No great danger, and the risk is worth the reward," von Stieff said. "While I was in Bordeaux, I was hoping perhaps to see you."

Ferdinand couldn't help but smile himself. "I'm not going to sell any cinnabar to Prussia."

Von Stieff laughed out loud. You're not?" he joked. "That's quite a surprise!" His external manner remained jovial, but his eyes narrowed and his voice became serious. "But that is why I wished to see you. It is not only Sarroche that you have offended by your refusal to sell cinnabar to the French. It is also your own ambassador. It is he as much as the French who wishes to force your departure."

"I offered to resign."

"He plays his games with the new government, and he waits for the optimum moment. But I wish to make an offer to you."

"Yes?"

"I can arrange with the Prussian authorities to invite you to observe the siege of Paris."

"I would be honored."

"As would we. The Prussian command has taken up residence in Versailles. You may expect to hear something from your ambassador soon." He stood. "Auf Wiedersehen, Herr Baron."

"Until we meet again," Ferdinand answered.

– 5 –

"I hear that Bazaine has surrendered his army in Metz," Prince von Metternich said. A week had passed, and Ferdinand's duties had been reduced to reading a few dispatches, the newspapers, and briefing the ambassador for a few minutes each day on the course of the war.

"Yes, Your Excellency. It had become inevitable."

"And will it bring the end of the war any closer?"

"No. The Prussian forces at Metz will be freed, but von Bismarck already has complete military control of northern France."

"And the new battles in central France?"

"The French continue to raise armies, and the Prussians continue to defeat them. The French farmers and villagers hide in the fields and shoot Prussian soldiers, and the Prussians burn the farms and villages in reprisal."

The subject was distasteful to the prince, and grievous. "How long will it go on, Baron?"

"Until President Thiers signs an armistice."

"Which would be a surrender. He can't, yet. I don't think France is ready to admit defeat. The war will just have to go on."

"Yes, Your Excellency."

"I have a new assignment for you." He said it casually, as if he was just asking for another report. "The Prussians have taken up residence in Versailles. I want you to go up there."

"Back to Paris?"

"Yes. To Versailles. It's already been arranged. You'll stay there to observe the siege and report to me on its progress."

"Yes, sir. For how long?"

"For the length of the siege, so you might as well find someplace to live there."

"When should I leave?"

"This afternoon, if you can. Or tomorrow. I need an observer up there, Baron, but I'm also just moving my pawn to get it out of the way."

"Pack everything again," Ferdinand said to Zoltan. "We're moving to Versailles."

Zoltan shrugged. "Another move. But near Paris."

"Very near."

"Will you go in the city?"

"I don't think I'll be able. We'll be able to observe the siege. Have you seen Versailles?"

"No."

"Even you, Zoltan, will be amazed."

Louis the Fourteenth, the Sun King, had ruled France as the sun ruled the day. The sun merely had the sky to rule from; Louis had Versailles. In his reign, it had been the greatest center of power on earth.

The palace was the greatest architectural achievement of its age, the most costly building ever undertaken, the highest statement of art, the vast bending of nature to man's glory, one specific man's glory. It was the essence and magnitude of the royalty of France condensed into physical form.

And now it was the Prussian headquarters for the siege of Paris.

The palace had been designed as a headquarters for a nation. Beyond the royal apartments, the kilometers of corridors and offices could house bureaucrats by the hundreds or even thousands, and the village of Versailles, which was generally an extension of the palace, could hold many more.

Baron Ferdinand Harsanyi, again searching for a residence, found his own small palace: a two-story cottage, smaller than his house in Paris but still with more room than he needed. As Zoltan unpacked trunks and bags, even without instruction he knew to set up an extra bedroom.

The cottage had a fine miniature garden in front, and was on a small street in sight of farms and forests. It had its own stable, and Zoltan was instructed to find two new horses and a carriage to replace the old ones, which had been sold off in Paris.

"We'll be country gentlemen," Ferdinand said. "But at least not idle."

They were not idle. Arrangements had indeed been made, and Ferdinand was accepted into the Prussian headquarters. Just as the French staff had earlier been anxious to show Austria its military prowess, now it was Prussia who was more than pleased to impress upon Austria the thoroughness of France's defeat.

The military order and Germanic regimentation in Versailles and in the Prussian lines were also in stark contrast to the French style.

The siege is a ring of iron around Paris, he wrote to the embassy in Bordeaux. *There is no chance of a French breakthrough, or relief by a French army from outside. The Prussian high command has no sympathy for a population of two million inside the city that will begin to starve soon. The main debate is whether to continue the bombardment of military targets only, or begin the systematic razing of the entire city.*

And to Therese in Vienna he wrote, *I am much more at home with military men and Germans. Though these Prussians are Austria's political enemies, I find their company more congenial than the excitable French. Zoltan and I have complete freedom to ride and observe, on our own responsibility to not be injured by the continual fire. I don't know how long the siege will last. I will send for you as soon as it is safe to return.*

The autumn turned to winter, Christmas passed, and the new year began.

"I had always feared this day," Prince Richard von Metternich said. Over seventy magnificent meters of crystal and gold, reflected and doubled by the wall of mirrors, were only the backdrop.

"It had to come." They were both in their most formal dress: Ferdinand in his uniform and the ambassador in a black suit; which matched his mood. It was the first that the baron had seen of him in three months.

Two dozen German kings, princes, dukes, grand dukes, and prime ministers were seated at the long central table. Richard and Ferdinand were in the rows designated for foreign diplomats, a very large section; every nation had come to witness, and fear, the history being made.

A short, heavy, old man with close but wild white hair sat himself wearily in the front of the section. "President Thiers," the ambassador said. "I didn't know if he would come. Tomorrow he'll begin the final negotiations for the armistice."

"I believe the city would rather starve than surrender. Paris will be as hostile to the French government as to the Prussians."

"Not Prussia," von Metternich said. "They won't be Prussia anymore. That word will be relegated to history. After today, we only have Germany. Who would have imagined? The German Empire finally re-created a millennium after Charlemagne, and of all places, in the palace of Louis the Fourteenth and of Napoleon. Only France could have prevented this." He was speaking from a reverie, contemplating an uncertain future. "It will be a new age," he said.

And in the center of the room, and the world, towering in every way over the ceremony, was the tall, commanding, walrus-like bulk of Otto von Bismarck, the peculiar heavy bags under his eyes detracting nothing from their power. He was standing behind the Kasier, Wilhelm, now the First, becoming more Kaiser with every stroke of the pens at the table as the dukes and princes signed their principalities and duchies out of existence and into the new Germany.

– 6 –

The new German Empire was only a day old when it took on its first major task, the surrender of the French government. The final negotiations were begun and the terms were harsh: the French armies were to lay down their weapons and be disbanded; the German occupation of France would continue until the final treaty was signed, including the requirement of a German victory parade through Paris.

But at least the gates of Paris would be opened and the siege ended.

"They have no choice," Ferdinand said to Zoltan. They were in the outside courtyard of the palace, which was always filled with officials coming and going. "The hostilities will finally end. I'm sending for Therese."

"It will take days for the trains to start running again."

"Or weeks. I'll instruct her to meet us in Brussels in four days. Then we'll come to Paris when the armistice is signed."

"Then everyone will be coming back."

"Yes. Everyone," Ferdinand said. "The prisoners in the German camps will be released."

"Perhaps even your son."

The voice startled Ferdinand completely. He turned to see the diminutive Sarroche looking up at him.

"What do you know about my son?" he demanded, angry as much from the surprise as at the person, and as from the subject.

"I know you have lost him."

"How do you know?"

"By the same methods that I know everything else," the Frenchman said. "And I am looking for him myself."

"Do not talk with him," Ferdinand said. "Don't go close to him."

"He is not your property to speak to me of him in this way. The war is ending and the preparations for the next war will begin. The stocks of mercury fulminate have been sufficient but now must be replenished."

"I was blamed for them being insufficient."

Sarroche ignored him. "And now your daughter will return from Vienna. At least your family will be partially restored. And you will be seeking your son in Paris. I agree. It is the reasonable place for him to seek you, and for you to seek him."

"You were listening to my conversation with my servant?"

"I would be informed of your telegram by the telegraph office in any case. And your daughter's escort, Captain de l'Imperator, will be with her."

Ferdinand was furious. "Why are you saying these things? Just to impress me that you have such complete knowledge about me?"

"To show you that you and your family cannot escape me. I will have the cinnabar from your mines, Baron Harsanyi. This time I will not negotiate."

Chapter Fourteen

THUS TO
ALL DREAMS

– 1 –

Upon her arrival in Vienna two weeks after Therese's, Princess Pauline von Metternich lost no time in seizing the reins of the city's social carriage. Her wealth, her highest noble rank, and her long practice in commanding the larger and more complex French high society made her unstoppable. In just weeks she was planning a reception, and the invitations were immediately the most sought after in the city.

Surrounding her center stage was the start of the Vienna Season, the vast milieu of operas, ballets, concerts, royal events, and innumerable salons and balls that marked the calendar from October to March.

Therese was dazed at the onslaught. "I'd expected you to be living in quiet exile here," she said as she accompanied Pauline on a search for an acceptable dressmaker. "Don't you think you'll be going back to Paris?"

"There is no more Paris," was the princess's curt reply. Not my Paris."

Between Pauline and Auguste, Therese's hours and days were full.

– 2 –

"Tell me more about Mother and Father," Therese said. She was having a rare quiet moment with Pauline in the princess's mansion.

"What should I tell you?"

"When we were children, Rudy and I, were they together much?"

"They were always together."

"Did they do the Season? Did they go to balls and the theater?"

"He went with her. He knew it was important for his career, but I don't think he enjoyed society."

"I'm sure he didn't!"

"He was more lighthearted back then, Therese. He wasn't so grim."

"Did they quarrel?"

"Never that I saw. It was just that he began being with her less, and being away more. As I've told you, I think they just realized they were friends, but not in love."

"No," Therese said. "I think it was the other way. I think they were in love, but they weren't friends."

"Who will ever understand love?" Pauline laughed. "I know that I won't."

"Was Mother ever in love with anyone else?"

"I would have been too young to know."

"Well . . . I mean . . ." Therese tried to use the correct words. "I mean after Father was gone."

"Oh. I don't know, Therese. I never heard any rumor of it. I was gone myself, in Paris, and she wouldn't have told me."

– 3 –

"The siege in Metz has ended," Auguste said, late in October. "Marshall Bazaine has surrendered his army."

"You would have been there," Therese said.

"And so, in the end, it makes no difference that I am not. The men are to be transported to the camps in Prussia where the emperor's army is already imprisoned. The officers will be paroled."

"What does that mean?"

"They are given the choice to swear that they will not take up arms again against Prussia in this war. If they give their oath that they will not, they are free to return to their homes."

"Would they?"

"Many will, I am sure. But always, an oath in these circumstances is not to be considered valid."

"What would you have done, Auguste?"

He smiled. "It is hard to know. And now I will never know."

Every few days Therese received a letter from her father. First they had been from Bordeaux, then from Versailles. They were short messages and said little, but they were reminders that he was still safe and thinking of her.

– 4 –

Early in November, Pauline had some news from Paris as she picked up Therese in her carriage.

"The newspaper says that your friend Pierre Beaubien has been killed."

"Pierre?" Therese was still settling into the seat, and the sudden start of the carriage caught her off-balance. Once she was securely sitting, she took the newspaper. "Does it say anything else?"

"It was just at the beginning of the siege. But there aren't any other details."

"Poor Pierre! It was on the same day we left Paris! What could have happened?"

"It may have been the bombing of the city."

"Pierre was killed!" Therese said when Auguste came by her house later that day.

"Pierre . . . ?"

"Pierre Beaubien." She'd cried earlier, and now she began again.

"It was perhaps in the defense of the city." Auguste tried to comfort her, although he didn't seem troubled himself. "He often took risks that were ill-advised. I feared that he would someday step too far."

For the rest of November, and through December, Therese slowly withdrew from the frantic pace of Pauline's preparations and entertainments and outings. She spent more hours with Auguste, and even more alone.

"Does some new sorrow distress you?" he asked one very cold day near Christmas, as they drank coffee in an ornate konditorei in her neighborhood. It had become their most frequent meeting place. "Or is it the long and cold nights? Or only the loneliness you have without your family?"

"I'm not sure, Auguste. I think I'm afraid."

"Afraid? Of what! I am with you."

"I'm afraid of what will come. Nothing that I trust seems to last. Mother is gone, Paris is gone, Rudolph is gone. I don't know when I'll see Father again. I don't know if I'm going to be in Vienna now, or if I'll go back to Paris. Is there anything that will be forever?"

"I am with you," Auguste said, putting his hand on hers. "That will be forever."

– 5 –

Finally, in January, the telegram she'd been waiting for came. Maria brought the messenger boy into the sitting room, where she and Auguste were playing cards. Therese took the envelope and read the message.

"It's from Father. He wants us to come back to Paris."

"Paris?"

"He says to meet him in Brussels in four days."

"From the reports in the newspapers, I thought it must be soon."

"I wonder if he remembers."

"Remembers what?"

"That day . . . it will have been a year ago that Mother died," Therese said.

The steam dissolved and the air cleared. As Therese watched through the train window, the Brussels station solidified from gray clouds to granite floors, iron columns, and high ceilings. And people. The platforms were filled, and through the whole station she could see no end to the crowds.

"Do you see him?" she asked.

"Not yet," Auguste said. "But he will be close, surely."

The doors were opened and the two rivers, the passengers and the platform crowds, merged into a churning ocean.

"Father?" Despite the pressure behind her, she paused on the train's steps where she was still above the crashing waves. "I don't see him. What is the matter? It's like a riot!"

"Something of importance, that is certain." Already standing on the platform, Auguste was still as high above the throngs as Therese. "Come. He is perhaps back, away from the crush."

Therese and Auguste pressed forward. They were close to the back wall, and at last the crowd had thinned.

"There!" Auguste pointed.

"Father!"

Auguste's was a double discovery. The baron was indeed standing in a corner, waiting, but he hadn't noticed them yet. He was completely devoted to his newspaper, which announced the reason for the melee of the crowds: *Armistice Signed! Paris Opened! Prisoners Released!*

"Father." Therese put her hand on his arm. "We're here."

He was startled and the paper fell, scattering. "Therese." And in his eyes she saw an immense relief. "We aren't staying in Brussels" was all he said, though, as they pushed back into the crowd. "Zoltan is getting your luggage to put onto the Paris train."

"Already, there are trains into Paris?" Auguste said. He had the wrinkled mass of the newspaper under his arm. "The armistice was only signed last night."

"The trains are going as far as Saint-Denis."

"The confusion will still be very great. Perhaps we should . . ."

But already Zoltan was coming toward them with Maria, two porters, and the piles of suitcases. Ferdinand had started forward to meet them, but he turned back for a moment to answer. "No. We'll go to Paris."

"What is the urgency?" Auguste said to Therese in a low voice. They were squeezed together in a second-class compartment. Her father sat in the opposite corner, Maria was even more tightly wedged in another corner, and Zoltan stood. A dozen other passengers were with them in the small space. "Saint-Denis on the outskirts of Paris will be fully in upheaval, and we have no certain knowledge that any road into Paris is truly open. Surely ten thousand of Paris's former inhabitants will be seeking to return on just this first day, and a hundred thousand as soon after as they are able."

Therese smiled. "The two of you will find a way."

"Assuredly." Auguste at least showed no doubt of his abilities. "But for what possible reason? What is this urgency? The French government will not return for weeks at least. The empty building of the Austrian Embassy is meaningless."

"No." Therese's smile was gone. "It said in the newspaper that the French prisoners are all being released. He hopes Rudolph will be coming back to Paris."

This troubled Auguste even more. "Do you believe in this possibility?"

"I don't know where else to find him."

Auguste took Therese's hand and said gently, "There is also the possibility, which must be confronted, that he is not alive. I have not said this before because of the pain that it would cause you."

"I don't want to think it's possible. But even if we don't find him in Paris, that won't mean anything."

"No. Nothing at all."

"You are anxious to find him, aren't you, Auguste?"

"Of course. How could it be otherwise?"

An hour later, the train passed over the frontier into France. French officials came aboard to check passports, while on the platform German troops patrolled beside the stopped train.

"It is a condition of the armistice," Auguste said, having read more details from the newspapers. "And I see that this is the crossing at Valenciennes, not Jeumont. We are taking the northern line through Amiens."

"What does that mean?" Therese asked.

"Perhaps that the Prussians are keeping the main line through Saint-Quentin and Compiegne to themselves." He shrugged. "The Germans will take many weeks to remove their forces. France will not have her own railroad lines back to herself until Germany is done with them."

The train continued to make good time for the next two hours, passing Amiens, but soon after Clermont and Beauvais it came to a stop in a small town. "See?" Auguste said. "Here this track joins the main one. Now we must wait for the Germans to give us usage of our own railroad lines."

"How far is it from here to Paris?" Ferdinand finally spoke. They had been stopped for twenty minutes.

"Perhaps forty kilometers," Auguste said. "It is possible that this is the limit of our travels today. And though unlikely, we may find lodging in this town—it is called Creil, and it is the junction of all the lines to Paris from the north and northeast."

"I will find a carriage," Ferdinand said.

Auguste was about to object, but then resigned himself to the finality of the baron's words. "Very well. It will be astonishing if indeed any carriage is available. But come, and if such exists anywhere in this village, we shall find it."

"What if the train starts while you're gone?" Therese asked as her father, Auguste, and Zoltan all prepared to leave.

"That it certainly will not do," Auguste said.

The train did not move.

It was after dark that the men returned. "Come," Ferdinand said as Auguste and Zoltan searched out the luggage from the baggage car.

"You found a carriage?"

"Auguste did. It must be the only thing on wheels left in the whole town."

The carriage would have been humorous in a different circumstance. "I'm going to Paris in that?"

"Yes," Ferdinand said. "It's an honest farm cart, and a sturdy horse, and I think they've made this trip many times. Our bags will be heavier than the loads they are used to, but by tomorrow we will be in Paris."

"The train will have gotten there before then."

"It may or may not, but then we'd be in Saint-Denis with no transportation at all."

"They have horses in Paris!"

"Not now," Ferdinand said. "There are never horses left after a long siege."

"Why not?" she asked.

Auguste leaned over to answer. "They've all been eaten."

Auguste drove through the first part of the night. The horse was sturdy and hardworking and slow. The night was very cold, clear as glass, freezing the roads and giving speed and distance to sound.

There wasn't enough room in the cart for all of them, and the weight would have been too great. Maria rode, but Ferdinand and Zoltan walked, sometimes pushing when the road led uphill. Therese slept most of the time, leaning on Auguste for warmth. Halfway through the night, Ferdinand and Auguste changed places.

At sunrise they were only past halfway. They stopped at an inn for breakfast and fodder, and Therese walked to loosen her stiff limbs. Her father and Auguste discussed the horse and decided that it looked strong enough to keep going.

And as they did go on, the road began to fill with other returning refugees. They had become part of a great movement of thousands, drawn to Paris as a whirlpool to its center, and through the day the current grew until the roads were unending streams of people.

Then at noon they reached the beginnings of the German lines. There had been no reduction of these in the two days since the armistice. The crowds were narrowed and funneled through only a few breaches made for them in the siege lines.

As the French nation drained back into Paris, the German conquerors watched silently like gray rock outcrops standing from their trenches and breastworks and artillery placements, from where they had been destroying the homes and city of the people they now watched pass.

The old farm cart that carried Therese blended with hundreds of others—men, women, and children flowing back into Paris. As the sun began to near the earth, they came at last to the actual walls of the city, but were not allowed in at the first gate at Saint-Ouen.

"Neuilly!" the German officer directing traffic shouted over the crowd. "Only Neuilly on the west is open for refugees! Vincennes and Neuilly only!"

"They tell us?" Auguste said angrily. "They dictate to us what roads we are allowed to use?"

They moved slowly down the dense, packed straight road to Clichy and then to Neuilly, and were crushed through the gate onto the Champs-Elysees. Mocking the crowds, pushing toward it was the Arc de Triomphe with a German watch post erected on its top.

"It is unforgivable," Auguste said.

All the great, ancient trees that had lined the Elysees had been cut down.

– 6 –

The Paris that the Parisians returned to was not the Paris they'd left. It had been reduced by the bombardment, and buildings they had known were damaged or gone; but more, Paris, joyous queen of Europe, city of light, fashion, art, and culture, had been insulted and hated and assaulted. How could anything ever be the same?

The people coming in faced the people they'd left behind, watching from the sidewalks and windows, and a new enmity was born between the refugees who had abandoned the city in her need, and the ones who had chosen to stay, or been unable to leave. Therese's entrance to Paris could not have been more different this time from her first time. It was a different Paris she was entering.

At the Arc, Auguste left the main crowds and turned south toward the Pont de l'Alma. Despite the sorrow that lay so heavily in the streets, Therese began to feel a hope growing in her as they crossed the river and came closer to the neighborhoods she knew. But then they passed one fine old house she had seen often before the war, which now was nothing but charred ruins.

"Will our house be like that?" she asked.

"Surely it will not be," Auguste answered.

"We'll know soon," her father said.

"One day," Auguste said, "one day, Berlin will pay. And Frankfurt, and Munich, and Hamburg, and every German city. Ten times they will pay." He faced Therese. "I promise you, they will pay."

"Don't promise me the sorrow of cities," she said.

"Then what should I promise you?"

"Promise me hope of no more sorrow."

"I cannot promise that. No one can."

"Then at least promise me Rudolph."

They traversed the length of the Avenue Bousquet to the corner of the École Militaire. Ferdinand looked up at the scars on the buildings, then faced forward again. "Even if he's not at the house, there will be some sign if he has been."

It was at the end of dusk and the beginning of twilight. They had just a hundred meters left before they turned onto the Rue Duroc, when suddenly the cart stopped.

"What are you doing?" Zoltan said to the horse. She didn't answer, and Zoltan snapped the reins. The horse took one step and stopped again.

"She's lame," Auguste said, but they'd all seen it.

Zoltan was beside the horse, feeling her front left leg. The horse shied from his touch. "A cramp, I think. She's gone too far for a day."

"Stay with her," Ferdinand said. "We'll go ahead."

They walked the last stretch and turned onto the Rue Duroc.

Immediately they saw. The street had been cleared and the rubble thrown back into the pile, but that was all that was left of what had for a few months been their home. The houses on either side were also destroyed; there was no sign of inhabitants in any of the buildings.

Therese moved closer to look into the debris. Her father was beside her, also searching the piles.

"There's nothing," he said.

Auguste was with them, also, and his anger was boiling. "All of Germany will be as this is, I swear it. It is my revenge!"

"No," the baron said. "It already has been a dozen times. This is the revenge they swore for that."

"I still call death down on them. Here, in this place, I call death and destruction on all with such evil in their heart!"

And as the echoes of Auguste's cry of *death* and *evil* and *heart* resounded in the dim and empty street, his cry was answered with the muffled report of a single rifle shot, and he was thrown backward into the ruins.

"Auguste!" Therese screamed and ran to him. She put her hand on him to help him up, but his heavy gray overcoat was wet and sticky, and in the dark the coat seemed to be growing darker.

"Therese," he said weakly. "I didn't mean . . . I didn't mean my own death."

"No!"

She pulled back his coat. There was only enough light to see that his white shirt was red, a great sea of red.

But he was looking past her, down the street, and she turned and saw her father also looking in the same direction, behind her. On her knees, with Auguste's head now cradled in her arms, she couldn't turn far enough to see, and so she bent to sit beside him and face the same way he was.

As she did, Auguste spoke again, louder than seemed possible, to whoever it was he was facing.

"And this is your revenge?" Then he coughed.

She looked toward the opponent. He stood ten meters away, a rifle in his hand, and his face a white blank in the darkness.

Auguste spoke. "My love . . . that I would have been with you always . . ." he said, and nothing more.

"Murderer!" she screamed at Rudolph.

Chapter Fifteen

EVERY KIND
OF WOUNDING

— 1 —

The wide emptiness of the Champ de Mars had answered Rudolph's cry with silence. He stood. The September evening was fading but still light and warm. His own hopes were midnight black and stony cold.

He turned away from the sunset and started walking again, toward the Rue Serpente.

He soon came to the narrow alley. The window above was dark. The street door was unlocked and the porter's door was closed. Rudolph mounted the two flights of stairs and came to the last doorway. As he had many other times, as if it were other times, he knocked.

And just as it always had, the door opened and Arpad Pock's sharp face and oil black hair stared out at him, and the firm voice said, "Come in, Rudolph."

"He only left two days ago," Pock said. "To Bordeaux. That's where the French government has fled." The table was set with dried beef and biscuits, and Rudolph was busy chewing them.

"What happened to our house?"

"I didn't know anything had. It must have been hit by a shell just yesterday or today."

"They can land that far into the city?"

"A few have. The Prussian guns in the hills above Saint-Cloud are only five kilometers away."

Rudolph had finished eating and sank into his thoughts.

"You could possibly get out, as an Austrian," Pock said.

"I don't want to."

"Why not?"

"Why?" Rudolph said "To go where?"

"Therese is in Vienna."

"I won't go to my family. I could go to Gravert's."

"Not in Belleville, Rudolph. It's far worse than it was in August. It would be very dangerous for you."

"There must be empty places. Everyone's leaving."

"Stay here," Pock said. "As long as you want. I have plenty more of that in the larder, enough for weeks."

"Weeks? Will the siege last that long?"

"Either Paris will fall, or it will be surrendered, and neither will happen soon."

– 2 –

Rudolph woke early.

"I never eat breakfast." Pock was rattling through cupboards. "But there's bread and cheese."

"I'll go out for coffee. Are the cafés open?"

"Do you think a small thing like a siege and bombardment would close the cafés of Paris? I'll come with you."

When they had a table on a peaceful street, and strong coffee and rolls, their conversation started.

"Tell me what's happened to you," Pock asked.

"Do you mean, where I've been?"

"More than that. You aren't the same as you were, Rudolph. Go ahead, tell me where you've been. I only know that you left home in July, and then you were in Metz two weeks ago."

"How did you know I was in Metz?"

"Auguste de l'Imperator was here. He told us everything."

"Everything?" Rudolph said, suddenly angry, and very skeptical. "Not everything. When did he come to Paris?"

"By his account, it was two days after he lost you near Montmedy."

"He lost me? He didn't lose me. He led me into a trap."

"He led you? But surely he wouldn't."

"Where is he now?"

"He's in Vienna with your sister."

"With her? Does Father know?"

"Of course. He sent them together."

Rudolph was getting angrier. "He sent them?"

"Yes," Pock said, taken aback. "Why shouldn't he? There was no possibility of Auguste returning to Metz."

"No. Not after he deserted."

"But he meant to return. He was prevented."

"Lies. He never meant to return."

"Please," Pock said, surprised at his vehemence. "Tell me from the beginning."

"It's too long to tell."

"Or too painful?"

"That, too."

"Wounds take time to heal," Pock said.

"I'm going to find Gravert." It was early afternoon.

"Belleville is a powder keg."

"I know my way around it."

From the Quartier Latin, it took less than an hour. As he walked along the dirt streets, between the dilapidated buildings, among the rough men and sullen women, he felt the unstable, unbalanced energy in the air, like an explosion just waiting. The glances were quicker and aggressive, and the feet treading the hard earth were always ready to race toward the fight, whenever it would come.

He went into the building where he'd lived and climbed the long flights in the windowless dark and stink that were always there. At the top, he knocked where he knew the door was, even if there was no light to show him.

The door opened. There was light in the room beyond from the one small window into the narrow space behind the building. The child looked up at him with her usual indifferent stare.

"Emile!" she wailed, and wandered back into the dark.

"Gravert."

"Harsanyi! Are you dead or alive?"

"Alive. Which are you?"

"Alive, too."

They walked down the steps toward the street and the light. "Did you go to Metz?"

Rudolph nodded. "And then Sedan. And I'm back now."

"Is your sister here?"

"No. Our house is knocked down and they're gone."

"You can't stay here." Gravert said it matter-of-factly. "No food, and my cousin is back."

"I'm staying with Pock."

"Is he still here?" Gravert was surprised. "Old Pock! Paris won't fall with him in it."

"What are you doing?" Rudolph asked.

"I'm going out." They had come out into the sun. "I leave here every day at three."

"Where are you going?" Rudolph asked.

Gravert had already been much changed from the clean, uniformed cadet of the École, but now he was even more so—bearded, his hair uneven, and his eyes burning.

"To the fort. De Noisy. I'm on the cannon."

"How long do you go?"

"From four until midnight, then the night men take over and I go back home."

"I'll come," Rudolph said. And with the brief conversation, Rudolph chose his role for the siege.

He followed Gravert through the streets to the Romainville gate in the city wall, and out into the fields beyond. "Who's organizing the forts?"

"General Trochu. The people trust him. They don't care if he's part of the government or not. No one trusts the government."

"Who's in the forts?"

"There's regular army," Gravert said, holding up three fingers. "They're precious few, and they're the only ones who know what to do." He touched the second finger. "There's the National Guard that was organized in the summer. They've had some training, but they're from the provinces and they aren't worth much. It was mostly National Guard troops in the battle at Sedan." The third finger. "And there's the Paris militia. They don't know anything about fighting, but at least they show up every day."

They had passed the small and empty fortress of Romainville, and then the village it was named for, and finally the larger Fortress de Noisy was above them.

Less than two kilometers to the southeast, another fortress came into view. As they watched, its guns let loose a barrage; first the billows of gray smoke, then the shaking thunder.

"Fortress de Rosny," Gravert said. "It's taken the most of the attacks from the east so far."

"I rode past it," Rudolph said, "on my way to Metz. It was so quiet that day."

Fortress de Noisy was crowded, mostly with men not in uniform and with no apparent purpose. But Gravert took Rudolph to the commander, who was smartly dressed in military blue coat and red trousers, with even a sword at his side, and from this person he received his assignment to do whatever Gravert was doing. The commander didn't seem to know what that was, or care. But in any case, Rudolph was accepted into the garrison, and into the defense of Paris.

Gravert showed him the twelve bright new cannons on the northeast wall, and then the thick walled magazine filled with shells. "Ten thousand," he said. "Enough for ten days' continuous fire."

They did not fire that day, though. They were issued a dinner of bread and boiled potatoes, and as they ate they watched the sun lower toward the city behind them and sink into its silhouette, and its thousand lights come on, and the thousand lights of the sky, also, and another thousand lights of the enemy east and north of them among the villages and farms beyond the ring of fortresses.

"Do they attack at night?" Rudolph asked.

"They haven't yet."

"Do they attack any other way than just artillery? Do the infantry ever come close?"

"They haven't yet."

The moon lit their path into the city only somewhat less than the sun had earlier lit their path out from it. At one in the morning, they reached Gravert's door.

"I'll be back tomorrow at three," Rudolph said.

"They don't pay anything, except supper."

"That's enough."

"And there'll be action sometime," Gravert said. "Sometime soon."

Rudolph looked up at the dark windows.

"Do you still have it?"

"Have it?" Then Gravert remembered. "Oh, yes."

"I'll come."

He walked behind Gravert up the steps in the pitch-dark. They opened the door to the apartment, and the black inside was the same. By hearing rather than by sight, Rudolph followed Gravert as he opened the door to the bedroom where the rest of his family was sleeping. Then he reached under the bed and pulled out something long and handed it to Rudolph.

"Thank you for keeping it."

It was another forty minutes' walk to Pock's apartment through streets quiet and silver under the moon. In the silence, the Seine was loud. He stopped on the Pont de la Tournelle to listen.

The water moaned and splashed against the centuries-old arches, speaking a language he didn't know. But on the bridge he opened the polished, beautiful wooden case. The moonlight found the perfect surface and leaped back from it. He ran his finger lightly down the length of his sword.

Whatever the river was speaking, the sword understood.

Pock was waiting when he got home.

"I worried you wouldn't return," he said.

"If I ever don't," Rudolph said, "it won't matter."

– 3 –

"How did you get to Metz?" Pock asked. They were again at their morning café.

"Therese wanted me to go."

"She urged you to be in the army?"

"I wasn't in the army."

"De l'Imperator said that you were. That was why you were in Metz."

"He knew that wasn't true. I was in Paris, at Gravert's."

"So you were after all. She asked me where Emile Gravert lived, and

I wondered if that was why. But then we were told you were in the army. How did she know where you were?"

"We saw each other once before at the beginning of August."

"She knew that early where you were?"

"I told her not to tell."

"Your father was very worried. He was trying very hard to find you."

"I didn't want him to. I knew why he was trying to find me."

"Because . . . well, because he's your father!"

"No." Rudolph's anger had returned. "Because he knew Sarroche was after me."

"Did you tell your father what Sarroche had said to you?"

"He found out. That's why he wanted to find me. He thought I was plotting with Sarroche."

"I'm sure he didn't!"

"He accused me of it."

Pock thought for a few moments. "And were you?"

Rudolph shook his head. "I wouldn't have. And then, it was too late."

Rudolph met Gravert that afternoon.

"Did you hear the guns this morning?" Gravert asked.

"No."

"You must be too far into the city. Everyone here could hear them."

They walked the four kilometers to the fort together, and as they did they saw three volleys fired by the far Fortress de Rosny.

"What are they firing at?" Rudolph asked.

"They can see the enemy camps."

"Does the enemy fire back?"

"I haven't seen them fire." They climbed to their own guns. Their metal was as silent and cool as the late September air. Gravert patted the smooth bronze like a pet dog. "Soon, my friend."

That night, Rudolph was issued a Chassepot rifle. There were thousands to spare in the city.

— 4 —

"I've been thinking about what you said yesterday." Pock was wiping the two plates and mugs they used each day for lunch. "About your father. He had been negotiating himself with Sarroche?"

"And with the other two: the Englishman and the Prussian."

"Whistler and von Stieff. Yes."

"He would have sold to the Prussians!" Rudolph said. "He didn't care anything but for the money."

"I'm not sure that's true. . . ."

"Why else would he have even talked to them?"

"He might have been trying to get a higher price from the French," Pock said.

"Too high," Rudolph said. "That was why Sarroche came after me. He was trying with Therese, too."

"No!" Pock was shocked. "How? He didn't approach her, also?"

"It was Auguste. He was Sarroche's agent."

Pock shook his head. "Auguste de l'Imperator. I never would have thought." He didn't seem greatly surprised. "And that's why you're upset that he would be with your sister even now. But how do you know?"

"He admitted it. I accused him."

"How long has Sarroche had him under his power?"

"Since he was in Vienna before we came to Paris."

"But I thought he only met Therese at the Austrian Embassy here in Paris."

"He had already known her for months. He came to Paris when we did."

"Does your father know this?"

"He didn't before. I don't know what he knows now."

Pock struggled with the new knowledge. "So . . . even then, Sarroche was planning to push your father aside so that you or Therese would have control of the cinnabar."

"He must have been." Then Rudolph had a new thought. "Unless Auguste was trying to influence Mother instead."

"Your mother?"

"He spent a lot of time with her when he came to the house."

"What a thought! That Sarroche could have tried to persuade her!"

"Nothing all day," Rudolph said as he and Gravert started the long trudge back to the city. This midnight was the least hospitable so far: a light rain was falling, and the cloud-obscured moon was a poor guide for the road.

"They want to starve us."

"The Prussians can't stay forever in the middle of a hostile country-side."

"The countryside is as hostile to Paris as it is to the Prussians," Gravert said. "They'll let the Prussians starve us."

"May I come with you someday?" Pock asked when Rudolph arrived back at the apartment. "I've seen most of the forts, but not de Noisy."

"Come tomorrow."

– 5 –

"Monsieur Professor!" For a moment, in his surprise, Gravert was rendered the respectful cadet of the spring.

"Gravert!" Pock showed his pleasure. "Well met!"

"Yes, sir." Gravert was recovering his poise. "Harsanyi told me that you were still in the city."

"If Prussia is at the gates of Paris, I am a Parisian. I want to see de Noisy."

"You vouch for him?" Gravert asked Rudolph.

"Of course I do. You know him, too."

"All visits must be vouchsafed."

"I vouch for him."

With these formalities complete, they began the long walk to the fort.

The commander of the fort could not be located to be informed of the visitor, so Gravert and Rudolph took it upon themselves to show Pock the walls and storerooms and the guns themselves.

"Is it new?" Pock asked as they admired the gleaming bronze.

"They've never been fired," Gravert said.

Pock was dismayed. "But the factory tested them! Didn't they?"

"They told us they had been."

"You should test them, Gravert."

Gravert bristled. "The commander would make that decision."

Pock bowed apologetically. "Of course. But I'm sure they will be fired soon."

"Yes," Gravert said, pleased at Pock's respect. "We all know it will be soon."

Even as he said the words, the air shrieked. Pock, from long experience, dropped to his knees, while Rudolph and Gravert turned dumbly to look out from the rampart toward the sound.

The rampart shook as the earth bank in front of it erupted in smoke and fire.

"Get down!" Pock said, and they both obeyed. But the impact was thirty meters away and far below them, and their slow reaction cost them only a shower of clods and dirt.

"Where did it come from?" Rudolph asked as they stood again, cautiously, and looked out at the horizon.

The answer was obvious, where a distinct smoky smudge was rising from beyond the village of Bondy, two kilometers away.

And behind them, in the center of the fort, the commander had appeared from his command room. Every eye was on him as he stepped smartly to the wall and peered out with a spyglass. His inspection of the enemy was not as intent as the stare the gunners had on him.

He was interrupted. The silence had only settled after the first shell when a second came at them. One lesson had taught everyone well, and every head was down, behind the wall, when the shell hit.

This impact was higher, on the lower reach of the wall itself, and shook them far more. But the wall was much stronger than one explosion.

"Prepare to return fire."

The commander had not lowered his dignity or himself, and he still stood tall and statuesque. At his either side, each long row of cannon was prepared.

"Load!"

Twelve shells were loaded into twelve breeches, and the breeches were closed and locked.

"Aim!"

Gravert stood aside. Honored, Pock put his eye to the sight and turned the crank. Every other barrel did the same, and twelve cannon in unison were shifted to all point directly at the far-off, telltale smoke.

"Prepare!"

A dozen lit brands were lifted to the fire holes. Pock stepped away as Gravert held his smoking wick.

"Fire!"

Rudolph was expecting the thunder and fire; for an instant he didn't grasp that he was thrown back, that a giant hand had taken him and lifted him, and then had hurled him into the rampart wall, or that he was blinded and choked by black smoke, or deafened by a metallic, smashing noise.

And then stunned, as he began to pick himself up, he had to remember what had just happened, and what it meant that the cannon was gone and its wheels were flat and broken on the ground. Then he saw the barrel.

It was three meters from where it had been and somehow deformed. From the shock, it was still taking him too long to realize the meaning of what he was seeing. But then he did. The breech end was opened out like a peeled orange. And there was something else.

Pock.

"Pock!"

In seconds, Rudolph and Gravert and the rest of the crew were pulling and lifting the thousand-kilogram bronze barrel. Underneath, Pock was flat on the ground, facedown, shuddering in pain.

He had nearly escaped. The cannon was atop his left leg, lying straight across it. The leg beneath wasn't straight.

For a moment, they had the bronze weight off the ground. Rudolph took Pock's shoulders and pulled as hard as he could, and pulled him free.

"Are you all right?" Rudolph asked.

"Not all," Pock gasped.

There was another crash as the rest of the cannon fired their second volley.

Rudolph and Gravert settled Pock into his bed. The journey had been arduous for them, leading the horse and cart that the commander had allowed them. For Pock, though, it must have been a nightmare. He had long given up speaking. But as they stood back, he managed a smile.

"Now I've seen de Noisy," he said. "I'll always remember it."

"What can we do?" Rudolph asked.

"There's brandy in the cupboard. Give it to me."

And later, Rudolph had found a physician, an elderly and patient man who left his dinner to come.

"He needs a surgeon. But the bone seems cleanly broken. Keep him very still and in three or four weeks it may heal back together."

"What about the pain?" Rudolph asked.

"The pain will ease," Pock said. "Don't be dismayed, Harsanyi. An old soldier learns to ignore the pain."

Rudolph sat up from a deep sleep. He was disoriented in the dark room and didn't know what had wakened him, until another loud wail came from Pock's room. Rudolph stumbled toward the door, still shaking off sleep.

The trembling light of a single guttering candle made the room tremble. Pock was not conscious, but not asleep. His eyes were open but blind, and his body thrashed in the bed. He called out, yet Rudolph couldn't understand the words, if they were words.

"Pock!" He touched the man's brow, and it was on fire, much hotter and brighter than the dying candle. "Pock. Wake up."

"It's dark," Pock answered, but not to Rudolph. Rudolph looked for a new candle, but there were none in the room. He went out into the hall, to the small closet, to the galley kitchen, looking for any taper, and in the bottom drawer of the large cabinet in the parlor he found four candles. They were long and heavy, meant for formal occasions, but they were all that could be found. Rudolph brought one back to the bedroom.

He lit it from the last gasp of the old flame. Quickly, its light grew and the room settled its motion into calm. Pock's agitation also lessened, and finally his eyes were seeing an unfevered world.

"Harsanyi," he said, a low moan. "You have brought me back."

"You're ill, Pock. It's a fever."

"I can feel it. I'm on fire." For a moment, his eyes rolled, and then he returned. "What is the time?"

"Three in the morning."

"Three in the fiery dark." He closed his eyes as the fever took him again. When he opened them, he focused, confused, on Rudolph standing above him with the lit candle.

Pock's eyes widened. "No! No! Put it out!"

"Put what out?"

"The light!" Pock was in a frenzy. "Put out the light!" He tried to sit up but couldn't.

Rudolph blew the flame away, and the blackness was complete. Rudolph could hear Pock, still breathing heavily, fall back into the bed.

"What's wrong?" Rudolph asked.

Pock's breath slowed. "I apologize," he said, and his voice was clear and normal again, only very weak. "The fever again. Leave it dark. The light rattles my brain."

"I'll leave it dark."

"Yes, that's right. But leave the candle so I can have light later, when I'm ready. And back to sleep with you."

Rudolph returned to the couch but not his sleep, and soon the morning light was coming through the window.

In the morning, Pock was awake when Rudolph came to see him, and his fever was subdued. His leg was bruised black, but the wounds were healing.

"It looks bad," Rudolph said. "Will you be all right if I leave for the afternoon?"

"Nothing can happen to me in my own bed."

– 6 –

The exploded cannon had not been replaced. But after the first attack, a number of the defenders chose not to return, so Rudolph and Gravert were attached to a new cannon crew, and the siege continued as it had. The fort began firing a few volleys each day, but they were very careful with their hoard of ammunition.

Rudolph also began to be careful with the hoard in Pock's larder.

Pock was only allowed to stay in bed, at least while Rudolph was home, and he was hardly demanding as a patient. The bruising subsided, and Pock claimed that the pain did, as well.

The days became a routine. Rudolph rose late, after sunrise on late autumn mornings when the sun rose late itself. Pock seemed to always be awake. Rudolph helped him out of bed to his chair, and as Rudolph ate, they discussed the events of the previous day: the forward and back of the attacks on the lines, and the rise and fall of the moods in the city.

Then Rudolph loaded his rifle and took his pack and before two he was in the street walking the kilometers to Gravert's apartment, and by four o'clock they would be at their places on the walls of Fort de Noisy.

The city behind him was not his.

"Why are you doing this?" Gravert asked one afternoon.

"What else is there to do?"

At midnight he left the fort and traced his steps back through a blackened city; the sun was retracing its own steps. Pock would wake, still in his chair, and Rudolph helped him into bed and then he finally climbed onto the couch to sleep.

And the weather began to cool, and their conversation continued.

"What happened when you were separated from de l'Imperator?"

Rudolph had been at Pock's for weeks. Slowly, he was becoming willing to answer questions.

"A Prussian patrol captured me."

"You, an Austrian?"

"They almost shot me just for claiming I wasn't French. They put me in a prison camp."

"Iges?"

"That's what they called it. There were thousands of French."

"A hundred thousand."

"It seemed like it. But no food. Just horses."

"I read about it in the newspapers. But you were released?"

"No. They didn't release me."

"Did you escape?" Pock's eyes were wide. "They said no one had escaped."

"I think it's time to leave," Rudolph said, although it was only one in the afternoon. "I'll be back tonight."

When Rudolph and Gravert reached their station on the walls, not all the walls were still intact. One section, three meters wide and two deep, had been notched from the rampart, and one cannon emplacement that had been in that position was gone.

"It was a lucky shot," the midday man said as they replaced him for their shift.

"Anyone hurt?" Gravert asked.

"Two dead. Not so lucky for them."

That afternoon, the fort was under attack for over an hour.

– 7 –

"I want to ask you an important question," Pock said the next morning. "Do you trust your father?"

"No. I don't."

"Why not, Rudolph?"

"Because I think I know now who he is."

"But you haven't seen him in months!"

"But I have seen so much else."

The day at the fortress was quiet. But late in the afternoon, the whole garrison gathered on the west side, facing Paris, to watch a small circle rise from the city; they were kilometers away, so the circle must actually have been very large.

"A manned balloon," Gravert said. "They're sending mail out, and orders from General Trochu to the rest of the army."

– 8 –

"What happened after Iges?" Pock asked. "From the time you were in the Iges camp to the time that you came here."

"There was an old farmer and his wife."

"What did they do for you?"

"They were poor as mice, but they gave me everything they had."

"I'm glad to know that someone in the world is still kind."

"They fed me and let me stay until I was healthy again."

"Had you been sick?"

It was hard to say it. "I was shot."

Pock quickly looked him over, head to foot. "Where?"

He put his finger on his side, above his waist. "Here."

"How did it happen?"

"When I was escaping."

"Tell me."

Rudolph shrugged and didn't answer.

– 9 –

"You must not know about Beaubien, the painter!" Pock said on another morning. "How would you know?"

"The man who painted Therese," Rudolph said. "What about him?"

"He's dead! It's quite amazing. He died in your father's house! Right in the parlor."

Rudolph's mouth dropped open. "How? When?"

"It was the day Therese and Auguste left for Vienna. When your father got home from the train station, the man was dead on the parlor floor. I had come home with him and I saw it myself."

"He just died?"

"He was killed. Murdered."

"How?"

"That great piece of cinnabar your father kept there? Someone had hit him on the head with it. We have no idea who!"

Rudolph's next question was immediate. "Where was Auguste when it happened?"

"Where . . . I think he was at the train station, the Gare du Lyon, with your father and Therese."

"No, he wasn't. He did it. Auguste killed him."

"Auguste de l'Imperator? Why?"

"That was the whole reason Sarroche had Auguste in his control. Auguste owed Beaubien money from gambling and he had to leave the country. Sarroche paid off his debts, and Auguste had to do whatever Sarroche wanted."

"But why would he have killed him? He wasn't in debt to him again, was he?"

Rudolph shook his head, angry and frustrated. "Beaubien had a letter I sent from Iges. It told everything about Auguste. Auguste would have killed him to keep anyone from seeing it."

"How could you have sent a letter from Iges?"

But Rudolph was too angry to answer. "Someday, I'll see Auguste again."

– 10 –

October ended and a much colder and hungrier November began. The word had finally reached the city that Metz had surrendered, and Marshall Bazaine and his army were marching to another set of newly constructed prison barracks in Prussia. As people realized that there was no army left to break their own siege, their rage against the new Republican government began to equal their hatred of the Prussian enemy.

"What happened to the bullet?" Pock asked.

"Which bullet?"

"*Which bullet?* The one you were shot with, of course."

"Oh. I think it's still in me."

"Can you feel it?"

"I think I can feel something hard if I push. I don't feel it any other time."

"Just like your father. That's about where his is, but higher up."

"What will happen to it?" Rudolph asked.

"Nothing, I hope. There are quite a few old soldiers carrying a bullet or two."

"Do you have any?"

"No. I've been lucky, at least in that. I was hit once, but it went clean through. I always wondered what happened to the man who fired it at me. That must be a more important question for someone who still has the bullet in them. Do you know who shot at you?"

"Yes."

"A Prussian?"

"One of the guards."

"What happened to him?"

"I . . ."

Pock waited. "What?"

"I killed him."

"Oh."

"I think it's time for me to leave."

"Be careful, then."

Rudolph may have killed other men that day. He and Gravert and their crew fired their cannon forty times.

"I think I agree with you," Pock said that night. "I think Auguste must have killed Beaubien. Nothing else makes sense."

"Beaubien would have been trying to deliver the letter I sent. It's the only reason he would have gone to the house."

"But Auguste was at the train station with your father."

"Or maybe my father did it."

"Rudolph! Why would he?"

"It must have to do with Sarroche. Maybe Beaubien was his agent, too."

"It was a brutal murder. His skull was crushed."

"I think it gets easier every time you kill," Rudolph said.

— 11 —

In the first week of December, the Paris garrison army was ordered to break out of the Prussian siege. Rudolph and Gravert were to be unaffected: the sortie was planned for the far side of Paris, toward Versailles. But then, on the day before, the orders were inexplicably changed, and in vast confusion, the army was moved through the city to the east.

Even before the move was complete, the first ranks were thrown against the Prussian lines, having to cross the frigid Marne and fight uphill into the most easily defended siege lines.

Rudolph and the other artillery crews used over two thousand shells in one day. They were expert at firing and eagle eyed with their aim, but by evening the French army was flooding back into the city, bloodied and furious.

"Why was the plan changed?" Rudolph asked.

"The government didn't want the rich villas of Saint-Cloud and Sevres damaged," Gravert answered.

"What does it mean to you, Rudolph, to have killed a man?"

"It means I'm a killer."

"You had no choice. It wasn't murder. I know it's a terrible choice, to die or to love your life as someone who has killed. I think many soldiers are disturbed by what they've done. I don't think you have any reason to regret your actions."

"I don't regret what I did."

"You shouldn't."

"Because I know now that I could do it again if I had to."

— 12 —

They were running low on food. December was cold and rain-swept; at least there was no lack of water. The trees were gone from all the parks and boulevards, and the Bois de Boulogne and the Bois de Vincennes on either side of the city had begun to feel the axe. The herds of cattle that had grazed there at the beginning of the siege were gone.

The Paris zoo was suddenly empty of animals.

With no trains in or out, the train stations were put to other uses. The Gare du Nord became a balloon factory. At least twice a week, manned balloons were launched over the lines, filled with letters and dispatches. They were blind shots. No one knew what happened to them once they floated away.

But there were heartening events, as well. In the first week of December, Pock was walking again. Very slowly, just from his bed to his chair, but walking.

"I've listened to all that you've said and thought it over and over," Pock said. "Tell me the truth. Do you really think your father killed your mother?"

"I do."

"I've known him for such a long time."

"I don't think people really know him at all."

"Would it have been to gain complete control over the cinnabar mines?"

"It would have to be."

"Why would he send Auguste to Vienna with Therese? Does he know Auguste is Sarroche's agent?"

"I don't know yet. Maybe he's using them both, Therese and Auguste."

"For what?"

"To get the cinnabar mines for himself."

"He has them now."

"I'll inherit them when I'm twenty-three," Rudolph said. "That's why I don't want my father to know where I am."

"He will find you, though."

"I'll be ready."

"If he tried to kill you, Rudolph, what would you do?"

"I'll be ready."

– 13 –

January came to Paris cold, hungry, and ill. The first starvations were occurring, and the first freezings.

The bombardment of the city itself, beyond just the forts, increased daily. Over one hundred Parisians each week were dying just from being in a place, at a time, that a flying shell landed and detonated.

Holding Rudolph's arm, Pock could get down the stairs to the street. He could walk the street without any help.

Then, as the month proceeded, Paris heard what it had hoped for and dreaded: The president of the Republic, Adolphe Thiers, was in Versailles negotiating an armistice. The hostilities would end, the siege would be lifted, and the treaty negotiations would begin. It would be complete surrender, but Paris would be freed.

On a cold day in January, a troop of cavalry and officers rode through the icy blue brilliance. The month was nearly over and the siege, as well. The horsemen of the new French government passed through the silent German lines and stopped at the outer Paris sentry position. From here, and farther and farther into the heart of Paris, they announced the siege was over.

They were met at the Place de la Concorde by General Trochu, and handed him the official orders from the government to suspend all hostilities. The garrison at Fort Mont Valerien would be allowed one final volley so that the French could claim to have fired the last shot; and then the fort was to be surrendered.

Rudolph and Gravert stood in the crowd at the Place and listened and watched. Food and supplies would be allowed in as soon as the conditions were met. No weapons would be allowed in or out of the city. The German High Command would continue to control all access to the city gates while the negotiations for the final peace treaty began.

The words they heard were about an armistice and treaty, but the words that Paris heard were that France had surrendered.

"Imbeciles," Gravert growled, along with the rest of the crowds. "No, not imbeciles. They're traitors. Thiers is in the pay of the Prussians."

Sensing the crowd's mood, the horsemen retreated back out of the city.

"Paris will never surrender," Gravert said as he and Rudolph walked beside the Seine. "We will never give in."

"What choice do we have?"

"We have our own militia, and we have two hundred guns."

"Will the militia fight against the government?"

"They will if they have to."

They parted at the Pont Royal, where Rudolph crossed the river toward

Pock's apartment. As he crossed, he heard a single low thunder from the west, the final volley from Mont Valerien.

"Imbeciles," Pock said, pulling himself up from the couch. "They can never fight the government. There is the whole National Guard, and now the Metz and Sedan prisoners will be released back to the government's command."

"They don't want to give up fighting the Prussians."

"Germans now," Pock said. "Not just Prussia. It's all of Germany, and Germany will be pleased to assist the French in putting down an uprising in the city. The two enemy armies side by side, bombing Paris. What an end to this war!"

By afternoon, the rumor of new supplies was racing through the city. If the food was bitter, it would still be accepted.

"So soon?" Pock said.

"At the Gare Montparnasse, they say."

"Trains are running?"

"That's what they said, and that the gates at Neuilly and Vincennes have been opened. I'll see what I can find."

"Be careful."

He walked the kilometer to the Gare Montparnasse to see what was being offered. He carried his rifle, and he was not the only one. But the crowd was vast and none of the rumored, promised trains had come, and he turned back.

He mounted the steps to Pock's apartment. As he put the key to the keyhole, he heard a voice inside, in French, which was not Pock's. He put his ear to the door to listen.

Pock seemed to be answering a question. "He might be back soon. He went out to get food at the Gare Montparnasse. I don't know."

The voice asked something else, too quiet for Rudolph to hear.

"He's been here since the siege began. He's been taking care of me; my leg was hurt."

Rudolph pressed his ear harder to hear.

"I want to find him," the voice said, and Rudolph recognized it.

He turned the key and pushed the door open.

"Monsieur Sarroche," he said. "What are you doing here?"

Pock was in his chair, but he seemed pushed back in, in a defensive crouch. His relief at seeing Rudolph was obvious. Sarroche was standing over him, his hands behind his back, miniature and threatening.

Sarroche turned. His face only showed his usual annoyance. "I am here to locate you."

"You have. What do you want?"

Sarroche paused. "For now, nothing more."

"How did you find me?"

"I presumed that Monsieur Pock would know if you were in Paris."

"I shouldn't have let him in," Pock said.

"I don't care if he knows where I am," Rudolph said. "Are you still trying to buy cinnabar? I don't want anything to do with you. You'll have to talk to my father, and I haven't seen him since summer."

"It is at his request that I have sought you. He may well be in Paris at this moment."

"In Paris?"

"I spoke with him at Versailles only a few days ago. He had planned to enter the city as soon as possible."

"What about Therese?" Rudolph asked, off-balance. "My sister."

"She will be with him."

Rudolph took a breath. "And Auguste? Captain de l'Imperator. He was traveling with her."

"I presume he also will be with them. I do not know."

"Yes, you do," Rudolph said. "You were paying him. You were after her just like you were after me, and he was your tool. He admitted it to me."

Sarroche didn't seem to care. "I am acquainted with Captain de l'Imperator, but I have not communicated with him in any way since the war began."

"Then you've lost control of him," Rudolph said. "He's trying to get Therese for himself."

"Your sister's romances are of no interest to me," Sarroche said.

"And why were you talking to my father?"

"He was looking for you."

"And he asked you?"

"He presumed I might have some information. That is why I came here, seeking you."

"Is there anyone you don't control, Monsieur Sarroche?" Rudolph asked. "Even my father?"

"That question is impertinent."

"You're impertinent. Now leave, before I throw you out." He picked up the rifle from the table. "Or before I use this."

"Rudolph!" Pock was anxious. "Be careful."

"I'm not afraid of him. Get out!"

"I will go," Sarroche said. "But it is likely that we will meet again. And your position might be greatly different at that time."

"What do you mean?"

"It may be that you will be making your own decisions. We have discussed this before."

"Nothing will change for me until I'm twenty-three."

"There is another possibility."

"If my father dies? Is that what you mean?"

"On a dark street, in a lawless city, anything might happen," Sarroche said.

"And if something did happen, you would be available to buy my cinnabar."

"Immediately."

"Leave," Rudolph said. "Immediately."

"I will leave. And I will very much anticipate our next meeting."

For a long time, Rudolph stared at the closed door.

"I shouldn't have let him in," Pock said again.

"No. It was useful to talk to him. I'm going out again."

"Where are you going?"

"To our house on Rue Duroc."

"To find your family?"

"That's where they'll go."

"Perhaps you shouldn't. They'll come here soon. Sarroche will tell them where you are."

"No, I'm going to find them." He picked up the rifle.

"Why are you taking that?"

"The streets are dangerous."

"Is that the only reason?"

"Why else would I take it?"

They stared at each other for a moment. "Leave it here, Rudolph."

Rudolph only shook his head, and with the rifle in his hand he left the apartment.

Now it was evening. From reflex, he found himself pausing at corners and looking around them, his gun ready, and soon he was nearing the Rue Duroc.

It was only a few blocks.

After nights of bombardment, the new silence was unsettling. He could hear so many other sounds in it, even in the bitter cold.

He'd seen few people on the streets, so at every sound he pulled his rifle ready. He himself was completely silent.

And he stalked the night.

At last, he was on the Rue Duroc, close to the old house. He could see the rubble, still collapsed into the street.

The moonlight was like mercury, all silver and liquid.

He saw a man standing in the street ahead, and even in the light without any color, Rudolph saw the gold hair and beard and knew who it was. Then he heard Auguste's voice. "Here, in this place, I call death and destruction on all with such evil in their heart!"

Auguste's words were still echoing. Rudolph stood looking on, still unseen. Then, from behind, a rifle fired and Auguste fell backward into the ruins of the house.

For the moment, Rudolph was stunned. He looked back to see where the shot had come from, but it was only dark shadows. In the instant, as he tried to decide whether to make chase, he heard his sister scream.

"Auguste!" He saw her run to him.

Rudolph stepped forward, half the distance.

He saw Maria, her hands to her mouth in horror. Therese was kneeling above Auguste with her back toward the street.

As he came closer, Rudolph could see Auguste's face, white in the gray light.

And Auguste saw him. "And this is your revenge?" he said.

Rudolph only stared back; he had no answer.

He couldn't see Therese anymore; someone else was standing in front of her, and somehow, whether from the dim light or a deeper reluctance, Rudolph couldn't tell who it was. And then he could. It was his father.

They faced each other for some amount of time; a few seconds or years. Rudolph still had the rifle in his arms. Then he felt someone take hold of him, and he turned to see Zoltan lifting the rifle from him. He didn't resist.

"Murderer!" Therese wailed.

"What have you done?" his father said.

Chapter Sixteen

A Man's Enemies Are His Own Household

— 1 —

Ferdinand had found his son.

Behind him, in the shadow of the ruin of his house, Auguste was dying. Before him stood Rudolph, in the shadows of everything dark.

"What have you done?" Ferdinand asked with every pain and rage and grief a man could know.

"Father!" Therese called. He turned away from Rudolph and stooped beside her only to see Auguste's eyes roll and his body sag in her arms. "Oh, Father . . ." she sobbed, and there was no comfort he could give her.

"Just hold him," Ferdinand said. "That's all you can do." Then he stood and faced his son again. "Why?"

"Why . . ." Rudolph seemed dazed. "Why?" Then his focus sharpened. "What? Do you think . . . do you think I shot him?"

Ferdinand looked at the rifle, now in Zoltan's hands. "I saw you."

"No. I didn't. I didn't! There was someone else—"

"Are you lying?" Therese shouted in amazement. "You killed him! Why did you kill him?" Her pitch was rising to a hysterical scream, even as Maria tried to calm her.

Ferdinand took a deep breath. "Go," he said.

Rudolph hesitated. Then he put his hand on the rifle that Zoltan was holding. Zoltan looked to Ferdinand.

Ferdinand nodded and Zoltan let go. Rudolph took the gun, but still only stood.

"Now," Ferdinand said.

"I didn't . . ." But then he gave up and turned.

"Where are you living?"

"Pock's," Rudolph said.

"I'll come tomorrow."

Then Rudolph looked back at Auguste with an unreadable expression. "They have coffins at Les Invalides. We used hundreds during the bombardment. They give them away."

"What do we do now?" Zoltan asked.

Ferdinand pulled himself back to the urgency of the moment. "How is the horse?"

"She can walk. It was just a stone in her shoe."

"We'll go to the embassy building to stay the night."

Zoltan nodded but didn't move from his spot. He nodded toward Auguste and Therese. "And him?"

"We'll put him in the cart and take him."

Zoltan left to bring the horse and cart. Ferdinand stepped closer to Therese and Maria. Maria was still whispering and singing into Therese's ear. There was nothing for him to say; he stood silently and waited.

"Gently," Therese begged as Zoltan and Ferdinand lifted Auguste's body into the cart. They'd made a space for him and now they set him into it, gently.

"To the embassy," Ferdinand said, and they began. Zoltan walked beside the horse to lead it while the others walked beside him. Only Auguste rode.

They were inside the courtyard, where Ferdinand turned and locked the gate behind them. Maria led Therese away from the cart and in, out of the cold.

"It would be best to leave him outside," Zoltan said quietly to Ferdinand. "Let him freeze. If we take him inside . . ."

"Take him into the stable and cover him."

– 2 –

The baron didn't sleep. Every hour he stopped to look into Therese's room, where she slept without moving, through the night. The rest of the time he paced the halls. The building was as cold as the night.

When the first, grayest light of dawn changed the black outside the windows to faint shapes and diffuse images of a Paris street, he put on his coat and went out.

Color had only begun to replace the gray as he reached Rue Serpente. The door to the building was locked and no porter was likely, but even as he stood in the street in view of the high window, the knob rattled and the door opened.

"Come up," Rudolph said.

Ferdinand followed his son's back up the steep steps. Rudolph opened the apartment door without looking back, and when Ferdinand entered the apartment, the first face he saw was Pock's.

"Harsanyi!" he said, trying to force a light tone. "But that won't do. I can't call you both the same name when you're together."

"That won't be often," Rudolph said. He was standing aside, nearly hidden by the entry door.

"You're wounded, Pock?" Ferdinand said, also seeing the bandaged leg.

"Just an accident."

"A cannon exploded," Rudolph said. "It's mostly healed, but it's not good this morning. He needs to be taken to a surgeon."

"Or bring one to me." Pock still tried to make light of all the tension in the room. "After three months, a few more days won't matter."

"I'll take him back to Versailles," Ferdinand said.

"Are you going soon?"

"Today. But first we'll bury Auguste."

"At least he deserves that. Not just to be left out in the street."

"Is that what you have to say?" Ferdinand asked angrily. "Will you tell me why you killed him?"

"I didn't kill him."

Ferdinand paused. "What reason would you have to deny it?"

"That I didn't kill him."

"I saw you! I saw you with the rifle in your hands pointed at him."

"Then believe what you want. I don't care."

"What has happened to you, Rudolph?"

He didn't answer.

"Where have you been?" Ferdinand asked.

"It's too long to tell."

"Why were you in Metz with Auguste?"

"You don't know?" Rudolph said.

"No."

"Then ask Therese."

"What does she know?"

"She sent me to get him."

Ferdinand shook his head. "I don't understand."

"I don't, either. I don't know what she wants, or what Auguste wanted, or what you want."

"What I want?"

"What do you want, Father? Besides all the money you can get from Mother's mines, and to get whatever use you can out of Therese?"

"I don't—"

"And to get me killed somewhere?"

"No." Ferdinand answered the accusation coldly.

"Where were you when I needed you?"

"Where did you ever need me?"

Rudolph shook his head. "I think I never did. I've done better without you."

Ferdinand swallowed his anger and tried to think of something to say.

"Please." Pock finally spoke. "Not like this, please. It's been very difficult and you may say things you would rather not."

"Who killed Auguste," Ferdinand said, trying to be calm. "If you didn't, who did?"

"I don't know. He deserved it."

"Why?"

Rudolph anger's was also gone, pulled inside. "Pock can tell you."

There was nothing else to say, or that Rudolph would listen to.

"We'll come to get Pock later this morning."

"I'll only have a few things to gather," Pock said.

Ferdinand stood. "There is one other thing," he said, moving toward the door. "The embassy staff won't be returning to Paris until the French government does. Someone could stay at the embassy building until then."

Rudolph nodded. "I'll stay there."

"Here's a key to the gate. The other keys will be in the porter's office."

"When will you be gone?"

"Before noon."

"I'll wait until you are."

It was still dim as he walked back home, and the gray light had formed into a gray fog.

But the streets were awake. Whatever relief Paris had felt at the end of the siege, and hunger, and war, was now being replaced as the realization came: She was a surrendered city. Even more, many people thought, a betrayed city.

The government of the Republic began the wooing of its capital city, but the bride was begrudging. Food finally began arriving. Paris accepted the gift, but not the giver.

And the suitor was pursuing her for more than her beauty. Whoever won Paris's heart would win her dowry of 200 cannon.

The details of the surrender had reached the newspapers that morning, and the scorn in the streets was swift. The occupation would continue. The German army would remain surrounding Paris, as guarantee that the treaty negotiations would move quickly. Even those negotiations would begin with terrible German demands: huge reparations, and even worse, the transfer of territory. And worst of all for Paris, the Germans had claimed the right to a victory parade. What a weak, cowardly suitor the new government was! To allow Prussian boots to march the Champs-Elysees of Louis the Fourteenth under Napoleon's Arc de Triomphe, this was the groom allowing his bride to be humiliated on the eve of her wedding.

And so the streets were well awake, even early. Empty carts, and carts full of food and clothing were moving through them, barely seen in the fog.

Nearing the embassy, Ferdinand met Zoltan with the horse and cart and a freshly cut pine coffin. "You talked to him?" Zoltan asked.

"For so long, I'd anticipated seeing him. And now I wish I never had. Is this how God does the things that only He can do?"

In the stable, Ferdinand found his daughter and Auguste together.

Zoltan had left him on the ground, covered with a blanket. Someone, either Maria or Therese, had uncovered his head and put a pillow under it. But he didn't appear asleep; his skin was blue and gray, even more ashen contrasting with his dull gold beard and hair arranged around his dead face.

Therese was beside him in a chair with her hand on his arm and her own face not much more live. She was staring, not at him, but just straight ahead. Her other hand held the necklace she'd given him on his way to war.

Ferdinand waited, but neither Therese nor Auguste moved.

"It's time to leave," he said at last.

She looked at him. "There's nothing to leave."

"But there is a place to go."

"There's nothing." She stood and some life returned to her eyes. "Where will we go?"

"To Versailles."

"And Auguste?"

"We'll bury him."

"His father is buried in the Cemetery Montmartre."

"We'll take him there."

The slow procession soon passed beneath the arch of the embassy courtyard into the Rue de Grenelle. Zoltan led with the reins in his hand, then the horse, with Auguste beneath his blanket in the cart. Therese and Maria followed on foot, and Ferdinand was last. The fog, stubbornly, clung to the city.

First they traveled east to the Boulevard Saint-Germain, to Rue Serpente.

With Zoltan, Ferdinand climbed the stairs for the second time that day and steeled himself for a second meeting.

But Pock was alone, still on the couch, and white with pain.

"Rudolph's gone" was the first thing he said, and it drained him.

"What do you have to take with us?"

"Those two." There were two chests, large and small, on the floor near the door.

"But everything else?" The room was cluttered with so many books and pictures and objects.

"I'll be back for them. In better times."

Ferdinand and Zoltan lifted the larger chest and carried it down to the street and the cart.

"Rudolph is gone," he said to Therese. Come up with us."

"Therese!" Pock brightened when he saw her.

"We'll take care of you, Uncle Arpad."

"I'm not leaving everything behind," Pock said to Ferdinand about the smaller chest. "Those are a few of the gifts I've received through the years."

Then Zoltan and Ferdinand lifted Pock and carried him as their last burden down the stairs.

"There's not room," Zoltan said. Pock, Auguste, the coffin, Therese's luggage, and now Pock's two chests were more than would fit.

Ferdinand and Zoltan took hold of Auguste and heaved him into the open coffin. But, from the cold or from his own death stiffness, the body didn't settle in; it held its pose between sitting and reclining, and the right arm was hung over the edge.

Pock was put in Auguste's place. Zoltan pulled the rein and the horse started, and the cart lurched forward, and Ferdinand, Therese, and Maria continued their cortege walk into the gray fog.

At Montmarte, Ferdinand and Therese chose a place as close as they could find by Auguste's father. Without ceremony, Zoltan dug into the cold ground. Ferdinand worked with him. No one bothered them as they worked. Together, in an hour, they had a shallow grave in which to lay the coffin.

Then Ferdinand led the horse back down the hill while Zoltan stayed behind to shovel the dirt back in. He caught up with them before they were out of the city.

Outside the walls, they turned toward Versailles. Therese walked with her father, and Zoltan led the horse, with Maria beside him. There had been so much walking in the last days.

The long-suffering old farm horse and her carriage finished the trip from Paris to Versailles at the door to Ferdinand's cottage.

Despite her sorrow, Therese took charge of the unloading and settling of Pock, as well as the rest of the luggage.

"I'll find a doctor in the morning," Ferdinand said. They were settled in the cottage on the edge of the village.

"Yes. When you can," Pock said. "I'll last awhile longer."

"I'm not sure that you will. Your leg looks much worse even than this morning. A day in a rough cart was hard on it."

For several minutes they sat in the silence of old friends. They might have even seemed asleep, but when Ferdinand spoke, Pock was listening.

"What was he like to live with for four months?"

"He's been made a man."

"He'd been becoming one."

"It's complete, and more."

"I want you to tell me about him."

"We'll have some time, Harsanyi, and I will."

The next pause was shorter.

"What did he mean when he said to ask you why Auguste deserved to die?"

"It's a long story, and I heard it over four months. But I can tell you the essence. Auguste was an agent of our friend Sarroche, and his purpose for the last year with Therese has been to acquire cinnabar through her. At least, that's what Rudolph believes. And you don't seem surprised."

"I can understand that he would think that."

"He says de l'Imperator admitted it to him."

"Then it's probably true."

"And he was in Vienna long before you met him in Paris. He and Therese were already close."

Ferdinand nodded. "Therese lied to me. There was always something that had seemed wrong."

"She knew what you'd say. A lone French adventurer chasing her without your permission? You'd banish him immediately. And he must have been whispering in her ear, telling her what to say to you. Don't be angry with her. She's suffering more than she deserves." Pock sighed. "I was afraid when Rudolph took his rifle with him. I was afraid he meant to use it."

– 3 –

The next morning, in all of Versailles, there was no doctor or surgeon. The German staff was still in the process of withdrawing, and the French government was just beginning to move in. For all the officials of every type, though, there was no one who could find a medic or even a nurse.

"Monsieur, every member of the medical profession is in the service of the military, tending the multitudes of wounded soldiers," a policeman told Ferdinand. "There is no possibility of obtaining medical help."

Ferdinand went looking for a different help.

Not all of the Versailles palace was marble and gold. At its creation, it had housed not only the glory of France, but also the machinery of its government. Now the machinery had returned to the hundreds of dreary and windowless offices that had been built two hundred years earlier for just such functionaries that every government, and especially every French government, also had had and always would have.

"Monsieur Sarroche," Baron Ferdinand said. "I have come to make a request."

"A request for what?" The little man was very busy. His desk was piled with papers and portfolios, and four clerks in his outer office were writing documents like madmen.

"I have a man who is wounded and needs medical help."

"You are asking me for medical help?" Sarroche said. "That is not my responsibility."

"It was not my responsibility to provide medical help to you," Ferdinand said. "But I did."

"I made a personal request. You are making an official request. It is not comparable."

"I would like to make a personal request that you find a doctor for him. All surgeons are assigned to the army and are not available to civilians."

"Their needs are much greater."

"This man was wounded in the defense of Paris."

"Then he should report to his own military unit."

"He is Austrian."

Sarroche frowned. "Austrian? Oh. You have Monsieur Pock with you?"

"You knew he was wounded?"

"Of course. I saw him only a few days ago, in Paris."

"Before the siege ended?"

"No. The evening of that day. I was looking for your son and I found him there."

"Did you tell my son that I was coming into Paris?"

"I did."

"Then that was how he came looking for me."

"So I have already done you a service," Sarroche said. "But as for Monsieur Pock, I will need to consider your request. I may be able to help."

"And I also want to notify you of the death of a French soldier."

Sarroche shrugged. "That is hardly of importance to me. There have been at least tens of thousands of deaths."

"This was Captain Auguste de l'Imperator."

Even Sarroche could not mask his surprise. But he tried. "Why do you tell me this?"

"He admitted to having been your agent. He admitted that you paid him to gain control of my daughter, and through her my cinnabar mines."

"That is only his claim. It cannot be proven."

"I think it's obvious," Ferdinand said. "Don't deny it."

"All right, then, I do admit it."

"And I should kill you."

"That would not advance your request of me for a doctor for your friend."

The baron's anger was growing. "And that was in addition to your attempts to turn my son against me. And your murder of my wife."

"Both of these were your own accomplishments."

Ferdinand regained control of his emotions. "Yes. You've said that before. Did you kill Henry Whistler?"

"I did not."

"Or Pierre Beaubien?"

"The painter?" Sarroche shrugged. "De l'Imperator was deeply in debt to Monsieur Beaubien. I did pay his debts in exchange for his work for me. But that is no reason for me to have ordered Beaubien's death. And I have had no communication with him since the war started."

"Have you ordered many men's deaths?"

Sarroche shrugged. "I am in the business of war, as are you, Monsieur Baron. I imagine you have killed many men."

"On the battlefield. Not in cold blood."

"They are dead either way. But I deny any involvement with any of these deaths."

"I wonder if anything you've said to me today is the truth."

"How dare you say that!" Sarroche's own control broke. "How dare you, you who offered for months to sell cinnabar to France when you never had any intention of doing so!"

"How do you know my intentions?"

"There was no cinnabar stockpiled at your mines. You had ordered all production stopped."

"You have just lied to me again."

"What do you mean?"

"You said you had no communication with de l'Imperator since the war began. But the only way you could know that I had stopped production at my mines in Idria was if he told you after he stopped there on his trip to Vienna with my daughter."

Sarroche ignored the accusation. "But why did you stop the production of your mines? Your cinnabar was worth more before the war began than it ever will be now."

"I will not sell it to you now, or ever."

"Why? Do you hate the French that much?"

"No. I hate war."

"Then you are a fool."

Ferdinand paused. "I appreciate your gracious help in procuring a surgeon for my friend."

"A surgeon will be at your house in the morning."

"The more quickly he can come, the better."

It was evident why the surgeon who was provided to the Austrians was still in Versailles and hadn't been conscripted by the military authorities. He was hale and hearty, but at least eighty years old. He wore a black coat, and a high hat on his hairless head, and he seemed none too pleased to be called out.

But he might have been the best doctor for the case.

"Do you have experience with injuries like this?" Baron Harsanyi asked doubtfully as the man stood next to Pock's bed. He looked quite wealthy, as if his clientele was more likely to have suffered heart palpitations or dry coughs than injuries caused by exploded cannon.

"Experience?" he retorted. "Young man, I was experienced in broken bones and saber wounds and bullet holes long before you were born."

"Then we are very pleased to have you."

"My first campaign was with the emperor in Italy."

Ferdinand frowned. "At Magenta?"

The man was insulted. "At Marengo!"

Pock laughed out loud. "He's got you there, Harsanyi!"

Therese was watching discretely from the doorway. "What do you mean?" she said.

"Magenta was twelve years ago. Marengo was more than seventy!"

"But he said it was with the emperor . . ."

"Napoleon the first," Ferdinand said.

"You do have some stories to tell," Pock said to the doctor, keenly interested. "Where else did you go?"

"I'm not here to talk," the doctor said, but he was obviously mollified by Pock's reverence. "You tell me your story."

"A cannon barrel was accidentally dropped on it," Pock answered as his leg was inspected.

"When?"

"A good long time ago. Just after the siege started."

"Four months?" The doctor shook his head. "And nothing else since?"

"It was improving quite well, but just in the last few days it seems to have taken a turn for the worse."

"Something has caused this turn," the doctor said. He put both his hands on the leg and felt it from foot to knee. "Yes, there was a break, and it's not healed. Or it may have healed but has been recently broken again."

"We carried him here from Paris," Ferdinand said. "Yesterday. It wasn't an easy ride."

"That could be the reason," the doctor said.

"Will his leg heal?" Therese asked.

"It should," the doctor answered. "If he is cared for. Are you a nurse, young lady?"

"No, sir."

"Then you'll have the opportunity to become one. Keep him in bed and don't let him walk without help, and not more than the length of the room. I'll return next week. And call me immediately if he develops a fever."

"Did you hear him, Uncle Arpad?" Therese said.

"I heard him," Pock answered, and laughed again. "And I don't think he knows a thing!"

— 4 —

"It hasn't improved," the doctor said a week later. Therese had been strict, and Pock compliant, but they all could tell that something was wrong. A bright, thin red streak had appeared running up the back of his leg, and even though he denied it, Ferdinand could tell that Pock was often in pain.

"What isn't improving?" Ferdinand asked.

"As you see, there is an infection. The wound isn't healing. Has there been a fever?"

"I had a fever after the first time it was broken," Pock said. "But it only lasted a few days."

"I'll return again next week. But something is wrong. And remember," he said as he was leaving, "if there is any fever at all, call me."

Ferdinand was awakened by someone loud and panicked.

It was a dark night, and he lit a candle to find his way to Pock's room. Therese was also hurrying from her room.

They stood over the bed watching. Pock was rolling side to side, his eyes open but not seeing, and his brow was covered with sweat.

"Pock, wake up," Ferdinand said.

"Now, now! Light them!" Pock was shouting at someone.

"Wake up!"

"Too close! Fire! Light them now!"

"Wake up." Ferdinand had his hand on Pock's shoulder and shook him strongly. Pock reacted violently, grabbing the hand and pushing it away. But then his eyes focused.

"Harsanyi?" Wherever he'd been, Pock was baffled at seeing Ferdinand there with him. "What are you . . . where . . . ?"

"You're in bed, Pock."

"And he has a fever, Father," Therese said.

"The Turks . . . oh." He took a few deep breaths. "Oh, I was dreaming."

"I'll bring some cold water," Therese said. "Should I get the doctor?"

"The morning will be soon enough," Ferdinand said.

– 5 –

"How is your friend, Herr Pock?" Prince von Metternich asked. Ferdinand had resumed his position as attaché, but he guarded his every word and action. There weren't many of either; the ambassador seldom spoke to him. But for once, the prince seemed congenial.

"Not well."

"My sympathies. I'm returning to Vienna for a few weeks to confer with Minister von Buest, and to collect my wife. Von Karlstein will manage the affairs here while I'm gone." The ambassador leaned forward to accent the importance of his words. "The negotiations between France and Germany are not going well. There may be trouble while I'm gone."

"I've read the reports in the newspapers, of course."

"Germany demands territory and reparations, and too much of each. They want Alsace and most of Lorraine, including Metz." He sighed. "Oh, and two billion francs."

"Von Bismarck is being cruel," Ferdinand said.

"It is worse than cruelty, Baron. It is a blunder. In fact, it might be the one positive outcome for Austria. Bismarck will get his new provinces, but the price is France's pure hatred. There will be another war with France. There will never be peace. In four years or forty, France will have her revenge." He leaned back in his chair. "But the next critical moment will be much sooner."

"The parade?"

"Yes, the German victory parade, straight down the Champs-Elysees. Right under the noses of two hundred cannon on Montmartre, which the French government does have control of. I'll want you to send me a telegram or two as the day approaches to let me know if it looks like anything might happen."

Returning home after sunset, Ferdinand saw the light on in Pock's window.

"He's just now fallen asleep," Therese said, sitting beside the bed.

"His fever?"

"It's much less."

"And how are you?"

She smiled. "Very tired. I've been with him the whole day." She looked around the plain room. "It's so cheerless in here."

At the foot of the bed was the smaller of Pock's chests. It hadn't been opened, and Ferdinand looked at it curiously. "He said these were gifts he'd received."

"We should put some out. He'd like that."

Ferdinand lifted the lid as Therese brought a lamp close to see in.

There were a dozen or so bundles in the chest, some of them wrapped in brown paper, and others uncovered: a miniature cannon, a lacquered box with French and Austrian flags painted on it, a silver candleholder. In the bottom lay four large red candles.

Ferdinand lifted the unwrapped objects out and set them on the room's tall bureau, and then he looked more closely at the candles. One had been lit briefly, while the wicks of the others remained untouched.

"You could go," he said. "I'll stay for a while."

"He's asleep anyway." She did seem very tired. She hadn't seemed very well herself since they'd reached Versailles, and she'd never again mentioned Auguste.

Ferdinand sat for an hour or more, watching his sleeping friend. Pock had aged. His face was thinner, and his jet-black hair had turned gray close to his scalp; it might have been guessed before that he dyed his hair, but now it was revealed plainly. In fact, all of his outward appearance seemed to be crumbling.

The few treasures in the chest were most of what Pock had from his life. Ferdinand looked again at them.

Then he looked closer.

Zoltan was passing in the hall, and Ferdinand called him.

"Yes, master?"

"Do you remember, in Whistler's hotel room?" He was trying himself to remember.

"I remember the room."

"What candles did he have? They were mostly burned down. But one was still burning."

"I remember," Zoltan said. "They were red. Dark red. And thick at the base."

"Were they like these?"

"Yes, they were just like those."

– 6 –

Ferdinand didn't sleep well that night, if he slept at all. In the first light of morning he was back to Pock's room.

Pock was already awake and sitting up in the bed, and greeted him energetically.

"Harsanyi! You don't look any better than I do!"

"I never have, Pock. We opened your chest last night."

"Yes, yes. We should have done it weeks ago. That was why I brought it."

"I want to ask you about some of the things."

"Where they came from? You know, as much as I like them, I forget over the years where exactly they all came from. But some I remember. The little cannon, that was from the Italian colonel . . . you remember, don't you? The 1856 campaign."

"Gaspari."

"That's it! Luigi Gaspari! And the broken bayonet blade. I don't see it out. Did I bring it or leave it in Paris?"

"It might be in the chest. We didn't open the things that were wrapped."

"Oh, you could. We'll do it later."

"Who gave you these candles?"

"The red ones?"

"Yes." Ferdinand held one up.

"Yes, yes. Those were from one of the students at the École. It was . . . well, it was Gravert."

"Gravert? Rudolph's friend? The one you said Rudolph lived with last summer."

"Yes. It was a somewhat odd gift. But his family's hardly wealthy, so he must have come across them somewhere, and they were all he had."

"Why did he give them to you?"

"A parting gift. It was after he'd left the École. He sent them to me. I wish he'd brought them personally, but he was probably embarrassed to be seen after his dismissal. I never wanted to burn them."

"No," Ferdinand said. "I think you should just keep them."

"Maria."

"Master?" She looked up from her breakfast cooking at Ferdinand and Zoltan.

He moved across the room to stand in the window. Zoltan stayed in the doorway.

"Back in Vienna. Do you remember the candles that were in my wife's room when she was ill?"

Maria smiled. "Oh, yes, master. It was a surprise, of course, but the mistress was so pleased."

"What do you mean?"

"That you'd send them to her."

It was completely unexpected, and Ferdinand was abrupt in his reply. "I would send them?"

"Well, yes, master." Maria was fearful at his reaction. "They came from Paris. The package had your name on it, to the mistress."

"I never sent any candles." Then he forced himself to be patient. "I'm sorry. I didn't mean to be harsh. How did they come?"

"Just in the mail. They were wrapped in a box."

"What color were they?"

"Red. They were beautiful candles."

"Was there a note?"

Now she was more disturbed. "Yes, sir."

"What did the note say?"

"It was . . . it was to the mistress."

"Did she show it to you?"

"Yes, master."

"What did it say?"

"It was an engraved card."

Ferdinand paused. Maria's reluctance and fear were hard to overcome, and he didn't want to frighten her completely. "It's important, Maria," he said very calmly. "Just tell me what you remember."

"Yes, master. It said, 'For your bedroom. May our love always burn as bright!' "

Ferdinand struggled to speak. "When did they come?"

"Just before she became ill, sir."

He choked the words out. "Maria, why did she send me the telegram that she was ill? Did she fear that she wouldn't survive the illness?"

"She never said that, master."

"Do you know why she did send the telegram? She had never before called for me to come home."

"I don't know, sir. But I think it might have been because of the candles. Because you sent them, I think she thought you would come to her."

All he could say was to thank her for her help, and he and Zoltan left the kitchen.

"Who sent them?"

The words came like a cannon exploding. Ferdinand and Zoltan were in the road in front of the house.

"The one who killed her," Zoltan said.

He started walking, pounding on the hard cobblestones of the street. "Who?"

Zoltan was with him but didn't answer.

"Who?" he asked again. "Who? And to Whistler, and to Pock."

"Sarroche," Zoltan growled.

"Who else could it be? No one else. It has to be. And Beaubien? And Auguste? Did he kill them, too? And why?"

"For cinnabar."

"Red candles with mercury mixed into them. Burning and filling the room with poison." A new thought stopped him. "And they were even colored red. Vermillion red like cinnabar."

"That is a boast," Zoltan said.

"Yes, a boast. A taunt. And Beaubien was killed by cinnabar."

"But not de l'Imperator."

"No. I still don't know everything, but I know much more. Zoltan, I feel this murderer more closely now, as if he is someone who has spoken to me by his murders." He started walking again, back toward his house. "It is time to speak back. It's time to speak to Sarroche. Will God fight evil? If He won't, I will."

The door to Sarroche's office was closed, and the head clerk blocked Ferdinand from even knocking.

"Monsieur Sarroche is unavailable."

"Is he in there?"

"He is in an important meeting and—"

But Baron Ferdinand Harsanyi hadn't come in order to be sent off by a clerk. He pushed past, set his hand on the knob, and threw the door open.

Two pairs of eyes were on him. From behind the desk, Sarroche's were irritated and cold as he recognized the interloper. The other pair, beneath a bald scalp fringed with gray and sandy yellow hair, were surprised, and more, embarrassed.

Karl von Stieff quickly stood to his full height, and then bowed down from it.

"Baron Harsanyi," he said in greeting.

"Baron Harsanyi," Sarroche said at the same time, in challenge. "You have intruded. Leave immediately."

The contrast between them would have been humorous, with von Stieff tall, thin-maned, and awkward, and Sarroche short, nimble, and with his luxury of hair. But there was no humor in the room.

"I won't leave," the baron said. "Not until I know what happened to my wife."

"It is absurd!" Sarroche exclaimed angrily. "To come here at this time and say such a thing."

"I'm accusing you of murder."

"You have done such before, and I have denied it. Now leave or I will call for the police."

"Please!" Karl von Stieff was alarmed by the sudden drama he was witnessing, but there was another look in his eyes.

"It is beyond endurance!" Sarroche said, his fury increasing. "I will protest to the Austrian government!"

"Monsieur Sarroche," von Stieff said. "I must beg your leave for a moment. Baron, please come. I must speak with you."

Only his utter seriousness kept the others from protesting. Before Sarroche could erupt again, von Stieff had pulled Ferdinand from the room, and to the outer hallway.

"What is it?" Ferdinand asked. His bewilderment had overcome his anger.

"He is not the one."

"Sarroche? What do you mean?"

"He did not murder your wife."

"But she was murdered!"

"Yes, but not by Sarroche." Von Stieff was speaking low and urgently. "I know this."

"How?"

"Sarroche was enraged when she died. His plans to purchase cinnabar were completely upset. I assure you, Baron, that her death was fully against Sarroche's hopes."

"Who told you?"

"I have a source."

"I must know," Ferdinand said. "I can't take your word for it."

"His name is Leander Wadsworth."

Ferdinand was stunned. "Henry Whistler's clerk?"

Von Stieff's face reddened in embarrassment. "I am ashamed to engage is espionage, but it is sadly necessary. He reported to me everything that

Mr. Whistler's agents reported to him. And I know that Mr. Whistler, and Sarroche also, were both convinced that you killed your wife."

"I didn't."

"I believe that. I know that you have been seeking your own revenge."

"Revenge?" Ferdinand stepped back. "No."

"Then why did you come here?"

He had to think. "Not for revenge. Just to know." And then he asked, "Why are you here?"

Von Stieff bowed his head, more ashamed. "If Paris revolts against the French government, the German army has agreed to assist the French army in putting down the uprising. I am discussing selling armaments to Monsieur Sarroche."

Your Excellency, Ferdinand wrote. *The mood in Paris is very tense. There has been no violence so far, but the possibility still exists that there will be with any provocation. The plans for the German victory parade are proceeding.*

I must also inform you that I have had a hostile confrontation with Monsieur Sarroche of the Bureau of Armaments. He has threatened to bring up the matter with the French Foreign Ministry. I apologize that I have complicated your relations with the French government.

Another week passed, and the doctor's call was pessimistic, just as Ferdinand and Therese knew it would be.

"It is deteriorating," the aged physician said. "Infection has only increased, and now there is a greater concern." He put his finger on the red stripe that was now wide and ran from Pock's foot to above his knee. The skin was broken in a few places.

"I clean the sores every day," Therese said.

"And the fever?"

"It comes and goes," Pock said, trying as he always had to minimize the seriousness.

"See how the color has darkened here," the doctor said. The place was obvious: a very dark red area, tinged with blue.

"A small hemorrhage," Pock said. "A little bruising is all."

"No, this is not bruising." They waited for the doctor to say the word. "It is gangrene."

"But it couldn't be!" Pock laughed and shook his head. "There's no reason for it. Of all people, Doctor, you must know that it isn't."

But the doctor remained grave. "Of all people, you know that it is."

"Well, then, what of it? It'll just be a longer recovery."

Ferdinand was also somber. "What do you suggest?"

"I would recommend an amputation."

"Oh, come, be serious!" Pock said, chiding the other two men. "The joke is wearing thin."

"You know it isn't a joke," Ferdinand said. "You've seen enough injuries to know you have no choice."

"I do have a choice, and I'm choosing not to have anything cut off." He turned serious and firm.

"Yes," the doctor said, "it is a choice to not treat the illness. But I will tell you that the necrosis will spread. As more tissue becomes gangrenous, the spread will accelerate. Surely, you know what follows?"

"What does follow?" Therese asked. She had been silent so far through the discussion.

"Death, of course."

"Uncle Arpad!" she said. "You have to do what they say!"

"That would be dying anyway." He shook his head. "I won't do it." He tried again to smile. "And the old fakir might be wrong, you know. Then I'd have lopped off a leg for no reason!"

– 7 –

Paris was so weary of parades, centuries of them. Armies marching out to war, armies marching through in victory—not always the same army that had left in the first place, as was this case.

The February afternoon was cool but tolerably pleasant. However, the German army's victory parade was sparsely attended.

The citizens who did observe had bitter motives: to pour what contempt they had left on their new government. None of its representatives were present.

And everyone, both in the crowds and among the participants, kept one eye on the height of Montmartre, crowned with cannon. Everyone knew the cannon and the city were under no government's control.

Rank on rank, the Germans passed, perhaps just a little hurriedly. They were finished before two thirty.

Ferdinand watched. He watched the people thinly lining the streets, he watched for movement on the slopes of Montmartre, and he watched the German troops. More than anything, he watched for Rudolph.

"I'll ride past the embassy building," he said to von Karlstein as the dignitaries were marching themselves back toward their carriages.

"Your son is still in residence?"

"Yes, he is."

Von Karlstein made one of his occasional attempts to be informal. "And your house is therefore empty?"

"My house was destroyed in the siege," Ferdinand answered.

"Was it? I apologize for asking."

"It was only a leased house, and we'd removed our valuable possessions."

"Where was it?"

"On Rue Duroc, near the Place de Breteuil." Then he suddenly frowned. "You didn't know?"

"Oh, of course I would have the information in my files."

"On the day before the embassy staff moved to Bordeaux, a man came to the embassy building and asked to see me."

"Oh, yes." Von Karlstein smiled. "He was an odd man."

"He asked for my address?"

"Yes. He demanded it."

"Did you give it to him?"

"By no means, Baron Harsanyi. I would never give such information."

The embassy building was deserted. Ferdinand looked through the offices, which were all untouched from when the staff had left. His own office showed signs of more recent use, but it was as empty as the others.

– 8 –

February passed and March began, but no progress was being made. Paris was less and less happy with the Republican government that was only an imitation of the old Imperial government. Negotiations continued in Frankfurt for the official end to the war, and every report made the worst seem more certain. The Germans had not left Paris, either. There was no further bombardment of the city, or battles elsewhere in France, but the war was not over. If the negotiations did break down, it could be resumed very quickly, and the siege of Paris immediately. Paris was the hostage for France's good behavior.

On the hill of Montmartre, the cannon were still in the hands of the Gardes Mobiles, the people of the city, and not in the control of the government.

When Ferdinand was called into the ambassador's office upon the prince's return from Vienna, the meeting was brief.

"I met with Foreign Minister von Buest and the French ambassador in Vienna. We have decided together that the Austrian Embassy to France will be better served by a different military attaché, one without the conflicts of interest that have impeded your effectiveness."

"Of course, Your Excellency," he said with no emotion. "I'll empty my office immediately."

The ambassador smiled. "Not quite yet, Baron. Please continue working. It will be a few weeks before you're replaced. In the interim, I'll need reports on the French forces around Paris. They may be needed soon."

That evening, when he got home, Therese was in tears.

"Uncle Arpad. He's been in terrible pain today. Can't we do anything?"

"Go ask the doctor for laudanum."

"Oh, not that, Father . . ."

"Pock wouldn't take it anyway. There isn't anything else to do, Therese. Has he slept?"

"Very little. He's asleep now."

"I'll look in on him."

"Is the ambassador back from Vienna?"

"Yes. I saw him."

"And Princess Pauline?"

"She is in Versailles."

"I'll go see her tomorrow."

Pock was asleep, but restlessly, and his face was bright from the fever, and pallid at the same time. It was another half hour before his eyes opened and focused.

"Harsanyi . . ." His voice had only an ember of the fire it had once commanded. "Let's take a walk, shall we?"

"Where do you want to go?"

"A café in Paris. The Fusillade. Did you ever go there?"

"No. Rudolph mentioned it a few times."

"I'll show it to you." But then he closed his eyes, and when they opened a few seconds later, it took them longer to find what they were looking for. "Or maybe another day . . ."

– 9 –

When he returned to the embassy the next morning, Ferdinand hadn't yet sat at his desk before von Karlstein came to get him.

"The ambassador needs you at once."

"Your Excellency?"

Prince von Metternich was much less condescending than the day before. "I need your opinion."

"Yes?"

"Tomorrow the French government will send a force into Paris to collect the cannon from Montmartre and bring them outside the city."

"How many men?"

"Fifteen thousand. They had to get specific permission from the German government to gather so large a force, because it's against the armistice agreement. They'll enter the city early in the morning."

"Who is leading the force?"

"General LeComte. Do you know who he is?"

"Yes. I know who he is."

"I don't. What's going to happen?"

"It's unpredictable," Ferdinand said. "It could be successful. It could easily not be."

"Please review all the information coming in. I need to report to Vienna. They are very concerned about the stability of the French government."

– 10 –

"Wasn't it Koniggratz?" Pock was propped on his pillows, staring off somewhere. "The Bohemian rebels came across the valley."

"Not Koniggratz," Ferdinand said at his side. "The Bohemians rebelled in the 1848 insurrection."

"Of course, Harsanyi. That's right. What am I thinking of, then?"

"The Prussians came across the valley and up the hill." It was past sunset and a single candle lit the room.

"Yes, yes. And we capped the cannon. What a bang. That was well done." Suddenly, he doubled forward and cried out quietly.

"Just rest, Pock," Ferdinand said.

Pock fell back on the pillows. "What a bang. Will you be with me?"

"I'm with you."

"At the end?"

"I'll be here."

"At Magenta, I thought that was the end. Who was the Italian?"

"Gaspari."

"Gaspari, yes. He gave me a memento. A miniature cannon. I thought that battle would be my end, but the cavalry saved us in time." Another pang forced a moan. "This is my end. This time there will be no cavalry."

"We didn't expect the cavalry at Magenta, either," Ferdinand said.

"No. Where will they come from? Through the door?"

He was trying to joke, and Ferdinand had to smile. And as they both glanced at the bedroom door, Therese appeared in it.

Her face was tear-stained, and her eyes had a deep longing for comfort. Ferdinand stood and went to her quickly, but she was already turning toward her own room. Maria was running after her.

Ferdinand waved Maria back and followed Therese to her bedroom. She was sobbing facedown on the bed.

"What happened, Therese?"

She threw herself onto him and wrapped her arms around him, still sobbing. He waited.

"She sent me away."

"She? Pauline? Why?"

"She said . . . she said everything's changed. Paris is changed. She said there is no more Paris."

As gently as he could, he said, "Why are you crying?"

"Because she doesn't want me anymore. They'll go back to Vienna. That's all she cares about now."

"It's been a very great shock to her, Therese. Don't think about what she said. She didn't mean it."

"She didn't care about me She only cared how she could use me. I'm nothing."

"All the answers to her cry seemed weak and meaningless. He could only say, "No. You're my daughter."

"Oh, Father." He waited while she cried. Finally, she said, "I wish Rudolph were here. Take me to Paris. Tomorrow morning."

He remembered what he knew about Paris. "It will be too dangerous tomorrow."

"Please!"

"No."

"I need him. I've lost everything. Auguste is dead, and Uncle Arpad is dying, and Pauline ridicules me, and Paris is dead. Pierre is dead. Everything is dead and lost. Rudolph is lost. I want him back, Father."

"We can't go to Paris."

"You don't want to see him!" Suddenly, he felt her anger toward himself. "Why don't you love him? You never have."

Ferdinand was surprised by the unexpected attack. "What do you—?"

"He ran away from you. You drove him away."

"And you lied!" Ferdinand's own anger burst out. "When I was looking for him, you knew where he was, and you lied. When Auguste came back, you knew why Rudolph had gone for him. You sent Rudolph into that danger and you wouldn't even tell me the truth that you had! You and Auguste together, deceiving me. When he asked my permission to call on you, it was all deceit and mockery. You must have laughed at me."

"No—"

"When you went to Rudolph to ask him to get Auguste from Metz, did you even think you were risking his life?"

"I had a letter from Auguste! It was so terrible. He was in danger! Pierre said he might never come back." The pain, and the fear of him, in her eyes at that moment were devastating. "I had to do something!"

And Ferdinand was regretting his anger. "Yes. You did."

"I had to."

But something had jarred Ferdinand's thoughts. "Pierre Beaubien?"

"When he saw the letter from Auguste . . ."

"You saw him after the painting was finished?" His voice was hard and frightened her even more.

"At a café. He drove me to Uncle Arpad's when I went—"

"Pock?"

"We drove to his building. Father?"

But Ferdinand had stepped back from her. "Pock."

"What?"

He turned away and stumbled out into the hall. Therese started after him, but he looked back at her.

"Don't come."

"Father!"

"Don't come." He forced himself forward into Pock's bedroom and closed the door behind him.

"Harsanyi." Pock looked up at him and tried a smile that was only ghastly. "You're back."

"You're still awake."

"Still awake. I think I won't go back to sleep. I don't think I'll wake up again if I do."

"Then you need more light to keep yourself awake."

Pock may have noticed something different in Ferdinand's voice, but before he could ask, Ferdinand was opening the chest at the foot of the bed and reaching down to its bottom.

"There's enough light," Pock said.

"We'll light these candles."

"Candles? No! No, I don't need any light."

"You do, Pock." He had two of the heavy red candles in his hands. "You need light."

"Not those."

But Ferdinand was removing the old, used candles from the holders and pushing the heavy red ones in.

"I want to use these."

"Harsanyi! Not those."

Ferdinand paused. "Why not?"

"They . . . were a gift."

"From Gravert, you said. No, I think he'd want you to use them here in your sickroom."

"I said no," Pock said, trying to be firm. "I don't want them used."

"We will use them, Pock." Ferdinand lifted the one small candle that had been burning through the evening. "We need the light that these candles will shed." He touched the flame to the wick of the first candle, the one that had already been burned once.

"I don't want light!"

"I know that." He lit the other candle. The flame sputtered a moment on the white wick, then grew larger and glowed. "But you need light, Pock. You've been in the dark too long. Far too long."

"Then not that light."

The candles were burning now. Ferdinand set one on the table near the pillow, just out of Pock's reach. Then he circled the bed and set the other on a high bureau. As he did, and the candles reached their full flame, the light in the room brightened until it seemed like day.

"Yes," Ferdinand said. "This light."

Then he stood beside the bed with his arms folded, and waited.

Beneath the blanket, Arpad Pock was still for a moment, all but his eyes. They darted from one flame to the other. Then, with an awkward jerk, he reached frantically out of the bed toward the closer candle and swung at it. His finger barely clipped the brass holder, and the candle tipped and fell in a slow movement, dropping off the table and hitting the floor with a quiet thump, followed by the heavier clatter of the metal candleholder.

The candle flickered and struggled to stay lit. The flame nodded and leaned, diminishing to a small blue globe hanging precariously onto the wick.

Pock was off-balance in the bed, half leaning out, waving his hand toward the flame that refused to die. With a heavier landing than the candle, he fell onto the floor. He swatted at the candle and extinguished the last spark.

"There's still another flame," Ferdinand said. "Just killing one isn't enough."

Pock looked up from the floor, where he was on his side in a misshapen mound. The bandages that had once been white, wrapped around his leg, were oily black and green. "Put it out," he said. Then he was convulsed in pain. Ferdinand waited for him to be still again.

"You know it takes more than a few minutes for the mercury to kill. It takes hours."

"Just put it out!"

"Tell me why," Ferdinand said.

"Because it's poisoning us."

"No. Tell me why you killed Irene."

"Put it out!" Pock said.

"Tell me everything, and I'll put out the candle."

"I'll tell you."

Ferdinand knelt and put his arms under Pock's and lifted him back into the bed.

"Tell me."

"It was Sarroche." He gasped for breath, but Ferdinand just waited. "He said he'd have me dismissed from the École if I didn't help him, and he'd pay me if I did help him."

"He told you to go to my wife. Why you?"

"He knew that I knew her. He knew that I . . . that I asked her to marry me. Long ago."

"But you didn't think she'd accept! There were dozens of suitors."

From beneath the pain and sickness, resentment appeared in Pock's eyes. "I did think she would."

"She never would have."

"But Sarroche sent me back to her! He told me to use my influence and her affection."

"She had no affection for you, not that kind. Just friendship." Ferdinand stared at the face on the pillow, dissolving and crumbling before him. "You lied to Sarroche. You boasted that you could influence her. You told him that Irene loved you. That's the only reason he would have ever sent you to her."

"Then I went to Vienna."

"And when you said you wanted her to sell cinnabar to the French, she refused."

"She was harsh."

"She would have been angered that you tried to use her affection."

"On the train back to Paris, I knew what I had to do. Sarroche was berating me and mocking me as a foolish old man. She . . . she had mocked me, also. So I told him that she had agreed to sell the cinnabar. And then I made her four candles in the laboratory at the École and sent them to her. And I knew she would burn them in her bedroom." He forced a smile, which was terrible. "I knew she would."

"You sent them in my name."

"And she did burn them. And when Sarroche was suspicious, I told him I knew that you killed her."

"How could you?" As before with Therese, Ferdinand's anger broke out, but ten times greater. "You old . . . evil . . . why? You'd kill just to save your position at the École?"

"For revenge against her! And you should have been pleased, as well! What affection did you have for her?"

"More than you could understand."

"Her death gave you everything. Her wealth, her mines, they were all yours. You should have thanked me!"

"For murdering my wife." His fury was ice-cold now.

"But instead you insulted me. What contempt you had for those who Sarroche 'destroyed.' And you still refused to sell him cinnabar."

"So you killed Henry Whistler."

"Sarroche told me to keep you away from him. I sent him candles."

"And you killed him. And Auguste de l'Imperator?"

"He was Sarroche's agent."

"You hadn't known?"

"I hadn't known." Pock seemed as if past the pain and weakness; he only seemed weary now. "I had to kill him before he, and you, and Rudolph talked. You would have found out."

"But how could you kill him?"

"I was walking then," he said. "I was walking. My leg had healed. I was slow, but could walk. I followed Rudolph. I was there in the dark."

"And you got back to your apartment ahead of him."

"But on the stairs, I fell."

Ferdinand shook his head. "And you are still fallen."

"Oh, you say I am?" Pock's anger flashed. "You say that? You who are such a . . . a judge of fallen men?"

"It was your fall that is killing you now. You broke your leg again, and this time it didn't heal. And what about Beaubien?"

"Ah, Beaubien! Yes, that was fate, that he came to me looking for you."

"Why did you kill him? You took him to my house. Why did you kill him there?"

"He had something."

"What?"

"If you wouldn't sell to Sarroche, your son would."

"He never would."

"He will. When the mines are his. Because he hates you. I told Sarroche I would give him your son."

"What did Beaubien have?" Ferdinand was suddenly desperate. There was one answer he needed.

"Power over you."

"What? What was it, Pock?"

"Put the candle out."

"What did he have?"

"He didn't know what he had." Pock's words slowed and slurred. "It could have saved you. Now only God can save you."

"Pock!"

But there was no answer.

The malignant light from the single red candle still shone in the open eyes, and Ferdinand put his fingers on the unmoving eyelids to close them, and then stood and with the same fingers crushed the flame.

Chapter Seventeen

LEAVING
EVERYTHING BEHIND

– 1 –

Therese's fear of her father's anger, and her confusion, only increased the drowning loneliness that overwhelmed her. As her father disappeared into Arpad Pock's room and the door closed, she was cut off from the only person left to her.

She didn't hesitate. Quietly but swiftly, she hurried past Pock's bedroom and out the front door, and into the night.

She fumbled with the saddle in the dark stable, then gave up and just fit the bit and bridle, and threw a blanket over the horse's bare back and rode out.

Outside the cottage, she stopped. Her father might find her room empty in just minutes, or not until the morning, and she was almost pulled back inside by the distressing thought of him seeing her empty and unused bed. But as she watched, the single candle burning in Pock's room was extinguished. She pulled the reins and the horse moved forward.

The road to Paris was twenty kilometers. The moon was bright enough for a while, but low in the west behind her, and she cast a shadow as she rode east. An hour took her to Saint-Cloud. It was very cold, but she had a heavy blanket over her shoulders and a cloak, also.

The Prussian siege lines of the winter were evident. No troops occupied the trenches and mounds. The earthworks were empty ruins, like an ancient castle, and they cast shadows with hers. As she passed through them, the moon set and the ground turned black. But the stars were bright enough.

From Saint-Cloud it was less than a half hour through the streets to the Boulogne Gate into the city. Paris was darker than it would have been at this time of night, but it was exhausted. By midnight she was at the Austrian Embassy on Rue de Grenelle.

It was as dark as all Paris, and the gate under the great entrance arch was closed. She pulled the bell rope and waited, then pulled it again. It had now reached the coldest early hours of the March morning, but she was warmed by the heat from the horse's back. There was no light anywhere except the stars. In the whole street, no gas lantern or window was anything but black. She pulled the rope again, over and over.

If Rudolph was in the building, he might be far from the bell, wherever it was ringing, if it was even ringing.

The bars of the gate were too close together to squeeze between. There were no windows onto the street that she could break in, and finally she gave up in frustration. But even as she turned the horse, toward what other destination she didn't know, a light moved in a window of the embassy building. A candle had been set to rest in an office, and it only took her a moment to realize the window was her father's office.

At first it seemed dreamlike and strange that her father would be there, in the dark and cold, especially on a night that she was fleeing from him. She quickly knew that it wouldn't be her father, but someone else who would choose that one office to sit in.

She pulled the bell rope again. It was still likely that Rudolph wouldn't hear it, but at least she knew he was there, just meters away from her.

"Rudolph!" Her voice was like feathers dropping slowly to the ground. There was no response from the window. She found a stone from the street. Her throw only reached the bushes in front of the embassy building. She found another stone and pounded it against the metal gate.

The sound was terrible, and loud enough to reach the window. The candle in the window moved, and the window opened a small white oval appeared by flame light in the black night. Of course, he couldn't see all the way to the gate.

"Rudolph!" Then she banged on the gate again.

"Who is it?" She heard his voice.

The candle disappeared from the window, and minutes later she saw it come round the side of the building. As he came closer, she saw him grow from a faint mask to a face, to a head and shoulders, to a man. Even when he stopped, with the iron bars between them, he didn't react to seeing her.

"Rudolph, let me in," she said.

"What do you want?"

"I want in. It's cold." She was cold, suddenly. Very cold.

"Why are you here? Don't they have any heat in Versailles?" Everything about him was closed to her.

"I want to talk to you. Let me in."

"We can talk here."

"No, Rudolph. Open the gate now."

"You called me a murderer."

"That was . . . that's why I want to talk."

"Do you want to scream at me more?" His face was hard.

"No. I want to ask you why . . . about what happened. And I have to tell you about Uncle Arpad."

"What?" There was at last an expression. "Is he better?"

Therese tried to keep her own expression empty. "You'll have to let me in."

"He's dead, isn't he?"

She took a breath. "Not yet. Just let me in."

It took a long time, but then he decided to open the gate.

In their father's office, Therese faced her brother. He sat at the desk, in almost the exact posture that Ferdinand had used, back straight, leaning forward, his forearms resting on the desk's surface, his hands folded together. And Rudolph had the same quiet, slightly clenched face.

"How soon will he die?" Rudolph asked, the first words since front gate.

"A few days," Therese answered. "It's his leg. It's gotten worse and worse. They wanted to cut it off, and he won't let them."

"Old fool." His voice had both affection and disdain. "But of course he wouldn't have. I could have told them that." Then he frowned. "Are you sure it's his leg?"

"What do you mean?"

"Is it his leg poisoning him? It isn't something else?"

"You mean Father?" She was furious. "Do you think Father would kill him? Why do you keep thinking that? You're calling him a murderer. You did before."

"You called me a murderer."

"But I saw you!"

"Then believe what you want."

She hadn't come to argue. "I want to believe you didn't kill Auguste. But you're different now. I don't know what to believe." She waited, but he was silent. "Would you kill someone?"

"I have. But not Auguste."

"Who did?"

"Zoltan."

Her mouth dropped. "But . . ."

"He'd do anything Father told him."

"Father? No! Why would Father—"

"Sarroche." Suddenly Rudolph's eyes lit. "Have you heard of him? He paid Auguste to . . ." Then he stopped. "No. I won't tell you."

She was frustrated, but no good could come from pushing him. "What have you been doing in here for two months?"

"Nothing."

"Have you gone out at all?"

"I've gone to meetings with Gravert."

"You're too pale."

"What?" For the first time, an annoyed spark of his old personality appeared. "Pale?"

"You haven't been outside enough. And why are you awake so late?"

"I'm awake at night. I sleep in the day. And you don't look very good, either."

"Rudy!"

"What have you been doing?"

"Taking care of Uncle Arpad."

"Is that all?"

She was angry at him, and for the moment, so glad to be. "Yes, that's all. What else would I do?"

"I don't know," he said. "There aren't parties anymore, are there?"

"No," she said, and the gladness was gone. "There's nothing. Everything's been lost."

"Lots of things were lost." Rudolph frowned. "What happened to the things in the house?"

"They were burned. Father had taken some things to Bordeaux."

"The painting of Mother?"

"No, Father had taken it. And my painting, too."

"Your painting . . . and the cinnabar stone from the parlor?"

"Father has it, too," Therese said.

"Pock told me about Beaubien in the parlor. Did he have anything with him when he died?"

"What?"

"A letter?"

"I don't think so. Father never said anything."

"He wouldn't. I sent a letter from Sedan. Beaubien would have had it."

"What did it say?"

"Nothing."

"It must have said something!"

"No. Where did Beaubien live?"

"Montmartre."

"I want to go up there."

"To his studio? Now, in the middle of the night? You don't even know where his studio is."

"Then you have to go, too."

"But its one o'clock in the morning!"

"This is when I'm awake," he said.

"Is anything happening today?" she asked.

"What do you mean?"

"Father didn't want me to come to Paris. He said it would be too dangerous today."

"I don't know anything."

Dawn was still hours away. Rudolph seemed to thrive on darkness. He looked at the horse that Therese had ridden from Versailles.

"Don't you know how to saddle a horse?" he asked.

"It was dark and the saddle was heavy and I was sneaking out," she answered.

"It'll be easier without a saddle for us both to ride." He swung himself up and pulled her up behind him, and she put her arms around his waist.

As they crossed the Seine, the wind increased. Therese pulled her cloak around herself more tightly. Far upstream, Notre Dame was a dim, gray glow.

Beyond the river they traveled north, crossing the Place de la Concorde and passing the Madeleine church. The eight pillars were phantom stone, barely present without light.

"Where did you go after Metz?" she asked.

"Sedan. The Prussians caught me and I was in the prison camp. I escaped." He took a sudden, deep breath. "I killed one of the guards."

She didn't know how to answer the pain in his voice. "Did you have to?"

"Did I have to?" He was angry. "Do you think I did it for play? What do you mean?"

"No, I didn't mean that. You had to, didn't you?"

"I had to." He was vehement. "He was going to kill me. He shot me. I have a bullet in me." She could barely see him put his hand on his stomach, on the left side. "Here," he said, calm again.

Beyond the Boulevard de Clichy, in narrower streets between sparser buildings, the butte of Montmartre rose abruptly. The starlight seemed brighter, enough to make the hill a black silhouette against the nearly black sky.

"And then I was at a farmhouse," he said, "and the farmer and his wife cared for me."

"Who were they?"

"Just an old man and woman. I think I can find them again. It was strange. They thought I was Prussian. While I was asleep I talked, they said, and it was all German. Of course it would be. The first time I woke up, the man tried to speak German back to me, and he couldn't." She could hear the amusement in his voice. "You've never heard such bad German, Raisy. But they thought I was Prussian, and they took care of me anyway. They could have just cut my throat."

"They wouldn't."

"No, they wouldn't. Not those two. They fed me—I hadn't had anything but a potato for days. At least it was cooked. Raisy, it was so lonely in the camp. I felt like I was already dead. They were killing people, and I thought maybe they'd already killed me and I was just dead and wandering."

"You're alive, Rudy."

"How can I be alive," he answered, "when there's so much that's dead?"

"I don't know. I'm trying to understand that, too." And then she had to ask, "Did you kill Auguste? Tell me."

"Would you believe me?"

"I will."

"I didn't," he said.

"I believe you." They started climbing the hillside. "What are those?"

"Cannon."

It was hard to tell how many. She could see two or three rows, and at least ten in each row. "Why are they here?"

"They belong to Paris."

As they approached the bottom rank, she could see there were more and more ranks behind it, stretching up the face of the hill. "How many are there?"

"Two hundred."

"I remember. We saw them when we were burying—"

"Auguste?" Rudolph said. "Is this where you buried him?"

"In the cemetery." In the dark, she was disoriented. "I don't know where Pierre's studio is from here."

"What street?"

"I don't know the name."

"Which side of the hill?"

"I think . . . on the left."

"We'll go that way." They reached the top row at the top of the hill.

"Stop here," she said. "Let me think. I'm trying to remember."

All was quiet. She could hear the wind rustling, and the light from the stars reflecting from the cannon was as faint as the sound. She tried to think where the studio was, but she was distracted by the dark and the obtrusion of such weaponry in the midst of the peaceful streets.

"What's that?" Rudolph whispered. He dropped down from the horse.

"What?"

"Do you hear it?"

"No." She lowered herself to the ground.

"Quiet," he said. "There's something down there."

Then she could hear it. It was more than the rustling of the wind; it was the sound of feet, of people moving through the streets on the far side of the hill. Many people.

"Come," Rudolph said. She followed him down the north side of the hill. He took them one block on a narrow street to a wider boulevard. Even before they reached it, they could hear and then see dark masses moving. "It's government troops."

"Why?"

"For the cannon. They're coming to get the cannon."

"What will we do?" Therese asked.

"I don't know."

"Shouldn't we get away?"

"Get away?" he said. "No. But should we raise the alarm?"

"Us!" She was shocked. "But why?"

"To stop them."

"We don't want to stop them!"

"We have to," Rudolph said.

"Don't." She was adamant. "Rudy, don't do anything. This isn't for you to do anything."

They moved back along their side street toward the hilltop. The first troops had already reached the top rank of cannon.

"Where are the guards?" Rudolph said.

"They must be asleep."

There were hundreds of soldiers, and then thousands as the long column slowly enveloped the hill. And still there was no reaction from the sleeping city. Many minutes passed, and finally the last men were positioned among the cannon.

"What will they do now?" Therese asked. Still in the dark and shadows, they had moved up to the very edge of the occupied zone.

"They will pull them out of the city."

"But where are their horses?"

"I don't know. I don't see any."

They weren't the only ones to realize the lack of horses. The troops had broken their disciplined ranks and begun drifting, staying close together but with a gathering confusion. And then, clearly, close at hand, Therese heard one soldier say the unbelievable to another.

"They forgot to send horses."

The very first light, not touching the ground, had begun to color the sky. Rudolph pulled Therese back deeper into a shadow.

"They need to leave," he said. "Now. Before anyone knows they've come. They can't take the cannon without horses, and they can't stay. There must be ten thousand soldiers there. They'll be seen soon. They need to get away before it's too late."

But it was too late. A scream pierced the quiet, louder than all the thousands of troops, then shouting, and then the bells from a church nearby began tolling. And the sky was swiftly gaining light, as if even it were raising an alarm.

The shouting stopped. The bell continued to peal, but it was the only sound besides the troops, who were shifting uneasily and speaking to each other nervously. It seemed there might still be no reaction.

Then doors began to slam, and lights went on in the windows, and more voices were heard, then more bells, and the street began to fill.

Within three minutes there were spectators, and in five minutes crowds, and in ten minutes throngs. Therese and Rudolph were swept into the swarm as every space was taken up by the people; the whole neighborhood was out, and from their vantage point and in the broadening light, they could see the streets below were streaming with people.

Then the troops were outnumbered. All the other crowds Therese had seen were small compared to this whole city gathering and surrounding.

Beside her, Rudolph was excited. He seemed to be anticipating something great, while she was fearing violence and blood.

"What's going to happen?" she asked.

"We'll see."

"Will they fight?"

"If they do, it'll be a massacre."

She didn't ask of whom, or by whom. "We need to leave," she said. "This is what Father was talking about."

"He knew?"

"He knew it would be dangerous." She was starting to panic. "I want to get out of Paris."

"I want to stay."

"I can't go by myself!"

"I'll take you to Pock's. You can stay there until it's safe." He hesitated. "But not yet. I want to see what happens."

"I want to go now."

"Then go by yourself."

Leaving by herself or staying with Rudolph in the crowd were both frightening. "I'll wait."

The standoff continued. It had been an hour since the first alarms, and still people were coming. There was still a space between the soldiers and the Parisians, but with the pressure from behind, and the lure of their own cannon before them, the first ranks of the crowd began to push into the troops' enclave.

In some places, the soldiers pulled back, but in others they didn't, and the crowd mingled with them. In a few minutes the soldiers were being merged into the multitudes.

"They're not real soldiers," Rudolph said. "They're conscripts and volunteers. They don't know what they're doing."

The soldiers and the people were merging. Pleas and taunts and revolutionary slogans were filling the air, and then one man in uniform, not far from Therese, lifted his rifle in the air, holding it by the barrel. The people roared, and then a thousand other soldiers held up their rifles in the same way, and the crowd thundered.

"What does it mean?"

"It means they surrender. It means they're refusing to fight. They're joining the people."

The confrontation was over. The army had been defeated without a shot fired, and finally, after the terrible year, after everything, with bells ringing, and the sun rising, Paris began to rise.

Chapter Eighteen

LOVE AND
REVOLUTION

– 1 –

Far after midnight, Rudolph climbed the stairs to Pock's apartment, not alone, and pounded on the door.

It opened a centimeter.

"Where have you been?" Therese asked angrily. She was very frightened.

"At a meeting," he said. "I'm tired. Let us in."

"Who's with you?"

"Gravert."

She opened the door. "There have been mobs in the streets all day."

"I was in them." Rudolph stepped aside for Gravert to follow him in. "I'm hungry, too," he said to Therese. "Is there anything to eat?"

"No."

"We'll find something tomorrow."

"What's she doing here?" Gravert asked.

Therese answered, "I came to tell Rudy about Uncle Arpad."

"You have an uncle?" Gravert asked.

"She means Pock. He's dying."

"What happened?" Gravert asked.

"His leg. It got worse," Rudolph said.

"I liked him." Gravert shrugged. "But he was old. Where will you find any food?"

"At the embassy. I'll go tomorrow."

"What's happening?" Therese said, impatient with them. "What meeting were you in?"

"They've overthrown the Republic."

She shook her head. "So what are they going to have now? They don't want an emperor or a king, and they don't want a republic. What do they want?"

"Liberty," Gravert said.

Rudolph blinked sleepily. "I'm too tired. It's all big, Raisy. The meetings are still going on. But I had to leave."

"What are they doing at the meeting?"

Gravert answered, "They've proclaimed a commune. A government of the people of Paris."

She didn't seem to understand. "What about the rest of the country?"

"That doesn't matter. Only Paris matters."

She turned to Rudolph. "Does the Republic know that it's been overthrown?"

"You take Pock's room" was his only answer. "We'll sleep out here. This is where I slept before. Do you want the chair or the sofa?" he asked Gravert.

"I'm going back to Versailles in the morning," Therese said. "You can have the bedroom tomorrow."

"No one's leaving Paris. The gates have been closed."

"From the inside or the outside?" she asked.

"Both," Gravert answered. "The city's already surrounded. I'll take the chair. I won't sleep anyway. It's too much! The Commune, Harsanyi! It's been done!"

– 2 –

The Austrian Embassy building was being looted when Rudolph arrived the next morning.

The gate was broken open, and two dozen men and women were carrying furniture and whatever else they could find out into the courtyard, or throwing them from broken windows. They were too intent on their work to notice as he joined them and looted his own belongings from the butler's bedroom he'd been using.

No one had found his food cache in the closet of the room, but he didn't want to be seen carrying it out, so he piled some rubbish over it and left it.

His father's office was already stripped empty.

Gravert was awake when Rudolph got back to Pock's apartment, and Therese's door was still closed.

"What's breakfast?" Gravert asked.

"Nothing yet. I can get something tonight."

Therese must have heard him come in, or heard him talking. Her door opened.

Her hair was tousled and her dress wrinkled, but the look she gave him was clear. "I want to get back to Versailles," she said.

"And good morning to you," Gravert said roughly. "You won't go back to Versailles today."

"Rudy. Get me out of Paris."

"I'll take you to the Boulogne Gate," he said, "but you won't get out."

They walked. A horse would have drawn too much attention.

By noon they had crossed the Seine at the Pont d'Iena, with the École Militaire far off at the other end of the Champ de Mars, and had walked the length of the Auteuil village. Like Belleville on the opposite side of Paris, it had been part of the city for only ten years, and it was opposite Belleville in every other way. It was pleasant, upper class, and well tended. At the far southwest corner of the Paris wall they came to the gate leading to Boulogne and Hillancourt, the rich suburbs between the city and the very wealthy Saint-Cloud.

They came to the Boulogne gate but went no farther. The gate, and apparently all the gates, were closed, and the city was again besieged.

There were two crowds at the gate. One was ordinary people, those who would have used the gate that or any other day, whose lives crossed the arbitrary line of the wall. The other crowd was smaller but radical, determined to keep the gate closed and the city isolated.

The larger group was middle class of the genteel Auteuil neighborhoods and sympathetic to the Versailles government. The smaller group was lower class, imported from Belleville and socialist to their core. The larger crowd was indignant.

The smaller crowd was armed.

Rudolph watched the drama play out between the two. The antagonism between them was as great as was possible in a single city, and the threat of violence was the strongest force. As the local Parisians saw the futility, and risk, of arguing, they withdrew, and the alien Parisians from the far end of the city held their place, and the gate remained closed.

"You won't leave Paris today."

"I'll stay if I have to," Therese answered.

"We all will. Everyone in Paris is together in this."

They walked by the Austrian Embassy on the way back to Pock's. The looters were gone, and they retrieved as much of the supplies as they could carry from Rudolph's closet. The gate was torn completely from its hinges, the windows were broken, and the chandelier in the grand ballroom was smashed on the floor.

And when they were back on the Rue Serpente, Rudolph found that the horse Therese had ridden from Versailles was gone.

"Now men, unfettered by authorities and rulers, will have their own lives!" The overfilled room responded with shouts and cheers. The speaker's fist waved, and his voice was like a hurricane, whipping the passions and emotions of the listeners. He was a politician, a well-known radical, wild-eyed and with hair like a tornado. "Now men, freed from the restraint and traditions of the past, will at last be truly themselves!"

Gravert, as ardently as anyone, joined the crowd's raucous approval. Beside him, Rudolph asked, "But what does it mean?"

"Now we have the chance to see what men are really like."

"But is that good?"

Another speaker, a leader of the working classes and no less a firebrand, replaced the first. Instead of a suit, he wore plain pants and a tunic; his beard was like an artillery shell explosion.

"Rise, Paris, rise! Defend your liberty! Now we will end the oppression! Now we will pull down the tyranny! We are now our own rulers! We are the Commune of Paris! Let the bourgeois, the rent takers, and the profiteers tremble! The people are free! The ones who exploited us will now taste our wrath! It is time for vengeance!"

"What do they do at your meetings?" Therese asked when he got back to the apartment.

"Mostly they talk."

"What do they say?"

"They just talk."

"Is Gravert coming back here?"

"Not tonight. But he might some other time."

"How long will I have to be here, Rudy?"

"I don't know." He was tired and didn't want to answer questions. "Maybe a long time."

"Then I need more clothes."

"Get more clothes."

"I don't want to go out alone. I want you to take me."

"Maybe tomorrow."

– 3 –

"This is where you buy your clothes?" Rudolph asked. They were on the Rue de la Paix, just a block north of the Place Vendome, and three blocks from the Rue Royale, near the Tuileries gardens and in the very heart of the wealthy commercial center of Paris.

"Princess Pauline always brought me here."

It was disconcerting to be in such a place. There was almost no sign of the convulsions the rest of the city had suffered in the last six months; everyone was well dressed, the shops were full, and there was no damage. It could have been that there had never been a war.

They were outside a shop that said *Worth Couturier*, and the dresses in the window made as great a contrast as possible with the dresses worn in the meetings and streets of Belleville. Every person within Rudolph's sight was probably a rent taker or a profiteer. They were certainly bourgeois.

And, more subtly, there might have been signs of the past and present troubles. The men in their top hats and the women in their bonnets passed worried glances, speaking together in low, anxious voices.

Therese was ready to go into the shop.

"How will you pay for anything?" Rudolph asked.

"They know me. Are you coming in?"

"No."

He waited outside. There was a café across the street, but it looked far too expensive and aristocratic. He just waited on the sidewalk, leaning against the building.

While he was waiting, an elderly man appeared on the street. He was elegantly dressed in a black suit and high hat, but most impressively, around his neck on a blue, white, and red ribbon was the five-chevronned white-and-gold medal of the Legion d'honneur. He walked slowly down the sidewalk, seeming befuddled, his white whiskers bristling like a windswept tree. When he reached Rudolph, he peered for a moment, and then asked, "Are you a Friend of Order?"

"Excuse me, sir?" Rudolph said.

"Is the march to come here?"

"I'm sorry, I don't know about any march."

"The march of the Friends of Order," the man said. "To protest the radicals! I've come to march to the Place Vendome."

A less likely protester could hardly be imagined, but at that moment there was a drumbeat from the far end of the Rue de la Paix, and indeed a protest march did appear. Even from the distance, Rudolph could see that the gentleman was perfectly matched to it.

This anti-mob was all men and women of the middle and upper classes, all respectable and well-ordered; they even carried a banner proclaiming them the Friends of Order. They were the people of Paris with the most to lose from the uprising and takeover.

Rudolph looked down to the other end of the street, and froze. The Friends were not conspirators to keep their march clandestine, and apparently the socialists in the militia were well aware of the protest. At the entrance to the Place, a hundred militiamen were forming into ranks to face the protesters.

"Are the Friends armed?" Rudolph asked the old man.

"We've been told not to be." But then he winked. "But there'll be a few pistols in pockets, I wager." He turned toward the marchers and nearly tripped off the curb. Rudolph caught his arm and steadied him. "Thank you!" The man adjusted his Legion d'honneur and began his slow walk toward the approaching marchers.

But Rudolph looked back at the men they were facing. They had the arrogant boredom of well-armed men opposing a weak and naïve foe.

"Sir, wouldn't it be safer to be inside?"

"Safe? From the rabble? They'll melt like snow! All they need is firm handling!"

There was a tense excitement in the air, as there had been at Montmartre. But instead of pulling him forward, it repelled him.

He pushed himself quickly into the dress shop. Therese was not to be seen, but all the mannequins and hat stands and mirrors made the place a labyrinth. "Raisy!" he called, and faces turned. "Raisy, come here!"

There was a rustle and then Therese appeared from a hall, wearing a light brown dress. "Rudy! I'm trying it on."

"We have to go," Rudolph said, and he grabbed her hand and started pulling her back down the hall.

"No! Wait," she said. "What's wrong?" She pulled her hand away from his.

"All right," he said, frustrated at her stubbornness. "Come look."

He took her hand again and pulled her toward the front window. There were already noises from the street: shouts, drums, and other, harsher sounds. Just as they reached the window, the first shots were fired.

"What is it?" Therese said.

"It is men killing," he said. Just in front of the door, the old man, his Legion d'honneur still around his neck, was lying faceup and twisted on the road, his white whiskers blood-soaked. Then the window was shattered, and he pulled Therese again, this time without any resistance, out the back of the shop.

– 4 –

"Massacre on the Rue de la Paix!" Gravert read the newspaper headline triumphantly. "Twelve reactionaries dead." Therese was in her room behind her closed door.

"There was no need," Rudolph said. "It was all old men, and they were unarmed."

"They fired first."

"No one could know who fired first."

"But it's useful. Now there'll be no more protest against the Commune."

"Some people in Paris don't want a commune."

"They want to oppress us," Gravert said fiercely. "So they can keep us living in ghettoes and starving. Why do you think there was an uprising? Those people in their rich shops are the ones who brought it on themselves!"

"But they still want their old lives back," Rudolph said.

"And I want my father back! The ones who died this morning were the ones who were themselves shooting protesters in the streets twenty years ago."

They hadn't heard the door open, but Therese was watching them. "And I want my father back," she said.

– 5 –

"What time is it?" Gravert blinked and stretched in his chair.

"Ten o'clock," Therese said. "In the morning."

"I can see that it's morning."

"Where were you last night?" Rudolph asked.

"The committee was organizing a new militia. I'm a captain now. You could have been too, if you'd come."

"What are you commanding?"

"A battery of artillery at Fort d'Issy, and I have to be there at noon."

"It'll take you two hours to get there," Therese said. "You should leave now."

"Come with me, Harsanyi," Gravert said. "It'll be like the last siege. But now we're fighting for ourselves, not for the government."

Rudolph shrugged. "I don't want to fight anymore."

"At the uprising, you were passionate for the Commune!"

"I lost my passion at the Rue de la Paix."

Later, he went out to see who else still had passion for the Commune; for it, or against it.

Most streets seemed the same. He wandered toward the southwest, across the Seine to Auteuil, where he and Therese had seen the confrontation at the Boulogne Gate. Now, several days later, the guard was smaller but better organized, occupying a house near the gate and no longer bothered by citizens challenging its authority.

But even walking the Avenue de Versailles from the river to the gate, he saw evidence that the government wasn't accepting its overthrow by the Paris Commune. The area hadn't been very much damaged by the Prussian siege, but now Rudolph saw demolished houses and cratered streets. The destruction was obviously by artillery.

He stood for a while near the gate, watching the sentries. He was in the middle of the road, in plain sight, but they paid him no attention.

His reflexes threw him to the ground before he even knew what he was hearing, the tearing scream of an artillery shell. He at least had learned to never fight his reflexes, but in this case he had not been in danger. The shell hit a safe block away, and he had to watch the building collapse from the discomfort of the street pavement.

The sentries did pay attention to the explosion, and the barracks house emptied a few dozen motley uniformed guards into the avenue, pointing and talking excitedly. Rudolph dusted himself off and approached them.

"Where are they firing from?"

"Mont Valerien."

"Government troops?" But then he remembered Paris didn't accept that there was a government outside its wall. "Versailles troops?" he corrected himself.

"Versaillard pigs!"

"They are bombing their own city," Gravert said that evening. "What is that but the worst tyranny?"

"But how did they get control of Mont Valerien?" Rudolph asked.

"It was treachery. As the militia took control of the gates on the day of the uprising, they also moved to occupy the forts. But Valerien was not occupied."

"Was it treachery, or was it just forgotten?"

"It must have been treachery. An investigation will determine who is to be punished."

"Executed," Rudolph said.

"Yes, executed. That will be the punishment. But now, Thiers and his Versailles dogs have Mont Valerien and they are bombarding the city." He laughed. "And the neighborhoods of Auteuil and Passy, where resistance to the Commune is strongest, are the neighborhoods that will suffer the most. So it is for the best. And the Prussians still hold the eastern forts, and the Commune now has the southern forts."

"Will the Prussians . . . the Germans join the government against Paris?"

"Why should they?" Gravert said. "They will just watch as the French kill the French."

– 6 –

"Why is he staying here?" Therese asked after Gravert had left. She seldom came out of her room when he was in the apartment.

"There's food here, and more room."

"I want him to leave and go back to his ghetto."

"He wants you to leave and go back to your life of oppressing the common people."

"I would if I could! I'm even going to try."

"Don't." Suddenly he took hold of her wrist and stared directly into her eyes. "Don't, Raisy. They'd shoot you." He let go. "Just wait. It won't go on forever."

"What will happen?"

"The government has to raise its army and be ready, and then they'll retake the city."

"What will happen when they do?"

"What do you think will happen?" Rudolph said, bitterly. "There will be a bloodbath."

"Couldn't someone stop it?"

"God could stop it."

"I don't like you to say that. You mean that He won't."

"Do you think He would? Has He done anything?"

Another week passed and March turned to April. Rudolph had returned to wandering. Gravert came and went and they talked less. Therese had proclaimed her own personal siege and was blockaded in Pock's bedroom, which was now her room.

When they did talk, Gravert told him news from the Commune. It was passing and repealing an abundance of laws, canceling rents for working people, renaming the months, and continually reorganizing its central committee and replacing commanders of the militia. The fight against the Versailles government was in a stalemate, and food was again becoming scarce just two weeks into the new siege.

Finally, Rudolph passed his own law.

"You are required to come outside," he told Therese, and she accepted.

He had a destination not far from Pock's apartment. They crossed the Boulevard Saint-Germain and continued south, Therese trudging beside him. They rounded the temple-like Theatre Odeon and came to a stop on the Rue de Vaugirard.

"There," he said. "Flowers."

Despite the war, despite the siege and the uprising and the whole year of tragedy, spring had unfailingly come, and the Jardin du Luxembourg was immense with flowers. The lawns were green and fresh-mown, the hedges trimmed, and the beds mobbed with bright colors. There were no trees, only stumps, and there were other signs of less than perfect care, but the blooms could hardly have cared. It might even have been that the aspirations of the tortured city had found a voice.

"Go look at them," Rudolph said, and Therese, opening like warmth after winter, flew into the garden.

"Thank you, Rudy."

An hour had gone by, just sitting on benches and walking, splendidly surrounded.

"You need to go outside more."

She laughed at her own words echoing back to her.

Gravert returned that night after several days' absence, a bloody bandage on his arm.

"What happened to you?" Rudolph asked.

"Don't you even know what's happening? The Commune marched on Versailles today." But the anger in his voice and his despondent collapse into the chair showed what the result had been.

"No," Rudolph said. "I don't know what's happening. You were pushed back?"

"We were pushed back," he said. "More treachery. Our plans were betrayed and the Versaillards were waiting for us."

"It didn't have to be treachery. Any general would have known to be ready for an attack."

"But now there's been a battle," Gravert said. "We are at war." He made a point of including Rudolph in his *we.*

"You're at war."

"Paris is at war, and anyone who is not on the side of the Commune is against it."

"I'm not French," Rudolph said.

"You were French in the last siege."

"I'm not now."

"As a friend," Gravert said, "I will warn you to be careful what you say. Remember, you are a foreigner and the son of a nobleman. You must be very careful what you say."

– 7 –

"It's always *treachery*," Rudolph said to Therese on what had become their preferred bench in the Jardin du Luxembourg. "They blame all their mistakes on traitors. Then they find someone and execute them."

"I wish we could get out of the city."

"But it's no better out there. The government of France is bombarding Paris, and Germany is helping."

"It's ironic," Therese said.

"I would have said that a year ago. But now I'm in it. It isn't ironic. It is . . . grotesque."

"Then what should we do? There must be somewhere we could go that's better."

"There can't be," Rudolph said. "They're the same men everywhere."

"But, Rudy! Not everyone. Not you."

"I am more than any of them."

"No, you aren't."

"It was Pock that always told me how much I'm like my father."

"You are . . ." Therese was unsure how to answer. "In good ways."

"In every way. I have no loyalty except to myself. I take what I want, and I kill when I have to."

"That's not the same . . . it's not . . . . Rudy, you're twisting everything." She set her jaw. "You say men are terrible, and you're blaming Father for it. You're blaming him for yourself because you're not perfect!"

"I'm blaming him because he killed Mother."

"Don't say that again."

"How much longer will it last?" Therese asked. She and Rudolph were in his bedroom in the Austrian Embassy, looking at the remains of his supply cache.

"Two or three weeks," he said. "But it's mostly potatoes and biscuits and dried meat now."

They gathered what they could carry, which was more than half, and trekked back to the apartment. It was night; it was safer to carry food through the streets in the dark than in open daylight.

"How much longer will this go on?" Therese asked.

"I don't know. You ask that every day."

"If Gravert didn't eat so much, all of this would last longer."

Gravert stayed two of the next five nights, and then he appeared with a bag of belongings.

"I'm moving in here," he said.

"What's wrong with your own apartment?" Therese asked.

"It was destroyed this morning. The Prussians are bombing the east side of the city."

"Where is your mother?" Rudolph asked.

"I don't know. Nobody has seen her or my sisters for a week."

Therese didn't seem to have any sympathy. "Couldn't you stay at your fort? Aren't you still the commander?"

He puffed up indignantly. "I command the artillery during the day. There are no barracks to stay in. They've been destroyed, too."

"Then if you're staying here, you need to find your own meals."

"Then I'll look for them at the Austrian Embassy. Don't you know it's illegal to hide food?"

"He'll eat with us," Rudolph said, breaking the confrontation. "There isn't any food to find. And we'll go out tonight and get the rest from the embassy."

But the embassy had been looted again, and Rudolph's closet was empty.

April dragged by. Gravert kept them informed of the new laws proclaimed by the Commune—that the cruel practice of night work in bakeries was prohibited; men and women both had the right to a free and secular education; and all property in the city belonging to a member of the Versailles government was to be destroyed.

"But the bakeries aren't doing any baking," Therese said. "And why are they destroying the buildings? Shouldn't they appropriate them for the people?"

Rudolph answered, "Because they know the assault is coming. The owners will just get them back."

"Paris will never fall," Gravert said.

In the first week of May, Therese showed Rudolph a newspaper.

"The Commune is going to pull down Napoleon's column in the Place Vendome."

"It's just another opportunity for something to be destroyed."

"I want to go," she said. "There'll be a band playing and everyone will get to watch."

"I'll go. But every time you go near the Place Vendome, there's a riot or a massacre."

There was a crowd in the Place, but it was a festive one, and only the band was riotous. Everyone's eyes were on the tall Column, with ropes tied to its top. At a signal the teams of men began pulling. The only open ground was the space where the tower was to fall.

But after several minutes it was obvious that there was no effect. An official inspected the base of the column. The teams resumed their work.

Over an hour had passed and the inevitable word began to circulate through the crowd.

"Treachery."

"Treachery?" Rudolph said. "How . . . why . . . what could anyone even do? The column is just too heavy to pull." The mood had turned from merry, to impatient, to angry. "We should leave."

But the next inevitability was already occurring. A troop of militia began to assemble.

"Now we'll leave," he said, and Therese couldn't argue.

In the newspaper that night they read that the column had finally been toppled, after a six-hour struggle. And when Gravert came back for the night, they ate the last of their provisions: one cooked potato for each of them.

Gravert brought them a huge bag the next evening, at least twenty kilograms.

"Carrots?" Therese said. "Where did these come from?"

He wouldn't tell them, and after a few days, they all three had learned to detest carrots.

It was mid-May. Each of them at different times had found scraps for their table: a molded cheese, stale bread, even meat of unknown origin bought on the street. Gravert seemed much older. His round cheeks were carved like dry apples beneath his shaggy whiskers and his forehead was prematurely careworn and wrinkled. Rudolph never asked what was happening at Fort d'Issy because he could see it in Gravert's face.

Therese, like all of them, was thinner and had somewhere found a collection of old dresses that fit in with the drab attire of the streets. She seldom went out, though.

And Rudolph himself, his own whiskers now a thick black cover for his jaw, was hardly the student cadet of the year past. He didn't feel that he was worn like Gravert. His own aging was caused by weathering from the inside, by his own black moods and disgust with his world.

– 8 –

Later in May, two months after the uprising, Gravert didn't return one evening, which was not unusual. But in the morning the newspapers, still being printed without interruption, screamed the latest disaster: *"Issy Falls!"*

Rudolph read the article thoroughly. Two months of bombardment had reduced the fort mostly to rubble, but it had fought on until just yesterday, when the last government attack had been overwhelming. The defenders had escaped, but their survival was itself proof against them.

"Treachery," Rudolph said.

"But they were trying to save their lives!" Therese said.

"The whole garrison has been charged with desertion."

"They couldn't say that! They couldn't!" Therese's sympathy for Gravert was as slight as ever, and yet she appreciated his loyalty and determination. "They've been fighting and dying to hold that fort!"

"Everyone from the garrison who could be found has been imprisoned and will be executed today."

She was shocked. "Even . . . ?"

"I'll find out where they're being held."

"I'll come."

"No. Stay here." Then he looked at the headline again. "If the fort at Issy has fallen, next they'll attack the Issy gate. The assault is coming, Raisy. The end of it all."

"When the gate is taken and the city is opened, Father will come for us? After the embassy, he'll look for us here."

"Then I won't come back."

"Then we'll find you, wherever you go."

"I'll be ready when you do."

"The Issy deserters have already been executed."

It had taken hours, and it was early afternoon before Rudolph found where the garrison had been imprisoned, in a police station near the Gare du Montparnasse.

"How many? Who were they?"

"Who are you to ask?" Three guards, dressed in rags, sat casually around the front room of the station.

"One of them worked in a stable with me. I want to know if he'll be coming back."

"Not if he was one of those."

"What were their names?"

"Find the names." A different guard, interrupted from his comfortable seat, began to look through papers on a desk.

"How many were there?" Rudolph asked.

"Twenty."

"Here are the names." The man picked up a sheet of paper with many scrawled signatures on it. "They signed it before they were shot."

"Gravert," Rudolph said. "Emile Gravert."

"Yes, he's here." The paper was held forward, and Rudolph saw the familiar signature.

"They're all dead?" he asked. Suddenly he couldn't speak. The room blurred.

"Yes, they're dead! They're all dead! Isn't that what you wanted to know?" The first guard, who he'd been speaking with, was becoming annoyed.

"No, they aren't," the third guard said. "There was no firing squad."

"Not dead yet?"

"They're still in the cells."

"But I ordered them executed." Now he was very annoyed.

"Then you do it. There's no squad."

"Find a squad. Ten men. Go!"

"We don't have ten."

The exchange continued like a nightmare, and Rudolph could hardly keep track of their argument over who should execute the prisoners, and then he asked, "Where are the cells?"

"In the basement," the leader said.

"I want to talk to them."

"Oh, you lazy goat," he said to the second guard. "Take him down to the basement, and I'll find a firing squad."

"Harsanyi?"

The two cells, each intended for a single prisoner, held ten times that many. The cells were windowless, the only light coming from a small window in the hall.

"Gravert? You're alive!"

"I'm not."

The men in the cells were reacting to Rudolph's visit; some were pushing forward, some were pleading, protesting, and cursing, while others ignored him.

"I can't let you die," Rudolph said to Gravert. "Can't someone stop this?"

"The orders are from the Central Committee."

There were footsteps on the stairs, and the two guards Rudolph had seen upstairs, and two others, came into the hallway, each carrying a rifle.

"Five of us?" Rudolph's escort asked. "That's not enough. Just five of us to take them all out to the courtyard?"

"We'll shoot them in the cells."

"But then we will have to carry them up the stairs."

"Then what do you suggest we do?"

The rifles hadn't yet been raised, and the bickering went on, and Rudolph was forgotten. Two minutes passed, and then, over the loud arguing and the louder voices of the prisoners, another voice was heard.

"Where are you?"

"Down here," the station commander shouted back.

More feet descended, in a hurry, and another man as ragged as everyone else came angrily into the crowded hall. He had no insignia, but the others, even some of the prisoners, straightened to attention.

"What are you doing?"

"The deserters," the commander said. "We're ordered to execute them."

"No, don't," the new man said. "Everyone to the Issy gate. Everyone, now."

"Why?"

"It's been taken. It's wide open and the Versaillards are gathering outside, ready to pour in like water. Everyone go, now!"

"What about them?" the commander asked, not happy with the thought of running toward the fighting.

"Take them. Everyone to the gate!"

"Are you going?" Rudolph asked once Gravert was safely out of the cell.

"Yes, I'm going. Will you come?"

Rudolph shook his head. "No! You'll be killed!"

"We'll all be killed," Gravert said. "This is the end, the last assault. Come with me, Harsanyi."

"No."

"Why? You'll go back to your father?"

"No."

"Come. We can die together."

"No."

"And we can kill a hundred enemy before we die."

"No."

"What else is there?" Gravert said. "Kill and die! What else is there now?"

Chapter Nineteen

THE BLOODY
WEEK

– 1 –

The horsemen came first.

The gate at Issy was open, the wall's first breach; and the horsemen gathered, rank on rank, to flood the exposed city.

The city had already suffered from war, bombardment, and destruction; from starvation, cold, and poverty; from sickness and disease. Now the fourth horseman—the horsemen—was ready. Cavalry, superseded by gunpowder, was no longer master on the battlefield; but where the streets of Paris were narrow, they were still the beautiful place for warhorses and their riders' swords.

Into the gate they rode.

Second came the cannon. They were rolled forward to the head of the Rue Lecourbe. The great rearrangement of Paris in the previous decade, cutting through the city in broad boulevards, had been for this purpose as much as for any other, to give the artillery a field of fire. Where the streets of Paris were straight and open, nothing could stand before the cannon.

Third came the infantry, and nothing could hide from them. They spread out through the side streets and the alleys and into the houses, like blood soaking a bandage.

Fourth came the masters: the police, the officials, the officers, whose job wasn't to conquer but to punish. They didn't mean to kill indiscriminately like the cannon, but to kill very discriminately. It was theirs to regain control and, by example, put an end to the next uprisings, as well.

Behind them came the last, the returners, the exiled, the fortune hunters, the opportunists, the separated, and the seekers. Ferdinand Harsanyi, and Zoltan with him, was a seeker.

Slowly, Paris filled with war. In the first blocks of Auteuil, Passy, and across the river in Grenelle, the invaders were met as liberators. One by one the gates of the west wall fell. By late afternoon the government cannon were wheeled into place at the Neuilly gate, and the Champs-Elysees was swept clean to Arc de Triomphe.

The seekers kept close behind the advancing line. Sometimes they were caught in crossfire and had to retreat, but the advance was steady. And whenever they passed an overturned barricade or blasted strongpoint, they looked at the bodies of the defenders to see if they recognized them.

And by evening the defenders still living had reacted and formed their lines, and the real warfare began.

In the twilight, Ferdinand and Zoltan stood in a doorway in the Place de Breteuil. The sounds of the day, rifle and cannon fire, had lessened. But not far away, almost at the ruined front steps of their old house on Rue Duroc, a makeshift barricade had brought the government advance, at least in this neighborhood, to a halt. The materials of the barricade had been easily found in the debris that lined the street.

"No more tonight," Zoltan said, watching the attacking soldiers put up their own wall of timbers and broken stone.

"It'll take cannon to open these streets. They'll wait until morning."

"Will we wait?"

"No," Ferdinand said. "I want to get through to the other side. Therese and Rudolph won't be here. We need to get to Pock's apartment."

They waited in an abandoned house, of which there were many, until well after dark. The moon was just rising, and its light hadn't yet reached the streets. Zoltan led, edging south, searching block by block for an opening in the fortified lines.

Finally, they climbed through the rubble of an apartment building that had once been four or five stories. Even as they crawled silently over the bricks, they had to stop. Four men, either sleeping or dead, were sheltered in a hollow of the ruins. They backed and found another path through.

The next street was quiet and seemed empty. Zoltan and Ferdinand kept to the darkest shadows, and paused again as a sudden fury of rifle fire erupted somewhere nearby and then faded. They headed toward the Quartier Latin, away from the combat lines.

It was a circuitous journey. The boulevards were systematically blocked by well-constructed fortifications. Apparently, the Commune had been planning for weeks for the defense of the city. The smaller streets were open but so blind and shadowed that a dozen men five meters away would have been invisible.

More than once, there were the dozen men, but Zoltan always sensed them before he was discovered himself.

Their groping motion forward brought them to the Rue Serpente in the last hour before dawn. They reached the building where Pock had lived, and Zoltan pointed up to the window.

"Someone is there," he said. Even with the shutters closed, they could see a crack of light from the room within.

The door was ajar, and light streaked the stairs and landing. Ferdinand put up his hand and gently pushed.

His first impression was of disarray. The large cabinet that had always stood against the wall in the front room had been pulled forward, and all its drawers were laid out on the floor. Every cupboard door was open, the cushions were off the couch and chairs. Only after seeing everything else did he realize who was standing in the door to the bedroom.

"Sarroche! What are you doing here?"

"I will not answer such a question!" Sarroche was just as surprised. "What are you even doing in Paris?"

But Ferdinand was no more willing to explain himself. "What are you searching for?"

Already angry, the question seemed to infuriate Sarroche even more. "You were dismissed from your embassy. You have no position in France. I demand you leave immediately!"

Ferdinand stepped forward and took hold of Sarroche's wrist and wrenched it violently toward him. "Candles? Is that what you're looking for?"

"Candles? I have no need of candles!" Sarroche tried to pull his arm free, but Ferdinand's grip was too strong.

"Then papers? Letters? Evidence of his murders? What could there be that you still don't know?"

"I know everything! Everything! His murders?" Sarroche broke free. "This man was no murderer."

"Then you know nothing."

Sarroche was defiant. "You are the murderer. Why do you accuse others? Again, I tell you to leave immediately!"

"You will leave," Ferdinand said.

"You have no authority!"

"We could kill you in a moment."

Sarroche backed away, but not from fear. "You will regret this. I promise you."

"Hold him," Ferdinand said in Hungarian. Zoltan was faster than Sarroche could react, twisting his arm behind his back. "Is he armed?"

"A pistol." Zoltan pulled it out from Sarroche's coat and handed it to Ferdinand.

Ferdinand looked in the chamber. "One bullet."

"You will regret this!"

"What were you looking for?"

"I will not tell you."

At a glance from Ferdinand, Zoltan jerked Sarroche's arm up behind his back. Sarroche yelped like a dog. "You will regret this!"

"The last time Zoltan had his hand on you, I told you he wasn't gentle. Now, what were you looking for?" Without waiting, he signaled Zoltan again.

Sarroche moaned. "There are papers here. Pock told me there were."

"What papers?"

"The day after the armistice. I came here and talked to him. He said they were his last power over you."

"What did he mean? What power did the papers have?"

Sarroche half turned toward Zoltan to relieve the pressure on his arm. Ferdinand nodded, and Zoltan released him.

"Power of life and death for you," Sarroche said to Ferdinand.

"For me?" Something in Sarroche's confident words shook Ferdinand. "How?"

"That is all I know." Sarroche was rubbing his shoulder.

"Why do you want the papers?" Ferdinand asked. "You couldn't still be desperate for cinnabar. Not this desperate."

"It is not desperation. My need for cinnabar is as great as it has been."

"But the war is over!"

"Another war will come. Do you doubt that, Monsieur Baron? Or do you believe that men will change?"

"Men will not change."

"Then as long as there is war and men will have need to kill each other, I will need cinnabar and all the materials of war."

"I'll never sell you mine," Ferdinand said. "No matter what power you have."

"Then I will buy it from your son."

"He wouldn't sell it to you, either."

"He may not be as foolish as you. And how would you know his thoughts? He has rejected you entirely. He is well aware of your crimes! Your every action has been to humiliate him and thwart him!"

"I haven't done that—"

"I know it well! He has said it often." He sneered. "I have reports."

"Pock . . . he was poisoning Rudolph against me, wasn't he?"

"He was only observing, and there was much to observe!"

Ferdinand fought off Sarroche's crowing. "He can't sell you anything. I'm still the guardian of the estate."

"As long as you live, Monsieur Baron."

Ferdinand paused, controlling his anger. "You would kill me to get cinnabar."

"You make it very plain," Sarroche answered, "that this would be my only choice."

"Right here? Now?"

"Your own son will accomplish this for me. It will be fitting, that he will avenge his mother. And then, without you to prevent me, I will gain ascendancy over him."

"Then I should kill you now." Ferdinand lifted the pistol in his hand.

"Kill me?" Now his anger was hot. "To add another murder to your deeds? You at least are deserving of death. I am not."

They stood, eyes fixed on each other until finally Ferdinand relented.

"Here is your pistol," he said. "I don't want it, and I'm sure you will find another anyway."

Sarroche's eyes narrowed suspiciously. He took the gun and opened the chamber; the bullet was still in its place.

Swiftly, he backed away from both Ferdinand and Zoltan, as far as the small room would allow.

"Do not move," he said, holding the gun forward. "It is plain that I have no choice."

"If you harm me," Ferdinand said, "Zoltan will kill you."

"Then I will kill him." Sarroche swung the barrel toward Zoltan. "And you later."

"Have you killed before?" Ferdinand asked. "By your own hand?"

"It is a simple matter of pulling the trigger!"

Zoltan had his arms crossed in front of him, waiting.

"So you haven't," Ferdinand said. "You've only ordered others to do it."

Sarroche was of course tense, but also very agitated. "There is no difference!" His stare was on Ferdinand as he answered.

Zoltan's motion was too fast to react to, almost too fast to see. For only an instant, a thin glint of iron sparked through the air, and then Sarroche shuddered, and gasped, and looked down at the knife hilt jutting from his chest.

"Oh . . ." he said, and folded, and fell, and made hardly a sound as he came to a final rest on the floor.

"I'm sorry," Ferdinand said. "I'm sorry you were in danger."

"It had to be done," Zoltan said.

"I wasn't sure. I had to know if he was bluffing or if he truly meant what he said. I'm sorry you had to kill him."

Zoltan leaned down and carefully withdrew the knife. Then, respectfully, he closed the staring, unseeing eyes.

"I hate to kill," he said.

They lifted the body onto the sofa. "What do we do with him?" Ferdinand asked.

"I killed him," Zoltan said. "I will take him."

"I'll wait." Ferdinand went into the bedroom and sat on the bed.

He heard Zoltan in the front room, and then the muffled sound of him descending the stairs.

Ten minutes later, Zoltan returned. Ferdinand didn't ask where he'd gone.

"Thank you," he said.

"Three bodies in Paris I've carried," Zoltan said. "This one was the lightest."

Ferdinand was ready to contend with the room around him.

"We'll put the apartment back together," he said.

"Pock will not come back here."

"I know. But if any papers are here, we'll find them. And it seems right. We had no funeral for him; this will be his service."

Zoltan lifted the couch. Nothing was beneath it.

"What are the papers?" he asked.

"I don't know any possibility."

The sun rose and reached its high noon, but in the drawers and books and cupboards, beneath the furniture and in every possible place, there were no papers. In searching, they reordered Pock's rooms to how they had been.

And in handling the possessions and all the accumulation of Pock's life; in cleaning the stains of Sarroche's death; in finding the evidence of his own children's presence in the apartment, Ferdinand was able to set his mind off the past and onto the future.

– 2 –

The streets were nearly empty and very quiet. They went first to the Austrian Embassy building, but it was vacant and ravaged. While they were searching, though, they heard closer sounds of battle: the hard rumble of cannon, and the brittle sharpness of rifle fire.

They ventured toward the sounds, walking the few blocks to the golden dome of Les Invalides; and as they looked to find the fighting, they realized they were in its midst.

The night's barricades had been broken through and new defenses hadn't been formed, and the fighting was a running engagement fought from windows and corners, from behind fences and from roofs. Some of it was invisible, and some too fast to recognize. Ferdinand and Zoltan retreated yet were still targeted twice and had to dive for cover.

On safer streets they paused. Here, the city was deserted. Everyone was inside hiding, or had fled. Ferdinand looked at the long street where they happened to be, with dozens of buildings and hundreds of windows.

"How will we find them?"

"In a whole city? We will not find them," Zoltan said.

Ferdinand stood looking again at anonymous doors, and intersections with other streets that led off in so many more directions. "The only place I know is Pock's apartment. Why would they have left it?" And then, in frustration, "Where are they?"

"Only God knows."

"Then we'll never find them." He looked upward to the sky. The heavens were at peace; they cared nothing for the desperation and violence beneath. "We'll wait at Pock's. They might come back there."

Ferdinand went out later, just before evening. Zoltan stayed behind.

The battle lines had again hardened, not far from where the fighting had been at noon. He used the cover of twilight to walk the line of barricades to see how the battle was progressing.

Les Invalides had fallen and was in government hands. To the south, the division followed a jagged line, nearly to the Place de Breteuil where Communards hadn't yet been dislodged from the Rue Duroc, and then back in a government salient all the way to the Gare Montparnasse.

As it had the night before, the ferocity of the fighting lessened as the light failed. It had been very fierce, though. As Ferdinand dogged the defenders line, he saw hundreds of dead. Some barricades were only manned by corpses.

Crossing the river was difficult close to the battle line. Snipers directed fire at anyone on the Pont de la Concorde, but the Pont Royal was far enough to the rear that Ferdinand could hurry across. Through the evening, he'd often seen companies or smaller groups of armed defenders moving from stronghold to stronghold, and the few single citizens like himself had been ignored. Now, as he crossed the bridge, he was passed by dozens of Communard soldiers running, in no order but like a mob, crossing from north to south. He wasn't challenged; there weren't sentries at either end of the bridge.

On the north side, the right bank, the Tuileries Palace was directly in front of him. It had become the forward command for the Communards. Many of its windows were lit, and there was continuous traffic in and out of the grand front entrance.

He turned left, back toward the fighting.

The Place de la Concorde was a staging area for the battle. There were thousands of men there: reserves, wounded, and supply runners. It was fully dark, a dozen bonfires making the square diabolical. The largest fire, at the base of the Egyptian obelisk, lit it like a beacon. At the corner of the Place, between the Rue Royale and the Rue de Rivoli, was the most formidable barricade Ferdinand had seen in Paris. It must have taken weeks to excavate and build, and 200 men were stationed in it, waiting.

From the Place, it wasn't far to the front line. Only 750 meters up the Champs-Elysees, at the Rond Pont, the fighting was still active and heavy, not dimmed at all by the darkness. A large barricade occupied the whole circle, manned by hundreds, and even reinforced by five cannon. Apparently the cannon from Montmartre had finally been put to use.

Ferdinand moved as close as he could and watched the battle. The defenders weren't organized but were effective, laying a continuous volley of rifle fire straight up toward the Arc de Triomphe. The fire was continually answered. An artillery shell landed just meters in front of the barricade and threw up street masonry, dirt, and smoke, but the rifles kept up their fire without pause.

North from the Rond, the line ran straight to the Boulevard Haussmann, and then bent away to the west. Every meter was contested.

"It'll take days," Ferdinand said to Zoltan. "A week to clear the whole city."

"We wait?"

"What else? If they look for us anywhere, it will be here."

– 3 –

The third day of the assault dawned with a massive cannonade. Ferdinand was already awake and he could feel the ground shuddering, besides hearing the thunder.

"Two kilometers away," he said to Zoltan. "Or less."

"The battle will come this far today."

"Which side of the line do we want to be on?"

"Will it matter?"

"I don't know." Hunger was sapping his energy, and even more, hopelessness was. "I begin to doubt that they will return," he said finally. "They were living here. We should have found them here. I can't think of any other place they would go, except that they could be anywhere." There was no answer. "We stay until the attack comes."

The progress of the government forces toward them was measurable through the morning and afternoon, first by the increasingly loud and close cannon, then by the approach of gunfire, and finally, in the early afternoon, by the sight of men and women running on the nearby Rue Danton and Boulevard Saint-Germain. Some were running from the attack and some were running toward it, but for the first time in two days, the streets in the Quartier Latin were not quiet.

Then, soon, from the window, they saw defenders positioned at the corner of the street, rifles ready, then firing.

The building they were sheltering behind suddenly disintegrated. First it shuddered as it was hit by the artillery, then it broke apart, and then the parts came slowly down onto the street corner in a huge pile of stone and dust.

"They won't fire this way," Ferdinand said. "That was from cannon in the Boulevard Saint-Germain. They can't reach this far."

"We stay?" Zoltan asked.

"No," Ferdinand said, watching the dust cloud the street, then settle. "No. Therese or Rudolph won't come back here now."

After the crash of the falling building, it was quiet. They had nothing with them to gather. But just before they opened the door to the stairs, Ferdinand stopped.

He heard footsteps. Someone was coming up the stairs.

They backed away from the door.

The person reached their landing and stopped. The knob rattled as a hand felt whether it was locked. Then it turned and the door swung wide.

Ferdinand wouldn't have recognized him except for his eyes, which were even more intense and magnetic than they had been. "Gravert?"

The eyes recognized Ferdinand.

"Baron Harsanyi."

He didn't seem surprised, but instead acted as if the meeting was what he'd expected. Even so, he didn't seem pleased. He was suspicious, and even hostile, and stood just staring at them.

"Do you know where Rudolph is?" Ferdinand asked.

"I came to get you. We don't have time to stay."

"I don't know where Rudolph is. Therese sent me."

The battle had reached the Rue Serpente. With Gravert leading, Ferdinand and Zoltan scurried toward the Boulevard Saint-Michel, away from the fighting. Bullets ricocheted from the walls above them. At the boulevard, Gravert stopped.

"We have to get across the river."

"Where are we going?"

"The Tuileries. She is a prisoner there."

But the boulevard was under full-scale attack. One block south, two cannon were positioned at the intersection with the Boulevard Saint-Germain. Facing the cannon, within twenty meters of Ferdinand, were the Communards.

Zoltan grabbed two shoulders, Ferdinand's and Gravert's, and pushed them north, toward the river. In a moment they were all running, putting distance between them and the imminent combat. They reached the river at the Pont Saint-Michel. Notre Dame was close-by, across the bridge and to their right.

"Don't touch me again!" Gravert exploded at Zoltan. "Keep your filthy hands off me, you monster."

"He doesn't speak French," Ferdinand said.

The bridge was wide, fifty meters across with no cover, and the rifle fire was everywhere. Behind them, they heard the cannon blasting. Ferdinand didn't turn to see. He and Zoltan leaned low and dashed for the far side.

It wasn't the far side of the river. Still running, they crossed the Ile de la Cite and the Pont au Change on the far side. Gravert had passed them, and they were finally all on the right bank, and in relative safety.

Out of breath, they walked the one block to the Rue de Rivoli. To their left, the road ran a straight two kilometers parallel to the Seine, to the Louvre and along it, past the Tuileries Palace and gardens, and finally to the Place de la Concorde and the massive barricade that Ferdinand had seen the night before. And even at that distance they could see the intensity and smoke of the battle around it.

When they reached the Louvre, Ferdinand had to rest.

"Why is she a prisoner?" he gasped.

"Because she is an enemy of the Commune."

"What did she do?"

"It is not what she did. It is who she is."

They started forward again. The long walls of the Louvre went on and on, nearly a kilometer, and beyond them the sky was turning black with smoke. When they finally came to the end, they could see the battle engulfing the huge Place de la Concorde barricade.

Even in the minutes it had taken to travel the Rue de Rivoli, the smoke ahead of them, to the right of the barricade, had dramatically increased. It was centered on the Rue Royale, the short street of shops and cafés between the Place and the Madeleine church.

"The Versaillards had snipers in the buildings," Gravert said. "All morning they were shooting into the barricade. This will put an end to them."

"They're burning the Rue Royale?"

"It should be burned anyway." He stopped to watch. They could see flames tearing into the sky, and the wind brought them the flames' acrid taste. "It's everything the Commune is against."

Ferdinand didn't waste time arguing. "Take me to Therese."

The immense Tuileries Palace was now the front-line command for the defense of the Commune. Its halls were supply depots, its salons were hospitals, its ballrooms were barracks. Its kitchens were preparing rougher meals than they once had, and there was still sufficient space for any other use the occupiers had, including the housing of prisoners.

Gravert led Ferdinand into a side entrance and soon to the main corridor. They made slow progress through the close-packed rows of wounded soldiers until they reached a narrower hall. Ferdinand had last been in the palace when Eugenie had fled from the mobs, and he saw they were taking the same path.

They finally came to the same room, the guardroom where Empress Eugenie had met them, where her son had been hiding in the cupboard. But this time, the room was crowded with men and women, from young to very old, most in middle-class suits and dresses, but all dirty and disheveled. They were sitting on the benches or on the floor.

He saw her first.

Therese was in a corner. Her knees were drawn up under her chin, and her arms were wrapped around them. Her dress was plain, her hair tangled and hiding her face. She looked as if she hadn't moved for hours, and everything about her was despairing.

"Therese," he said.

She looked up, then leaped to her feet and ran and pushed her way to the door.

"Father!"

Her expression was hope and terror together; in an instant, Ferdinand read in it what nightmare she must have been living.

But a guard shoved her back, while another put himself in the doorway to block Ferdinand.

"Her father?" the guard said. "What are you doing here?"

"He's a foreigner," Gravert said. Apparently, he was at least known to the guards. "Can he talk to her?"

"No."

Therese shoved back at the guard and got past him to the doorway.

"Father," she said. "Help me—"

"Quiet!" The two guards together faced her. She backed away, but her eyes were on Ferdinand.

"I'll find the commander," he said.

"Don't leave!"

The guard was only concerned that his prisoner was communicating with someone outside the cell. "Get away, you," he said.

Ferdinand stepped back.

"I'll come back for you," he said again to Therese. It was a weak, worthless promise. Then he pulled himself away.

"Could the two of us get Therese out of that room?" he asked Zoltan. They were back in the main hall of the palace. Everywhere was chaos.

"It would be risky."

"I don't want to take a risk. Not yet. Who can tell the guard to let her go?" he asked Gravert.

"There might not be anyone."

Many more wounded were being carried in, overflowing the foyer and the halls and rooms, and those who had already been settled on the floors were being picked up or forced to stand. Other men, not the injured, were carrying boxes of supplies, stacks of rifles, and other materials toward the back of the palace. Ferdinand realized the building was being evacuated. The smell of smoke was much stronger.

They pushed past the stretcher bearers and nurses and the injured soldiers who could still walk.

"How did she get in there?" Ferdinand asked.

"She was in the palace looking for Rudolph," Gravert said. "Someone recognized her, some serving boy who'd seen her, and he denounced her."

"Is that all?"

"That's enough."

"What will happen to her?"

"I don't know."

"The fighting will come soon," Zoltan said. "We need to see what is happening outside."

Gravert was still with them as they walked out the front door, and they stood and watched the battle at the far end of the Tuileries gardens, a kilometer away. The barricade, and the whole Place de la Concorde, were invisible from the smoke of the fires and the bombardment. Ferdinand looked to the left, at the Seine.

Across the river on the south bank, government troops were positioning cannon.

"You're being flanked," he said to Gravert.

"We will fall back when we must," Gravert said.

"Why are you fighting?" Ferdinand asked. "There's no chance that you can win."

"Then we'll all die."

"Not if you give up now."

"Give up?" Gravert answered in an immediate rage. "What? And be executed? We're already dead."

"You could get away. You could hide and wait."

"And then what? This is what I have lived for and hoped for. I cannot go back to how it was before. None of us can."

"There must be something else, something besides this!"

"What?" Gravert demanded.

"I don't know," Ferdinand said. "But I have to find it. I have to find my children. What will happen to the prisoners?"

"They are nothing!" Gravert said, angry again. "Not compared to everything else! Why should anyone care? We'll shoot them. It isn't for me to decide."

"Then get my daughter out."

"I can't." Gravert's anger was more than Communard idealism. Ferdinand saw frustration, and even sorrow in Gravert's intense eyes, besides the anger. "I can't get her out."

"How did you know she was there?"

"She persuaded a guard to find me."

"Why did you come for me?"

"She persuaded me to."

"Thank you that you did."

Receiving gratitude was too much for Gravert to accept. "I wasted time! I should have been there, at the barricade. Now it is too late to go back."

"Help me get her out," Ferdinand said.

"I cannot, I said."

A sudden thunder of artillery shook them. Ten Communard cannon brought to the middle of the Tuileries gardens had let loose a volley against the government cannon still being positioned across the Seine.

"There!" Gravert said. "We attack them before they attack us!"

At least four of the government cannon had been destroyed from the close-range fire, but the many others opened their fire in return. Ferdinand and Zoltan fell backward against the wall of the palace. Within a minute, the Communard cannon, without any cover, had been blown to pieces.

Then, from the far end of the garden, from the Place de la Concorde barricade, there was an even louder, more terrible explosion. The flames of the burning building were dwarfed by the eruption of fire and smoke and flying debris.

"The ammunition pile," Zoltan said.

"The enemy could never have reached it," Gravert said. "The garrison must have exploded it. They are abandoning the barricade."

And the remnants of the garrison were already retreating, running through the gardens toward the palace. The cannon across the river rained shells on them.

"Back inside," Zoltan said. Gravert didn't follow.

Inside the palace, the evacuation had accelerated.

Those of Place de la Concorde garrison who had survived the explosion and retreat were filling in the front windows of the palace and pouring a murderous fire on the advancing government troops, who now had their own turn at crossing the open gardens.

"Ten minutes," Ferdinand said. "That's all before the cannon begin blowing the palace apart. We'll have to get her out ourselves."

He and Zoltan ran through the front hall, which was even more frenzied and panicked, toward the prison cell.

Each hallway was pandemonium. Everyone was trying to escape, in every limping, crutched, staggering gait.

They finally reached the cell. It was empty and the guards were gone.

He went in straight to the corner where Therese had been sitting and began rummaging through trash, looking for a note, a sign, anything. The room was filthy, like the whole palace, and he sifted through the clutter.

There was nothing.

"Where did they go?" Ferdinand gripped the shoulder of a wounded soldier leaning against a wall close-by. A white bandage circled his head and covered one eye.

"They went away," he said in a slow whisper.

Ferdinand looked for anyone else who might have seen. The hall was less crowded, and everyone was moving.

"I shouldn't have left her," he said to Zoltan. "We have to find them."

"If they're to be shot, they'll do it outside."

"I know," Ferdinand said. "You look for her there, out in the courtyard. I'll look through the halls."

No one could have found anyone in the palace halls, but at least they were emptier than before, as most of the wounded had been removed. Those inside were filling the rooms that faced the battle. There were women as well as the men, and everyone had rifles.

The first artillery shell crashed into the front of the palace, blowing apart the door of the room that had been hit. Billows of smoke and flame followed it, and the sound was almost visible. If anyone had been in the room, they did not leave.

Four more explosions shook the building in the next five minutes, though none as close to Ferdinand. But even after the first, the defenders were beginning to pull back. They made no attempt to stop the fires. In some places, the impoverished laborers and destitute homeless who found themselves being driven from the opulent palace fanned the flames instead, or set new ones. They seemed determined that no new emperor would ever oppress them from the Tuileries.

After several minutes of fruitless searching, Ferdinand met Zoltan at a side kitchen entrance. "Keep looking" was all that Ferdinand could say. "As long as the palace is still standing. We have to find her."

"Only God can find her," Zoltan said.

In the tension and frustration of the moment, Ferdinand was angered by the words. "Then if we find her," he said, "we'll know there is a God."

Zoltan chose not to answer.

Ferdinand returned to the main foyer of the palace. He stopped. He didn't know where to go.

The great staircases on either side seemed to draw him upward. It was unreasonable to search for anyone on the higher floor. But he walked anyway, slowly up the stairs. Huge closed doors faced him at the top landing. He'd passed the doors in years past, at imperial and diplomatic functions. He opened a door now and entered the Imperial Grand Tuileries Ballroom.

A thousand couples had danced in royal spectacles in this room, and kings and queens and emperors had held court. A thousand soldiers had bivouacked here, and Communard generals and commissars had held their councils.

But now only the detritus of sleeping pads and mess tables and extinguished cooking fires covered the floor. Above the floor, the ballroom was an immense, dim, hazy cavern. The air was still and the smell of smoke was very heavy.

"Therese?" he said.

The only light was hard shafts from the windows high in the front, and a vague gray glow from those in the rear. A balcony gallery circled the perimeter of the room on stone pillars.

"Rudolph?" His voice penetrated the smoky, dense air and echoed back diminished, as if from a distance. The room was empty.

There was no reason to stay, but he couldn't force himself to leave. He walked out into the room, moving between piles of rubbish. Above him, strangely, the crystal and silver chandeliers still floated, unlit but catching the sunlight and scattering it through the mist.

He stared at the fragments of light. One streak, refracted from the lowest pendant of the central chandelier, stabbed down toward a table on the far side of the room. He walked toward it.

He reached the place where the light, nearly solid in the haze, shone perfectly on a long, narrow, wooden case of dark polished wood.

It was impossible.

Ferdinand unlatched and opened the lid, and another voice came to him for a moment, Prince von Metternich's. *"War isn't fought with these anymore. This is only its symbol."*

The case was Rudolph's. It might have been an identical case, but it wasn't. It was just as it had been that afternoon a year ago, except that the sword itself was gone.

He looked up again. It was too hard to see.

"Are you here?" Ferdinand said.

The room was silent. The only sound was the muted roar of flame elsewhere in the building.

"Speak to me, Rudolph."

"I'm here."

He was above, somewhere. There was movement in the raised gallery, on the far side. But it was too far and smoky to see.

"Will you come down?"

Rudolph didn't answer, but Ferdinand could hear his progress around the balcony, then to the stairs that flanked the main entrance. As he descended, he could finally be seen.

He had a thin beard. His hair was overgrown, its black curls over his ears and collar. His white shirt had the same black smears and stains as every other white shirt in Paris that had once been clean now had. As he came closer, and less smoke hid him, Ferdinand could see his son's face: the square cheeks and chin beneath the beard, the strong brow, the empty eyes. And in his hand was the sword.

He came to a stop still a few meters away.

What was there to say?

"I've been searching for you."

"Why?" Rudolph said.

"Because I want you to come back."

Rudolph shook his head. "I can't come back."

"Why?"

"Come back to what? To you?"

"Yes, to me."

"How can you ask me?" Then he was trembling, and his voice broke. "You killed my mother!"

It was an accusation that he must have been practicing and waiting to make for months.

"No," Ferdinand said.

"You went into her bedroom and you killed her."

Every sound spread slowly through the huge room and reflected back, like a whisper.

"Rudolph—"

"Deny it, Father. Say it to me, face-to-face, and I'll believe you. Say, *I did not kill her.*"

"She was already dead."

"And you didn't tell us?" he shouted, and the echoes shouted. "We welcomed you home, and then you left the house, and all the time you knew what we'd find?"

"I had my reasons. I can tell you what they were."

"I know your reasons! I know about your secret meetings and selling cinnabar! You did it all for money!" He lunged, swinging the blade in a wide arc.

But the attack was only a warning. Ferdinand stepped out of the way.

"I've never done anything for money," he said coldly. The charge had cut him sharper than the sword could have.

"How many francs? How many pounds? That was all you talked about!"

"I was trying . . ." He stopped and forced his anger down. "How can you even believe I would murder my own wife?"

Rudolph had a ready answer. "Because of how you've treated me."

Ferdinand waited, slowing and calming the conversation. "How have I treated you, Rudolph?"

He answered calmly. "You've hated me."

"I never have."

"Do you think I can't tell?" He stepped forward, brandishing the sword.

"What are you going to do?" Ferdinand asked.

"I'm going to kill you with this."

Ferdinand stepped back again. "I'm not armed."

"Would you kill me if you were?"

"No."

"Then it doesn't matter."

They were talking again, not shouting.

"How did you know you'd find me here?" Ferdinand asked.

"I saw where you left the case," Rudolph answered, nodding toward it. "I knew you'd come back to it."

Ferdinand was perplexed. "But I didn't bring it. I didn't even know where it was."

"It was at Pock's."

"Therese must have brought it."

"Therese?" Rudolph said. "Why was she here?"

There was a crash somewhere in the building, not far away. It might have been cannon fire, or it might have been something collapsing.

"I don't know," Ferdinand said. "I thought she was looking for you. Did she know you were here?"

"No. But everyone's here, she could have guessed." The questions were irritating him.

"Then why would she bring the sword?"

"It doesn't matter!" Rudolph jabbed the sword at him. "God brought it here for me," he said angrily. "It doesn't matter who brought it or why! Ask her if you want to know. Where is she?"

"I don't know. They had her in a cell, and now the cell is empty."

"In a cell . . . ?" Now Rudolph was perplexed. "I don't understand."

"She was arrested."

"Then they'll shoot her. They're shooting everyone."

"She's your sister, Rudolph! Is that all you can say?"

"There's nothing to be done."

"I want to find her!"

"They'll shoot you, too." Despite the distractions of the questions, he was still and ready. Ferdinand edged back another step.

"Why did you come here, to the Tuileries?"

Rudolph shrugged. "There was fighting and food and a place to sleep."

"What are you going to do after we're finished."

"Just wait."

"Here?"

"I'll wait here," Rudolph said.

"The palace is burning."

"I know."

Time was passing. They could feel heat from the fires. The air was becoming turbulent.

"And what are you going to do now, Rudolph?"

Rudolph held the sword vertical, the point jutting upward. "Since I left home, every time I thought about you, and Mother, I thought about this moment. This whole terrible year. I planned what I'd say."

"What will you say?" Ferdinand asked.

"It doesn't matter now."

"Say it."

"I was going to tell you what I've learned, what you taught me. I've learned that men are only evil. I know that every man is a murderer."

"How do you know?"

"I've seen it. I've seen so much killing. I look in any man's face and I can see that they would kill."

"I've seen it, too."

"I'm looking into you, Father. I see it."

"Yes," Ferdinand said. It was only the truth.

"I know it's in me." It was an angry, forsaken cry from his heart. "I don't have to see it."

"Then what will we do?" It was almost a whisper.

"I don't know," Rudolph said.

They faced each other. Everywhere else was smoke and flame, war and battle. In their room there was only emptiness that could be seen and felt, and silence beyond the fire.

"Only God can save us," Ferdinand said.

"Then we're lost."

A door behind Ferdinand opened. He turned to see Zoltan, alone.

"Did you find her?"

"No." Zoltan saw the father and son. "No one knows where the prisoners were taken. Maybe to a wall." His eyes were on the sword in Rudolph's hand and he edged closer.

"Just stay back," Ferdinand said.

A swirl of hot air from Zoltan's open door swept through the room, lifting papers and shreds of cloth.

"The fire is coming," Zoltan said.

"Let it come," Rudolph said.

"No." Somehow, face-to-face with the dark, Ferdinand broke away. One thin stream of light was still touching the chandelier, wreathed as it was in smoke. "There must be a way to escape."

"We can't escape ourselves."

"There must be more than just evil in us."

"How could there be?"

"If God put it there."

"There is no God!" Rudolph said. "Show me that there is."

The far side of the room was only a vague darkness, but something opened in the dark, and sunlight, finding its way through windows or fallen walls, pierced the shadow; a white rectangle framed a dark shape. The shape approached and became two figures.

"Father?"

"Therese?"

"Father!"

She flew across the room, swerving between obstacles of cots and piles of rubbish. When she reached him, she threw herself into his arms.

"Therese," he said. There was too much to say; he couldn't speak.

"Oh, Father."

"How did you . . . ?" He didn't even know what to ask.

"Gravert found me."

The second figure had reached them. Gravert, with his rifle slung over his shoulder, stopped a short distance away.

"They were taking us somewhere," Therese said. "And Gravert came and told them to let us go. And he said he'd shoot them if they didn't." She looked toward Gravert. "So they let us go."

But Gravert had seen Rudolph. "What are you doing?"

"Nothing."

"You found your sword!" Therese looked at Rudolph and saw his dead expression, and Ferdinand's own anguish, and she stepped back from them both. "They took it from me."

"Why did you bring it?" Ferdinand asked.

"Because of the letters."

A vast new explosion shook the room. The main doors to the front foyer and stairs burst open, and a billow of smoke and flame blew through them.

Therese was thrown off her feet, and the others stumbled back. Zoltan was the first to speak.

"Leave now," he said.

Their actions were reflex. All five turned toward the door behind Zoltan. He waited as Rudolph pulled Therese up from the floor. In turn, she snatched the sword case from its place on the table.

Gravert was last. As he reached the door where Zoltan was still waiting, another wave of flame poured into the room from the foyer.

Gravert put his hands on Zoltan's shoulder and shoved him out of the room.

In less than a minute, the five of them were outside in the courtyard of the Louvre, and the palace behind them was a screaming torrent of flame. They paused long enough for Rudolph to put his sword back in the case, and then they ran.

They didn't stop. Gravert took the lead through an arch to the Rue de Rivoli. The battle had moved forward to the front of the Tuileries Palace, but they lunged across the road into the blocks beyond, moving north and east, away from the fighting and toward the Commune strongholds of Belleville and La Villette.

Long before they reached those neighborhoods, though, they stopped, in a small square.

"We can't keep going," Ferdinand said. "We need to stop." He began looking for an open door.

A large, old church, the Eglise Saint-Eustache, made up one side of the square, and it had an unlocked door. Ferdinand took them in.

Inside, the sanctuary was crowded, full of old women and men, mothers and children. Priests and dozens of nuns were trying to keep peace amid the panic and crying.

They found a space in a side chapel where they huddled together.

"What will we do now?" Therese asked.

"Just wait. The battle will pass by."

"What will you do?" she asked Gravert.

"He'll wait with us," Ferdinand answered.

Gravert didn't protest. He seemed too exhausted to think or move.

"What will you do?" Ferdinand asked Rudolph.

"I don't know."

The low murmur of the refugees, even the cries of babies, seemed to make the air of the church itself quieter and more still. The only light was coming through the colored windows. Movement was subdued, also, as people moved slowly and fearfully up and down the aisles.

"What letters did you find?" Ferdinand said.

"They were in the case," Therese said. "Didn't you put them there?" she asked Rudolph.

"I don't know of any letters."

Rudolph didn't move or care, but Ferdinand cared very much. "What letters?"

"Uncle Arpad must have put them in the case. Didn't he tell you, Rudy?" She opened the latch.

The sword shone, even in the dark. But Therese felt beneath it, in the silk lining. "After you left," she said to Rudolph, "I found the case under the couch and the letters were in it. When I read them, I had to find you." She had two sheets of paper in her hand. In the dim light she held them close and began reading. " 'Dear Father, I am a prisoner . . .' "

"What is that?" Ferdinand was bewildered.

" 'They threatened to kill me,' " Therese continued. " 'I've been terrified. I'm hungry. There is no food. I am alone here. I am an outsider. I've always been an outsider and I've always been alone.' "

Rudolph was even more amazed. His blank stare was gone now. "How did you get that?"

"It was in the case. It says that Auguste was an enemy."

"Don't read the rest," Rudolph said.

But she kept reading. " 'I am in a terrible place. Men are dying around me. I don't know what will come next for me.' "

Even in the gray light, Rudolph's tears glistened on his cheeks. "I should have died then!" he said. "I could have. I could have easily."

"No!" Therese said. "You didn't want to! You wanted to live!"

"I didn't. I couldn't have."

" 'Father, I want you. I need you. Please help me. Father, please come and take me out of this place. I want to come back home. Please forgive me.' " She folded the paper. "That was what you wanted."

"Father." Rudolph looked toward him. He could hardly speak. "Please forgive me."

In amazement, Ferdinand laid his arms around his son. "I do," he said. "Forgive me."

" 'God bring you soon Rudolph and safely.' " Therese was reading the other letter. " 'I pray for our restoration. I am sorry for the mistakes I have made. I want you back with me. I want this more than anything else I can imagine. Your Father.' "

"I will come back," Rudolph said.

There was an altar above them, with a painting of a man holding a sheep. Ferdinand's eyes were drawn to it; the man was in the same posture as he was, leaned forward and with his arms encircling the sheep's neck. There were words below the scene. *The thief comes only to kill and steal and destroy.*

He moved his head to see the rest.

I came that they might have life and have it abundantly.

"Then there is a God," Ferdinand answered.

Historical Note

The Franco-Prussian war of 1870–1871 caused both the fall of Louis Napoleon's Second Empire, and the rise of Otto von Bismarck's and Kaiser Wilhelm's German Empire, and laid the foundation for the World Wars of the twentieth century.

Many of the characters and events in *Dark in the City of Light* are historical. The Archduke Albrecht's visit to Paris; the Bourse Swindle; Princess Pauline receiving Empress Eugenie's jewels, and Eugenie's escape through the Louvre; the Spanish Throne Candidature; the Ems Telegram; the Iges Peninsula prison camp; the Proclamation in the Hall of Mirrors of the German Empire; General LeComte's raid to retrieve the Montmartre cannon; the Massacre in the Rue de la Paix (even the death of the elderly Legion of Honor recipient); and all the battles and sieges and greater events are all lifted straight from the history of that tragic year. Richard and Pauline von Metternich were much nicer than I've made them. Pauline's memoir *My Years in Paris*, written in 1920, is delightful.

The Austrian Embassy building on the Rue de Grenelle is now a French government office. The École Militaire houses offices of the French army. Rudolph would have been in his mid-thirties before construction of the Eiffel Tower began at the far end of the Champ de Mars. Some of the forts around Paris are still intact as military or government offices; some have become parks; and some have disappeared. The walls of 1870 Paris (the Thiers Wall), built thirty years earlier, were demolished in the 1920s and replaced by the Boulevards des Maréchaux and the Boulevard Peripherique motorway.

The *Semaine Sanglante*, the Bloody Week, that ended the Paris Commune was all too real. The number of deaths in Paris in those seven days is estimated at between 10,000 and 50,000. Paris was rebuilt after the war, with the exception of the Tuileries Palace. Its blackened shell was pulled down in 1882. It stood between the two wings of the Louvre, closing off the large courtyard that is now open toward the Champs-Elysees and contains I. M. Pei's glass pyramid.

Photographs from the time show the impressive array of cannon on Montmartre. The same location was later chosen to be the site of the new Church of Sacre Coeur, built to "expiate the crimes of the Communards."

I've modified the effects of mercury poisoning to meet the needs of the story, but not by much. A bedroom would reach vapor saturation, far above the lethal level, with as little as one gram of mercury—the weight of a paper clip. The chemistry of mercury fulminate, as demonstrated by Professor Pock, was well known at the time. The cinnabar deposits in Idria have been mined since the Middle Ages.

Pierre Beaubien is fictional, but his peers of the impressionist age were also caught up in the war. Degas and Manet fought in the Paris Militia; Renoir was nearly lynched during the Commune by a mob who thought he was a government spy; Monet fled to London. There's a pretty series of watercolors by Isidore Pils that shows military and civilian life in Paris during the siege.

Emile Zola's novel *Debacle* follows several common soldiers through marches, battles, and the Commune, including the burning of the supply depot being burned at Chalons and a horrific description of the Iges Peninsula. A French soldier, Leonce Patry, wrote a memoir of his actual experiences, including the Siege of Metz, in *The Reality of War,* translated by Douglas Fermer. Elihu Washburne, the American ambassador in Paris during the war, wrote his very detailed *Recollections of a Minister to France.*

The standard modern histories of the Franco-Prussian war include Michael Howard's and Geoffrey Wawro's, both titled *The Franco Prussian War*, and David Wetzel's *A Duel of Giants: Bismarck, Napoleon III, and the Origins of the Franco Prussian War.* And there are many others. Alistair Horne has written several books on French history, including *The Fall of Paris: The Siege and the Commune,* and a wonderful, large, illustrated *The Terrible Year: The Paris Commune,* with amazing pictures of the city through all the disasters of that year.

Acknowledgments

Thanks to Andrew and Denyse Sanderson and their family for being British; to Wayne and Betty Coleman for their patronage to Sharon Diller and her ilk; to Mill Mountain for their tea; to David Long and Bethany House for more than everything; to all the authors and historians of the Franco-Prussian war for loving their work; and to all my encouragers.

About the Author

Paul Robertson, author of the acclaimed novels *The Heir*, *Road to Nowhere*, and *According to Their Deeds*, is a computer programming consultant and a part-time high school math and science teacher. He is also a former independent bookstore owner. Paul lives with his family in Blacksburg, Virginia.